EXPOSURE

London, November, 1960: The Cold War is at its height. Spy fever fills the newspapers, and the political establishment knows how and where to buy its secrets. When a highly sensitive file goes missing, Simon Callington is accused of passing information to the Soviets, and arrested. His wife, Lily, suspects that his imprisonment is part of a cover-up, and that more powerful men than Simon will do anything to prevent their own downfall. She knows that she too is in danger, and must fight to protect her children. But what she does not realise is that Simon has hidden vital truths about his past, and may be found guilty of another crime that carries with it an even greater penalty . . .

EXPOSURE

HELEN DUNMORE

LARGE
PRINT

First published in Great Britain 2016
by
Hutchinson

First Isis Edition
published 2016
by arrangement with
Penguin Random House UK

A catalogue record for this book is available
from the British Library.

ISBN 978–1–78541–245–5 (hb)
ISBN 978–1–78541–251–6 (pb)

Published by
F. A. Thorpe (Publishing)
Anstey, Leicestershire

Set by Words & Graphics Ltd.
Anstey, Leicestershire
Printed and bound in Great Britain by
T. J. International Ltd., Padstow, Cornwall

This book is printed on acid-free paper

Prologue

It isn't what you know or don't know: it's what you allow yourself to know. I understand this now. I'm on my way home, in a second-class smoker from Victoria. I stare out over the network of roofs, shining with rain. The train wheels click into a canter. I have to change on to the branch line at Ashford, but that's a long way yet.

It turns out that I knew everything. All the facts were in my head and always had been. I ignored them, because it was easier. I didn't want to make connections. I've begun to understand that I've been half-asleep all my life, and now I'm waking up. Or perhaps I'm kidding myself, and it's like one of those nightmares where you push your way up through sticky layers of consciousness and think you've woken. You sweat with relief because it's over. You're back in the waking world. And then, out of the corner of your eye, you see *them* coming.

I dream that I'm back at Stopstone. It's night, and I'm huddled in bed. At last I manage to tip myself over the border into sleep, and it's then that my door bursts open and my brothers crash into the room. They pull the bedclothes off me. They don't need to tell me not to cry out. One grabs my feet and the other grips me under the shoulders, drags me half off the bed and then lets go and takes hold of my wrists instead. They swing me and my shoulders burn. I'm afraid they will pull my arms out of their sockets. I can smell the sweat of them. It's stinky, like grown-up sweat. They lug me to the window. I see that the sash is right up and I don't know how they did that. They push and shove until they have bundled me on to the sill. Now they are each holding one of my arms. The terrace is below me, two floors down. They will drop me and tell everyone that I was sleepwalking. They say nothing but they work together. There is a push in my back and I scrape over the sill and dangle from my brothers' hands. Now I hear them counting: "Ten, nine, eight, seven, six, five, four, three, two . . ."

Soon it will be over. Perhaps I will fly. Perhaps they will let go of me and I will fly over the grass and the dark trees and the lake and they will never see me again. But my animal breath pants out of me and urine trickles down my leg.

"... one ..." They shake me, as if they want to shake me wide-awake in case I miss any of what they are doing to me. Perhaps they want me to cry out now, but I can't.

"BLAST-OFF!"

I never went beyond that in my dreams. I woke in my cell.

2

* * *

I never spoke about it to anyone but Giles. I opened myself to him. I don't even know whether I trusted him or not. The word didn't apply. There was nothing Giles didn't know about me. Nothing in me that he couldn't touch.

I'm not sure about love. What it is, and what it means. But now I think that nobody is sure. Instead, we conspire to convince one another. That winter afternoon in my digs on the Madingley Road. Giles was sitting on my bed, reading. Every so often he would turn to me. He didn't smile. He would take me in, and then he would go back to his book. I was sure then.

Once the train reaches Ashford, I have to change on to the branch line. There is a little train to the coast. There are any number of stops before it reaches the last one. East Knigge. Lily, and the children.

I've got some time yet. I tell myself I'm going home, although I've never seen the place before.

CHAPTER
ONE

The Whistle Blows

November, 1960

It starts with the whistle of a train, shearing through the cold, thick dusk of a November afternoon. Lily Callington hears it as she digs over her vegetable patch at the bottom of her garden in Muswell Hill. For a second she's startled, because the whistle sounds so close, as if a train is rushing towards her along the disused railway line at the bottom of the garden. She straightens and listens intently, frowning. The whistle goes through her, touching nerves so deep that Lily doesn't even know where they are. The children! They aren't here. She can't see them, touch them, keep them safe —

Stop it, you fool. They are not babies any more. Paul is ten, Sally almost nine. Even Bridget is five. They're at school. What could be safer than a primary school in Muswell Hill? She'll walk down there for three-thirty, and wait in the Infants' playground with the other mothers until the little ones spill out of the doorway. Always, there's a half-second when the appearance of Bridget startles her, as if the daughter in her head

4

doesn't quite match the boisterous schoolchild whom her teacher calls "a chatterbox". Lily wants to kneel down and open her arms for Bridget to hurtle into them. She wants to fold herself around the sturdy little body. Of course, she never does. She smiles, and waves, like the other mothers. She smoothes Bridget's dark curls, and asks if she has remembered her PE bag.

They're not babies. She, Lily, is a married woman in her thirties with a house and a job. Her feet are planted in safely mortgaged earth. Lily smiles at herself, a little derisively, as the wind shifts and the noise of the train whistle is carried out of hearing. The train is far away now. She puts her right foot on the shaft of the fork, jiggles the handle slightly and eases the tines deep into heavy clay. Her heart steadies. You should drink less coffee, she tells herself. All those years and still the old panic blazing up in her veins. She looks down at the clods of London clay that cling to the fork. There's three-quarters of the patch left to do, and she likes digging. The soil must be opened up for the winter frosts to work on it. You are standing on your own patch of earth. Your name is Lily Callington. You are in England now.

Giles Holloway hears the train whistle too, as he mooches through Finsbury Park. He's close to the main line and the sound is clear. There it goes, getting up speed for the race to the north.

Giles wears a midnight-blue overcoat which might have been elegant on a more elegant figure, but even the skill of his tailor hasn't been able to overcome

5

Giles's crude bulk of chest, shoulder and belly. In these streets, he and his coat draw second glances. He might be a landlord, in search of a couple more houses to cram with Irish labourers. Giles hears the train whistle, and to him it says, as it always does: *Elsewhere*. He knows exactly which train he will catch, if ever he needs to disappear. He won't go anywhere near the Channel ports. King's Cross to Newcastle, and then the ferry to Bergen.

Everything that surrounds him is provisional. It won't and can't last: history has already decided that. But it's decades since Giles was introduced to that way of thinking, and, like his overcoat, the cover of such thoughts doesn't quite fit over the weight of what life has done to him — or, to be fair, what he's done to life. From time to time, he stubs his mind against the solidity of this world that history has *decided against*, as they used to say in secret, smoky, ardent meetings all those years ago. They were so certain then. Nothing had touched them. What they believed was as fresh as a sheet of paper with nothing written on it. Fascism must be defeated, and be replaced by a new and better world.

Of course they had no illusions. They understood that omelettes couldn't be made without breaking eggs. Sacrifice — even the sacrifice of others — was heroic, correctly understood. How they struggled for the correct viewpoint, overcoming the handicap of their class origins and bourgeois culture. Actions that appeared grubby, even furtive, would be revealed in all their clarity once history had swept away the debris of capitalism. For the time being, there must be secrecy. Concealment was an art you had to learn, and then you saw it everywhere, although you'd never suspected its existence until you began to be part of it. Giles remembers Julian Clowde's rather cold, self-satisfied smile as he took stock of Giles and made him understand what was what.

It was passionately exciting, but you never showed it. An inner ring within an inner ring. If you didn't know that the inner ring was there, you saw nothing. It was there in plain sight, but camouflaged. You saw a group of friends on the summer grass by the river, laughing, and you passed on with a quick, ignoble pang because you were not one of them. You had to be beckoned in. Initiated. Julian had beckoned him in. Julian had watched Giles, got to know him, tested him as you test an inner tube in a bowl of water to see where the puncture is. Giles had had a lot to learn. First of all, he had to learn to become silent about his opinions. He became humorous about his young self and its ludicrous pronouncements on politics. Now he'd grown up and seen the world as it was. He knew that others were doing the same, and that they wouldn't necessarily even recognise one another for what they were. They had learned everything about concealment in the open.

Julian smoothed Giles's way, and Giles glided into place. Lunches were had in quiet clubs, overtures were made and accepted, and there you were, old boy, lodged in position, vouched for by men who had the ear of everyone who mattered. *Have you come across Giles Holloway? I'd like you to meet him.*

There you were, and no one knew what you were. Giles was a pirate then, flying his own flag under the very bows of the great ship of state. He'd always rather fancied that notion. And then there was the war.

Nineteen forty-seven. Back to London. Back to the Admiralty and back under Julian's wing. Older now, though. The years were going by. On it all went: those documents, those damned dingy documents, on and on. The sails of Giles's little ship hung limp.

Here he is still, after all those years. On goes the world, blithe and satisfied with itself. London is more grey and massive than ever, and it's tiered with chaps whose opinion of Giles Holloway is no longer as sanguine as it once was. Giles has not fulfilled his early promise, from any point of view. When he catches sight of himself in shop windows he turns away. He isn't fifty, for Christ's sake, but he looks old and paunchy, his cheeks purpled, his eyes . . . Well, it's never a good idea to look into your own eyes.

No need to do so. We aren't meant to see ourselves as others see us. In fact it would be a bloody dull world if we did, because no one would ever make a fool of himself again. We might as well accept that we're put on this earth to make unwitting entertainment for our fellow men, and get on with doing so. The thought eases him, as it always does. Whatever balls-up he might have made of things, it can't matter much. The train whistles for the last time, hurtling into a future that the dull streets can't imagine.

He crosses the road, glancing up at the pale, cold sky, and then down at his watch. It must be later than he thought, because he begins to walk rapidly and with purpose. He comes out on to the main road, passes the dairy and turns into a pub. At the bar he orders a double Black & White before glancing casually around. Most of the tables are empty. A young man, a clerk perhaps, nurses his half-pint in smoky peace. In the corner farthest from the window, another man sits reading the sports pages. He looks up as Giles approaches, then down at his paper. He reads on, absorbed. From time to time he reaches out an automatic hand to lift his glass to his lips.

Giles settles himself with his whisky. The fire in the grate is made up, but not lit. If this were any other pub, Giles would have the barman over and the fire going in no time. But today, in this place, Giles doesn't choose to exert his personality. He doesn't even tell the barman to keep the change, with the habitual easy generosity that gets him remembered next time.

The man at the other table reaches for the packet of Senior Service on the table in front of him, fumbles out a cigarette and strikes a match. But he's awkward, and the match snaps in a fizz of flame. It's out before he can light his cigarette. And it's his last match. The box is empty. He shakes it, annoyed. The business has drawn Giles's attention.

"May I offer you a light?" he asks courteously, taking out his lighter. The man half rises, cigarette to his lips, but Giles is too polite for him, has already left his seat and is leaning forward to proffer the lighter. His bulk blocks the table from the bar. His thumb flicks the lighter catch and a perfect small flame, like a crocus, appears. The two men's faces are illuminated as they lean towards it. Their hands are in shadow. They are worshippers at a nativity, come from far away. The packet of Senior Service on the table moves a fraction, and then is still again.

The two men are back at their separate tables. Giles drinks off his whisky. The bar is cold and stuffy, not a place to linger. The other man has sunk back into the sports page. Giles looks at his watch again, stands up, and with a nod to the barman he is out of the door. He walks briskly now, towards Finsbury Park station and the Piccadilly Line to Green Park.

Paul Callington hears a train whistle too, but he's not sure if it's in his head or outside it. He's been daydreaming about Top Shed at King's Cross. He's a practical boy, and knows that school is probably too far from the main line for him to hear the train in reality. If the wind is from the east, he might just catch the sound. Luckily, old Craven insists on open windows throughout the winter.

Paul has already finished the Practice Intelligence Test, but he doesn't want old Craven to know this. Craven is not fond of what he calls "clever clogs", and is happy to enforce the point with a knuckling from his bony fingers. If you finish a paper early, you should spend the remaining time checking methodically through your answers. But there's no point in checking; Paul knows that his answers are correct.

He bends over his paper, all apparent concentration. Ten minutes more for thinking about trains. The

10

10.00 a.m. *Flying Scotsman*, King's Cross to Edinburgh Waverley, gathering speed . . . Maybe Dad will take him to King's Cross again soon. They buy platform tickets and watch the trains. Paul's dream is to visit Top Shed. He tastes the names of the locomotives: No. 60113, *Great Northern*; No. 60052, *Prince Palatine*; No. 60103, *Flying Scotsman*. It's only Paul and his father who go on these trips. Sally isn't interested, and Bridgie is too small. Mum gives them sandwiches and a flask of tea. Dad knows a lot about trains, but Paul knows more. He can tell Dad how the German smoke deflectors work on the modified No. 60059, *Tracery*. He hopes there'll be another Saturday like that soon.

The whistle shrieks again, but this time Lily, Giles and Paul hear nothing. The train is already beyond the confines of the city.

CHAPTER
TWO

The Oddity of the Flat

It's the oddity of the flat that does for him, in spite of all the years he's lived here. It's not really a flat at all. Flats should be on one floor, and his is not. You go down the bedroom corridor, open what looks like a cupboard door, and there's a narrow flight of stairs which twists round on itself as it rises steeply to a landing. From the landing, further steep steps rise to an attic room.

The whole place is an absolute bloody death-trap. Giles Holloway has always known that. But he likes the attic, and it's useful. As far as he knows, from his discreet enquiries, no other top-floor dweller in the block of mansion flats has a secret attic. It was a quirk of the builder, no doubt. The possession of this tucked-away space pleases him.

He knows the place like the back of his hand, but still he falls. He had a bottle of '52 Pomerol at dinner. Giles has little interest in wine, but he knows what to order. Afterwards, at home, the usual bottle of Black & White on his desk, and the soda siphon.

Giles works on into the night, feeling rather than hearing the vibration of Big Ben's chimes through the walls. Suddenly, it is two o'clock. He gets up, stiff-legged, and crosses to the window. He pulls up the blackout blind that for some reason he has never taken down, and stares across the roof-tops. Rain falls steadily. The tiles glisten. He thinks of what it would be like to cling to those tiles, scrabbling for a foothold, sliding inexorably downwards to the gutter. *Get a grip*, he tells himself.

He is the only one awake to see the wet roof and hear the tick of rain on the tiles. Everybody else is asleep. Giles likes to be the only one on the qui vive. Even more than this, he likes to be awake here, in his eyrie, high up and hidden. Oddly, he thinks, tapping a fingernail on the window-frame, one never feels that there is anything wrong with being alone once it's past midnight. In fact, one feels more alive, as if one has scored, somehow, over the sleeping world. Earlier in the evening, at dinner, say, it can make Giles uneasy. Not that he is often alone then, unless he chooses to be.

My little room, he thinks sentimentally, glancing back at it under the strong downpour of light from the unshaded bulb. The wood beneath his finger-tips is spongy. The frame is rotting and at some point he'll have to have the window replaced. But not yet. He's been putting it off for years. He doesn't want workmen up here.

The utility desk at which he works was already here when he first bought the flat. Someone must have hauled it up the stairs, God knows how, and decided there was no point in ever trying to get it down again. Giles has added a single bentwood chair and a narrow corner cupboard, like a school stationery cupboard. The floorboards are bare. On the wall behind the desk there is a small painting, no more than eight inches square, and poorly framed. It's a very early Kandinsky, painted with meticulous realism. Few would recognise it as a Kandinsky at all. There's a river, a haystack, a long flowing horizon. Giles likes it all very much, just as he likes everything in the room. Soda siphon, bottle of Black & White, Waterford tumbler. There's a file on the desk, open. If it were closed it would be possible to read the words stamped in red on the cover: "Top Secret".

Giles remembers the days of *Most Secret*. That phrase was more attractive, somehow. He preferred it to *Top Secret*, which has always struck him as rather childish. Minox next to the file. Such a perfect little camera for the job; you couldn't improve on it.

No need to tidy things away, up here. No one else ever comes. Pigeons walk up and down on the window-sill sometimes, crooning noisily on summer evenings. He supposes that they are there all day long, when he's at work.

No one ever comes, but the attic is not what it once was. Even the bloody pigeons get on his nerves. Watching everything. Winged vermin. Once they laid an egg, just one, exposed on a little pile of rubbish they'd put together. He swept it away.

These last months, he's been jumpy. He has nailed the window shut. There's been one too many of those carefully casual, probing conversations. A character called Frith seems to be everywhere these days. Julian calls him "Mr Plod". Frith even had the nerve to drop in to Giles's office for what he no doubt thought was a "discreet chat" about Giles's visits to the Nightshade. As if Giles hasn't been going there for years. It was pure officiousness. What the hell were they playing at? He broached the question with Julian, but you might as well try to have a word with the Cheshire Cat as with Julian when he doesn't want to be pinned down.

"You're not getting nervy, I hope, Giles?" Julian barely breathed the words, but there was a touch of scorn in them that stung.

He can't make Frith out. Cool as an oyster, not very bright you'd think, until you caught the oystery gleam behind his glasses. Frith has been dropping in more and more frequently.

"Try to be a little more discreet, my dear Giles," said Julian in passing, at a party.

Giles stopped taking files home, but not for long. He couldn't stop for long. He's always known that. He waits a few weeks, then once again, as evening comes, he puts his briefcase on his desk, and then, leisurely, places into it the file that he requires, before snapping shut the lock. Giles is all serenity at such moments. The art of hiding in plain sight used to be second nature, and now it has become the whole of him. But this file, tonight, is rather different. It ought never to have been on his desk at all. Julian had signed it off earlier today; yesterday, now. He was leaving for Venice at noon, but he had come in to deal with one or two urgent matters. There were his initials: JRC, the last of three sets of initials. The three pairs of eyes that were cleared to see the file. Julian had sauntered into Giles's office, dropped the thing on his desk and chatted for a few minutes about the *prossimo spettacolo* at La Fenice. As he insisted on calling it. Julian was no linguist, thought Giles; he ought to stop trying to talk Italian.

"Get it back to Brenda when you've finished with it." Brenda was Julian's secretary. "Absolutely trust-worthy and discreet," was the way Julian described her. Or, more accurately: *Deaf, dumb, blind and quick with her hands*. And then Julian had buggered off in his tweeds, and there was the file, at which Giles then looked closely for the first time. Christ, he thought. *Christ*.

Quarter past two. Time for bed. Even so, he watches the rain. It's not that he couldn't survive if he had to leave London. But Moscow . . . Those leaden winter days, those awful clothes and the still more awful perfumes that women wore to cover the fact that bathrooms were in short supply. The monstrous, garish architectural ensembles. Endless ballet. Taking his holidays on the Black Sea and grateful for it. "Moscow? It's like Birmingham, my dears, but without the bright lights." Cue gales of laughter. Good old Giles. He speaks frightfully good Russian, you know. After the war he was in Special Intelligence in Berlin, all very hush-hush . . .

As usual, they'd got it all wrong, but that suited Giles. They flitted around him, filling his glass, talking about *I Puritani* — they'd absolutely loved it but it was a thought too long, didn't he agree? — and how they'd adored *The Country Girls*. Giles said the kind of things he'd always said. Outrageous, that was Giles. Witty,

16

shocking, quotable: *Have you heard Giles's latest?* Cue more gales of laughter.

Or did they laugh? He frowns. He seems to remember being alone, in the middle of the party. A joke that didn't come off. He'd slopped more whisky into his glass — there was never any decent whisky at these parties — and gone out on to the terrace. It was dark and quiet. He looked back into the lit-up room and the party that went on without him. Mouths opened and closed, heads were thrown back in whinnies of laughter, hands were put out to trap an interlocutor. He was losing his touch, but, more than that, he couldn't care less, even when that booby Firclough raised his eyebrows prissily and turned away. Giles leaned against the stone balustrade. He was cold and sad, as he sometimes was after sex. It was passing from him, that erotic, delicious pleasure of being at the heart of things.

Parties are not what they were, thinks Giles now, looking out at the rain from his attic window. Everyone is so bloody dull these days. Stuffed shirts. He'd once made the mistake of taking Princess Margaret's elbow to steer her across the room. It was pure courtesy, for God's sake. There was a crush in the club and he knew a discreet little exit. The way she'd looked at him had sent him three paces backwards. My God. Nicky in Istanbul had told him she was pure poison, her visits the dread of embassies all over Europe. Now he believed it. But she'd liked him. She'd leaned forward and laughed at one of his jokes.

To hell with her. To hell with the lot of them. He glances at his desk. The file and the Minox are there as ever. He works so hard, twice as hard as anyone realises, and he gets no credit for it. He's never cared before. Self-pity: can't have that. Should be a cold fish like Julian Clowde. You'd never catch Julian feeling sorry for himself.

Giles has always had a strong head, but lately he's been waking with a jolt of panic, as if something too dark to remember has taken place during the night. Slowly, the day takes care of it. He follows the same routine every morning. He draws a cold bath, takes the chill off it, plunges in and scrubs himself vigorously with Pears Soap and a loofah. He wraps himself in a towel and walks around his flat like a Roman emperor, eating toast and marmalade and whistling songs from the music hall.

His days appear fixed. The early walk to the Admiralty. His sprawling notoriously untidy desk, his high-handed carelessness, those breakfast cups of scalding tea at regular intervals, the fug of Senior Service that slowly fills his office. He lunches on a bench in Green Park. It's a well-known Holloway eccentricity: "Giles is a fresh-air fiend." Sometimes he will meet an acquaintance. Sometimes he will sleep for an hour in the sunshine. He never drinks during the day. Evenings: dinner, the club, then perhaps going on to other little clubs with a quite different clientele. The Nightshade, for instance, or Bobbie's. Occasionally he'll bring someone back, but he's cautious about that.

All the boys know one another and are terrible gossips. He doesn't want the flat to become common currency.

Time for bed, old son, or you'll be like death warmed up in the morning. Time to do something about those sodding pigeons, too. Rat poison? Would that work? Carefully, Giles tucks the Minox and measuring chain into a drawer and puts tumbler, siphon and whisky bottle on to a tin tray painted with the face of Father Christmas wreathed in holly. He uses this tray year-round. Upstairs and downstairs it goes, with everything that he needs to sustain him through the night shift. He could keep the whole caboodle up here permanently, he supposes, but he can't be fagged with washing up. He'll leave it in the kitchen and Ma Clitterold will sort it out in the morning. She never comes up here. He keeps the staircase door locked in case she should take it into her head to explore.

He hooks his foot around the attic door to close it, and that's when it happens. The bottle slides. His quick reflexes come to his aid and he grabs it before it falls. But the door is in the way. The bottle is now in his hands but the tray tips. As it crashes to the floor Giles loses balance, misses the step, falls backwards on to the landing and thumps down the twisting staircase.

He is at the bottom, huddled into a corner. He sees drugget and a stair rod which is at the wrong angle because somehow Giles is wedged so that he's looking up at it. A ferocious red pain grips his leg. His right knee is at the centre of it. He knows at once that something is broken. Nausea rushes through him. He is cold, he sweats, he wants to empty his bowels. He groans and his head knocks against the skirting board. He must get out of the staircase. He cannot climb. He's got to go downwards, out of the corner where he's somehow got jammed.

There are four stairs beneath him, then a square of drugget and the closed door to the corridor. He can get down those stairs. Once he is in the corridor he can crawl to the telephone. There's an extension in his bedroom.

He assesses himself; calmly, he thinks. There is blood in his eyes. He reaches up and wipes it away. More blood trickles down. He knows that any wound to the head bleeds profusely, and he's unconcerned. He has hit his head hard, at the back, but the bleeding is coming from his forehead. He doesn't remember how he fell. Another curtain of blood comes down over his eyes.

There's nothing to hold on to, but he can roll over. The pain makes him hiss through his teeth but now he is on his hands and one good knee, pointing upwards, shaking away the blood so that he can see. He'll let himself down the remaining stairs backwards, he thinks, but then finds he cannot, because of the knee. He rolls farther round, on to his left side, and pushes himself down, using his hands. He thinks he might faint or vomit, but does neither.

At the foot of the stairs he lunges upward and gets the door handle to turn. He pushes hard, and works himself through, using his hands, until he is in the corridor. His bedroom is the next door on the right. He ought to be able to reach the telephone.

It's not going to work. He feels deadly sick. He huddles himself up on the carpet, shivering. He's very cold. There's a strong smell of whisky: the bottle must have smashed and perhaps that's how he got cut. He can't get to the phone. He has got to shut and lock the door that leads upstairs, before old Ma Clitterold gets here. She'll seize her chance. She'll be up there poking about.

> Twankydillo twankydillo dillo dillo dillo
> And he played on his merry bagpipes made
> from the green willow
> Green willow green willow green willow
> green willow

He has the song trapped in his head as he struggles on to his good knee, catches hold of the doorframe and lunges to close the door. The pain is so bad that he can't see, or maybe it's the blood. There is the doorknob. His fingers find the key and turn it, then take the key from the lock. As he does this he caves in on himself, weight twisted on to the bad knee. He is down on the carpet, making a noise. He has the key. He feels the key pressing into his hand. Blackness rushes in front of his eyes.

He is still for a long time, and empty. He's not feeling so sick now. He needs to give himself a few minutes and then try for the bedroom. He sees again the surface of his desk, and the file. Ma Clitterold won't go up there now. He's safe. But then it flashes over him, as if he's opened the door of a room on fire: he took Julian's file home overnight, as he did with all of them. He's always in early, no matter how late the night before. He slides the files he's been working on back into the chaos of his desk. But this file has got to go back to Julian's office. Those initials. Christ. He can't pass this one off.

He could have done it easily. Taken the file along as a sandwich filling between a couple of duffers. Brenda would have dealt with it.

Not now. He won't be in early tomorrow. *Today.* He must get that file back before Frith comes looking for it.

He can still do it. Get to the phone. Ring Julian.

Fuck it. He must have hit his head harder than he thought. Julian's in Venice. Christ, Holloway, *think*.

It's got to be someone who'll do it but not grasp what he's doing. Someone who'll do it for him, Giles Holloway. Someone who knows the office, and Brenda, and won't be noticed —

He knows. Of course he does. Another qualm of sickness goes through him as he knows who it is.

CHAPTER
THREE

Nil By Mouth

Giles is in a bed at last, in a private room, wearing a hospital gown. His own bed, blessedly flat and white after the ambulance's red blankets and the slippery lurch of the trolleys that have carted him from one department to the next. The hospital porters whistled like coal-men heaving sacks on to their shoulders. They braced themselves as they lifted him: "Got your end, Ron? Here we go. One, two, three, upsidaisy."

"Is there someone whom we could telephone?" the Sister asks.

He gives her Ma Clitterold's name, and his own number. "My housekeeper comes in at nine."

All night, it seems, he has been wheeled from one desolate room to another. He has been X-rayed, prodded, bled. Porters wheeled him down corridors and backed his trolley expertly into lifts. They slid him on and off examination couches.

Now the nurses refuse to give him a cup of tea: he is NIL BY MOUTH. He has concussion, it seems, but his skull is not fractured. They are going to operate on his leg.

"There is someone whom I must telephone urgently," he says, but the Sister only nods. He will be going into theatre at eleven. Mr Anstruther is coming in specially, she announces, as if this is a rare privilege.

"Surely there's a telephone you can bring to me?"

"I want you to lie perfectly still. You have concussion."

They are running a tank over his head. Pain comes in regular, complete pulses. He turns aside and vomits into a kidney dish held by a student nurse. He smells whisky. She takes away the bowl. Now the Sister is back. She won't let him drink but she wipes his mouth. "I want you to lie quite still," she says.

It's Simon he has got to see. He struggles to raise himself on his pillow so that he can look at his watch, but his watch has gone. Simon Callington. He said the name aloud, he thinks, but it doesn't matter. "What time is it?"

"It's five to ten, Mr Holloway. You'll be going down to theatre in an hour. Just keep nice and quiet for me."

They'll wonder where he is. He's never ill. Never even has a hangover, no matter how much — His desk at the office will be just as he left it, with a worm of cigarette ash on top of the pile of papers. So carelessly, carefully dropped there. Files shoved in anyhow, or so it appears. Giles has his own system.

Ma Clitterold will ring the office, full of the drama of his accident. The secretaries will pass on the message. Frith will hear it, and whoever Frith's working for. Quietly and without any fuss, they'll take advantage of his absence.

Frith will pop in. He'll stand over Giles's desk, oyster eyes gleaming behind his glasses. Giles pictures the slow smile spreading over Frith's features. He can't remember ever seeing him smile.

Those carefully casual, probing conversations over the past few months were a warning, and meant to be taken as such. But they don't want to push him too far, not yet. They don't want him to panic and fly off. They want him to lead them to Julian Clowde, even though Giles very much doubts that they even know it's Julian they'll find at the end of their long trail a-winding. But if he gets the file back . . . Once Brenda's got it, they won't be able to prove anything . . .

"What time is it?" he asks.

"I want you to keep nice and still while I take your blood pressure."

He is ill, really ill. He hears mutters above his head but doesn't open his eyes.

"You're going to feel a little prick in your arm now."

There is someone he must see but the name is gone. He cannot get to the places in his head where he keeps the right words. His eyes are sealed, as if someone else has his thumbs on the lids. With a rush of relief he gives in, as if he's giving in to death.

It is light. Giles lies beached on his bed. He can see the fold of the sheet. There is a vile, rubbery taste in his mouth. He gags, and someone lifts his head. His teeth chatter on the rim of an enamelled dish; he heaves and vomits. He is alive and out of surgery. Now he can see the nurse's hands taking away the kidney bowl. Another nurse kneels by the side of his bed and takes his hand. Her young, fresh voice goes in and out of his consciousness. "You are back from theatre, Mr Holloway. It's all gone well. Mr Anstruther will be coming to see you shortly."

They are giving him blood. He doesn't care about anything. He is empty. He has vomited out all the filth of the night.

"Simon," he mutters. "I must see Simon Callington."

The nurse puts her fingers on his wrist. "Mr Anstruther will be coming to see you presently. Try to sleep now."

He sleeps and wakes. Mr Anstruther stands by the bed, a glorious pinstriped column. Giles raises his eyes and sees at once that Mr Anstruther is someone who will understand. He listens, gathering his forces, as Mr Anstruther explains about the internal bleeding that made the operation a little more tricky, and its satisfactory conclusion. In a day or two Giles will be in the pink.

Giles strikes. He opens his eyes, gives a small, apologetic smile, says, "You've been marvellous. This is all a frightful bore. I need to ring up a couple of people quite urgently — is that in order?"

Anstruther glances down at his notes. "You're at the Admiralty, I gather."

"Yes. Hellishly busy at the moment, too, more's the pity."

They are in it together, two men at the top of their profession, self-deprecating, knowing their own worth. Very probably Anstruther *is* at the top of his profession.

Giles can still gather it to himself, the manner that makes things happen, even though he's falling, not rising — falling right through himself . . .

"I'd be most awfully grateful," he says through closed eyes.

Giles's bed is right by the nursing station, because they need to keep a close eye on him after the anaesthetic. But yes, he will be moved back into his private room as soon as possible.

The telephone. The clanky old trolley with the phone and trailing wire that plugs into the wall. Here it is by the bed, within reach. And here is a bottle of Lemon Solo squash beside his water jug, a pile of clean handkerchiefs and his wallet. Ma Clitterold must have visited while he was asleep. He is not in the ward any more, but back in his private room. He must be better, or else more time has passed than he realised. Blood is still going into his arm. He wants to lie here, thinking of nothing, listening to the hiss of traffic far beneath the window.

It's dark outside. The day is over. They've moved around him, sponging him and emptying bags. His left leg, in heavy plaster, hangs suspended from the ceiling. There is the blood transfusion tube going into one arm, and for some reason they've left a blood-pressure cuff on the other, slack but ready for service. Why on earth have they done that? How do they expect him to make a telephone call with that thing on his arm?

He rings the bell. A very young nurse pads in and takes the thermometer from the case above his bed.

"Before you start on that," he instructs her, "I need you to get a number for me, and then pass me the receiver."

"I must fill in your chart first," she says.

It hurts him to look up at her face. She is so young. Her face is smooth and pink, obstinate. He'll have to be careful.

"All right, my dear, you go ahead." She frowns with concentration as she takes his temperature and blood pressure, and fills in his chart, but she doesn't meet his eyes. Give me the sodding telephone, he thinks, and bugger off. But no, he needs her to dial the numbers for him.

She wedges the receiver rather cleverly so that he can speak without having to hold it. A wave of exhaustion catches him. Concentrate, Giles. After four rings, the phone is picked up. No one speaks.

"Oh hello, it's me," he says, the usual tired, automatic formula. "You know, George's cousin. I've had a bit of an accident and I'm in the Latimer. There are a few things I'd like you to pick up from the flat, if you would. Don't bother about the file; someone will be coming from the office to sort out all that. You've still got the keys, haven't you? Thought so. Excellent. You know my study. I'll tell my Mrs Thing."

Still got the keys, he thinks, eyes closed, as the nurse replaces the receiver. Fatigue and nausea wash through him again. They've got the keys all right. The keys to everything, lock, stock and barrel. Sometimes, when he comes home, he's pretty sure they've been in the flat. They keep an eye on him. Nothing is obviously

28

disturbed, but he can sense it. They want him to sense it. They know he knows they know.

That's sorted out the Minox and the other stuff. Now for the file.

"I'm not sure . . ." says the girl doubtfully. She's worried about Sister. Mr Holloway is a head injury and needs to be kept quiet.

"One more brief call," says Giles. With an effort, he opens his eyes. The silly pink face gapes at him. Will she, won't she? Of course she will.

It's after eight o'clock when the telephone rings in the hall of Lily and Simon's house. The children are all in bed. Lily hurries, in case the ringing wakes them.

"Lily Callington speaking. Yes. Yes, he is. Just a moment, please."

Simon is reading the latest number of his son's *Railway Magazine*. He looks absurdly serious over it, just as Paul does. Simon assumes that the caller will be one of Lily's friends — Erica, probably. Simon hates the telephone. He has quite enough of it at work.

"It's Giles Holloway for you."

"Bloody hell. I thought he was in hospital. There was a memo round this afternoon saying he'd had an accident."

"Was it serious?"

"Can't have been, can it, if he's ringing me up?"

Lily dislikes Giles Holloway. Or perhaps she's been unfair. The first time they met, long ago, he'd had too much to drink. His eyes flickered over her. She thought, or perhaps imagined, that there was something hostile there. But since then he has always been civil. He's an old friend of Simon's. It was Giles who got Simon his job.

She watches as Simon pushes back his chair, already preoccupied. The magazine drops to the floor. Simon goes out of the room, pulling the door to behind him. Lily picks up the magazine and smoothes its cover. Paul won't like to see it creased. He is a collector, a careful saver of railway tickets, postcards and memorabilia.

Simon picks up the receiver. He speaks quietly, aware of the sleeping children and the bedroom door left open upstairs, because Bridget likes to see the landing light.

"Hello."

"It's Giles."

"I thought you were in hospital."

"I am. Simon, dear boy, could you do something for me? I was working on some documents which need to go back to the office — to Julian Clowde's secretary. If you come down now, I'll give you my keys. I'd be enormously grateful . . ." The voice weakens. He's in a bad way, thinks Simon, his irritation swallowed in concern. "I'm in the Latimer, in a private room. Let me ask the nurse for the ward number —"

"But surely it's too late for visitors?"

A flash of impatience. "For God's sake, Simon, I'm not asking you to sit at my bedside."

Typical Giles, thinks Simon, as he puts the receiver into its cradle. He always wrong-foots you. And now, somehow, Simon has agreed to cross London, pick up

Giles's keys and collect whatever work it is that Giles has taken home so that it can be returned to the office the next day. That's the evening gone. He and Lily were going to listen to the play on the wireless, and then go to bed early.

"Why are you wearing your coat?" asks Lily.

"It's bloody annoying. Giles left some work at home which needs to go back to the office asap apparently. That's why he was ringing. What an idiot."

"What do you mean?"

"I don't know what's up with him. He wants me to pick up his keys and then collect a file from the flat."

"Now?"

"He said it's urgent."

"Surely you could do it tomorrow, if you go in early."

"I know. He's the limit, but he's smashed his leg badly. They had to operate. He's lost a lot of blood and he's got a head injury. He sounded all in. You know how obstinate he is when he's set on something."

"I don't really know him at all," says Lily, and picks up another exercise book. "I suppose he was drinking when he had the accident. He's like a child, Simon, and you all cover for him."

Simon's face darkens. "Don't wait up for me, Lily. I'll creep in quietly."

She looks up, looks him full in the face. "Be careful."

The door clicks softly, and Simon's gone. Lily thinks of him hurrying through the dark streets and all the way downhill to the Tube station. She hears the wheeze of the train doors as he is swallowed inside. He's going to the hospital and then Giles Holloway's flat. She can't picture either place, but everything to do with Giles makes her uneasy. If only he hadn't rung Simon —

She squashes the thought. In a couple of hours Simon will be back and everything will be as it was before. You have to feel some sympathy for a man on his own, with no one to look after him. A smashed leg and concussion sound quite serious.

But I don't sympathise, she thinks. I don't want Simon to have anything to do with Giles Holloway.

She looks up at the clock. There are eight more exercise books to correct, and then she'll switch on the play. According to the *Radio Times* it's about a woman who loses her memory and doesn't recognise her own children. Ridiculous. However, it'll take her mind off Simon out there in the dark. Her hand reaches out for the top exercise book, but instead of opening it she stands up, kicks off her shoes and goes lightly through the hall, up the stairs and on to the landing outside Bridget's little slip of a room. The door is ajar, as always. Inside, the room is dark, still, warm. Lily thinks that she can smell Bridget's sleep. She's the only one of the three who still has that baby-smell.

She stands there for a while, then goes to Sally's bedroom door, and listens. There's no sound, so she moves on to Paul's. They are all asleep. Lily is smiling as she moves noiselessly back downstairs.

CHAPTER
FOUR

I Am a Friend of Giles

There's a pulley thing attached to Giles's leg. The leg itself is cased in plaster and hoisted into position. It doesn't look like part of a living body. Giles, in a hospital gown, lies flat on his back with his eyes shut. The hospital smell reminds Simon of when Paul was born, and Simon was allowed in at the visiting hour to see a strangely unfamiliar Lily, with a burst blood vessel in her right eye. They brought in the baby, wrapped up like a caterpillar in a cocoon. He can still see that baby, as clear as clear, quite separate from his son asleep at home. As if somewhere, if he opened the right door, he could find them again. Lily would smile and say in a voice that had a crack in it: *Simon.*

Giles is asleep, snoring lightly. His face is slack and his mouth open. He won't like Simon seeing him like this. The nurse is outside, visible through a glass panel, at her desk, writing under a shaded lamp. There's a bell by Giles's left hand. Tubes run from his right. Simon glances at the bag of blood, suspended on its own scaffolding. The blood crawls down the tube and into Giles. There are dressings on Giles's forehead. The hospital gown has a number stamped just below the neck. Giles wouldn't like that either. The numerals are so blurred with washing that you can't read them.

The hospital smell catches in Simon's throat. An animal instinct sweeps over him. He's got to get away. Back out on tiptoe so there's no chance of rousing Giles, turn to race along the corridors and then take the stone stairs two at a time, faster and faster, chasing the echo of his own footsteps. He wants to burst out into the night, and run all the way to the Tube, head back, legs pumping, even though there's no one after him. Later, he'll remember that instinct.

"Giles?" he says tentatively. He has absolutely no idea whether he's talking at normal volume or not. This place is far too quiet. Giles snores more deeply, as if he's heard Simon's voice but is determined to take no notice. Bugger this for a game of soldiers, thinks Simon in sudden annoyance. He should be at home, reading Paul's magazine so that the two of them can talk about it over breakfast. He should be listening to the play with Lily. Giles, with his telephone call, has put a stop to all that. Now that he's dragged Simon out, Giles can bloody well wake up.

He leans over the pillow and says loudly, "Giles, it's Simon. I'm here."

Slowly the eyelids unglue themselves. Giles's gaze, perfectly blank, is revealed. Even more slowly, he focuses. Simon sees the big darkness of his pupils contract: whoosh.

"What are you doing here?" asks Giles hoarsely. "Stuck a bloody tube down me." He clears his throat loudly. His eyes glint with the old conspiracy.

"You rang me up and asked me to come," says Simon. Yet again, in Giles's company, he experiences the sheer hopelessness of trying to impress on Giles that he, Simon, has an entirely separate life that is worthy of not being interrupted. Giles always knows where to put his hand on Simon, reclaiming him. Or trying to: Simon is stronger than Giles now, not because the other man is lying in a hospital bed, injured, but because he, Simon, has moved on to his own territory. He has Lily. He has the children. The past is the past. "You telephoned. Don't you remember?"

"So I did," says Giles. His voice is stronger now. He blinks, wrinkling up his face, and starts to cough. As the spasm develops, Simon grabs the glass of water from the locker and holds it to Giles's lips. He bats it away, spilling water on the bed. His skin darkens, dusky red and soon purple. Just as Simon's about to ring for the nurse, the tide of colour starts to ebb. The coughing fit is over. Giles wipes his mouth with his free hand. "It's that damned gas they give you. I was sick as a cat when I woke up."

"What kind of operation was it?"

"Surgical repair of a comminuted fracture of the right tibia and fibula," says Giles, with a flicker of pride. "Bloody nuisance, but as long as I keep my leg elevated the sawbones says I'll be as good as new. Or, to translate, with any luck my leg won't drop off."

"That's good. What happened? How did you do it?"

Weariness curtains Giles's eyes. "Lost my balance going downstairs."

"Did you have to wait ages before anyone came? No, I suppose not, there are always people coming and going in those flats."

Simon assumes that he must have fallen on the common stairway. "No," says Giles, "I was in my flat." He can't be bothered with explaining. Sleep, that's the thing. Tides of it washing over him. But first, Simon . . . He gathers himself. "I've left a file at home, like an idiot."

"You said. What file?"

"Julian asked me to go through it. You know he's in Venice. Shouldn't have taken it home, I know, but I'm up to my eyes at the moment. Left the wretched thing in my study. Oh, you don't know my study, do you? There's a staircase up to it, off the bedroom corridor. Door looks like a cupboard." The gaff is blown. The study is already a thing of the past. It will never be used again. Move on. "I'll give you the keys."

"You want me to bring you the file?"

"Not *here*," says Giles, with the old impatience, as if only a halfwit could ever have thought this. "Take it to Brenda in the morning. She'll deal with it."

Please, Simon nearly says aloud, so used is he to drumming manners into the children, and as if Giles has heard his thought, he wrenches out one of the old charming smiles and says:

"I'd be most awfully grateful, Simon. My name will be mud if that file isn't in place first thing."

What the hell do you mean, I don't know your study? I never knew you had a staircase in your flat. You haven't mentioned it in all these years.

36

What the hell do I think I'm up to? Is that what you want to know? Go on then, ask me.

They are both silent, bristling. Another door opens in Simon's mind, on to a grey January day years ago. He was in his digs, lying on the bed, huddled up, all the blankets piled on him and his winter coat on top of that. He was freezing cold, shaking with it. He'd got the flu, like everybody else. The night before he'd been so hot he'd chucked all the bedclothes on to the floor, even the sheet. There was a sick, sour smell around him and he ached all over. He was thirsty, but the glass by his bed was empty.

There was a knock at the door. Simon turned his head. The door opened and Giles stepped into the room. Simon wanted him to go away. He didn't want Giles to see him like that. But Giles put his hand on Simon's forehead and said, "You need aspirin. I'll go and buy some."

There was more muddled time, with Simon not sure if he was asleep or awake. Later, when it was dark, he woke up for sure. The gas fire was on, and Giles was sitting under the lamp, reading. He looked up and said, "You've got a touch of flu, dear boy." He lifted Simon's head and helped him to drink the lemon barley water that had appeared from somewhere. Two more aspirin. "You'll be as right as rain tomorrow. I'll sleep in the chair."

Simon wanted to protest, but said nothing. He was glad to have Giles there. The shadows seemed to be staying in their right places now, instead of reaching out for him. Later, Giles brought a bowl with soapy water and a flannel, and washed Simon's face and hands. Imperial Leather, not the cheap white soap that Simon's landlady supplied. He unbuttoned Simon's pyjama jacket, sponged his chest, and dried him carefully with the threadbare towel. Simon closed his eyes and went down deep, dark, into a sleep that lasted until it was light. Giles helped him to the lavatory and supported him while he peed a thin dark stream into the bowl. He was so weak that Giles had to half carry him back to bed.

"That was a bad idea," said Giles. "I'll ask your Mrs Thing for a chamber pot."

Simon lay with his eyes shut, exhausted. There were voices on the stairs, and then footsteps. He felt Giles come back into the room.

"I've told her to look in on you. Your meter's fed as high as it'll go and there's a pile of shillings beside it. Don't play the fool and overdo it. You'll be as weak as a cat for a day or so. See you next Saturday." He stroked the hair back from Simon's face then, and smiled at him.

The door to the past closes. Here is Giles, lying hooked up to the pulley. Poor old Giles, it really was a rotten thing to happen. He'll be laid up for weeks, if not months. He's not asking for much. It's a perfectly simple matter to fetch the file and get it back to Brenda.

"Bloody careless of me. I'm sorry, dear boy, I really am most frightfully tired."

He looks it. Drawn, yellowish, all the purple drained to the lees. He looks as if he might be going to die, Simon thinks, and then doesn't know what to do with this thought, or the slight but pungent relief that it brings. What kind of a selfish bastard am I? I'll have to say yes, even though it's probably just Giles flapping. The file can't be all that important, or it would never have left Julian's office.

"All right. I'll go in the morning."

Giles lifts his head, winces, drops back on to his pillow with closed eyes and mutters, "Tomorrow's no good. You might as well not go at all."

"You mean you want me to go now?"

"You were the first person I thought of," says Giles.

Simon has the keys to the flat in his hand when the nurse comes in, frowning, to take Giles's temperature and pulse. "I think you'd better go now," she says to Simon, rather severely, "Mr Holloway needs to be kept quiet."

Chastened, furious, Simon says, "Goodbye, then, Giles." There's no response. Perhaps Giles is already asleep, or unconscious, or, now that he's got what he wants, he has switched himself off.

Simon knows the flat well, but tonight it's strange to him. Everything is extremely tidy, and there is a strong smell of disinfectant. He switches on the hall light and advances past the sitting room, past the kitchen and the dark, narrow little dining room that Giles never uses, into the bedroom corridor. There's the door, just like a cupboard door, as Giles said. He's either not noticed it

39

before, or assumed it was the linen cupboard. The key fits. How on earth did Giles manage to lock it, with his leg in that state? He might have asked the ambulance men to do it, Simon supposes. Inside the attic stairwell, the smell of whisky is strong. There are dark splotches on the drugget. The stairs are steep and narrow. Servants' stairs. Why have a study up here? It was an accident waiting to happen. Giles must have been half-cut to fall like that. He usually was, any time after six o'clock.

The single bulb on the landing is unshaded and gives out a sallow light. The study door is open. Simon feels like a burglar, going in without Giles here.

The attic is cold, and stuffy. It smells of whisky in here, too, and the fug of trapped cigarette smoke. The ceiling is yellow with nicotine. He might open the window for a minute, to clear the air . . .

How extraordinary: the bottom of the window-frame is nailed to the sill. Giles is such a fresh-air fiend. He must be worried about cat burglars, coming over the roofs. You'd have to be a bloody good climber to get up here, thinks Simon, looking at the wet, steep tiles.

There's the file, on the desk. He picks it up, turns it over, holds it as if weighing what it contains, and then opens it. He is still. His son Paul would recognise the look of extreme concentration on Simon's face. It's how he looked when he tried to mend the broken piston on Paul's steam train.

His breath hisses through his teeth. What an ocean-going idiot, to leave this kind of stuff lying about. What the hell was Giles doing taking it home? *Up to his* eyes . . . Yes, in whisky. He's in a bad way. Worse than anyone knew. Losing his grip completely.

Suddenly, Simon's memory flashes back to a crowded pub years ago. He's sitting with Giles, crammed into a corner table. He's talking too loudly, and heads are turning. Giles is trying to shut him up: *Get a grip, Simon.*

Giles is the one who has lost his grip; or who simply doesn't care any more. No wonder he was so keen for Simon to get the file safely back. He must be getting slack, not keeping up with things, taking files home . . .

The explanations circle in Simon's head, going faster and faster, tightening like a band. He sees the stiff hospital gown with the number stamped on to it. Giles's face, discoloured against the white hospital linen. He looked shrunken — reduced. Giles would hate Simon to pity him.

Better get on with it. The file ought never to have left Julian Clowde's desk, except to be locked away. He'll get the bloody thing back to Brenda and that'll be the end of it. Never to be spoken of again, or even acknowledged between them, like so much else.

He can't go on the Tube with something like this tucked under his arm. Better find a bag. Or better still . . .

Beside the desk there are two briefcases. One, he knows: Giles's familiar dark-brown leather. The other is a dusty, battered pigskin, not at all Giles's style. It looks like the kind of thing a father might give to a son. He'll put the file in there, get it back to the office and then he can return the case to Giles later on.

Simon looks around for something to wipe off the dust, but the room is bare. No curtains, no rug. Just a small picture on the wall. Never mind. He takes out his own handkerchief, but then sees that the area around the fastenings isn't dusty. He opens the case, which is empty. In goes the file.

At that instant, he is sure that there's someone else in the flat. Did a door shut downstairs? Another sound comes, muffled, indistinct but closer. Simon is on the balls of his feet, skin prickling. Probably it's the cleaner, come to take a last look round. She's devoted to Giles, apparently.

Simon knows that's a nonsense. What cleaner would come at this hour of night? He scans the room for something heavy. Nothing. Downstairs, another creak as if an internal door is being opened, quite softly —

In a rush, briefcase in hand, Simon swarms down the stairs and through the cupboard door, barking, "Hello? Who's there?" Burglars are damned cowards, he knows that. All they want is to get away.

But it's not a burglar who appears at the door of Giles's bedroom. It's a heavy-set man with a curiously blank face, dressed in a suit. Frightful cut, thinks Simon automatically.

"Hello!" he says sharply. "Are you a friend of Peter's?"

"Peter? No, I don't know any Peter," says the man. "I am a friend of Giles."

Are you? thinks Simon. I rather wonder about that. You don't look in the least Giles's type. However, the

42

man clearly knows whose flat this is. "Just checking," he says. "One can never be too careful."

The man is looking at him intently, frowning. "Giles asked me to bring some personal possessions to him at the hospital."

"Oh, I see."

"He has perhaps also asked you to bring something for him?"

"Not exactly." Simon feels a sudden flush of annoyance. Who does this character think he is? "Have you got keys?"

In answer the man lifts his right hand and opens it, revealing a set of keys. They look the same as the ones Giles gave to Simon. How many spare sets has Giles got, for God's sake? He seems to scatter them about like confetti.

"I'm going now," says Simon. "Lock up after yourself, won't you? We don't want any burglaries."

"You are going to see him now?"

"As a matter of fact, I'm going home." The unspoken words *If it's any of your business* hang in the air between them. He doesn't want to leave this man in possession of Giles's flat, but short of marching him out of the door, he's going to have to. The man seems at ease; not at all furtive. But then, Giles has always had some pretty odd friends, although most of them are a lot younger.

"Goodnight," says Simon. The man looks down, very deliberately, at the briefcase Simon's carrying, but Simon is damned if he's going to offer any more explanations. Let him think what he likes.

* * *

How good the air tastes. Fresh and damp. Rain glistens on the pavement, but none is falling. He swings the briefcase in his right hand.

Walking has always been the way Simon makes sense of things. He beats his way on up the empty pavement, and it all takes shape inside him. He thinks of the man at the flat, with his own set of keys, quietly going through things. Making sure. Had he even seemed surprised to see Simon? He was a bit of a brute. Giles had poor taste, true, but usually the poor taste was a lot younger.

Simon lopes up Whitehall. Lily will be asleep by the time he gets back. No point in worrying her. She's never liked Giles. Maybe, if *he* met Giles now, for the first time, he wouldn't like him either. That bloody file. How could anybody be such an idiot?

He says the word over and over to himself, as if that will make it true. Giles is an idiot, and he drinks too much. He doesn't know what the hell he's doing, half the time. That's why he rang his old friend Simon.

Bloody careless of me. You were the first person I thought of.

Charing Cross. Simon accelerates along the tiled corridor, thinking he hears the whoosh of air that means an approaching train, but there's nothing. There are one or two others on the platform. Now he can hear a train. The briefcase swings. If he turned, like this, and just before the train came, chucked the case on to the rails —

But the train is here. The doors open, and the briefcase is still in his hand.

44

CHAPTER
FIVE

The Cartridge Burns

Simon closes his front door softly. All the downstairs lights are off. Upstairs, the dim landing light still burns, in case Bridgie wakes.

He's tired, but keyed-up. If the water tank weren't so noisy he would run a bath to relax. He wants to wash off the hospital, Giles's flat, that man padding about in Giles's bedroom. He goes into the kitchen, lights the gas and puts on the kettle, then takes it off again. He wanders into the dining room. Lily has laid the table ready for breakfast, as she always does. Bridgie dropped her rabbit plate, but he mended it: you can hardly see the join.

There's a bottle of cider on the dresser, back in the kitchen. Lily must have opened it, as a treat while she listened to the play. Her frugality frustrates him sometimes, but more often it moves him to tenderness. She is absurdly careful. If there's a glut of plums at the market, she makes jam. Their own apples, potatoes, carrots and turnips are carefully stored in the garden shed, well protected from frost. He takes the stopper from the cider bottle and pours himself a glass.

The mortgage is heavy. His parents gave them nothing, and Lily's mother had nothing to give. Her father, the mysterious father in Morocco whom Simon has never met, sent a cheque for a hundred pounds when Paul was born. A huge sum. Lily frowned at the cheque, scrutinising it as if it might be a forgery.

"What a piece of luck," said Simon.

"Let's see if it clears."

It did, and she bought the pram, the twin-tub and the sitting-room carpet. Simon's career — if you could call it that — was not exactly progressing. Now, years later, he's begun to understand that it never will. He'll plod on while the high-flyers flap their wings above his head. Already, some of them are a good bit younger than he is. Let them get on with it. He'd rather leave on the dot to do a tricky bit of soldering with Paul. His salary is solid, and Lily has her part-time teaching job. Her job paid for the stair carpet and the scarlet leather sofa and armchairs.

It's calming to think of money. It worries Lily, though. She makes lists, draws up budgets, calculates whether or not they'll be able to rent a holiday cottage next summer. But after an hour's frowning concentration she gets cross with herself, throws down pencil and paper and exclaims, "We forget how lucky we are. Look at the garden! Look at this house!" as if she'd never expected to be allowed such things. And, probably, she hadn't.

Lily looks so solemn when she's doing her sums. She must have looked like that when she was a little girl. Serious. Trying to be good. But then, suddenly, everything changes. He's always loved those summer days of cloud and light. When he's on a train he likes to watch the shadows fly over the landscape, chased by the sun. Lily throws down her pencil, shakes back her hair and smiles at him. You can't make Lily smile. He used to try, but it never worked. Her smile comes when you don't expect it, changing her face utterly.

He pours a second glass of cider, cuts a chunk off the loaf and fossicks about in the larder for the cheese. There's no pickle. Paul eats everything. He'll eat pickle out of a jar, with a spoon. Lily says it's his age and the rate at which he's growing. Simon tries to think back to himself at that age, but cannot. Doesn't want to. Touching on his childhood is like pressing a bruise.

He was never much of a Callington. His brothers called him "Milkman" because he was small and dark, and Callington men were big-boned, fair, blue-eyed. He told Lily that once, expecting her to laugh, but she drew her brows together. She's never thought much of the Callingtons, and in his heart he's glad of it.

The briefcase squats on the kitchen tiles. He'll have to put it away, or Lily will want to know whose it is. That damned file.

He opens the briefcase, watching his hands as if they are someone else's. The file is as it was. *Top Secret*. It ought to have been locked away. It certainly ought never to have left the office in Giles's briefcase.

But it did. Simon's hands hesitate, move, are still. His fingers want to open the file again, and read it. No, he tells himself. It's absolutely off to go poking about. Giles trusted him to collect the file and take it back to the office. To Brenda. Easy-peasy. Obviously Giles hasn't stopped to think about how bloody odd it might look if Simon were to parade into Julian Clowde's office and hand his secretary a file like this. No, Giles wouldn't think of that. Simon can almost hear him: *Surely you can employ a touch of discretion, dear boy?*

With sudden decision, he plunges the file back. As he does so, his fingers catch on a side-pocket he hadn't noticed before. There's something in there. The briefcase wasn't empty, as he'd thought. There's something in it, right at the bottom.

He draws it out, frowns, focuses. Again, his face takes on that look of extreme concentration. He turns the cartridge over. There's a serial number on the left-hand spool, and on the right it says: "36 EXP".

Very rapidly, face shuttered, he turns to the stove. The good old coke stove that he riddles night and morning. He bends down, picks up the forked-end tool and unhooks the plate. Inside, the coke burns sleepy red. He weighs the cartridge in his palm, then quickly drops it into the fire and replaces the plate. He hesitates again, and then takes the file from the briefcase and opens it. Very quickly, he flicks through its pages and then back to the first page, where three names are typed. By each name there is space for a set of initials. None of the names is Giles. The last of the three names is Julian Clowde's, and his initials show that he has read and returned the file. But he hadn't returned it. The file is in Giles's possession.

There could be any number of perfectly good reasons for that.

Simon takes the file between his hands, and attempts to tear it, but cannot. He glances at the door, then pushes the file back into the briefcase, takes it into the hall and shoves it to the back of the coats in the hall cupboard, behind the row of wellington boots.

That won't do. He pulls out the briefcase and rearranges the wellingtons. He'll take the case to a left-luggage office. He should have thought of that before. Much better than having it at home. He can leave the case in left luggage until he's decided what to do with it.

His heart is beating fast, as if he's run a race with Paul. He can still run faster than his son. "That's torn it," he says aloud as thick, noisy heartbeats push their way up into his throat. Already, he knows that he won't be handing the file to Brenda.

He must think. Giles will be in hospital for several days at least. How soon will the file be missed? Clowde's on leave, but . . . As for the cartridge . . . No, he's not going to think about that now. And why hasn't he burned the file? Deep in himself, shamefully, he knows that he needs it. It is evidence.

He's in a state, as Lily would say to the children. He glances up at the clock. Ten to twelve. Only a few hours since Giles rang. None of it has taken long at all, but it seems to Simon as if his whole life is rushing away from him like a train disappearing down the line. But of course that's nonsense. Here he is, in his own house, with Lily and the children asleep upstairs. Husband and father, breadwinner. Those words are true and safe but at the same time they don't sound real. He sees

49

himself: a tiny figure set down in a life he doesn't really understand, like one of the models who wait for the trains on the platform of Paul's railway set.

Simon Callington. Look where he is now. All this has come about through his own fault, through not seeing what he ought to have seen, not asking the questions he ought to have asked, refusing to recognise what was right in front of him. That Giles, his old friend Giles — But now, at ten to midnight, with the cartridge melting to nothing in the stove, he might as well call a spade a spade. Giles has been batting for the other side in more ways than one. There may be a good reason for taking such a highly restricted file out of the office, but try as he may, he can't find one that explains away the film cartridge. How could he, knowing Giles so well, knowing him for so long, have failed to see what was going on?

Failed . . . Or chosen to fail. It's the old story he's been hearing since he was eight years old. "Simon is a boy who could go far, but is hampered by his own sheer mental laziness." Simon will never climb past the middle of any ladder, let alone to the top. Simon is a reasonably competent civil servant. He quite likes his work. The sense that not too much is expected of him is a relief rather than a goad. Simon is a good chap. One of us. If a copy of the *Railway Magazine* strays from Simon's briefcase at lunchtime, it does him no harm.

He ought to have stayed at Cambridge. He might have written a book.

Idiotic. He didn't get his First. He'd always known he wasn't going to. He hadn't a first-class mind.

50

He must put the briefcase in the shed in the back garden for now, and leave the side gate unbolted. In the morning, he'll nip up the path and fetch it, after he's said goodbye to Lily and the children. Then he'll go straight down to King's Cross, to the left-luggage office. After that the bloody thing will be out of the way and he won't have to think of it again.

He listens. Sometimes, even now, Lily gets up to check that the children are all right. But tonight everything is still. They are all fast asleep and they know nothing. Simon looks around the room. There is Lily's pile of marking, all done. After that she would have laid the table for breakfast. She doesn't like a mad rush in the mornings . . .

There are a few twigs of winter-flowering cherry in a blue jug by the toast-rack. She must have gone out in the dark to pick them.

He thinks that he can still smell the cartridge burning.

CHAPTER
SIX

One Way Out

Simon picks up the receiver and hears heavy breathing. There's a scrabble, followed by a grunt of annoyance. "Dropped the sodding receiver in what passes for breakfast," says Giles.

"How are you feeling?"

"Bloody awful."

"You must be getting on all right, if they let you have breakfast."

Another grunt, then: "I can make a telephone call, if that's what you mean. How did *you* get on?"

"At your flat, you mean?"

"You found the file all right?"

"Yes." Simon runs the telephone cord between finger and thumb, then squeezes it hard in his left hand. The silence develops. He should say something, but what? He nearly gave his own name at the left-luggage office, but remembered just in time and wrote "Stephen Cartwright" on the form. The briefcase is in the left-luggage office at King's Cross. The cartridge is in the stove. Simon is at his desk. It all reminds him of Bridgie's school reading books and he finds he is smiling.

"I can't hear you."

"I said, 'Yes'." He is not in Giles's world, whatever Giles may think. He is in his own. "I found it all right."

And it must all be there in his voice, because Giles is silent, breathing. In the background, Simon can hear hospital sounds.

"Have you taken it back?" asks Giles at last, and Simon is back in prep school Latin, learning the form for "Questions expecting the answer 'No'".

"Not yet."

"Why the hell not?" He's querulous now, but also, Simon thinks, relieved by that weaselly "yet".

"It's a bit awkward."

"It'll be more than a bit bloody awkward for me, if you don't pull your finger out. Or" — his voice changes, becomes charged with something Simon doesn't quite want to name — "do you mean that it's awkward at this particular moment?"

He means, is anyone else within earshot? Or is the business of putting the file back turning out to be trickier than Giles thought, for some other reason? Brenda away, for instance? Complicity, that's what it's called. I was mistaken, Simon thinks. It hasn't crossed Giles's mind that I won't do as he wants. He thinks he's got me. Am I going to go on letting him think that?

The plaited telephone cord is printed into Simon's palm. "No," he says. "It's always going to be awkward, Giles, as far as I'm concerned. The file's in a safe place. I shan't discuss the matter with anyone. But I can't muck about with a file like that."

53

There's a hissing, whistling silence, as if the line has been cut. This goes on for a few seconds, and then the receiver clatters into its rest.

And now, drugged to the eyeballs and woozy as he is, Giles swings into action. He is black with fury against Simon. Christ! He sounded like a headmaster chiding some boy about a confiscated dirty book. Who the hell does he think he is? Ask him to do the simplest thing, and he not only cocks it up but has the temerity to make it sound as if Giles is the one at fault. Rage and self-righteousness course through Giles. Simon has left him no choice. Now, if he can get that telephone into position, it should be perfectly possible to take off the receiver, dial and then lift the receiver, all with one hand. He won't be forced to rely on that fool of a girl to dial for him.

It is bloody difficult. By the time he gets the connection, he is sweating and exhausted, which does nothing to improve his temper.

"Good morning, is that the Sunbeam Laundry?" asks Giles.

"I'm afraid you have the wrong number. This is Wilkes' Tea Importers."

"I beg your pardon. Good morning." He replaces the receiver. Time to go through the whole childish performance again. "Good morning, is that Wilkes' Tea Importers?"

"Yes, Wilkes' Tea Importers, which department, please?"

"Put me through to Mr Thompson, would you?"

A series of clicks and whistles. The nurse outside Giles's room glances incuriously, professionally, at her patient on the other side of the glass. Pulse, temperature and fluids chart in twenty minutes.

Without announcement, a different voice speaks in Giles's ear: "You should not call me on this number. Brown has been to the flat. Everything else is organised. Your chum has taken the subject back?" It's the man Giles knows as Alex. *Chum*. Where in God's name do they learn their English?

"The thing is, there's been a slight hitch." And then he hears himself go on, stupidly — because of the bloody anaesthetic, that's what it is; the real Giles would never talk like that: "I'm sure I can sort it out. Just give me a chance —"

Alex's voice sharpens. "Go on."

Giles goes on. The man at the end of the line doesn't speak until Giles finishes, and then all he says, quite softly, is, "How long will it be before the subject is missed?"

"I'm not absolutely sure. Just possibly tomorrow morning." Even as he says it, he knows that Alex knows it's a lie.

"This really is a frightful nuisance, old boy."

Giles hears his own tone coming back at him, mocking him. Now Alex can show his contempt. *Unreliable*, that's Giles. Bloody drunkard, falling downstairs, risking everything, and then making another balls-up when he tries to put things right. Alex will sacrifice Giles immediately. He's always known that.

The bed is rank and sweaty. His leg itches. Silence hisses through the telephone line, but he knows that Alex is still at the other end. Silence is also a weapon. Here Giles lies like a pig on a spit, unable to do a bloody thing. His mind clicks on, measuring the distance it must travel to safety. What the bloody hell did Simon think he was playing at? *I can't muck about with a file like that.* Too pure to pretend you don't know what you're doing, for the sake of good old Giles. You won't sully yourself. You don't want to be down in the dirt.

Now it's rising in him, a groundwater of anger that's been gathering for years. You married a woman called *Lily*, for fuck's sake. Pure as the lilies in the sodding dell. *You didn't want me*, says his mind, lifting layer after layer, finding the raw place. Long-ago rages and humiliations, fresh as the paint on a canvas hidden behind another canvas for decades. And the fear. He's always had his get-out more than half-fixed, but he won't be slipping away to Bergen with half a ton of plaster and pulleys attached to his leg. He's trapped. A sitting duck.

Frith will have him. He'll sit at Giles's bedside, night and day, implacable, until Giles is well enough to be taken into custody. Mr Plod. All Giles's brains and wit and quickness — *all that he is* — won't help him. They'll pull out the coils of his double life — all those years, his *cleverness* — and by the time they've finished his guts will be all over the floor.

Everything falls away. Oscar Wilde stood on a platform at Clapham Junction for half an hour, in shackles and prison uniform. Presumably, those in charge of his transfer made sure that there would be that half an hour of utter disgrace. It wasn't enough for them that he'd lost everything and was on his way to pick oakum. His gaolers looked the other way and left him to it as a crowd gathered to shove and shout and jeer. One man spat in his face.

"I, once a lord of language, have no words in which to express my anguish and my shame."

A man in prison uniform covered with arrows, jailed for sodomy. That's what comes of trying to be so funny. Who's laughing now?

Have you heard the latest about Giles Holloway?

Marigold says she always knew that there was something not quite right about him.

He'd have cleared off like Burgess and Maclean if it hadn't been for his accident.

Oh, come on, surely you're not saying Giles Holloway was in the same league as those two. From what I gather, he was just an errand boy. Yes, I know, getting a bit old for an errand boy . . .

It's all rather seedy.

"I must say to myself that I ruined myself, and that nobody great or small can be ruined except by his own hand."

A fat, queer traitor, a drunkard and a bungler. Who's laughing now?

"I hope that you have got a bright idea," says Alex.

Giles has only got one. There's one way out. Simon.

All day it has been streaming wet, but now ragged holes have appeared in the cloud cover. Sometimes they show the moon. It looks as if it's racing across the sky, but of course that's an illusion. Simon has been working late for once, and was just about to go home when he had a message that old Firclough wanted him. After what seemed like hours of Firclough's mouth opening and shutting, it turned out to be something perfectly trivial: a list of submarine movements that wasn't completed correctly by some underling who was apparently, suddenly, Simon's responsibility.

Lights are still on, high up in the buildings; policemen change shift. There are always lights burning, and always policemen on guard.

It's only a step from the Admiralty to Charing Cross, but he's going in the other direction, down Whitehall. He'll go as far as Derby Gate, then along the Embankment as far as Northumberland Avenue, and back up again. The smell of the water will clear his head. He doesn't want to go home until he has decided what to do. He doesn't want to bring all this home with him.

He never takes the bus from Highgate: always walks. Up the hill, then along Woodland Gardens and The Chine, across and upward through the narrow grid of streets until he reaches the terrace where he would never have imagined himself living. *All the way uphill and home.* That's what Lily tells the children, when they tire and pull on her hands. Lily believes in walking. But he's forgetting: only Bridgie is still young enough to whinge. When he's away from Lily, the image that comes when he thinks of her and the children dates from years back: Lily pushing the big pram up the road

58

to the shops against the wind, with the baby as fat as an emperor under the canopy, Sally on a seat across the body of the pram, and Paul alongside, clutching the ivory pram handle. Sally was a hopeless walker, until she went to school. Lily leans forward as she pushes the weight of the pram uphill. Her hair whips over her face. She presses her lips together and pushes harder.

A muscle twitches in his cheek. It's been the hell of a day, he tells himself, and the banality of the words almost calms him. Once or twice a year he'll come home and burst open the front door, raging against the whole damned lot of them and how the office is eating up his life. "It's been the hell of a day," he'll explode, and she'll advance, pushing back her hair, not at all disconcerted, saying something like, "The collar on that shirt's worn, I hadn't realised — and they've given me an extra half-day's teaching. That's good, isn't it?" and she'll smile. No matter what his day is or was, her smile says it's over and it can't follow him here.

That won't work tonight. He has got to fetch the briefcase from the left-luggage office. He can't think why he was such a fool as to take it there in the first place. He filled out the form and took the ticket, and then suddenly, hours later, while watching the end of Firclough's nose as he spoke — a little twitch every sentence or so, he'd never noticed it before — Simon realised what he'd done. If Simon didn't come back for the case, they would look inside it for a name and address, and then they'd find the file. Why the hell hadn't he burned it, along with the cartridge? But that wouldn't have solved anything: Giles would have asked where it was, the file would be missed — and that file is the only evidence that Simon hasn't dreamed up the whole business.

There's a bit of a flap on about Giles. Comings and goings down the corridor. Rumours that the piles of fag ash and papers on Giles's desk are being sorted out at last. That man Frith has been in there all day. Giles has come a cropper, they say. Poor old bugger has fallen downstairs and smashed his leg. He won't be back for weeks. Simon says nothing. The talk of the office washes around him while his heart beats with uneven strokes.

He can't remember when he last felt like this. Uneasy, as if something toxic is bubbling away inside him. Not knowing, for the life of him, what to do. Maybe it was that first night at Bradenham, after his parents had driven away, when hundreds of other boys surged around him, shoving him out of their way as if he weren't Simon Callington of Stopstone House, Stopstone, Norfolk, England, the World, the Universe, Outer Space, but anyone or anything at all. If he'd looked down at his hands and seen them transformed to a pig's trotters, he wouldn't have been surprised.

It seems a hundred years since he put on his clean white shirt that morning, upstairs in their bedroom, at half past seven. The light was murky, and the street-lamps were still on. Simon went to the window as he always did, tying his tie with automatic fingers, gazing over the city and its lights.

60

"You can see as far as the Surrey Hills," the estate agent had boasted when they came to view the house. Simon had never set foot in Muswell Hill in his life. He didn't know what to make of the narrow hall and long strip of garden that ran down to a disused railway line. Whether or not the house was worth two thousand pounds, he hadn't the faintest idea. But Lily had gone straight to the bedroom window and leaned out.

"It's beautiful," she'd said quietly, so that only Simon could hear, and then she'd turned to the estate agent and begun to bargain. He had put out his hand to stop her, before he realised that the estate agent was listening, really listening, as Lily discussed with un-English frankness what they would pay and what they would expect for the price.

Hundreds and hundreds of clean white shirts, a fresh one each morning. How many years of clean shirts? Paul was two, Sally one, Bridgie not yet born when they moved into the house. The children had loved it from the first minute. Lily kept a dustbin full of clay in the kitchen, and they modelled birds and animals and queer little families to which they gave names he couldn't remember. They would play like that for hours on end, and then they'd be out in the garden in their siren suits in all weathers. He used to have tiger hunts with them in the dark, when he came home, and then he'd bring them in, Paul and Sally standing on his shoes and clinging to his legs, Bridget in his arms.

Every morning the faint smell of Imperial Leather, and a splash of the cologne Lily bought him at Christmas. Lily seeing him off, rubbing her cheek against his smooth face, kissing him on the lips. And then he was out of the front door, swinging down the steep steps and on to the street. He always turned and waved to the children. But now they're too old for clustering at the window in their pyjamas. They're busy, clattering up and down the stairs, getting ready for school. Bridget can't find her shoes; Paul hasn't got a shirt —

His body is clammy with sweat and his shirt sticks to him unpleasantly. He can't go home like this. He'll have to do something. Once he's got the briefcase back, he'll know what to do with it. He thought that the man behind the counter at the left-luggage office looked at him strangely when he deposited the case.

He has reached the public gardens and can smell the dirty brown spoor of the river through the traffic fumes. The Thames looks dangerous as it slides about in the dark, sucking at its bridges. Some days, even as far upstream as this, he tastes salt. Today is not one of those days. He turns left, then hesitates. But what can he do, if he doesn't go home? What else is there? He is what he appears to be, a reasonably well-regarded civil servant in his thirties, in dark suit and tie, dark overcoat, no hat. He glances sideways into the trees, and then, as if he's found no answer there, he strides out along the path that goes east, parallel to the river. A gust of rain blows in his face but he doesn't put up his umbrella. The wind is rising again, thrashing branches, whipping the piles of wet leaves. It blows the shadows about so that even if Simon were to look round he might not see the two men in dark overcoats and trilbies who are walking fifty yards or so behind him, keeping pace with him. The wind covers the sound of their footsteps. They follow him for a short distance, and then they peel away.

At the left-luggage office, Simon hands in his ticket. The chap at the counter disappears into the back. Simon waits, glancing around. Outside, a policeman walks past with slow, steady gait. *He's on his beat, you fool. Nothing to do with you.*

"Here you are, Mr Cartwright."

Simon stares at him, absolutely blank, the words, "My name's not Cartwright," as near as damn it on his lips. On the way home, grasping the case, he reassures himself. That chap won't remember anything; he must have hundreds of people through his office every day.

The truth is, Simon's no good at this sort of thing. Using his own initials in a false name was idiotic, and he hadn't even realised it. He might as well have laid a trail to his own front door. He's got to get a grip. Lily and the children mustn't be dragged into all this.

CHAPTER
SEVEN

A Contamination

Lessons are over, and the girls are going home. By the netball court, Miss Davenport claps her hand at a bunch of stragglers as if she is herding geese. The second team hasn't yet given up the idea of holding an extra practice, although it's raining and almost too dark for them to see the ball. Lily, standing at the staff-room window, watches idly. This is the rarest of moments for her: a corner of time when she doesn't have to do anything. Bridget is going to tea with her friend Lucy. Even better, Lucy's mother will collect both children from school. Sally and Paul are old enough to walk home on their own and look after themselves for an hour or so. They are sensible children.

"Cigarette?" It is Barbara Watson behind her. Lily turns, and takes a cigarette from the offered packet. They light up, and both turn back to the window, which has darkened, it seems, in the few seconds since Lily last looked out. A squall spatters the glass. The netball players have had enough and they run for shelter, shrieking. Everything girls do at this age is exaggerated, thinks Lily. There are chrysanthemums in the flower bed opposite the window, held up by bamboo canes but battered by wind and rain. The flowers will have lost their scent.

"You're usually off straight away," says Barbara.

"I'm waiting for my timetable. They have to fit in the private lessons around the classes. It's very complicated, apparently."

"Next term's, you mean?"

"Yes. I've got an extra morning's teaching."

"That's good, isn't it?"

"Yes, it will be useful."

Barbara Watson draws luxuriously on her cigarette, head back, eyes half-shut. This is the moment she's been waiting for all afternoon: the quiet sense of camaraderie between old soldiers who have served another day. Or is it time in prison that is served? She slides a sideways glance at Lily, who seems rather out of sorts. It's the weather, perhaps. Children are always restless when the wind blows. Perhaps her lessons have been difficult this afternoon.

Lily stares into the gathering darkness. Simon is not himself. That telephone call from Giles has upset him. Why should he go out in the night like that? He came back so late that she was asleep. He is keyed-up. But perhaps it's only because he is tired. He was boisterous with the children this morning. Too boisterous. Bridget cried after he'd gone. Usually he knows better than to get Bridget worked up before school —

"Why the sigh?"

"What?"

"Is anything the matter, Lily?"

For a second, in the dusk, as they stand together with the red tips of their cigarettes brightening and fading, Lily thinks: She is a friend. Not a friend like Erica . . . But I can trust her. The spatter of rain on the thin glass makes the room private. She knows that Barbara Watson is discreet. She has a dry humour that Lily likes very much. Barbara isn't one of those women who suck your secrets out of you and then treat them like their own private property, to be shared out at will. But to trust or to like, Lily also knows, is not the same as to speak. She learned that long ago; had it drummed into her.

The light snaps on behind them.

"Here you are, all in the dark!" announces Miss Harrold, the school secretary, as if they'd have had no way of knowing this without her. She surges forward with a sheaf of papers in her hand and a smile that shows her teeth. The little ones are often fooled in their first term, because Miss Harrold looks so motherly. They soon learn that she enforces school protocol to the letter. Her ample bosom, should you try to repose on it, would be iron-hard.

"Thank you," says Lily, taking the papers. Yes, it's the timetable. She glances quickly across the hours.

"It was all rather complicated, I'm afraid," says Miss Harrold with an edge of blame to her voice.

"I'm sure it was." Lily will not blunder into apologising to this woman because she has had to do a job she is paid to do.

"This is Week A and this is Week B. As you see, I've had to slot in a single Week C at the end of term, in order to equalise the times."

66

"I'm sure it will work very well. Thank you, Miss Harrold."

God knows what the woman's Christian name is. No one ever uses it. The older members of staff refer to her as "Harrold", but Lily is not on such terms.

There's a pause, as if more should be said or done, and then the secretary makes for the door, turning off the lights as she leaves, apart from a single bulb above Lily and Barbara's heads. Barbara Watson raises her eyebrows, and Lily pulls a little, conspiratorial face.

Barbara is fond of Lily. If someone — she can't imagine who — were to ask her, she would reply, "Oh yes, I'm very fond of Lily Callington." Suddenly Barbara is oppressed by her own emotions, muffled by a sense of possibilities that will never be realised. Perhaps, if she and Lily were to meet outside school, things would be different . . .

She's only seen Lily outside school once. You'd think you would always be running across people. West Hampstead isn't so far from Muswell Hill, for heaven's sake. Lily was on the other side of the road, with her little girl holding her hand. Lily was bending down and the little girl was saying something to her. Lily's hair blew about her face and when she straightened up again she was smiling in a way she never smiled at school. Instead of crossing the road to greet her, Barbara stepped back into a shop doorway.

"Really, you wouldn't think it was a job she does every term," says Lily.

"I know. What a performance." Barbara's lips ache as they quirk into a dry smile. "Another cigarette, Lily?"

"No, thank you. I must go."

Barbara Watson glances at her watch. "Good heavens, is that the time?" she observes, as if she, too, is in a hurry. Rain streams down the windows. All the children have gone now. She must buy coffee beans from Enzo's on her way home. She is very particular about her coffee. A cup of steaming coffee, her fire lit, the pile of marking, curtains drawn against the beating of rain and wind. She will have the wireless on. She'll mark the odd, artless little compositions of the Upper Third. Sometimes she'll glance up as if to share the joke with someone.

Perhaps she shouldn't have asked Lily if anything was the matter. There *is* something wrong, she's sure of it. Just for a moment, it seemed as if Lily might confide in her, but then that wretched Harrold came in, and the moment was gone. Lily is so reserved, she thinks to herself quickly, and then, in a flash of bleak insight: *She will never tell you anything.*

Lily's children sit around the dining-room table, doing their homework. She watches their bent, shining heads. Sally looks up, eyes blank as she counts on her fingers under the table, where she hopes Paul will not see. Even Bridget has invented some school task for herself and is crayoning a magic castle. Simon hasn't come home yet. Lily waited to serve the beef casserole, but when he had not arrived by seven, she ate with the children. Eight o'clock. It's late for Bridget. She'll send them up to bed in a minute. The dining-room fire is uneasy too, as the wind blows down the chimney.

"I want to show Daddy my drawing," says Bridget.

"He's going to be late tonight," Lily says. Earlier she had made a mistake, wondering aloud why Simon was late until she saw the flash of anxiety in Sally's eyes. She must seem certain. Their family life must not appear to be blown about by forces she cannot control.

"But he was going to paper the front bedroom of the doll's house! He promised!" bawls Bridget, tears spurting off her cheeks.

"Dad didn't promise," says Paul, bored. "He just said he might if there was time. Why are you such a baby? Can't you see that Mum's tired, Bridget the Pidget?"

At last, Lily gets Bridget upstairs, and baths her as if she really *is* a baby, soaping her back and drying her on her lap in a towel that has been kept warm in the airing cupboard. All the while she watches herself with a touch of irony. She knows that she is doing this for herself, to comfort herself with the firm sweetness of Bridget's body, and the logical rigmarole of Bridget's thoughts. Sally is already in bed, reading. Paul has his *Railway Magazine* and is saying for the hundredth time how much he wishes they hadn't closed the railway line at the bottom of the garden.

"But if it hadn't been closed, you wouldn't have the copse to play in," Lily points out, as she always does.

"I know, but . . ." He wriggles in his bed, unable to explain himself. It is the romance of it he wants. The rails singing long before the train comes into sight, the thunder of the locomotive, the blur of light from the carriage windows. The whole house would vibrate with it. He bends over his magazine again and traces the outline of Britannia Standard Class Locomotive *Evening Star*. He will cut out the picture. Dad said that it was the last steam locomotive that would ever be built in Britain.

He'll be home soon, Lily thinks as she settles herself with her marking. She works quickly and with method, making notes in a separate small book where she records each child's progress. Each time the wind slams against the glass her nerves crisp, but she works on calmly. The telephone rings in the hall, and she jumps up quickly, in case its ringing wakes the children. But it's only Erica, asking if Lily will be able to have Thomas after school while she takes the baby to the clinic. After she's put the receiver back in its cradle, Lily picks it up again, then stands irresolute. There's no point in ringing Simon's office number now. She puts the receiver down softly, goes upstairs to their bedroom and pulls back the curtains. On nights like this the house is like a ship, surging in the wind above the sea of London. She clasps her elbows, then rubs her upper arms to warm herself. She thinks of Simon walking uphill, head down against the rain, doggedly making for home.

As if her thoughts have brought him into being, she sees him, away down the street, under a swinging pool of lamplight. Now he has walked on into the darkness but she can still see him, head down, briefcase in hand. It is his shape and walk; she'd know them anywhere. She's about to go down and open the front door when there is a cry from Bridget. She goes to the bedroom door, and there is Bridget, reared up in her bed, staring. Still asleep, Lily knows. It happens sometimes. She waits. The thing is not to wake her, or she will start screaming. There's Simon, coming in downstairs.

"Lie down, darling, and I'll tuck you in," says Lily, as she says every night when she puts Bridget to bed, and through her sleep Bridget hears the words and lies down on her side. In a few moments more, she is breathing peacefully.

Lily kisses Simon's cold face.

"Bridget had one of her night wakings," she says. "You go and have a wash. There's no hurry. I haven't put your rice on yet."

She listens to his heavy tread as he mounts the stairs, then she goes to the kitchen to warm up his share of the casserole and cook more rice. She wants to give him time. Something is wrong. The feeling of wrongness is all around him.

"Here you are. Sit down."

"Aren't you going to eat?"

"I had mine with the children. It's almost ten o'clock, Simon."

"Oh. Is it?" He doesn't apologise. He smells of soap now, but there is something else too: metallic, gunny. Has he been drinking? She doesn't think so. Lily carries a dish of finely chopped and steamed Savoy cabbage to the table. She cooks it with caraway seeds and finishes it with butter. The children are beginning to realise that the food they eat at home is quite different from school food. At their friends' houses, tea might be slices of Spam with beetroot salad, salad cream and bread and butter. Only the Jewish homes offer the intensity of taste and texture with which they are familiar. Bridget loves Spam, however. She can cut it into any shape she wants, as if it's a more malleable form of Plasticine. Lily smiles, safe for a moment behind thoughts of the children.

Simon eats a little, then pushes his plate aside.

"Aren't you hungry?"

He looks down at the casserole, the rice and cabbage. "Sorry, Lil," he says. "Hold on, I bought a book for you. I've been carrying it about all day."

It is a copy of *Lady Chatterley's Lover*.

"The full, unexpurgated edition," says Simon.

"Could you get it so soon? Have they published a new edition already?" It's been only two weeks since the Lady Chatterley trial finished.

"No," says Simon, "I got it from a bookseller who had stockpiled copies from the first edition. He's safe to sell them now, so good luck to him. I thought I would bring one home for my wife."

She smiles, takes the book, flicks it open and begins to read:

Connie was sorting out one of the Wragby lumber rooms. There were several: the house was a warren, and the family never sold anything. Sir Geoffrey's father had liked pictures and Sir Geoffrey's mother had liked cinquecento furniture. Sir Geoffrey himself had liked old carved oak chests, vestry chests. So it went on through the generations. Clifford collected very modern pictures, at very moderate prices.

So in the lumber room there were bad Sir Edwin Landseers and pathetic William Henry Hunt birds' nests: and other Academy stuff, enough to frighten the daughter of an R.A. She determined to look through it one day, and clear it all. And the grotesque furniture interested her.

Lily looks up and smiles. "Like your family."

"But I don't collect very modern pictures at any price."

"Are you all right, Simon?"

"Of course I am. What are you talking about?"

She sighs. "I wish you'd ring when you're going to be so late. Bridget was waiting for you to wallpaper the doll's house with her. She wouldn't go to bed. She's done all these tiny paintings to hang once the walls are finished."

"Couldn't you have done it?"

"I could. But it was you she wanted."

At once, a black mood overtakes him. He frowns, hunching over the drink Lily has given him. Such moods are familiar to her and they always pass. It's not his mood that worries her, but the tension around him, the almost audible zizz of his nerves. Something has certainly happened.

"There's Bridget now," she says suddenly, looking up at the ceiling. "She must have woken up again."

Simon puts down his drink and goes upstairs. She hears Bridget's voice, cheeping, instantly sociable, and

Simon's, deeper. She guesses that they are coming up with a plan about the doll's-house wallpaper. Lily takes the plate into the kitchen, but does not yet throw away the food. That, for her, is the hardest thing in the world to do.

As he comes downstairs, Simon notices for the first time that Lily has replaced the cherry blossom with burnt-orange and brown chrysanthemums. The room is full of their bitter autumn tang.

"What happened to the blossom?"

"It got knocked over, and Bridget stood on it. Fancy you noticing." She's pleased, he can tell, and he's flooded with compunction. Lily gave him beef casserole with rice, at ten o'clock and without comment. Lily's cooking makes him feel as if he belongs to a secret society because it is so unlike the meals that his colleagues describe. He wishes now that he had eaten his meal. He isn't hungry, but he says, "Could you warm up the casserole again, Lil?" and sees her face brighten. He can almost hear her thoughts: He's hungry; he must be feeling better.

While he eats, Lily sets the clothes horse in front of the dining-room fire. "Your coat is soaked," she explains, and spreads it out carefully. It is a good coat, a charcoal-grey Crombie. A Callington coat. A present from his mother, for his thirtieth birthday.

He watches her. She's frowning, not because she's worried now but because she's thinking about his coat. She kneels down and adjusts the legs of the clothes horse to make it more secure under the heavy weight.

74

She always handles his things carefully, and in just the right way, as if she is touching him.

Usually he rings the doorbell, for the pleasure of hearing her come to the door, but tonight he used his key. Lily was upstairs. He pushed the briefcase with the file in it right to the back of the coats again, behind the children's boots. It would do for now. If Lily was looking for something — one of the kids' gloves, say — she might find it, but it's probably all right. Perhaps he wants her to find it. He wants her to say: What's this, Simon? and then it will all come out. *A trouble shared is a trouble halved.* Lily says that, without irony. It's one of the little sayings that make you realise, as nothing else does, that she wasn't born speaking English. Well, of course, no one was, but Lily's ear is almost faultless. That's why she's so good at languages, because she can hear what sounds right. But sometimes, she misses a beat. He doesn't correct her. He likes her moments of slightly old-fashioned bookishness. He likes her sudden foreignness, which only shows for a moment before it disappears, and Lily is a Londoner again.

He's smiling in spite of himself, thinking of her. Lily mustn't know anything. Lily and the children must be kept safe.

He won't think about the damned file any more tonight. He'll find a better place for the briefcase. With luck, it will all die down —

"Simon!"

"What?"

"I thought you hadn't heard me. Are you all right?"

75

"Of course I'm all right. I'm tired, that's all." He makes an effort, and smiles. "Let's have an early night."

She isn't fooled. She won't ask him, though. His mother said that Lily was cold.

"She doesn't seem awfully interested, Simon."

"Interested in what, Ma?"

She meant that Lily wasn't giving her what she wanted. There was no touch of deference, no shadow of eagerness to join the Callington world. Lily wanted nothing that the Callingtons could give or withhold. He can see her now, in the shrubbery at Stopstone, in the winter coat she'd made herself from a *Vogue* pattern. She had found a bolt of tweed inside a chest in a junk shop — old stuff, pre-war quality. Lily loved things like that. His mother was talking at her, while Lily rubbed between her fingers a leaf of bay.

"Your poor shoes," said his mother. "It's frightfully muddy this way." She meant: *Don't you know enough to bring suitable shoes to the country?*

Lily glanced down at her black suede shoes. Her best, he knew. "They'll be fine," she said indifferently, as if she had fifty pairs.

So why doesn't he confide in Lily? He trusts her completely, far more than he trusts himself. Lily is everything. She is the still point in his turning world. Again those ridiculous tears that will never be shed prickle at the back of his eyes and throat. Get a grip, Callington. Get a bloody grip.

The briefcase with Giles Holloway's file in it has entered the house, like a contamination. He doesn't know what to do with it. He can't return it now. Its absence must have been noted. He can't get rid of the file, because it's evidence. But that works both ways —

He rubs his forehead, pushing up his hair. He has forgotten Lily. He is thinking of Giles Holloway. *Giles* . . .

CHAPTER
EIGHT

The Single Bed

He can't even remember the first time he saw Giles.
When he first met Lily, she seemed to fit a place within
him that had always been there, waiting for her.
Through Lily he learned what he was. But Giles
claimed him, as if he'd lost Simon long ago and simply
stepped forward to say, "This is mine, I think."

Afterwards, Giles said he'd noticed Simon a few
times, around Cambridge, when he was visiting Ali
Ferguson. But although Simon often looked back to
those days, trying to remember when it was that he had
first caught sight of Giles, he always came up with the
same, original image: Giles standing there, one foot on
the fender of the pub's fireplace, with a glass of whisky
in his hand. The fire wasn't lit because it was June.
Light spilled in through the low doorway, showing up
motes which danced like gnats. The others were all out
in the garden, drinking beer and eating pickled eggs
because there was nothing else to be had.

"You're Simon, aren't you?" said Giles.

Simon coloured slightly. Giles knew perfectly well
who he was. Ali had driven Simon and three others
from Cambridge in a crammed, clapped-out Austin 7.

Giles Holloway had arrived in his new Wolseley 4/50, straight from London. Simon liked cars. He'd gone over to have a look at the Wolseley, in the pub car park. Giles had arrived first. He was older, and rich enough to drink whisky instead of beer.

"Aren't you coming outside with the others?" Simon asked.

"I like it in here," said Giles.

The bar was empty. The publican was polishing glasses, slowly, with a blue and white cloth. His profile was carved, remote.

"D'you want a drink?" Giles asked.

"I've got one outside."

There was a shout of laughter from the garden. It sounded exaggerated, Simon thought. There was a clock on the wall, stuck at half past seven. The floor was brick, in a herringbone pattern. If the clock were ticking, thought Simon, or if the fire were lit, it might be pleasant in here.

Giles had crossed to the bar, and was tapping a half-crown on it. The publican moved slowly towards him, as if underwater. Simon heard Giles ordering more whisky, and he turned away to rejoin the others.

Outside the pub door there was a bed planted with violently red salvias. He stared at them until the colour throbbed. His mother was always marching about the garden, telling the gardener what she wanted, going down on her haunches to point out some disease in the fiercely coloured beds. No gardener stayed long. When he was younger he'd had such an overwhelming desire to kick her in the backside while she knelt that he had to race past her, full tilt. He had to get away from her and from himself.

Giles Holloway touched his arm and Simon just managed not to jump. He looked Giles full in the eyes and then away, as if the salvias and his mother might be visible in his own pupils.

"What were you thinking about?"

It was such a curious question that Simon answered it truthfully: "My mother."

Giles Holloway looked around the pub garden with its flaring, brassy flower beds and dry lawn. "Not much of a place," he observed.

"No."

"You still haven't got a drink."

"I don't need two drinks."

Half-hidden from them by the hedge, Simon's friends yelped with laughter.

"They sound as if they're having a good time. Why don't you join them?" asked Giles.

"I don't know them very well, except for Rod."

"You don't know Ali, then?"

"Hardly at all." Simon knew that Ali was Giles Holloway's reason for being here. They'd been at school together or something like that, although Giles was years older and had gone through the war. Ali said that Giles worked at the Admiralty now.

"Is she beautiful, your mother?"

"Good God, no!" said Simon before he could help himself. He glanced round and there were the salvias, glaring at him.

"I'm surprised," said Giles, and his eyes moved over Simon's face, his neck, and down over his body. There was neither lasciviousness nor speculation in his gaze, but something Simon hadn't come across before: certainty.

Is she beautiful, your mother?
Good God, no.
He could tell the truth to Giles. The more lacerating, the more ridiculous the truth, the more Giles went for it. He positively roared with laughter when he heard that Simon's brothers had given him the nickname "Milkman" because of a supposed doubt over his paternity. Callington males ran to flesh as soon as they were over thirty. They had pale blue eyes which they screwed up against the light when they took aim. Simon was dark. He was strong but lightly made, and at five foot nine he was four inches shorter than his father and brothers.

Giles ran one finger down Simon's spine. They were jammed into the single bed in Simon's room. Simon couldn't often get to London, and anyway Giles seemed to like coming here, to the digs Simon had found on the Madingley Road. Simon couldn't stand living in college. Everything about it rubbed him the wrong way, from the freezing dash to the bathroom to the procession of dons to High Table, all wearing the look of exalted sheep. Spiritually they belonged to the tribe of the Callingtons, although intellectually, of course, they were in a different league. At least, he hoped that they were, because if they weren't then it was all, the whole pack of it, a gigantic sham where people kept telling other people how brilliant those other people were, in the hope that the same would be said about them.

"Your sheets are extraordinary," said Giles.

"They're utility."

"Remarkable."

What was remarkable was that the landlady had sides-to-middled them, so that a ridge ran down the middle of the bed. Even so, Simon loved his room. He cherished the worn lino with its bald patch by the bed, the single gas ring in the corner, the strong iron bed, the ticking mattress, the gas fire and the curtained hanging-rail for his clothes. He'd bought a desk and chair in a junk shop. He didn't want pictures or decorations. His landlady, Mrs Chapman, never troubled him. She had no time for the university or its rules and restrictions. As far as she was concerned Simon was a grown man. He paid for his room and could do in it what he wanted. She provided breakfast, take it or leave it. Simon usually left it.

"I don't think I've ever been to bed in a room quite like this," Giles observed, rolling on to his back and lying with his head pillowed on his arms. Simon got up, wrapped himself in a dressing gown and went over to his desk to start work.

"What are you doing? Come back to bed."

"I've got to finish this."

Giles reached down the side of his bed and picked up his whisky glass. The bottle, also on the floor, was a quarter full. More there than he'd thought. Giles poured himself a drink and lay back again, watching the cold, whitish sky and listening to the sound of Simon's pen.

"Do you think that this can possibly be the high point of our love?" he asked suddenly. "Friday the twenty-third of January, two-zero-six pip emma. Look at those clouds. Write it down, Simon. Damn, it's two-zero-seven already."

"Could be," said Simon, not really listening, writing hard. Giles could not see that he had pushed aside the sheets of his essay, and was writing a letter.

"You're only going to get a bloody Third, you know. Why don't you stop that and come here?"

"In a minute . . ."

But he wouldn't, they both knew that. Giles drank his whisky, slowly and luxuriously. It would be dark before long. He had to get back to London but there was no need to think about that now. It was something he'd learned in the war: only think about what is directly in front of you. No, that wasn't quite right. He'd had to plan ahead all the time . . . But not to *feel* ahead. For a man of Giles's far-seeing, intricate temperament, that had been a hard lesson. But Simon, he could see, knew it by instinct.

"I shan't get a Third," said Simon now, as if informing Giles of something that had already been decided.

"Oh?"

"It'll be an Upper Second. I haven't worked hard enough for a First."

"And then what?"

Simon shrugged. "I'll leave Cambridge. No point staying, unless you get a First. Do my National Service, then find another room like this. In London probably. Find something to do."

"Any idea what?"

"No idea. Something'll turn up."

I bet it will, thought Giles, watching him turn back to his work. "Who's that letter from?" It lay on the floor: a thick, creamy envelope covered in sharp writing.

"My mother."

"So you don't open her letters."

"Not always."

"I see."

"I doubt if you do."

"You don't read their letters. You live in this room, which must be one of the least attractive the city has to offer, even though it's perfectly obvious that you could do better."

"I don't agree."

"This sheet . . ." Giles ran his hand down the lumpy seam. "Is this your flag of rebellion, Simon?"

Simon swung round on his seat. "Rebellion! Hardly. I'm at Cambridge, remember?"

"So you are." The whisky sang and burned inside him and he was — as he sometimes was in Simon's company — for a moment, perfectly happy.

"I could help you find something," he said. "I think you'd do well in the Admiralty. There's a chap I'd like you to meet."

"That would be good," said Simon, but again, he wasn't really listening. Everything outside Cambridge still seemed unreal. "But I warn you, I'm not very ambitious." As he said it, he discovered that it was true. He didn't want to do well and make his mark. He wanted to live peacefully and privately, far away from Stopstone, Norfolk, the World, the Universe and all that. Not wanting things made you free.

"I don't have to go back tonight," said Giles, to push away the black thoughts that were beginning to swarm in him. He had plans for Simon, even if Simon hadn't any for himself. He wanted to stay. Simon stretched back in his chair, eyes blank, tilting the chair legs. A yawn went over his face like an ecstasy, and he pushed his papers into a heap.

"Finished," he said. "What did you say?"

"I'm staying tonight. We'll get drunk at the Ram."

The Ram was out at Emberley, more than ten miles away.

"Fine," said Simon, "but we're having something to eat first. I've got a tin of baked beans."

"For heaven's sake, if you're hungry we'll go and have dinner —"

But Simon was already assembling plates, cutlery, his one saucepan, half a loaf. Giles watched as he toasted slices of bread at the gas fire while the beans bubbled on the ring. He was as handy as a matelot.

"Butter!" said Simon. He thrust the toasting fork into Giles's hand, leaped to the window and pulled up the sash. On the broad sill he kept a pint of milk, a packet of margarine and a small lump of cheese wrapped in greaseproof. He unwrapped the paper, regarded the cheese, then wrapped it up again. Suddenly he drew back his arm and hurled the cheese as far as it would go, into a neighbouring garden.

"For God's sake, shut that window," said Giles.

Simon spread margarine on the toast, poured out beans lavishly and heaped salt on the sides of their plates. Both of them shovelled in the food.

"What was wrong with the cheese? Maggots?"

"Christ! It was my mother's ration. She doesn't need it at Stopstone, *of course*. Do you like milk?"

Giles watched as Simon poured milk into two cups, and drank his own down in one draught. He smiled. "Have mine as well. I don't drink milk."

"Are you sure?" In a second draught, the second cupful was gone.

He was young and hungry: two things Giles liked. But as for finding something for Simon in London, he still wasn't sure which way the cat would jump. Simon, with his anger and his baked beans, his desire to tear down a world that was old, soiled, falling apart at its promises: Simon had possibilities. He hated the world into which he'd been born. Well, that was fine, that was what was required; but Giles was coming to think now that the hatred was all too real and thoroughgoing. Simon hadn't the grace to appear part of what he detested, to bide his time as it was necessary that he should bide his time.

Or did he simply loathe his mother? And that father of whom he never spoke?

Before the war it would have been easier. Everything was so much more clear-cut then. A young man like Simon would have realised, by the end of his first Michaelmas term, that he was on the side of the future. With his temperament he'd probably have rushed off to Spain. But now, with Nye Bevan and the National Health Service, the Bank of England nationalised, the Coal Board, the Gas Board — all those things that made Giles deeply weary and impatient and as if the wrong people had got their hands on the levers of power, even though it was what he'd always wanted and worked for — but not like this, not now, not here — Giles's thoughts stopped him, in their confusion.

And there was Simon, naked in the middle of the room, pulling his vest over his head, and then his shirt. He knew, he must have known, that there was nothing Giles liked more than this: the shirt over the head, the face invisible, buttocks, cock, balls exposed as if even their possessor possessed them less than did Giles himself.

They were in the Ram by seven, and by half past eight Simon had three pints inside him and a fourth on the table. The fire was too hot and for once the pub was crowded. Payday, Giles supposed, although he knew little about such things. Men seemed to have come in off the farms from miles around. The air was thick with smoke and the barmaid pulled pints as if she were stoking a furnace. The pump's brass handle flashed through the fug. They'd never been in on a Friday night before.

They didn't belong here; Giles knew that. They ought to be in the snug, on the tight leather chairs that looked as if they should be set in rows in a funeral parlour. Bugger that. Everyone who came in glanced at Giles and Simon, noted their strangeness and then went on to the bar. Simon was sitting back in the shadows, watching ash gather on the end of his cigarette. He looked half-asleep. Time to be getting back, Giles thought.

"Let's have another drink," said Simon, getting up clumsily and knocking the table. He reached his hand into his pocket and peered at the coins. "Same again?"

"I've had enough," said Giles. He didn't want to drive the Wolseley into a ditch on one of those godforsaken Fenland roads.

"I've never heard you say that before," said Simon, and laughed loudly. A couple of heads turned. Giles watched as he made his way to the bar. It was all right. He must have given one of his smiles, because a man with a pint in his hand stood aside with a nod of recognition to let Simon get past. All the same it was time to get him home.

This time Simon didn't knock the table. He put his own brimming pint down, and a double whisky in front of Giles. Carefully, he edged round to the bench where Giles sat, and settled himself. They were touching. The heat of their bodies travelled up and down them, inside their clothing. Giles moved away, just a little. The pub was packed and they were in their corner, hidden away, but all the same . . .

Simon put out his hand, his right hand. He laid it over Giles's left hand, where it rested on the table, loosely clenched.

"For Christ's sake, Simon." Giles swung round to look into Simon's face. It wasn't flushed — Simon's skin didn't flush — but it was dark, mantled with blood as it became during sex. His eyes glistened.

"You're drunk!" barked Giles. "Come on, we're going."

"I haven't finished my drink."

"You don't need another sodding drink."

"Don't tell me what I need."

Giles looked at him. Simon wasn't twenty-one until the spring, but he was old enough to know what could be done where. This was sheer bloody-mindedness. Simon needed some sense knocking into him. The thought came from nowhere, surprising Giles. He saw himself standing over Simon, Simon on the ground, both of them panting, Simon's knees drawn up, his arms shielding his face.

"As long as I'm out with you, you'll fucking do as I say," he said.

"You're wrong about that," said Simon. He was half smiling now. "Don't you want me to put my arm around you?"

"For Christ's sake," said Giles again, and heard his own impotence. "Get a grip, Simon."

"Why not? Don't you like it?"

"You know fucking well why not."

"No one's looking at us."

But they were. It wasn't Simon's touch on Giles's hand that had drawn their gazes, but an intensity between the two men that instinct told them shouldn't be there. Two men glanced over their shoulders as Giles looked up. A third was openly watching them, with a flat, stubborn interest that might easily turn nasty. And here was Simon, smiling, reckless, intimate, crossing the line as if he didn't even know there was one.

"Do you want to get beaten up? We're going," said Giles in a savage undertone. Without looking at Simon again he stood up, pushed the table aside and shouldered his way through the crowd towards the door. Behind him, the mass of bodies closed up again. It must be market day, there were so many. He was sweating.

He stood in the cold, wet dark and waited for Simon to emerge. His heart was still thumping with anger. He wanted to get in the car, slam the door, reverse it over the muddy verge and turn for London. Put his foot down and let the black night stream by, faster and faster. Let Simon walk back to Cambridge. That would cool him down. Who did he think he was?

It was probably only five minutes before Simon came out.

"What were you doing?"

"Talking about the price of turnips."

"What the hell do you know about the price of turnips?"

"Enough to hold a conversation."

Giles eased the car off the verge. He felt cold now, and tired. Simon's narrow room wasn't amusing any more. Giles wanted to be back in London, among people who knew how things were done.

"Christ knows how you'll cope with National Service," he said as he swung the car round a corner — too fast, but he knew what he was doing.

"I'm taking a three-year short-service commission in the RAF," said Simon. He was angry with himself as well as Giles. He wished like hell that he hadn't slid the letter he'd written into Giles's overcoat pocket.

"When was that decided?" demanded Giles.

Simon didn't reply. His head slipped sideways. He was asleep.

Giles drove on. It wasn't raining any more, but there was mud on the narrow roads. It would be the easiest thing in the world to take a corner too fast and slide into a ditch. Or lose control altogether and smash into a tree. Then there would be nothing. One moment of huge exploding silence and then he'd know everything there was to be known.

Simon's head slid further, and sank on to his shoulder. Giles drove slowly now, carefully, as the weight and heat of Simon came through to him. His anger was gone. He was calm now and melancholy, heavy with a burden that could never be discharged. This was what Simon had wanted in the pub. All that he'd wanted; Giles knew it now. Their two bodies touching.

And then there was that evening in Giles's club. When was it? Months later, it must have been. The plane trees in the square were putting out their leaves.

"The trouble with you, Giles," said Simon, "is that you like feeling you're part of a secret society."

Giles's pupils contracted. He was shocked and Simon knew it.

"What the hell do you mean by that?"

"You like going straight from here" — he made a gesture that included the hushed tables and the elderly waiters trundling babyish puddings around the room — "to Bobbie's."

"Why not?"

"No reason. I'm not criticising you, it's just an observation."

"And you don't?"

Simon looked at the white damask cloth, considering. "It's necessary, I understand that. But I don't like it. I like things simple."

"How the hell you are going to get through three years in the RAF, I don't know."

"Drinking in the mess."

"There is that."

Simon smiled. He sat quietly smoking as Giles ordered his pudding. Each table sat in its own small weak pool of light, so you didn't have to think about any of the others. Sometimes another member would have a word as he went past, but usually they were left alone. Quite why Giles wanted to bring Simon to his club, it was hard to determine. But Simon thought it was part of the same thing. He liked the sense that within this cocoon there was a small, flickering touch of risk. He liked to think about what the club members who spoke to him so affably would say if they knew that

92

he and Simon had been in bed together not an hour before.

But probably, thought Simon, they all had their own secrets. You keep your secrets, and I'll keep mine. That was the way things worked. If he reached out, though, and touched Giles's hand — if he kissed him on the lips —

It was a game; that was what it was. Giles would have a word with a tottering old waiter, then, if Simon wasn't available, he'd be off to pick up boys at Bobbie's or the Nightshade. It had all seemed so different from Stopstone at first, but it was the same. He was cold with weariness.

"Do you want cheese?" asked Giles. Simon shook his head. "You don't seem very hungry tonight."

"I'm not. Listen, Giles, I'm sorry, I'm not coming on to Bobbie's. If I go now I can catch the last train back to Cambridge. I've got to see my tutor in the morning." He stood up as he spoke. Suddenly tiredness swept through him, as strong as sexual desire. He stretched and yawned as if he were alone in his room, and Giles watched the inside of his mouth as it opened.

"You can't go now," he said. "You'll have missed the train."

"I'll thumb a lift."

There Simon stood, faintly smiling, with the distance of a traveller whose train is about to depart. And I shan't fucking run after him, thought Giles, and he nodded and looked down at his plate as Simon loped away, a hundred times younger than anything else in the room.

Giles's pudding sat sloppily in its puddle of custard, and he chucked his linen napkin on top of it. It was a quick, grand gesture, and he almost stood up to leave. But suddenly he wanted that pudding. He hadn't even touched it. Under the napkin he knew that the pudding was a pale golden brown, spotted with currants. The custard was soaking into it. Giles glanced quickly around the room. No one had noticed. Airily, he flipped up the napkin and crumpled it beside his plate. He picked up his spoon and broke the surface of the pudding. There was just the right density of currants. He took the first mouthful. Perfect, luscious, vanilla-sweet custard, just as he liked it. Not too thick, and not so thin that it ran off his spoon. The pudding was thick, warm and lemony in his mouth. He took another spoonful, then another. He was eating fast now, shovelling it in, the custard, the currants, the suety, sugary flesh of the pudding itself.

It was over. A fine sweat had broken out all over his face. He picked up the napkin, folded it so that the stained part was hidden, and wiped his forehead. He sat back, pushing away his pudding plate. As he did so he caught the eye of the man at the next table. A gross fellow: Giles couldn't remember his name. Red-faced. What was it? Crickling? Stickling? A silly sort of name. But all the same, a fellow club member, to be encountered over and over again for years, so Giles said loudly, "Frightfully good spotted dick."

"You were tucking in all right," said the gross fellow, and Giles knew he'd seen it all. Simon's departure, the throwing down of the napkin, the subsequent guzzling of pudding and custard. The fellow was grinning conspiratorially, as if they were two greedy schoolboys. His plate, too, was smeared. "Nothing like good old spotted dick."

"No," said Giles. He thought of Simon, at the side of a dark road, arm stretched out, thumb up. He thought of Simon folding his body into another man's car. "No," he repeated. "Nothing."

CHAPTER
NINE

You Are in England Now

It's one of the days when Lily doesn't teach. Bridgie insisted on walking to school with her brother and sister, like a big girl, and off they went, Bridgie's hand in Sally's, Paul walking ahead, determined not to arrive at school holding hands with his little sister. At once, as shockingly as if a machine has been turned off, the house is quiet.

Lily goes into the kitchen. Everything looks grubby. She will give the whole of the downstairs a thorough clean, she decides, and then she will feel better. Everything seems disturbed and out of place. Simon had woken her in the early hours, sliding into bed, his feet icy against her. He must have got up in the night. She muttered, protesting.

"Lil?" he said. "Lily? Are you awake?"

Sleep pulled her down like a tide. Her mouth and eyes were full of it. She knew she should answer but she couldn't — not now. She thought he said "Lil" again as she sank away from him.

She could hardly wake him at seven-thirty. Downstairs the children were squabbling over the hamster. Was he ill, or simply, as Sally thought, not very frisky this morning? Paul held him under the standard lamp to examine his ears, but Sally thought that was cruel . . . And then, at breakfast, Bridgie spat on the last piece of toast just as Paul was reaching for it.

"I'm the only one who can eat it now, because it's got my spit on it," she was fool enough to say. Paul lunged at her as Lily lifted the child from her chair.

"Go and put your coat and shoes on, Bridget. You are not having that toast, and I am going to make a fresh slice for Paul."

How Bridgie roared. It was the rain, and the wind. Children were always like this when the wind blew. And here was Simon, standing by the table, gulping tea while his egg and toast cooled.

"Don't you want your breakfast?"

"Sorry, Lil, I'm late."

She would have the egg for her lunch, with the rest of the soup.

"Do you think the children need their wellingtons?" she asked him.

"It's not as wet as that."

They were all barging into one another in the narrow hallway, arguing again, tugging coats and scarves off their pegs. Already, Simon was in the doorway. Tall and clean — distinguished, she thought suddenly, although how could that be? Distinguished in sharp outline against the grey morning and scuds of rain. Suddenly she longed to hold him, be held by him, smell his smell, taste him for a second before he was lost to the day. If only she'd woken up properly last night. But she couldn't get to him through the children.

"Simon!" she said, and for a second he held her eyes and half smiled.

Lily thinks of her mother as she drags out the ash-grey vacuum cleaner. It snuffles along the skirting board, spitting out as much dirt as it sucks into its belly. There's something wrong with it again. Suddenly the sound changes to a high, skirling whine, and there's a stink of burning rubber. The vacuum cleaner has swallowed something too big for it to digest. Lily unplugs it, takes off the front of the cylinder and pulls out a mangled sock.

Her mother dreamed of other things for Lily: scholarships, university education, a profession. Elsa had learned English from books and conversation classes, before she came to know England's dirty floors and crusted lavatories. She arrived in England with Lili, in the winter of 1937, to work as live-in help for a family in Finchley. It was a condition of the guarantee under which they had been allowed to emigrate. Lili knew all about that. They shared an attic room, with Lili on a bed that the lady called "truckle". Lili repeated the word. *Truckle*. Who knew which words would be useful? That was the way to learn, her mother said. Don't be afraid of the words. No, Lili, I am not going to speak German to you, even when we are alone. You have to think in English. You are going to school and if you don't speak English well they will think you are stupid and put you into the bottom class. For *dunces*. From the way her mother brought out that word, Lili knew what it meant without being told.

"And when you go to school, tell them that your name is Lily. L-i-l-y. This is how you spell your name now, in England."

It wasn't a grand house. There were six bedrooms, three children and endless work. A charwoman called Mrs Brennan came in twice a week to "do the rough", but otherwise Lily's mother did everything. The first winter, she had chilblains so badly that her hands swelled up, cracked and bled. She was frightened, in case she couldn't work. Mrs Brennan made her tea from hawthorn berries. "That'll get the blood moving in you," she said. Lily's mother drank off the tea, and pulled a face.

"Is it working?" Lily asked.

"It was very kind of her." Elsa took her daughter's hands, turned them over. "You have my hands."

Her mother became ill when she was forty-seven, before Lily's children were born. Lily was already engaged to Simon. The two women were drinking coffee when her mother said, "These days, when I'm walking up the street, I am more like a shadow than a person who makes a shadow."

Lily protested.

"It's not a bad thing. I suppose that when you are young, you believe that all the things in the world have been put there for you. The sunlight, the shops. The whole fabric of it. It's all there for you and you are equal to it. But then, later on, you see it differently. The post office or the library — this coffee shop — will exist for much longer than me, let alone those trees. Even a piece of paper in the gutter may be here for longer."

"You're only forty-seven." *And this is England*, she wanted to add. *Nothing bad will happen to you here*. But there was no point in saying such things. Her mother, she knew, didn't believe them. Belief was not part of the picture for her. She had no interest in religion. As long as people could be brought to behave with decency to one another, what more could you ask? Lily's father had not, perhaps, behaved well, but there were extenuating circumstances.

He had almost stayed in Berlin too long. He had been too confident. He had only one Jewish grandparent, and had divorced Elsa. The divorce was agreed between them. It was the only way, her father said, that they could protect their property. *Mischling* of the second degree as he was, he would be counted as legally Jewish if he remained married to a Jew.

Why should he give up the apartment, his elderly parents, the business, everything that belonged to him?

"The trouble with your father was that he thought he was one step ahead of everyone. That is the weakness of clever men, Lily. They think that cleverness is everything. A little common sense and understanding of human nature would have been more to the point. A man called Strasser wanted the business. Your father refused, because the offer price was too low. Instead of raising his price, Strasser

100

lodged a deposition that our divorce was a sham. We were trying to deprive the authorities of the assets of a Jewish business. So, your father should be considered *Geltungsjude*. You can understand how dangerous that was. The business would be taken. The Government would get its share, and Strasser would take the rest. At a low price, far lower than what he offered first. That's how it went."

"*Kanntest Du Herr Strasser, Mama?*"

"Speak English, Lily!"

"Did you know him?"

"Of course. He often came to our house. He had a little girl your age."

Lily's father made his way to Spain in late 1938, and spent the war in Morocco. There, as Lily's mother explained, he had "met someone" during their long separation. One day, perhaps, Lily would go there and see her father.

"I don't want to go to Morocco," said Lily.

"You don't know what you are talking about," said her mother, but in spite of the sharp words Lily could see that she was consoled.

"I want to always stay with you."

"You're going to live for years and years," said Lily, that day over the coffee. "You're only forty-seven."

How could she have said anything so stupid, Lily asks herself now. It's true that she was very young, and probably quite immature. Taken up with her own world, with Simon, the future . . .

Three months later, her mother had a stroke. It was completely unexpected, but fortunately, the doctors said, it wasn't too serious. Not this time. With care, her mother would make a complete recovery, although she ought to give up work. By this time, Elsa was a solicitor's receptionist, a job that she appeared to enjoy. Lily had done brilliantly in her Higher School Certificate, and now she had a good degree from UCL. Not a First, but . . . She was going to teach.

Elsa had wanted her daughter to study law, or medicine. Even now she hadn't given up hope. *Teaching is all very well, Lily, but there are plenty of other things you could do with a good degree.* But Lily had met Simon, and seemed to have lost her ambition. And now this stroke, and the tiredness that crept into every fibre of Elsa's body. London was suddenly too big, too noisy, too shapeless. She was afraid of crowds. She had to hold on to Lily's arm when the swirl of the streets threatened to separate them. She tried not to cling to her — she must not frighten Lily —

"I am going to live in Brighton, Lily."

"Brighton!"

"Yes. You remember the Lowes? They have been living there for five years and are very happy. It's a nice town. Cheap, too. I can buy a little flat there."

The stroke must have affected her mother's mind more than the doctors had said, thought Lily. How did Elsa imagine that she could suddenly buy a flat?

"Your father has sent money."

"Sent money!"

"Please, Lily, do not repeat every word I say. Papa has a business in Fez, he has money, he sends some of it to me. Is that such a miracle?"

"Why didn't you tell me before?" If only her mother wouldn't say *Papa* like that, when neither of them had seen him for years. Lily could not remember his face.

"It never happened before. And you are qualified now, Lily. You will get a job and a home of your own. You and Simon."

"You always say Sadie Lowe never stops talking. She's like a parrot, you said, but there's no cloth to put over the cage."

Her mother sighed impatiently. "Don't be childish, Lily. Why should I care if Sadie chatters? The Lowes are old friends. Besides, the fresh air will be good for my health."

A little flat. A one-bedroom flat ten minutes from the sea front, close to the shops. A put-you-up bed in the sitting room for Lily's visits. Lily was soon married and almost immediately she was pregnant with Paul. She could hardly lie down on the put-you-up bed.

Even with the ferocious light that beat off the sea front, the flat was dark. Her mother filled it with furniture. There were little tables that toppled if you moved carelessly and a bureau with a photograph of Lily, Max and Elsa in 1934. In the photograph, Lily wore a coat with a fur collar, and the three of them were walking along a wide, tree-lined city street. Her parents held the child's hands. So who took the photograph? Lily didn't ask. She avoided the eyes and smiles of the photographed family on the pre-war street. They had nothing to do with her now. Her mother said she was thinking about acquiring a dog. A very small one, she said. There was enough room in the flat for a little dog.

Once Simon had left the RAF and he and Lily were living in London, Elsa said, "You can come for the day, Lily."

Bus and Tube, train from Victoria, bus again. Sally in the pushchair and Paul trotting alongside. Heaving the pushchair on and off trains and buses. The potty, the changes of clothes, the carrier bag with sandwiches and fruit.

"Take them down to the sea front for an hour, Lily, so that they can run about. Children need exercise."

"Why don't you come up to London, Mama, and spend the day with me? The children have all their toys at home, and the garden. It's so much easier. They can play, and we'll have time to talk."

"Surely Simon could look after them for one day, so that you can come and visit me on your own?"

"I don't think he's ever looked after them on his own for a day."

A sudden volte-face from her mother. "Well, he is at work all week. Men need time for themselves."

They most certainly do, thought Lily. Fifteen years in Morocco, for example, without once seeing their daughter. Her mother seemed to think Lily should accept that, just as she should accept the fact that her mother would not come to London. How was it possible to feel such a pure, burning jet of dislike for someone who had done so much for you?

* * *

There. The vacuum cleaner is running again. She'll
finish the hall, and then have a cup of coffee before she
tackles the bedrooms. The air smells of dust. But who
likes housework? At least it's her own house, her own
dust, her own children's muddy marks on the strip of
hall carpet. Lily kneels to tackle the area under the
coats. They ought to get a proper shoe rack. She starts
to sort out pairs from the heap of boots and shoes, and
that's when she sees the briefcase, tucked back against
the wall. For a moment she thinks perhaps it's an old
case of Simon's, from when he was at school, but of
course it can't be. She'd have seen it before. She pulls it
out. It's light, almost empty, but something rattles
when she shakes it.

She never looks at Simon's letters. It's a point of
principle. She would never go inside a drawer or wallet
that belonged to him, and nor, she knows, would he
invade her handbag or the files where she keeps the
certificates: their marriage, the children's births, her
own naturalisation papers. But this briefcase isn't
Simon's. It's old, but it's expensive, so it must belong to
someone. Perhaps Simon has brought it home by
mistake. But she knows that's not possible. He would
have mentioned it to her: Simon is so open.

Lily stands stock-still. Is he so very open, or is that
just something she's got used to taking on trust? In her
mind she sees Simon coming in soaked through, late,
on edge. Not saying anything to her. If she hadn't
known better, she would have thought he was up to
something.

105

Already, her fingers are feeling for the lock on the briefcase. Now they are pressing in on both sides. There's a click. It wasn't locked. The catch unsnaps. The briefcase opens.

And here she is, at the kitchen table, with the file in front of her. *Top Secret*. She knows immediately that it ought not to be here. Simon has never brought anything like this home. He rarely brings work home at all. Perhaps it's got nothing to do with him, perhaps someone just —

Crept into their hallway with a briefcase while her back was turned?

The case can't have been there long. The children barging about for boots and dropped gloves would have found it.

For some time Lily sits there, looking down at the file. A blank, blind space surrounds her.

She no longer speaks German. It has all disappeared. She speaks English, French, Italian. She cannot remember. Even her father's face is a pale disc.

"Surely you must remember Strandbad Wannsee, Lily! When you were three — four — five — you would pester me every day to go there. Of course that was when it was still permitted to us . . ."

No. She can remember nothing. Not a twig, not a drop of lake water, not a grain of sand. Her mind fumbles, but it is all blank. Sometimes, now, her mother would like to speak German with Lily: "Surely you can't have forgotten the language you spoke every day until you were nearly ten years old!"

"You always said: Speak English. If I spoke in German you wouldn't answer."

"There was a war on, Lily. How could I have you speaking German in the streets? Better that you forgot."

"I did forget."

Her hands reach out. She opens the file. On the front sheet there are three typed names, with initials handwritten against them. She recognises only one name: Julian Clowde. He has read this file. Here are his initials: JRC. She finds herself wondering what the "R" stands for. Simon doesn't like him.

"Why not?" she asked him once.

"He's a cold fish. But I don't have much to do with him these days."

"He's too important now, I suppose."

"It's not just that."

"I thought he was a friend of Giles?"

"Yes," said Simon shortly, and the subject was closed.

She has made a mark on the cover of the file, because her hands are dirty from emptying the vacuum cleaner. They will notice it. What is this file doing here? Julian Clowde signed his initials, after the other two men whose names she doesn't recognise. And then, for some reason, the file was passed to Simon. He brought it home in a briefcase which isn't his, and tucked it away behind the children's boots. Never, not once, has Simon brought home any file like this. She feels again the coldness of his body as he slid into bed beside her, in the early hours.

Lily turns to the back of the file, and then forward through the pages. Statistics, diagrams, tables, acronyms. A swarm of words and figures that mean nothing to her. And then, at the front, a page written in plain English. A briefing document. Words jab out at her. What they describe are underwater surveillance and detection techniques. The diagrams and graphs are illustrations to the text. "Ref. Fig. 1, acoustic field sweep. Ref. Fig. 2, sonar directional plotting range. Ref. Fig. 3, bearing and feed calculation."

At the foot of the briefing document is written: "Admiralty Underwater Weapons Establishment".

England is an island, Lili. That is why we will be safe there. England is surrounded by the sea, and armies cannot march across water.

It had made her feel very safe. Hitler will not get his boots wet, her mother said, when Lili was most frightened. The sea is England's strongest weapon.

This file. This file in her hands. This is a weapon. Simon ate nothing this morning. He wanted to talk to her when he came in last night, but she fell away from him into sleep. In the morning it was too late. They looked at each other over the children's heads, and he was gone.

No one but Simon can have brought this file into the house.

Lily sits with the file in front of her and her thoughts drumming. She will put it back behind the boots. She will wait until the children are in bed and then she'll bring it out and say to Simon, "What's this?"

A train whistles, and the sound goes through Lily's bones. *Don't be frightened, Lily. You are in England now.*

She is in England because her mother would not wait, not even for Lily's father.

She must hurry.

Lily gets up, puts the file back inside the briefcase, and clicks it shut. It's no good just getting rid of the file. The whole thing must completely disappear. No one must know that it ever came into the house.

Lily empties the sack of kindling that they keep in the cupboard under the stairs, places the briefcase in it and knots the sacking. She dresses herself in raincoat, hood, wellington boots, and goes to the back door. She looks all round, carefully. The garden is very private, but there are back windows, and now that the leaves are off the trees there might be someone looking out — No. All is quiet. She walks briskly down the crazy-paving path beside the lawn. Beyond the rose-trellis, there is her vegetable patch, the apple and pear trees, the gooseberry patch, and beyond it the wild, overgrown part of the garden that leads to the copse. No man's land. She puts down the sack, and fetches the spade and fork from the shed. Here, by the compost heap, the soil is soft and there is garden rubbish piled up, waiting to be burned when everything is no longer sodden with the autumn rain. She shoves the rubbish aside with her spade, and begins to dig.

Digging a hole deep enough for a briefcase to be buried is harder than she thought. God knows what it would be like to dig a hole deep enough to bury a man. The topsoil is soft, fed with ash from years of bonfires, but below it there's clay. She sweats inside her raincoat even as the rain falls harder. Rain is good. It keeps people indoors, not looking over their garden fences.

The spade hits something hard, and won't go deeper. Lily gets the fork and levers out a chunk of concrete. Brambles whip at her and she shoves them aside. She'll pull them forward afterwards, to hide where she's dug. She chops at roots with the edge of the spade and hacks her way deeper.

At last, she thinks the hole will do. She stands, easing her back. The sacking is dark with rain. She drops the case in the bottom of the hole, and treads it down, crushing it into the dirt, before she begins to fill in. Every so often she tramples the soil down again. At last it's level with the rest of the earth. She fetches the garden fork and pulls rubbish and undergrowth over the grave of the briefcase. When she's finished, she walks backwards, smoothing away the marks of her boots. By the shed, she stops and looks back. There's nothing to see. No one would know.

Lily takes off her boots before going into the shed, so that she won't leave muddy footprints. She finds a rag and with it carefully wipes the tines of the fork and the metal blade of the spade; then she replaces these on their hooks before shutting the door. Even now, she doesn't put her boots back on, but walks in stockinged feet to the water butt, where she rinses off her boots

110

carefully. At the back door she undoes her suspenders and strips off her stockings. She'll wash them, and dry her raincoat on the clothes rack by the kitchen stove. With luck, her stockings won't have laddered. Now, she must find another bag for the kindling.

She looks back over the garden. Her feet have left no prints on the grass. The rain falls more gently now, in a mist that almost hides the copse. She'll have that cup of coffee now, and afterwards she'll vacuum the bedrooms. Everything is just as it was.

CHAPTER
TEN

Sunday

A rainy November afternoon, and cold with it, but deliciously so now that the curtains are drawn, the fire lit and the sitting room's clutter basks in soft, yellow, flickering light. Paul and Sally kneel on the hearth rug, taking turns with the toasting fork. Bridget isn't old enough to toast crumpets yet, but she has her doll's tea set with real tea in it, and is content. They have been out all day. Paul and Simon went to King's Cross, Sally on a trip to the zoo with her friend Katie (Sally is a child whom other families are always eager to invite), Bridget and Lily to Highgate Woods in macs and boots, with Erica, Thomas, the baby and Coco, the King Charles spaniel that Bridget craves.

Erica let Bridget hold the lead, and Bridget took it reverently. Now, she was a girl with a dog. Anyone who saw them might think it was her own dog. The spaniel is appealing, although Lily has never taken to it. The glassiness of its eyes repels her.

Bridget raced ahead: "Come on, Coco! Good girl, Coco!"

"How are you, darling?" asked Erica. "Christ! I wish this rain would stop."

"Oh, you know. Fine."

"You look a bit down. Time for the convalescent home?"

This had been Erica's fantasy, when Thomas was little. Thomas, although a lovely boy, as everyone quickly says, is not quite like other children. He is immature, perhaps. Slow to learn in most things, fright-eningly quick in others. Although he is Sally's age, he naturally plays with Bridget. As a baby, he slept perhaps six hours in the twenty-four. His temper, then as now, was explosive.

Worn out by sleepless nights and hours of screaming, Erica would dream aloud of a convalescent home deep in the country, wide-lawned and wreathed in wisteria, staffed by kindly nurses in white-winged caps who would wheel the mothers' beds into the sunlight, bring them tea and cups of soup, murmur soothingly, "Your children are perfectly happy in the nursery. Your job is to rest."

But even after all that, Erica had the courage to have another baby. Clare slept from seven to seven and cried only, it seemed, to remind her mother that she was a human child and not a particularly delightful doll.

"You're the one with the baby," pointed out Lily. "The rest of the children are quite civilised now."

"They look it," said Erica, as Thomas snatched the dog's lead and Bridget roared and flailed at him with her fists.

"I mean, they use the lavatory and eat at the table. Bridget, stop that *now*."

"Give me the lead, Thomas. If you two can't behave nicely, then you can't have Coco."

Sullen, united, the two children slunk behind the adults.

"But there is something, isn't there? Or perhaps you don't want to talk about it," added Erica hastily, for she had a horror of intrusiveness and the gossip of the playground.

"I can't, really." Erica was so quick: she always knew when things were wrong. Lily would have liked to confide in her, but it was impossible. And Erica would not press her.

"Never mind, darling," said Erica. "Let's go to the kiosk and buy ourselves a huge bar of fruit and nut." She raised her voice and glanced behind her. "The children will just have to watch us eating it."

Lily lies back in her chair by the fire, eyes half-closed. Today, more than ever, she has been glad to draw the curtains and shut out the world. But who is she kidding, as Simon would say. The world has battering rams if it wants to use them. She heard those words: *dirty Jews*. It took time for her to apply them to herself. At first those words wouldn't connect from her ears to the place where she understood herself and knew what she was. Their apartment in Berlin was small: kitchen, living room, her parents' bedroom and a room for Lili that was big enough for her bed and chest. She had to put her toys away into boxes that fitted under the bed, and her bookshelf was in the hall. But their apartment was in a very good area, her mother said, and that made up for everything.

To go home was to be entirely safe. There was the thick outer door, the lobby, the entrance hall, the lift with its gates that folded up like concertinas, the row of letterboxes with their polished brass name-plates. Lili traced their own name with her finger before she could read. She was allowed to go down all by herself to fetch the post, and up again three floors in the wheezing hush of the lift. Their own front door was made of oak, her father said. There were three locks, one at the top, one in the middle, one at the bottom. One day, when Lili and her mother came home, Mama took out a key Lili had never seen her use before. She reached up and turned the key in the top lock, and then she bent down to the very bottom, almost on the floor, and turned that lock too. From that time, if Lili came home and one of her parents was already inside the apartment, she had to wait while all three locks were opened. Soon after that, when she was on her way home from school, she heard it for the first time: *Dirty little Jew*. She turned. But it was a nice lady in a summer dress with yellow and purple pansies on it. She looked straight at Lili. Had she said those words? She looked like one of Mama's friends. In fact Lili was certain that she recognised the face. A neighbour perhaps. But the lady's face was cold. She twitched her eyebrows and turned away. Her skirt swished from side to side as she walked off down the pavement in her high heels.

Lili went home. She felt hot and ashamed, as if she'd wet herself and there was a patch on her skirt. When she rang the doorbell she waited for the sound of the three locks being turned, one by one. Once she was inside, she said nothing about the lady.

The crumpets are ready now, piled on a plate by the fire to keep warm. Two each, and one left over. Paul and Sally have already eaten theirs and licked the butter off their fingers with cat-like neatness. Bridget's voice badgers her gently: "Mum, do you want more tea, Mum?"

"Lovely," she answers, without stirring from her own thoughts, and takes the minuscule cup with its dregs of cold tea.

"Mum, you're not drinking it."

"Yes, I am. Give Dad a cup too."

Paul looks up from his pile of *Railway Magazines*. "It says here, Dad, that derailments, broken rails, earth slips and engine failures are the most common mishaps that close the line. Do you think that the ten-thirty-six was diverted because of an earth slip?"

He can see it in his mind, Lily knows. The drama of it: the train panting to a stop; the piled, quivering earth. She remembers reading *The Railway Children* aloud to them.

"I should think it's more likely to have been routine maintenance. They do most of that on Sundays. Does anyone else want that last crumpet?"

"You have it," says Lily.

He spreads the thinnest possible film of Gentleman's Relish on to the crumpet, and bites into it. How young he looks, suddenly. Eager, and almost happy. He can't

116

have looked for the briefcase, or he'd have seen it was gone, and asked her about it. It can't have been anything serious, not really. She won't think about it any more. It is Sunday afternoon, and their door is closed on the world. Simon bites into his toast, and smiles at her. She'd never heard of Gentleman's Relish until she met Simon. Those Callingtons. His mother and father and his brothers, all so full of themselves, knowing what is right. "It was a bit off," they'd say of someone's conduct, and everybody was supposed to nod. None of them has Simon's yellow-brown eyes.

"What colour are your eyes?" she asked him, not long after they first met.

"Hazel," he said, but the word was too soft for their jewel-like brightness. They are not easy to look into. Bridget has exactly those eyes.

In the hall, the telephone rings.

"I'll get it," says Lily.

"No, don't get up. It's probably for me."

He goes out, shutting the door behind him. She hears the murmur of his voice but can't make out any words.

"Put some more coal on the fire, Paul," she says, more sharply than she intends, so that he looks at her in surprise.

The fresh coal makes the fire smoke. It must have got wet in the bunker. The smell catches at the back of Lily's throat, and she gets up to clear away the plates and cups. The empty crumpet plate swims with grease.

"Five minutes until bedtime, Bridget."

The murmur from the hall stops. Simon will come back in a minute. She looks away into the guttering fire as the door opens. She turns quickly, and then, as if scorched, her eyes drop. There is something in his face that is all too familiar. It's like the look on her mother's face when she turned the three locks with her key. Fear.

"Who was that?"

"Giles Holloway."

"What did he want?"

"I don't know," says Simon slowly. Her runs his hand through his hair until it sticks up. "I don't know why he rang."

"I thought he was in hospital."

"He is. They're hoping to move him to a convalescence place quite soon. He can't manage in the flat yet."

"What does he want you to do?"

"Why do you say that?"

"Isn't that why he rang last time? He wanted you to do something for him? So now what does he want?"

They are face to face now, locked, staring. Around her she feels the children's silence. They sit as still as hares on the carpet. They know. Just as she always knew. When her parents talked together, all those frightening words. She listened while she pretended to read or to play. They talked about the documents that were needed, the embassies that must be visited, the forms that must be filled in. Endless forms. She listened to their desperate urgency, cloaked in the everyday.

118

"You might be going on your travels, Lili! Just you and Mama. To England, right across the sea. How would you like that?"

"You know, Lili, like in *Peter Pan*!"

Peter Pan! Did they think that they were going to fly to England? She watched their mouths, their eyes. They'd always told her not to be afraid. Of the dark, of the Kirchners' dog that raved at the end of its chain. The dog would never be able to get at her. "See, Lili, how strong the chain is!"

Now her parents were afraid, and she soaked in their fear through the pores of her skin. People think children know nothing, that they forget, that they don't feel things. But she knew everything. Her mother said, when they had been in England less than a year: "Lily barely remembers Berlin. She can't speak a word of German these days."

She stands up. She must put Bridget to bed immediately. "Simon," she says, with all her tenderness, putting her hands up to touch him, and she sees his face change, soften, dissolve, come back to her.

"Lily," he answers, recognising her and opening himself to her again. He is about to speak, to tell her. Everything is going to be all right again.

The doorbell rings. A long ring, a short pause. It rings again. They are pressing on the bell. They don't intend to go away.

"I'll get it, Mum," says Paul.

"No! No." She collects herself. "Paul, Sally, I want you to go upstairs straight away, with Bridget. Sally, get Bridget ready for bed. Make sure she cleans her teeth properly. She doesn't need to have a bath. Bridget, you must be a very good girl tonight and do exactly what Sally says. Quickly now! And shut the bedroom doors."

Her children run upstairs without a word. She hears one door slam, and then another. Paul has gone into his own bedroom. Bridget is with Sally. It has all taken perhaps thirty seconds. The bell peals on and now they are rapping on the wood of the door.

"I'd better go and see who it is," she says, but already she knows. Her heart thuds up in her throat, quick and hot. The briefcase is buried. No one will be able to find it.

All the lines and bones of his face stand out. He lifts his right hand as if to touch her, but it drops to his side.

"I'm sorry, Lil," he says.

The hours stretch. The children are at Erica's. Lily telephoned her, and she came immediately, swathed against the rain, her eyes big and fearful in her pale face. She thought there'd been an accident.

"It's all right, Erica, no one's hurt —"

"Your friend should wait at the front door, madam. No one must come into the house." He set Lily aside, and said to Erica, "We shall need your name, address and telephone number."

"My God, Lily, what's going on?"

"Madam, as soon as I have these details we'd like you to take the children and leave."

Earlier, under supervision, Lily put the children's overnight things in a bag, with their school uniforms for the next day. A policeman watched her all the time.

"Excuse me, madam, I shall have to look through that bag before it leaves the house."

He thought she had slipped something into the bag. His hands were practised. He picked through Paul's pyjamas, Sally's and Bridget's nighties, the rabbit slippers, the toothbrushes and flannels, and he ran his fingers rapidly up and down the seams of their clothes. "You may close the bag now."

Thank God that happened before Erica arrived. As it was, they'd treated her as if she, too, might be part of this. Whatever "this" was. They wouldn't answer any of Lily's questions. When she offered them a cup of tea, they looked at her as if this were yet another of the gambits with which they were all too familiar.

"Are you Lily Elsa Callington, formerly Lili Elsa Brand?"

"Yes," she said, "Brand was my maiden name." They had made it sound as if she'd changed her name to conceal herself. They wrote it down, even though it was clear they knew it already. She saw her place of birth further up on the form, which was already partially completed in a different hand. Perhaps they had intended her to see it.

The door shuts. The children are gone. Simon has gone. He has accompanied two officers to Scotland Yard for questioning. He went so quickly, so undramatically that she barely had time to understand that it was happening. He looked at her as he was led down the hall. She saw the shock in him, the fear and shame that they were doing this to him and he could do nothing to stop it. "I'm sorry, Lil." He said that when they came to the door. He said nothing more, but he looked back at her.

Through the open door she saw that there was a car outside. It was black but not a police car, and there was someone in the driver's seat. The rain was still falling, the same rain that had fallen on them earlier in Highgate Woods. Simon went down to the road with the two officers, and another man got out of the car. He was a policeman in uniform. He opened the door for Simon to get into the back and he put his hand over the top of Simon's head as he climbed into the car. The engine was running now, and the car was moving away from the kerb.

Lily sits on the red sofa, as she has been told. "Please sit down here, Mrs Callington." There's a policewoman with her now, but no one has asked Lily any further questions. They tramp purposefully around the house. She hears the lifting of the metal plate on top of the stove, and the unlocking of the back door. They'll go down the path and into the shed, and search all around it. Lily rehearses in her mind all the steps she took to conceal the burial of the briefcase. The scuffing of leaves, the covering of garden rubbish, the brambles pulled forward. There's nothing to see, but her heart beats fast and there's a lump in her stomach, as if she has eaten too much.

She draws her knees together, and straightens her back. There they are, overhead, in her and Simon's bedroom. She can't help glancing upwards, and the policewoman does the same. She's wearing very thick make-up: pancake, Lily thinks. Probably she has a bad skin. But it's surprising that she is allowed to wear so much make-up on duty. It makes her look like a man in drag.

They have searched Lily's handbag, and all the downstairs drawers. When she first saw the police-woman, she was afraid that they meant to search her personally, but nothing happened. She wonders exactly what it is that they are looking for. The file would be too big to fit into Lily's handbag. They are going through everything: the cutlery drawers, and the kitchen cabinets. She listens. One by one she identifies them: creak and swing of cupboard doors, chink of knives and forks, rattle of pans. All the everyday sounds of her life. It's Sunday evening. She should be in the kitchen, laying the table for breakfast, preparing everything for the week that lies ahead.

Policemen are going through her kitchen cupboards. Nothing can be put back in its right place now.

CHAPTER
ELEVEN

Do You Speak German?

The sitting-room door opens, and a man in a dark civilian suit enters. He sits down in the armchair opposite Lily — in Simon's chair — and puts his hands on his knees, giving Lily a small smile which she cannot read. Possibly it is apologetic. It looks as if he is separate from the uniformed officers who are tramping up and down her stairs in their boots, over the turquoise carpet that she bought with her first year of part-time earnings. She expects him to introduce himself, but instead he opens his mouth and addresses her. She cannot understand a word of what he says. He stops speaking, and raises his eyebrows.

"I'm sorry," she says, "I don't understand you." Belatedly, it comes to her: she knows that mesh of sounds. He's speaking German.

"But you are German," he says. His voice is flat and strong, reasonable, sure of itself.

"I am British by naturalisation." He hasn't told her his name. Why hasn't he?

"You were born in Berlin. You went to school there. Of course you understand German."

"I left Berlin when I was a child. Since then I have spoken nothing but English."

"And you are married to an Englishman."

She glances round, and sees that the policewoman has a shorthand pad on her knee, and is taking notes.

"You are married to an Englishman," he repeats.

"Yes."

"And your husband works at the Admiralty."

"Yes."

"Do you understand the work of the Admiralty?"

Lily hesitates. "To some extent."

"To some extent. You know the nature of your husband's work?"

"He doesn't discuss it with me."

"Never?"

"I suppose — Sometimes a man will mention something about his office life."

"Of course he will." He seems pleased with her.

"But it's nothing," she says quickly. "Only that it wouldn't be natural for a man to — not one word about his work —"

"It wouldn't be natural for a man to — not one word about his work," he repeats. "You know, Mrs Callington, you *do* sound a little German. Perhaps you were being modest when you said you couldn't speak it?"

"I've said already that I don't."

"So. We've established that your husband sometimes talks to you about his work at the Admiralty."

"That's not what I said —"

"He talks to you. Does he also talk to others?"

"Of course he doesn't."

"You know, I am sure, that he has signed the Official Secrets Act?"

"Yes."

"He has discussed that with you?"

"No! It's just that I knew — I assumed —"

"You knew, and you assumed."

"Simon would never discuss with me anything that was covered by the Official Secrets Act."

"Do you mean that he might discuss such things with anyone else, Mrs Callington?"

"Of course not. Of course that's not what I mean. You are deliberately misunderstanding what I say. I think you misunderstand my husband's work as well. He is not in a senior position." Even as she said it, she felt a stab of betrayal. It might sound as if she were belittling Simon.

"I am not quite sure, Mrs Callington, that *you* perfectly understand what I am asking you. Perhaps your English is not quite as excellent as you believe it to be." Again, suddenly, he switches into another language. This time she knows it's not German. It isn't French, Italian or Spanish.

"You don't understand me, Mrs Callington?"

"I don't even know what language you're speaking."

"And yet you speak English, French, Italian. You speak French well enough to teach it. You are quite a linguist, Mrs Callington, and yet you don't understand a word of your mother-tongue and you don't even

126

recognise the language in which I've just been speaking to you."

Lily says nothing.

"Well? Is that correct?"

"I don't know if it is *correct*," she says, laying a slight emphasis on the word. "But it is the case."

At once, sweat starts out under her arms. A blunder. She used that word because she was thinking of the briefcase. Can he see her thoughts? If she hadn't been thinking of the briefcase she would have answered, "It is the truth." She must be careful. This man knows what he is about. She is on the defensive and likely to make mistakes.

He doesn't take her up on the word. He is quite relaxed, it appears. He watches her face closely, but without obvious suspicion. This is England, she thinks. They cannot throw you down the stairs or lock you into a standing cell until they get the answers they want. They don't do things like that here.

"Has your husband changed his habits recently? Home late, different routine *und so weiter?*"

"No."

"Did you recognise the words I just spoke?"

"No."

"They were German. Do you consider yourself English, Mrs Callington?"

She hesitates just a moment too long. "I'm married to an Englishman. My children are English. My life and my work are here. I am a naturalised British subject."

"That's not what I asked."

"What right have you to ask me such a question?"

He sighs, and crosses his legs. "This is a perfectly normal part of our investigation, Mrs Callington. I'm sorry if it upsets you. What were you doing on April the eighteenth this year?"

"April the eighteenth?" She can't help an upsurge of relief. That was months ago. It can't be anything to do with the briefcase or the file. "I'm sorry, I don't remember. I'd have to look at my diary —"

"You keep a diary?"

"Just for my work and the children's appointments."

"Where is it?"

"In my handbag. It has already been looked at." One of the policemen took it out of her bag, opened it and riffled the pages with his thumb, then put it aside.

"I'm surprised you don't remember what you were doing on April the eighteenth. It was a big occasion. You were at the CND rally in Trafalgar Square."

She had forgotten the date. They must have photographs. She signed a petition, too. She didn't want to go at first, because, as usual, her instinct was to keep her head down. But Erica was going. They talked about it one cold afternoon, outside the school. Erica was taking the baby, even though Clare was only two months old.

"It's her future. All the children's future. We've got to do something, Lily. Those idiots are quite capable of blowing up the whole world." Erica for once not smiling, not ironic, but lit up with anger.

"I'll come with you," said Lily, and Erica let go of the pram handles to hug her.

"You were there with a friend," says the dark-suited man now. "Not your husband?"

we have brought our children? Young men and women chanted with upturned faces: *Ban the Bomb! Ban the Bomb!* She watched their happiness, their passion and innocence, as if she were a thousand years old. The surge and mass of it, and the April sun much too bright.

"All kinds of people, indeed. What kind of person would you describe yourself as being, Mrs Callington?"

"Why are you asking me these questions? Why have you arrested my husband?"

He sits back, as if at last she has said what he wants. "I was wondering when you were going to ask me that question. You might have shown some curiosity on that point earlier, to be frank. But perhaps there was no need."

"What do you mean?"

"I think, Mrs Callington, that with your excellent grasp of English you must know what I mean. You did not ask because you were not curious. You were not curious, because you knew."

"Of course I didn't know! How could I? I don't know what any of this is about."

"Very well. We'll leave it at that." And he actually stands up, still faintly smiling, and steps forward. He towers over her as she sits on the red sofa.

She is at Stopstone. Callington land. It's a hot day, and she and Simon have planned to take a picnic to the river, but there is something wrong with his car. He's gone to the garage in the village to see if it can be fixed. He thinks it's something quite simple, the spark plugs perhaps. Lily wanted to go with him, but he said it would be a lot of standing around in the heat. Better to stay here and relax in the garden.

She's lying on one of the steamer chairs in her brown linen shorts and yellow Aertex shirt, book at her side on the grass, eyes half-shut. It's too hot. In a minute she'll have to pull the chair into the shade. Flies are buzzing. There's a lake at the bottom of the slope beyond the lawns. The water draws the flies. When Lily first saw the lake in the distance, she was delighted. She and Simon could take a boat out. Perhaps they would swim. But when she walked down to it, she saw that it was murky, tangled with weed. There was a jetty with broken and missing planks. She asked Simon why the lake was so neglected and he shrugged and said, "We used to fish in it a lot."

"Didn't you swim?"

"Yes. There wasn't all this weed then." He hesitates, then blurts out: "The gardener's little girl drowned there, about ten years ago. After that, no one much fancied swimming. And then I suppose we got out of the habit."

"How terrible."

"It's a pretty filthy place now. It's an artificial lake, you know. The drains are clogged. I keep telling them to get it seen to, but no one can be bothered."

The flies buzz. There are bees, too, in the nearby beds. The colours of the flowers here are so violent. She ought to get out of this sun —

Shadows fall, blocking out the light. Her eyes snap open.

132

"Well, if it isn't Lily. Where's the Milkman?"

Simon's brothers. Not like him: big-built, fair-haired, with small, inexpressive eyes. She doesn't like them.

"Simon has taken the car to the garage."

"We'll have to do our best to entertain you, then, shan't we, Rupe?"

"Absolutely, Rog. Got any ideas?"

"It's bloody hot, isn't it? How about a swim?"

"In the lake?"

"Why not?"

"Off we go then. Upsidaisy!"

As one, they swoop on Lily. Rupert has her ankles, Roger her wrists. She struggles fiercely, but they are much too strong for her, and she is afraid. They could run her into the woods and do whatever they liked. No one would believe her. What if she screamed? Simon wouldn't hear. The parents might but they would do nothing. Besides, she is already too far from the house.

"I don't want to swim," she says furiously. She twists, trying to bite Roger's wrist, but she cannot reach. The ground bumps and rushes below her. They're carting her down the slope now.

"Oh, we think you do, really."

"Put me down now!"

They're laughing. She twists in their grip and they tighten it, burning her flesh. They are running her down over the lawn, over the rough ground below. They can't be seen from the house here.

She jerks and thrashes once more, then goes still. She shuts her eyes and mouth, and goes deep inside herself. She is not here. The sound of their feet changes. They are not on land. They've taken her out on the rotting jetty. Now they are swinging her.

"One! Two! THREE!"

She is flying. Her eyes open, catch wheeling sky and lake. Her right foot bangs against something hard. She hits the water on her back and her hair rushes up beside her. She strikes out. Weed catches her hands. She fights it off, swallowing down her horror.

Lily pulls up to the surface, treading water. She puts down a foot, fearful of tangling into weed and slime, but she's out of her depth. Mud churns around her and something whips against her foot. She draws up her legs, shuddering. She mustn't swim for the shore or she will get caught in the dense mat of weed and pulled down. The men will catch her if she heads for the jetty. She lies flat along the surface and very slowly sculls herself out, into clearer water. There they are, on the jetty, looking at her. She doesn't think they will plunge after her into the lake. She swims deeper.

"Come this way, you little idiot!" yells Rupert. She tips her face up to look at him along the oily skin of the water.

"You're going in deeper, you fool!" bawls Roger.

Lily pushes her hair out of her eyes. A coil brushes against her leg. Weed, she tells herself. Only weed. She mustn't put her legs down. She must scull on the surface. She can float for a long time, perfectly safe, and the water isn't cold. For half a second she's exultant, with the sun in her eyes. The exultation of the one who has gone in. The sand, the sharp, sparkling water, all those crowding bodies, her mother pacing the water's edge.

Nicht zu weit, Lili!

Of course the brothers wouldn't harm her. They would probably reach down from that jetty to haul her out. They would say, *Can't you take a joke? We were only mucking about.* But all the same she'll stay here. There must be another way out of the lake, where the weed is not so thick and there aren't all those reeds growing along the shore. She'll keep her head and swim around until she finds it.

They are getting worried now. Clearly, they didn't mean actually to drown her.

"Lily!" they shout. "Lily!"

She lies completely flat along the surface of the water. It isn't cold. She breathes through her nose while the water laps at her lips.

"Lily!"

But that is their mistake. They bellow too loudly. Suddenly she hears another voice. She turns and sees the gardener running down the slope, shading his eyes.

"Mr Fitton!" she cries out. "Mr Fitton!"

"You all right there, miss?"

"If I swim to the jetty, can you help me out?"

"You hang on now, miss. Go careful. I'm coming." He does not so much as look at the brothers.

The jetty seems a long way off but Mr Fitton is down at the end, waiting for her. The brothers have stepped back. Lily swims slowly, keeping herself to the surface, sculling her way around another mass of weed. Mr

Fitton is kneeling down, holding out his arms, encouraging her: "That's the way. Go careful now."

She listens to nothing but his voice. A few more strokes. His face swims above her.

"Get your elbows up on the wood. That's the way. I'll pull you over."

A last trail of weed catches at her as she rises. He seizes her elbows and pulls until she has her right knee up on the wood, and then pulls again, dragging the lake off her. Now she is on hands and knees, drenched, panting.

"Get something to wrap her in," says Mr Fitton to the men behind him.

"I'm all right."

"They ought to of told you. This lake's not safe for swimming."

One of the rugs from the steamer chairs is put over her shoulders. She doesn't look at the brothers. Her mind is closed tight against them. She can no longer breathe them in.

"You want to go and have a hot bath."

"Yes, I will."

"It's a shame," he says, low, helping her up.

"Thank you for your help," she says.

They are talking quietly: the brothers won't be able to hear.

The brothers move aside as Mr Fitton helps her up the jetty. Without looking at them, she says clearly, "That was a bit off, wasn't it?"

Mr Fitton walks her all the way to the house.

By the time Simon comes back from the garage, Lily has bathed and washed her hair. She has rinsed out her clothes, which smell of the lake. Rupert and Roger, she knows, will say nothing. Mr Fitton, perhaps, might mention it; but she thinks not.

The next day, her right foot is bruised over the arch. There are scratches on her thighs from the rough wood of the jetty. She examines her wrists carefully: they are unmarked.

The man who hasn't introduced himself towers over her as she sits on the red sofa. He says nothing, just makes her feel his dominance in her own house. She understands him. She knows his type, and he doesn't know hers.

"Why are you standing so close to me?" she asks in the clear, authoritative voice that she uses in the classroom. The policewoman snaps her a quick glance. He can't help himself: for all his training and determination, he steps back.

"Thank you," says Lily. "Are you intending to arrest me as well as my husband?"

"What makes you think that?"

Lily is silent.

"We may need to have another chat later on."

The policewoman has her pencil poised. He nods. She closes her notebook and snaps a band over it. I should have asked for a solicitor, thinks Lily. He has been interrogating me. But to do so might be read as an admission of guilt. If you have nothing to hide, then why do you need a solicitor? Besides, she can't think where she would find one, on a Sunday afternoon in rainy Muswell Hill.

"Where have they taken Simon?"

He doesn't answer straight away, and she thinks he means to balk her, but then he replies, matter-of-fact: "Scotland Yard."

"When will he be allowed to come home?"

"That's not my area, I'm afraid. He is helping with inquiries. He hasn't been charged. My advice to you now is: Go and collect your children, bring them home and give them their supper. It's school tomorrow, I believe. We're finished here for today. I'll drop in another time."

He has wrong-footed her again. She is to expect him at any time. She is not to relax for an hour. He's inserting himself into her house, her life. He keeps on being much cleverer than she expects. Be careful, Lily. *Go careful.*

He's gone, and the uniformed officers with him. They have taken all the papers from Simon's desk in the bedroom and Lily has had to sign for them. They don't seem to understand that the papers are only insurance policies and bank statements. It is nine o'clock by the time they leave. Bring the children home and give them their supper, indeed. They have been at Erica's for hours. She goes to the telephone.

"Erica?"

The children are still up, playing bagatelle with Thomas. They can stay over, says Erica. She's already put Clare's cot into her and Tony's bedroom, and made up three beds on the floor in the baby's bedroom. The children will be fine. She's got plenty of sofa cushions, and there's the camping mattress.

"It's all right, Erica, I'll bring them home."

"Are you sure? Is everything — I mean, are they still there?"

"They left a few minutes ago."

"My God, they were there for hours. Is Simon back yet?"

"Not yet."

Erica is silent. The line hisses. Does it always make that noise? This is craziness, Lily. No one's listening to you. But perhaps you should talk as if they are.

"I'll be round to fetch them in ten minutes," says Lily.

It's Tony who opens the door. He doesn't quite look at her as he says heartily, "Come on in. Let me take your coat."

Erica rushes downstairs, clutching a nappy bucket.

"Here you are!" She kisses Lily, and the smell of ammonia from the bucket mixes with Erica's Jolie Madame. "They're all playing in Thomas's bedroom. You're freezing. Are you all right?"

"Yes, I'm all right." She feels dazed, coming into the light of Erica's hall.

"And Simon —?"

Lily shakes her head.

"It's all some ridiculous mistake," says Erica quickly.

"I know."

Tony has hung up the coat, and is watching her. Yes, there is a reservation. He would be happier, really, if Lily weren't in their hall, *dragging them into it*. Tony's not like Erica.

"I don't really know what's going on," says Lily.

"Do you want a cup of tea?"

"Gin might be more to the point," says Tony nicely, and Lily melts. She's started to suspect the worst of everyone and she's got to stop it.

"I'd love a drink, but I must get the children home," she says. "School tomorrow, and Thomas needs his sleep too."

"I only wish he did," says Erica. "Darling, at least come and get warm. You look awfully tired. Come in the dining room; there's still a fire there."

As always, the laden clothes horse is up, the baby's pram wedged against the piano, and Thomas has made another elaborate den under the table. Tony and Erica usually have to eat their meals on their knees. Erica drags a dining chair to the fire.

"Sit down. Tony'll get you that drink."

Lily spreads her hands to the heat. She knows Erica's house almost as well as her own. Even the smell of it. She should tell Erica about the two of them being watched at the CND rally. But Tony is back, with a gin and tonic for her and a saucer of peanuts.

"I don't suppose you've had anything to eat."

Lily swallows her drink gratefully. Tony has made it strong. She can feel it going into her veins. They are her friends: good friends. The gin eases her.

"What did they want?" asks Tony.

140

"I don't know. It's to do with Simon's work."

"The Admiralty, isn't it?" Tony's eyes are dark and inward. He is no fool. He knows perfectly well that Simon works at the Admiralty and it's all a bit hush-hush even though, as Simon says, he's really just one of the back-room boys. Tony likes Lily; always has done. He likes coming home to find the two women thick as thieves, laughing over some idiotic joke that they can never explain while Thomas and Bridget roister over the furniture. But there's no question about what comes first. Tony likes reading newspapers and is always quoting from articles: "Would you believe it, this chap Burrows was really called Buryakov? No one had the faintest idea, not even the next-door neighbours." Spies aren't cloak-and-dagger types at all, not in real life. They're dull as ditchwater. They keep themselves to themselves, leave notes for the milkman and take the same bus to work as you do.

But Erica hasn't read those articles. "It's absurd!" she bursts out. "Simon, of all people. Haven't they got better things to do? You only have to *look* at Simon. I hope you get a proper apology, Lily. They can't behave like stormtroopers." And then she blushes deeply, all over the smooth even skin Tony loves. Erica, in the heat of it, has forgotten about Lily. Damn silly thing to say, anyway; as if a British policeman could ever be anything like those Nazi thugs.

Lily, too, sees the blush. Erica; her dear friend Erica. She isn't naïve at all, and in fact she would call herself well informed about politics. Committed, even. She was so determined about the rally: *We've got to do something, Lily. Those idiots are quite capable of blowing up the whole world.* Her eyes glowed as she signed petitions, delivered leaflets, attended rallies. Sharp, funny Erica even knew all the words to "Don't you hear the H-bombs' thunder", and sang along. And yet Erica knows nothing, because she has never been afraid.

"Of course it's all a mistake," says Lily. *Es ist alles ein Mißverständnis*, says her mind. Did she speak aloud? Did she really say those words aloud in German? No, all's well.

"Of course it is, darling," says Erica, dropping to her knees beside Lily's chair, taking her left hand, chafing it between her own. "You're still cold . . . It must have been a most awful shock for you. Are you sure you're up to taking the sausages home?"

It's nothing to be scared of, Lily tells herself. Of course there was always the German language in her mind. You don't forget things. You put them away, out of sight and sound, and think that you have forgotten them, but they are still there. They come out when you least expect it. It's the shock. She and Erica haven't called the children "the sausages" for years.

"We'll be fine," she says, and gently disengages her fingers. Tony proffers the gin bottle, but she shakes her head. "I must get them home."

"What an absolute bloody nightmare," he says, his face flushed by the gin or the heat of the fire. He splashes gin clumsily into his own glass. "Isn't there somewhere you could take the kids until it all dies down?"

142

At once she realises that Tony doesn't believe it is all an awful mistake. In Tony's world, the police do not turn up to ransack a house for no good reason. A man like Simon would not be arrested and taken in for questioning unless there were solid grounds for suspicion.

"Of course she can't take them away. It's the middle of term," says Erica. "She'd lose her job."

"All the same. The papers will kick up a hell of a stink if they get hold of it. Might be best to go to ground for a while."

Both women stare at him. "Why should the papers get hold of it?"

Tony shrugs, avoiding their eyes. Lily understands. Simon hasn't been charged, the man said, but the papers would soon get hold of it, if he were. Tony doesn't want to say that. "The police talk to the press all the time, off the record," he says.

"How on earth do you know that?" asks Erica.

"Common knowledge. The baby's crying, darling."

"I know." Both parents listen, looking up at the ceiling. "I thought she'd settled." The cry swells to a roar. "She's standing up again."

"She used to be such an angel, but now she pulls herself up, and then she can't get down again."

"She stands there screaming until one of us goes up."

"I'll go."

"No, it's all right. I'll go."

The stairs creak, the door opens, the volume of crying rises and slowly, sobbingly, declines. "He's picked her up," diagnoses Erica. "He always does that.

He's hopeless. You have to sit by the cot and pat her until she goes back to sleep, but Tony hasn't the patience. Oh God, he's bringing her down."

And here they are. Tony smoothes back the baby's feathery hair, which is damp with sweat and tears. She stares around. A hiccup shakes her and she buries her face in her father's shoulder. Her arms go around his neck.

"She knows I'll put her straight back in her cot," says Erica. "That's why she won't look at me. Nine months old, would you believe it? She plays him like a violin."

"It won't do her any harm. She's just a baby."

"So you say. Come here, lambkin, let me wipe your face."

Lily watches them. Their tender, absorbed faces. They can't feel this for anyone else, only for Clare and Thomas. Tony would do anything — or *not* do anything — to keep his own baby safe. It's natural. Lily has always known that this is how it works. But usually she has Simon at her side and they are united as Tony and Erica are united, for all their differences. Now, though, there is only Lily.

The children huddle alongside her as they walk home along the wet, glistening pavements. It has stopped raining at last. Bridget stumbles, half-asleep on her feet.

"Thomas cheated at bagatelle," she complains, her voice blurred.

"Never mind."

"He always cheats," says Paul. "You should be used to it by now, Bridgie."

144

"We'll soon be home, and then we'll all have cocoa, and you can tumble into bed," soothes Lily. Bridget, she knows, isn't listening to her words, only to the tone of them and the comfort of her mother's voice. She was frightened. Sally whispered that, gravely, in her mother's ear. "Bridget was scared, Mum. She wet herself. I told Erica and she gave her some clean knickers."

And she, Lily, had stupidly forgotten to pack clean underwear for the children. At home, she takes Bridget upstairs and kneels to undress her. Bridget stands still, shivering with tiredness. She is wearing, incongruously, Erica's lace underwear.

"Thomas didn't know I wet my knickers," she says.

"Of course he didn't. Anyway it doesn't matter. Let's get your vest off. Arms up, knees stretch, rah rah rah."

That's what Simon says to them. She's learned all the English children's sayings from Simon.

"I don't like these knickers. They're scratchy. Take them off me." She starts to cry, not the usual Bridget bellow but a whimper that draws at Lily's heart.

"It's all right, sweetheart. Look, here's your nightie, all nice and clean."

"I didn't like it at Erica's. I wanted you to come and get me."

"I did come, didn't I?"

"Not for ages! Thomas was horrible to me! He said I was a stinky pinky pee-pants."

"You know what Thomas is like. He'll have forgotten it all by tomorrow."

Bridget stops crying as her face flushes with rage. "I hate him," she screams. "I don't ever want to go to his house again. If he tells anyone I'm going to kill him."

"That's my girl," says Lily, laughing in spite of herself.

"Mum . . ."

"What?"

"Could I really kill Thomas? Would you let me?"

It was years before Lily told Simon that his brothers had thrown her into the lake. She did so the summer that Simon's mother pressed for Sally to visit Stopstone on her own. Sally was a favourite with the Callingtons.

"Why not let her? My mother's fond of Sally, at least that's something."

Lily told him about the lake.

"Why didn't you say?"

"It would only have made trouble. Don't get angry, it was years ago. But I don't want Sally going there without me. It's not a safe place for her."

She hadn't cared about making trouble. It was because of the shame that she had kept quiet. She, Lily, picked up like a bag of rubbish, dangling from his brothers' hands and then heaved into the lake. She didn't want Simon ever to see that humiliated figure.

Bridget presses against her mother. Lily holds her, rocks her, lifts her, puts her between the sheets like a baby and tucks her in. With her eyes tightly closed, Bridget puts her thumb in her mouth and begins to suck rhythmically. She'll soon be asleep.

146

CHAPTER
TWELVE

The Charge

Simon is to appear at Bow Street Magistrates' Court tomorrow morning, at 10a.m. The charge is that between 30 November 1959 and 20 November 1960 he unlawfully conspired with a person or persons unknown to commit breaches of the Official Secrets Act 1911. Pargeter, Simon's solicitor, has already explained that since bail is highly unlikely to be granted, he won't be making an application.

The police had enough evidence to charge him.

They must have found the briefcase. It's the only possible interpretation. They'd have ripped the house apart, looking for more evidence. Christ knows what damage they'll have done. What did they say to Lily? She'll have kept the children out of the way and made sure they didn't see anything that frightened them. She wouldn't have let anyone know that she was frightened herself. For a second Lily is before him. Their bedroom and the new green eiderdown. Lily's face buried in the pillow. Her hair spread out and the ribbon strap of her nightdress slipping off one shoulder. He winces, and shuts off the thought.

Simon has been brought from his cell for this meeting with his solicitor in the interview room. It's Simon's father who has instructed Pargeter, who is apparently "an absolutely top man". He's not from Blyth & Corston, the local solicitors who have handled Callington affairs "for generations", as the Callingtons like to say. Simon and Lily wouldn't be able to afford Pargeter, but the bill is going to Stopstone. He mustn't betray himself, if Pargeter mentions the briefcase. He must seem to be open, but to know nothing. He can't trust Pargeter.

Simon's father has acted fast, in that crushing way of his.

When Pargeter came in, he was so clean that he made Simon feel dirty. He must be used to prison. He didn't bat an eyelid. The green paint on the walls of the interview room was flaking, and the single bulb in its metal cage buzzed intermittently, like a bluebottle. Simon felt as if he'd brought the tang of his cell with him. The touch of the prison blanket and the taste of his metal mug made him dirty to himself.

Pargeter wears an old, smooth watch which purrs through the minutes of his appointment with Simon. It was probably his father's watch. He writes down Simon's words with a heavy silver fountain pen. He smells, faintly, of cologne.

Simon isn't going to give him Giles's name. Christ knew where that would lead. The file must have been missed pretty much straight away, he thinks. Brenda must have said Giles was working on it. They'd have rung Giles and Giles had clearly panicked. They'd have gone into the Latimer to question him about it as soon as possible, broken leg or no broken leg. Giles must have caved in. The anaesthetic . . . Giles was in a hell of a state when he saw him in that hospital bed — For God's sake, what can he have told them? Surely not that he, Simon, filched that file from Julian Clowde's office. The most basic inquiry would show that wasn't likely. That file would have been locked up. Simon has still not sorted out in his mind why Giles had it at all. Those three names and three sets of initials. He sees them all the time, as if they've been written on his mind.

Even if the file was supposed to have been lying on Giles's desk, for some reason which was absolutely against every security protocol he'd ever heard of, then how the hell was he, Simon, meant to have known the exact moment when Giles had left it there — and then, presumably, managed to walk out with it, without anyone noticing?

If only he had kept out of Giles's office. But, for old times' sake, he keeps the habit of dropping in. The air is always thick with cigarette smoke, and there are rings on documents from Giles's endless mugs of tea. The chaos of his desk is a byword. Old Giles is a law unto himself. A brilliant eccentric, people said, in the old days when his brain seemed to work in a different dimension from everyone else's. He spoke near-perfect Russian, played chess like a demon and could date any painting you had in your house. He'd tell you it was a fake into the bargain. He'd get roaring drunk but never drop a line in one of those marvellous stories of his.

Not so much now. They will say that Simon has made use of him, trading on old friendship. Dull, plodding Simon, glorified clerk Simon, exploiting flawed but brilliant Giles to turn himself into an actor on a bigger stage than he merited. Milkman.

Is that the story? Poor old Giles, they'll say. He deserved better. That shit Callington knew his weaknesses. If that's the story, then the police already knew what they were looking for when they came to the house. They'd have found the briefcase in five minutes.

But have they got the briefcase? He can't ask Pargeter. The solicitor is still writing away on his pad. Simon clears his throat. "This charge against me," he says, and stops. If he asks about what evidence the police have got, then it might sound as if he knows there is some.

Pargeter caps his pen. Instead of meeting Simon's eye he stares somewhere past his left ear, and frowns. "Something's come up," he says. "I've had information that certain material has been found in the course of further police investigations."

"Where?" asks Simon, instantly. Pargeter's face changes. *You fool, you bloody fool. Why did you say that?* A man who'd never seen the briefcase wouldn't have asked "Where?" He'd have burst out: "They can't have found anything! There's nothing to find!"

"They can't have found anything," he says, but it's too late. Pargeter won't meet his eye.

"It's highly unusual for Special Branch to let anything slip at this stage," he says. "But I happen to know one of the investigating officers pretty well.

150

Known him for years, in fact. He's a decent type." He smiles faintly, in appreciation of the world of decent types to which he also belongs. "It was quite a coup for him." Simon stares. What the hell was this man talking about? Quite a coup? You're supposed to be my solicitor, for Christ's sake, he thinks. Angry words burn on his tongue, but he says nothing. "This chap led me to believe that the material was found during a search of your office," Pargeter continues.

"In my office!"

"You seem surprised."

"Well, of course — Of course, for God's sake, I'm surprised." It's the truth, so why does he sound as if he's acting? "Whatever this material is, it's got nothing to do with me." He isn't saying any of this right. He is telling the truth and he sounds like a liar.

Pargeter places his hands on his knees. His fingers drum once, twice. "Look here." He's avuncular now, playing the twenty or so years that he has on Simon. "Cards on the table. I can't help you, you know, if you don't help me. No, no" — and he holds up a hand, to forestall an interruption that Simon hasn't been about to make — "I don't need to know everything. But don't, I beg of you, send me barking up the wrong tree and expect me to make a case out of it."

"It's a pretty easy case to make, as far as I can see," says Simon. "I know nothing about whatever it is they've found in my office. I have done nothing to contravene the Official Secrets Act. I don't believe there can be any evidence against me that's going to stand up in court."

Pargeter leans back. Without looking at Simon, he says, "If you'll forgive me, that's not a case. That's an assertion on your part. Where was it you were at school?"

"Renton."

"Renton. Of course. Splendid. I've a nephew there. Look here, about this barking-up-the-wrong-tree business. One develops an instinct, if you'll forgive me."

"For when someone's lying, you mean?"

"I didn't say that, and I didn't mean it. But it tends to become clear when a client is holding something back. Sometimes, it has to be said, in order to protect others."

"You think I am part of a ring of spies, is that it?"

Pargeter glances at the door. "That's not what I said."

"If they've found something compromising in my office — a file, say — I can assure you that it has nothing to do with me."

"Is there any reason why it should be a file?"

"No, of course not, it's just that offices are full of files —"

"It wasn't a file."

"What was it?"

"A Minox. A type of camera. You may have heard of it."

"Was there a film in it?"

Pargeter gives him a glance. "I believe so. Possibly my contact was cleverer than I thought. He must know the implications of disclosing such evidence to the defence."

Simon feels something awful happening within himself. His stomach loosens. He's going to shit himself. He bends forward, tightening every muscle, breathing shallowly.

"Here, have some water."

The mug with its taste of dirty London. He drinks. He is sweating but he has got control. He burned the cartridge. He didn't burn the file. Why not? Evidence, his mind said. He'd thought that, there in the kitchen, with the cartridge burning. The file was evidence, and he might need it. And why think that at all, unless another thought lay under it? That Giles, perhaps . . .

That Giles was not to be trusted. His mind knew enough, but he didn't listen to it. Instead, he'd let Giles know what he'd done. He'd said: "I can't muck about with a file like that." That was what he said to Giles, those exact words. He told Giles in so many words that he wasn't going to do what Giles wanted, wasn't going to get the file safely back into Brenda's hands. And now a camera has been found in his own office. A Minox with film in it. But Giles, for God's sake, Giles is strapped up to a pulley — He can't get out of bed, let alone to the office — He can't have planted the camera. Giles wouldn't —

But someone has planted it. Simon remembers the man in Giles's flat. He wasn't English. He'd never have got into the Admiralty. But how many others are there? My God, if they've got someone else inside the Admiralty — someone whom no one would suspect, or more than one . . . But in that case, why didn't Giles ask that person to replace the file in the first place? All this could have been avoided. Giles wouldn't have needed to ring Simon.

Another thought goes through him like an electric charge. They haven't found the file. They can't have found it, or it would have been the basis of the case against him. A top-secret file discovered in Simon's own house: that'd make it easy for them. So they don't know where it is, unless Pargeter's hiding something —

No. You'll go mad if you start thinking like that. They haven't found the file. But they should have done. An old briefcase tucked behind the children's boots: they'd have found it in no time. Someone got rid of it. There's only one person who can have done that. Lily.

Pargeter is waiting. That same look is on his face, watchful.

"It's got nothing to do with me. That camera. I've never seen it in my life. Someone must have put it in my office."

"You know what kind of camera a Minox is?"

"Of course I do. My work involves handling classified information. My clearance —" He stops himself.

"Yes."

There they are, the two of them. Pargeter's face is set; rather a beefy face. Neutral. Frowning. He doesn't like this. He's not going to help me. Why should Pargeter believe that the Minox was planted? It sounds like something out of the *Boy's Own Paper*.

Soon Pargeter will get up to leave. His way will be opened for him through all the locked doors, and he'll walk out into the rain. He'll put up his umbrella and hurry to the Tube. Buy the *Standard* if he feels like it,

154

or a pomegranate from a stall. Lily likes pomegranates. Simon always buys one for her when they are in season.

There isn't enough air. Simon breathes shallowly again. In a minute Pargeter will stand up and go. Simon will be taken from the interview room, back to his cell. The cell door will clang shut. There'll be the rattle of keys and then heavy boots walking away. The warder will say something to Pargeter about the weather. Call him "sir". They are in it together, professionals. Pargeter will do his job. He thinks I'm lying.

"I've been giving some thought to the question of your barrister," says Pargeter. "Unless you have someone in mind? A family connection possibly?"

"We don't go in for being on trial."

"Absolutely not. Absolutely not," he repeats, almost dreamily, tapping the cap of his pen on the table. "Your family place is in Norfolk, I gather?"

"Stopstone."

"I've talked things over with your father, of course. It would be best if your wife and children were to go down there straight away. Things can get pretty hot once the press get hold of a story."

They're parcelling him up between them. His father and Pargeter. Now they want to get their hands on Lily.

"I don't think that's a good idea."

"Oh. Don't they get on?"

"Not particularly. Besides, Lily will want to be here in London."

"Oh. Pity. Never mind: back to our muttons. The chap I have in mind is very good. Peter Learmonth. Come across him at all?"

"No."

"He was briefed in the Shelley Gold case. I dare say you remember."

"No."

"Really? It was in all the papers. Marcus Shelley and Ruth Gold."

"I don't remember."

"He's not flashy, but he's got a terrific grasp of detail. Nothing gets past him. Learmonth's the man I'd choose."

"If you were me?"

Pargeter gives Simon a look of pure, unguarded surprise. "I suppose so."

"Not that I'm suggesting you ever could be."

Pargeter's rather heavy-lidded eyes are hard to read. He is still tapping that damned pen cap. Doesn't he know how it gets on a man's nerves?

"Let's have Learmonth, then," says Simon.

"I'm glad you agree. Well, then." The pen is capped, and replaced in the silky inside jacket pocket. The chair scrapes back. Pargeter is seized with energy. He's going to leave.

He's going and I am staying here. That's how it is and how it has to be. If I put my hand on his arm and said, "You know what, old boy, I think I'd rather come along with you," he would be embarrassed. He would try to shrug me off. Make a joke of it. If I didn't do the decent thing, I'd be pulled off him.

Rain. The unguarded wetness of it on his face. The children's wellingtons. Have they found the briefcase? He daren't ask.

156

"I hope it's stopped raining," Simon says.

"Raining?" asks Pargeter, a little suspiciously, as if Simon is talking in code.

"Outside, I mean."

"Oh, I see. No, no. Lovely day, in fact." And he looks quite bright at the prospect of it. He'll go out, in just a few seconds, into that sharp low sunlight you get at this time of year. Simon has always thought it's the light that suits London best.

He'll appear in the Magistrates' Court tomorrow. And what will Giles do? Lie there in that hospital bed with his leg slung in a pulley, and wait for events to take their course? Giles. Christ. There was I feeling sorry for him. Giles was ahead of me. *I can't muck about . . .* Simon mimics himself savagely, under his breath. What kind of a cocksure tosser would give himself away like that? He'd as good as said to Giles: *You're screwed. I'm not going to help you.* He should have kept Giles guessing. He'd have gained a day. Two days, maybe. What a fool he's been, all the way back. Not wanting to know . . . If he hadn't been convinced that Giles was losing his touch, if he hadn't felt sorry for him — Christ! Sorry for him? Always feeling stronger than Giles, surer than Giles, because Giles was letting himself go and he, Simon, was holding on . . .

Vanity. That's what it was. Thinking himself such a bloody wonderful decent chap. The same vanity as Pargeter's. Vanity of thinking he was doing the right thing by old Giles. If he hadn't been such a blind bloody fool he'd have seen what was under his nose. He did see it, most of it, years ago, but he pretended that it didn't matter or that somehow Giles had changed and all "that old stuff" didn't have to be thought about now. How could anybody as frankly devious as Giles really be leading not one but two double lives? Giles half-cut, Giles rambling, Giles embarrassing at parties, Giles with his odd assortment of friends; *Old Giles was a bit of a Red in his misspent youth . . .*

Giles has been shouting what he is from the housetops for years. Everyone has heard but no one has listened. It's unspeakably clever. Good old Giles — poor old Giles — has been batting for the other side in more ways than one. He may look a shambles — he may *be* a shambles, an embarrassment, even — Giles may have wanted Simon when Simon no longer wanted him —

But none of that matters, not now.

He should never have telephoned Giles. He should have gone straight to Julian Clowde. He could have done it all without dropping Giles in the shit. Everyone knows about Giles's drinking; Clowde most of all. Simon would only have had to say a word or two; Clowde would have picked it up, and no harm done. He would have acted quickly, in that cold, decisive way of his. Clowde would have taken it on. Giles wasn't keeping on top of his work and he took home a file he shouldn't have. He wasn't thinking straight, and then, after the accident, he panicked —

Even though it was impossible that Giles could fail to be saturated to the bones with security, after all these years — Giles, who knew to a shade what each grade of

158

clearance permitted — Clowde would have made sure it was all hushed up, because Giles was Giles.

The thing was, they were all so much in the habit of making allowances for Giles.

Simon isn't sure what time it is, except that it must be getting late. The clanging and footsteps are muted. He shifts position on the hard bed. In the morning they will take him to court — to the Mags, as Pargeter called it. They'll charge him with conspiring with a person or persons unknown to breach the Official Secrets Act. If that person is unknown, then he can't be Giles Holloway. Giles is off the hook. Scot-free. In the clear, old boy. Off he goes while Simon jumps up and down protesting that it wasn't him, it was one of the big boys —

A wave of humiliation makes Simon groan aloud. He hears the noise he makes. Steady. Get a grip, Callington. Don't be such a drip. *Callington's so wet you could shoot snipe off him.*

He sees himself in another bed, in another room. He is lying on his back, lazy, drowsy, replete. Giles is sitting on the edge of Simon's narrow student bed, reading. His weight bears down on the mattress. He looks like a Buddha in wool-and-silk underwear. Simon's eyes are almost shut.

"Wake up and listen to this, dear boy:

"I have got to make everything that has happened to me good for me. The plank bed, the loathsome food, the hard ropes shredded into oakum till

159

one's finger-tips grow dull with pain, the menial offices with which each day begins and finishes, the harsh orders that routine seems to necessitate, the dreadful dress that makes sorrow grotesque to look at, the silence, the solitude, the shame . . ."

"Did you know that they made him stand for half an hour in convict dress in the middle of Clapham Junction? Half an hour of spitting and jeering. He had dysentery. He must have been terrified he'd shit himself in front of all of them."

"Who? Who was terrified?"

"Oscar." And after a pause, "Oscar Wilde."

"Oh. Did he shit himself?"

"Not as far as we know."

"You wouldn't think he'd want to write about it."

"You've got a lot to learn, my dear boy. It's from *De Profundis*."

Simon closes his eyes again and recites:

"Out of the depths have I cried unto thee,
O Lord.
Lord, hear my voice: let thine ears be atten-
tive to the voice of my supplications . . ."

"Just so. Were you a chorister?"

"I sang in church at home."

"I wish I'd heard you."

"If thou, Lord, should'st mark iniquities,
O Lord, who shall stand?"

"My view exactly. Do you still sing, Simon? There are so many things I don't know about you."

"Hardly at all. My voice broke. There was some idea that a fine baritone might emerge from the wreckage, but it turned out not to be the case."

"I shall imagine you in a red cassock and a white surplice."

"We wore black."

"I wonder why he didn't kill himself."

"Oscar Wilde?"

"Yes. He could have done it before the trial. He had time. Or during it, when it became clear things were going wrong. The trial lasted for several days, so he could easily have done it then. Or he could have killed the wretched Bosie. That might have been more to the point. Queensberry would have left him alone then. Do you know, the old bastard couldn't even spell 'sodomite'? He left a calling card: 'To Oscar Wilde, posing somdomite.'"

"How on earth do you know that?"

"Education, my dear Simon, education. The trouble with Oscar, he didn't believe it was really going to happen to him, until it was too late. He didn't believe they were going to find him guilty. One of his friends had a yacht waiting to take him off to France, but he didn't go. I suppose he must have imagined himself in court, giving marvellous speeches, and then going home at the end, just as he'd always gone home from the theatre when the play was over. That was his mistake."

And so it went on. Giles pondering, reading out more passages, scratching his back.

Once, he turned and stroked Simon's hair, tenderly, almost as if he were sorry for him. Simon couldn't have cared less about Oscar Wilde, but he thought it polite to take an interest.

"How long did he go to prison for?"

"Two years."

"You wouldn't kill yourself, surely, if you were only going to prison for two years."

Giles had looked at him strangely. "You don't know what you are talking about, Simon."

You tell yourself you've forgotten things, but you haven't. It's all there, under the lid he's crammed down on it since he met Lily. Lily must never know. Lily mustn't suspect, and so Giles must be absent even from Simon's thoughts. But now it seems that not thinking about those days for so long has only made the memories stronger. Giles on the bed in his old-fashioned underwear, about which he was as unselfconscious as a baby, telling Simon what he feared most in the world. And also telling Simon that he, Giles, wouldn't make the same mistake as Oscar. He would know when the play was over, and he would get out. But Simon hadn't listened. Giles's voice buzzed on, like the knocking of a bee inside a flower. Simon lay there, drowsy, sated, half hoping Giles would go home soon so that he could have the bed to himself — he used to guzzle sleep then — and half coldly wishing that Giles wouldn't talk about "Oscar" like that, because it made him sound like an old queen.

> If thou, Lord, should'st mark iniquities,
> O Lord, who shall stand?

He thinks he can sense, far below him, the rumble of the Tube. It feels like a kind of freedom, as if he's still part of that outside world of weary office workers swaying as they strap-hang their way home. He wouldn't care how packed the carriage was.

He used to lie and listen for the trains, when he was eight or nine. There was only a branch line to Stopstone, so that was no good, but his prep school was half a mile from the main line. When he couldn't sleep, he used to pretend he was on the train and rushing away through the darkness. Sometimes he became the train itself. Rushing and rushing into the dark, until he slept.

CHAPTER
THIRTEEN

Shadows under the Lamp-posts

Desks and chairs are set out in the hall. It's to make the final practice Eleven-plus for Paul's class — Top Class — as much like the real exam as possible. The lower panes of the internal classroom windows that overlook the hall have been covered with sugar paper. No one can look in or out. Top Class lines up by the door. In five minutes, not a minute more or a minute less, they will march into the hall and take their places. The desks are set far apart. Old Craven has spoken to them about trying to look at someone else's paper. Anybody who does so will be sent straight home in disgrace, and a letter will be written to the Local Authority. As he spoke, Craven flexed the cane which he always brought out at such moments. It was called "showing the cane".

Old Craven walks up and down the line of children, and flips Danny Coughlan's head with an exercise book for not standing still. Several of the girls have brought in their mascots, even though this isn't the real exam. None of the boys have mascots.

This time last year, Paul was sent to fetch the crates at milk-time with David Alexander. They were both trust-worthy boys, Mrs Wilson said; they were in her class then. Paul and David were told to carry the crates across the hall in absolute silence. Don't look at the children doing the exam, because it might distract them. Straight there and straight back, and make as little noise as you can. Don't rattle those crates!

Now Paul is in Top Class, and everybody else in the school is keeping quiet for them, even today when it's only practice. Last year only one boy and one girl passed for the grammar, and four boys and one girl to the technical school. Mum says this is because there was a bulge of babies born around the same time as Paul, and there aren't enough grammar school places. Craven says it is because last year's Top Class was full of thickos. This year, at least six are capable of passing for the grammar. They know who they are: Paul Callington, Richard Cemlyn, Andrew Dodds, Joseph Lodge, Penelope Fawley, Anne-Marie Gorman.

"I don't see what there is for you to smirk about, Daniel Coughlan. If you weren't bone idle you might be on the list, instead of going off to Payne's Wood."

Penny is best in the class at Comprehension. Paul is best at Mental Arithmetic. The Intelligence Test is the part Paul doesn't like. If he thinks about the questions for too long, he makes them more complicated in his head than they really are. You have to be quick. You have to allow the right amount of time for each section.

"It's no good knowing the answers. It's what you put down on the paper that counts. The examiners aren't mind-readers."

The examiners aren't code-breakers either. "A spider with DTs could write better than that, Joseph!"

Old Craven says that if he had to choose between being deaf and being blind, he would choose to be blind. He knows about both, because he was shelled during the war.

They sit at their desks. Everybody looks neater and cleaner than usual, as if they have been polished, ready for the exam. This is not like all the other practices they've done in the classroom. This is the dress rehearsal. Alison Wigley throws her plaits back over her shoulder. On your marks, get set —

A long time later, Paul surfaces, dazed. He has finished. The clock on the wall shows that there are eight minutes left. If you have time left over, use it to check your answers. Go right through the papers. Don't sit there staring round and wasting time.

Alison Wigley is crying. Her plaits have fallen forward and her shoulders are hunched. She isn't making any noise. Her papers are messy on her desk. The minute hand on the clock shivers, then bumps forward. Paul shuffles his own papers without looking at what is written on them. He cannot read through everything. He cannot check his answers.

Seven minutes. Dad has been gone for three days. Four if you count Sunday as a day and today, Wednesday, as another day. But if you count it in hours, then it's not even three days. Sunday afternoon to

Monday afternoon, Monday afternoon to Tuesday afternoon, Tuesday afternoon to eleven-fifty-three on Wednesday morning. That's not even sixty-eight hours.

Their house is the only one he knows that the police have been to, apart from Danny Coughlan's. That was because of Danny's big brother. Martin Coughlan is twenty and he's a mod. He goes down to Brighton and gets into trouble.

Five minutes. Paul arranges his papers. They are messy because he was writing fast. That doesn't matter too much. Craven keeps switching about whether or not neatness is important. Sometimes slow and neat is worse than fast and untidy. "The Eleven-plus isn't a handwriting competition, Susan Trudgmill!" That was because Susie only wrote half a side for her composition —

A flash of heat goes over Paul. It's all right, he tells himself, calm down, you idiot. There isn't always a composition. Sometimes they put in a long Comprehension question instead — he wrote loads for Comprehension —

But his hands don't believe him. They blunder at the papers in front of him. Read through the question papers. Don't rush at the exam like a bull at a gate. The examiners have put every word on that paper there for a reason.

"Write a composition on ONE of the following subjects: The Life of a Horse, Grace Darling's Daring Rescue, The Holiday I Will Always Remember, A Winter's Day, The Race to the South Pole."

How can he not have seen it?

"Two more minutes, children," says Mrs Liddell from the front.

Everyone walks soberly out to the playground. Their milk has been kept for them in the crates by the wall. Paul stabs through the silver-paper top with his straw and sucks up his milk. It's cold. He likes it cold. In summer the milk tastes of old cheese by playtime. He doesn't want to talk to anyone. A knot of girls has gathered around Alison. Some pat her cardigan; one holds her milk bottle so she can drink.

"It doesn't matter, Ali," somebody says. "It's only the stupid old practice."

"And next time it'll be only the stupid feckin' Eleven-plus," says Danny to Paul. He grins around his straw. "It's well for you."

"I left out the composition," says Paul.

"You never."

"I didn't see it."

"Nerves," says Danny professionally. "Our Martin had so much nerves before his trial, he was sick in a bucket four times."

"Was that for the Gunners?" asks Paul, although he knows.

"Yeah, the Youth, when he was fourteen."

They sit on their heels, backs against the wall. Even though it's a cold day, the sun has left some warmth in the bricks. It was only the feckin' practice.

"It'll be gas at Payne's Wood," says Danny, and digs Paul with his elbow.

168

Paul hangs around playing football after school, until he sees Craven at the door, peering about as if there's someone he wants. He's been in the office all afternoon, going through the exam papers. Paul slips to the gates.

He has threepence ha'penny. He goes into the sweet shop, buys fourteen Black Jacks and puts the bag in his pocket to warm up. They have to be soft and chewy.

Now he's at the top of their road. It's so steep that when he was little he used to think that if he ran as fast as he could and flapped his arms he would take off like an aeroplane.

He slows. There are men in the road. Some of them have got cameras and they are walking backwards, in the middle of the road, pointing the camera at the houses. They are jostling each other. One is almost in the hedge outside his house. Another is leaning over the gate with his camera.

He sees his mother at the window, dodging behind the glass. She disappears and a moment later the front door opens. He can't see her, so she must be standing behind the door.

"Paul!" she cries sharply. "Paul."

He runs, with his head down and his satchel bumping. By the gate he nearly trips but he saves himself by grabbing the post. A man catches hold of his arm and he tears himself free.

"I was only trying to help, sonny!" the man shouts after him as Paul jumps the steps. He is inside. The door slams and Mum shoots the chain into its slot.

"Where're Sally and Bridgie?"

"In the back."

Mum pulls the curtains across in the sitting room. As the curtains swish together, he sees faces bobbing over the hedge.

"Do you think they'll break in?" he asks.

"No. They're newspaper photographers, that's all. They want pictures."

"Why are they here?" he asks, but he knows, just as he knew even before he found the unanswered composition question in his paper. Mum turns to him. It is darkish in the hall but he can see her face.

"Dad was remanded in custody this morning."

Mum thinks he knows what that means. Sometimes she thinks he knows more about English words than she does, because he was born here and she wasn't.

"Are they going to let him come home?" It's a stupid question. Childish. He knows that as soon as it comes out of his mouth, just as he knew it would be worse than useless to write out one of the essay titles and underline it, in the couple of minutes he had left.

"No. In custody means in prison."

"Custody," says Paul.

"Bridget thought he had been put in a big pan of custard."

"Did you tell Bridget?"

Mum frowns. "I said the police were talking to Dad about an accident. She'll be more frightened if she hears things that she doesn't understand. Or if people say things to her."

Paul doesn't agree. Bridget is only five, and blurts out everything. "But why custody, Mum?"

170

"Dad didn't get bail, which means he can't come home. They're keeping him in prison until the trial."

"But Dad hasn't done anything."

Mum looks down at Paul's hand and says sharply: "Come into the light."

In the kitchen he too sees that his hand is bleeding.

"How did this happen?"

"I caught it on the gate." He thinks he remembers, now, a pain he didn't feel at the time. There's a scrape across the back of his hand, and a deeper cut. Mum reaches up to the shelf where she keeps the Dettol. She pours a capful into a cup of water, takes down the cotton wool and bathes his hand with the cloudy liquid. He likes the ordinary smell of the Dettol.

Mum reaches up. "There should be some plaster in the tin, if Bridget didn't have it all for her knee . . ."

She finds the plaster, and snips it to size with her kitchen scissors. Now the cut is hidden.

"There," says Mum. "Remember to keep it out of the water when you have your bath."

"What do they say Dad's done?" he asks, his voice small and casual. What he thinks is that Dad must have killed someone by accident, when he was driving the car. Dad always drives too fast.

Mum has her back to him as she reaches up to the shelf again to replace the tin. "They say that he has given important secrets to the Russians."

It is so unexpected, so extraordinary, that Paul can't take it in. Mum must have gone mad.

"You mean, like a spy?"

"Yes. They think he has taken information from his work and given it to the Russians."

"But Dad doesn't know any Russians."

"They think he does."

"If Dad was doing anything like that, we'd know about it."

Mum pushes back his hair from his forehead, and strokes his head as if he were as young as Bridget. "Sally is playing Ludo with Bridget in the dining room," she says. "I'll come in a minute and hear Bridget's reading while you and Sally do your homework."

"Mum, you didn't tell Bridget, did you? About them thinking Dad was a spy?"

"No. Oh, Paul, I forgot all about your exam. How did it go?"

"It was only the practice, Mum."

"Didn't it go well?"

"I missed out the composition question." He pauses. Mum knows what that means. She's a teacher. She'll be angry that he did something so stupid.

"It wasn't the real exam, was it?"

"No. I think I did the rest OK. Craven will go mad when he sees my paper."

"Take no notice of him," says Mum. "He's been in that school too long." Mum has never said anything like this about his teachers before. "Take no notice of anything that anyone says. They will say things, you can be sure of it. Ignore them."

"What kind of things?" he asks, although he already knows.

172

"Lies about your father."

Behind them, the doorbell rings, and goes on ringing.

"Aren't you going to answer it, Mum?"

"They're journalists. They've been ringing that bell all afternoon. They're trying again because they saw you come in."

"I could disconnect it," says Paul.

"Could you?"

Paul picks out the small screwdriver from Dad's toolbox in the cupboard under the stairs. He's watched Dad replace the batteries loads of times. First, he must twist off the bell's metal cover by hand. Luckily, it has stopped ringing. Paul undoes the two screws that hold down the bell's connections, and pulls out the ends of the wires. Easy-peasy. He replaces the cover, and scoots down the hall to put the screwdriver back in its exact place. Mum is pleased.

"Did you put the bolts across?" Paul asks.

"Yes."

He likes feeling together with Mum, doing jobs for her. She has shot both bolts across, top and bottom.

"I've bolted the back door too," says Mum. "I don't want Bridget to play out in the garden tonight."

Bridget always plays out after supper, even when it's pitch black. She's scared of dark in the house, but not of dark in the garden. She has a camp down by the apple tree, with the cushions from the old sofa they had before Mum bought this one with her teaching money.

The door-knocker bangs against its metal plate. It's the dolphin door-knocker that Dad found for Mum in a junk shop. They shouldn't be touching it.

"They'll stop soon," says Mum. "I'm going to make corned beef hash. I haven't been able to get to the shops."

"Did they stop you going out?"

"No, but they'll take photographs, and try to talk to me. Don't worry, Paul. Tomorrow they'll be somewhere else."

The children are in bed. Lily stands by her bedroom window, screening herself with the curtain even though she is sure that all the press people have gone. One of them came up to the letterbox and shouted through it, but that was before the children came home from school. His dirty voice filled her hall.

"What do you think about your husband, Mrs Callington? Is he a Soviet spy?"

Maybe he wasn't even a journalist. All kinds of people jump on the bandwagon. He might have been a neighbour who has always, secretly, wished them harm.

The hearing was so short, less than five minutes. She'd thought it would be longer. Simon was brought in with a policeman on either side of him. He wore the dark grey suit and navy tie that Lily had chosen for his court appearance. He looked straight ahead as he confirmed his name and address. His face was very still, as if he were making himself absent. He didn't look round for Lily. If you didn't know him, you would think he was arrogant. She wanted to say to him: *Simon, don't look like that. They are watching you.* The charge was read. The ridiculous, incredible words were read aloud.

"The case of Simon Paul Everard Callington, charged with offences under Section One of the Official Secrets Act 1911, that he did conspire with a person or persons unknown to breach the said Act on one or more occasion between the thirtieth of November 1959 and the twentieth of November 1960."

There was no application for bail. The magistrate remanded him in custody. One moment Simon was there, and she could look at him, and then they had turned him away and he went down the steps and disappeared. It was over. One of the clerks said something which made the other smile.

The glass of the bedroom window is cold against her face as she looks out. There's London, all the lights of it spreading beneath her. When they first came here, you could see nothing of it some winter nights, because of the pall of smog that hung there. Often smog crept all the way up the hill to where they were. It stank for weeks, yellowly, and people went out with handkerchiefs over their faces. How Sally coughed that winter. Lily would sit up with Friars' Balsam melting in the steamer, and hold Sally so she could breathe more easily. But now Sally is as strong as can be.

The house is a ship, riding the waves high above London. This is what Lily has always told herself at night, when she's afraid and the noise of the city becomes forlorn, even terrifying, as if anything might happen.

Lily no longer speaks a word of German, but she still hears the noise of thousands and thousands of throats, open, baying. It's only the traffic, or the wind.

She was allowed to visit Simon in prison before the hearing. His hands shook. It was very slight, just a tremor. Although the men — the guards, the prison warders — were sitting very close, she doesn't think they would have noticed it. Simon looked all wrong. It reminded her of when Bridget was a baby and Erica looked after her for a couple of hours. She came back smelling of a different house and of Erica's perfume.

Simon made a grimace when he saw her. It wasn't a smile, but a way of controlling his face in case it gave him away. She had seen that look before, on her father's face, on the day he had to report to the local police station with his papers. Of course, her father came back. He made light of it. They were idiots, fools. But he had been away for hours. They'd kept him waiting, he said.

She always loved Simon's hands. They were fine and long-fingered, unlike her own workaday hands. He had almond nails. But his hands were not too soft, because he liked doing jobs, liked getting out the oil and screwdrivers and little spanners, and working on the train set with Paul. Or he would put a new hinge on the shed door. He liked it when she had a little job of work for him to do.

176

He folded his hands together and put them on the prison table. She was afraid he would be handcuffed to the guards, but no. They sat a little way off, one at either side of him.

She ignored the guards. She knew there was never any point in trying to propitiate such men. She was there for Simon, only for him. She told him some things about the children, bringing him back to her. The grimace that held his mouth began to relax. There were brown stains of sleeplessness under his eyes. This is what can happen to a man, she thought, in a few days. She didn't allow herself to wonder what they had done to him. She knew — she believed — that there were rules here in England. There was the rule of law and Simon would be treated according to it. She smiled at him, and said, "The children talk about you all the time."

She wanted to say: *You are just the same to us. We think of you in exactly the same way as always. We haven't changed.*

She said, "Have you got enough cigarettes?" and one of the guards stirred and looked at her closely, as if he suspected that Lily had cigarettes hidden somewhere and was about to give them to Simon. But she knew that wasn't permitted.

"You know I was trying to cut down," said Simon.

It's two in the morning, and the children have been asleep for hours, but Lily can't even think of sleep. She is lit up. Her body is full of ferocious energy and she cannot sit down. Earlier she caught herself pacing up and down the hallway like an animal, taut for sounds from outside or a stir from the children in their bedrooms. They have no protection now, except for her.

Behind her, on the bedside table, there is an envelope covered with figures. She has to calculate how they are going to manage. She may lose her job. Once next morning's papers appear, the news of Simon will be everywhere. There was a piece in the *Standard*'s late edition which gave details of the charge against him. Erica rang to tell her. But it was on an inside page, quite small. Tomorrow will be worse. They wouldn't have sent so many reporters and photographers to the house otherwise. Once the morning papers are out, her school will know. They might not even wait until the trial. They will sniff the wind. There will be low-voiced meetings in the Headmistress's study. Miss Harrold will come in with a tray of tea. She will enjoy being part of the excitement, and demonstrating, yet again, her discretion. Besides, she has never liked Lily. Perhaps parents will telephone the school, or write letters of complaint about a teacher with such connections being allowed into the classrooms. Miss Harrold will open those letters, read them, and place them in the middle of the Headmistress's desk. She will field the telephone calls, and pass on every word. Parents read the newspapers, and quickly work themselves into a lather of indignation if things aren't to their liking. They won't want their children to learn French from a woman whose husband is in prison. They are the ones who pay the bills.

And the children, her children; their children. What will it be like for the children? Will women turn round after them as they walk home from school, and spit on the pavement? *This is England, Lily. You are safe here. Their school cannot make them leave.*

She was a fool when Simon was arrested. When the police took him away, she believed that in a few hours it would all be over. The authorities would come to their senses and understand that they had made a mistake. It was a case of mistaken identity. The evidence really referred to someone quite different. They wouldn't apologise, but they would find a way to let Simon come home. Even after that prison visit, she still believed it.

His court appearance has changed everything. She's seen the big smooth gears of the law begin to move around Simon, meshing him in. He was the defendant now. A policeman stood on either side of him, so that if he tried to run they could prevent him. That was their job. There was whispering and conferring before the proceedings opened.

She doesn't like Simon's solicitor. She doesn't think he is the right man to defend Simon, but the Callingtons are paying, and they have chosen Pargeter.

The famous English legal system was at work in front of her, and she didn't understand it. She knew hardly anything about it. She was a foreigner. She knew that they couldn't possibly have a case against Simon, and yet there they were, standing up, sitting down, saying things in quick, smooth voices, moving Simon further and further from Lily and the children and all his life before. It was all so polite and quick and almost off-hand. They remanded Simon in custody until his trial. She understood that. They were sending Simon back to prison. He looked quickly all round the courtroom then, his gaze blurring over Lily, not seeing her. But he didn't struggle. He bowed his head in acquiescence, and went down.

Simon's solicitor came over to Lily. He was fresh and cheerful, as if everything had gone according to plan. He took her elbow to guide her out of the court, and she understood that Simon's case was only one of a run of cases this morning. In the corridor he said to her, quite nicely, "Sit down for a moment. You are very pale."

"I'm always pale." She didn't want to sit down with him standing over her, like the police officer who had come to their house.

"You understood that no application for bail would be made?"

"Yes."

"In a case like this, bail won't be granted. There's no point in having a refusal on record, in my opinion. Now, I have a spot of news which may cheer you up. Learmonth has agreed to take the case."

She must have looked at him blankly, because he said, rather impatiently, "He's the barrister we wanted to instruct."

"Oh — of course. I'm sorry, I didn't recognise the name for a moment . . ."

"Of course not." He was gallant again. "A very tricky morning for you, Mrs Callington. You're not used to this sort of thing, I suppose."

180

"Hardly," she said, with all the dryness she could muster. Did he imagine they were a family of criminals?

"It's not so bad, once you grasp what's going on."

"What happens next?" she asked him. "When will he be tried?"

"Oh, it's early days yet. There's a tremendous amount of preparation for a case like this. My money would be on late Feb, early March, but it could be later."

"Have you been involved in a case like this before? When someone has been accused of spying?"

He looked surprised. "Cases of alleged espionage are quite rare, Mrs Callington. A solicitor who specialised in them would be twiddling his thumbs for nine-tenths of his time. However, I can assure you — Why don't you have a word with your father-in-law? He'll be able to put your mind at rest."

She'd offended him. He thought she doubted his professional competence, and that she was an ignorant fool. No doubt he was a top man. The Callingtons would have made sure of that. But she still didn't like or trust him. He was much too much at home in the court. That was his world, and Simon was incidental.

"Have you got anyone with you?" he asked.

"No."

"If you'll forgive me, you do look most awfully pale. There's a coffee place about a hundred yards down the road. Go right and right again."

He was dismissing her. He didn't like her, either. She knew it. He was the kind of man who would always know, without even having to think about it, that Lily was a Jew.

There's London, spread out below her window. Somewhere in it is Simon, but she can't see him or touch him. Twenty-five past two. Perhaps he's also awake, but she hopes not. To be awake, in a cell with no window that you can open, to be unable to get up and walk downstairs, make a cup of tea, or drink a very small glass of whisky, as Simon might do when he couldn't sleep . . . To be unable to choose a book from the shelves, or a biscuit . . . Or go out to stand for a moment on the doorstep, breathing in the cold night air —

She feels a sudden, physical anguish of separation from him, as if he were one of the children and had been torn from her arms.

What did her mother use to say, when Lily curled up in a ball on the truckle bed they had given her, at the foot of her mother's iron bed-frame? "You cannot carry on like this, Lili."

There's enough money in Lily's savings account to pay the mortgage for three months. Before she even considered a stair carpet, let alone the sofa and chairs, she made sure that they had money saved. Simon was more relaxed about such things, but Lily had insisted. If the trial is in late February or early March, as Pargeter thinks, then that is three months. Or wait! The mortgage is already paid for November. It was paid on the first of the month, so she has enough saved to pay

December, January and February. She supposes that Simon's salary will stop immediately, but they must pay him for the part of November that he has already worked. She isn't sure, even if he is acquitted, that they will let him have his job back. She must look for a full-time job. Sally's old enough to bring Bridget home from school, and look after her for an hour or two.

Lily's mother won't be able to help. Elsa manages, but her grandchildren's birthday and Christmas presents require careful saving throughout the year. Lily always tucks a five-pound note into her mother's birthday and Christmas cards, along with the sensible presents of a jumper or a scarf. The money is never mentioned. She would like to give Elsa perfume. Elsa loves perfume, and always comments if Lily is wearing it. Lily bought some for her once: L'Air du Temps; but when Elsa opened it her face snapped into annoyance: "So extravagant, Lily! I asked you for a navy cardigan. My old one won't last through the winter."

Lily has said nothing to Elsa about Simon's arrest. She tells herself it's because she doesn't want her mother to be frightened. Elsa doesn't read the English papers. She likes Simon, of course. She has come to love him, in a way. But that means nothing. All her feeling for Simon would be blown away in an instant, if he failed Lily.

"I always thought there was something not quite right," she'd say, putting her lips together, daring Lily to defend her husband. Her mother likes such English phrases. There they sit on her lips, while her eyes are dark with the swamping, visceral, critical love that she feels for Lily and no one else. Even the grandchildren come nowhere near it.

Simon's mother, of course, knows everything. She rang up to say that the solicitor was charging an absolute fortune. It didn't occur to her to ask how Lily would manage without Simon's income.

"I simply don't understand how Simon could have got himself into such a pickle," Julia Callington announced in the tone of one who has no intention of trying to do so. Before the three minutes were up, she'd rung off.

Perhaps it's a form of courage, thinks Lily now. Your son is in prison, accused of espionage, and you talk as if he's an adolescent who has got into trouble at school. You pay for the solicitor, because he is a Callington. When Julia meets an acquaintance, does she say, "I expect you've heard that Simon's got himself into a frightful pickle?" Lily touches the cold glass of the window. She must go to bed. She has lessons in the morning. Everything is marked and prepared. Twenty to three. Four hours' sleep, maybe four and a half. It'll be enough.

She can go to bed now. No one will come at this hour, and those are only shadows under the lamp-posts.

CHAPTER
FOURTEEN

Who Can Tell Me
What Patriot Means?

They tell him everything is going well, but he knows they are lying. Liquid seeps out of the drain in his leg. He catches a smell like wet sawdust on a butcher's floor. The kind of butcher who doesn't sweep out his shop often enough. He remembers: that's how wounds smell, when they go bad. Last night a nurse came with a syringe and jabbed morphine into his thigh. She gave him a roguish look as she straightened up, and he turned his head aside. His leg throbs in the pulley.

He wants to see the charts they fill in every four hours. Sister puts the thermometer into his mouth, looks at it, shakes it down, writes, puts the clipboard with his chart back on to the end of his bed. The blood-pressure cuff wheezes on his arm.

"Is there much fever?" he asks, detached and professional. But Sister isn't fooled.

"You are doing splendidly, Mr Holloway. Mr Anstruther's coming in this afternoon."

"Are you going to take off my leg?"

"Good heavens, what an idea! Whatever put that into your head? Your leg is coming along nicely. You have an infection, but the penicillin is dealing with it."

"It smells pretty high to me."

The walls are nearer than they ought to be. If he keeps very still, with his eyes wide open, everything is fine. As soon as he moves, the walls begin to close in on him. He holds on for as long as he can, but at last, with vast, exquisite relief he lets go. How deep it is. His leg, the pain, all of it gone like the light as you fall down a shaft. He sleeps.

When he opens his eyes, a new nurse, one he doesn't recognise, is writing on the wall. Big, looping words appear across the paint, in a script Giles can't read. How extraordinary that nurses are allowed to write on the walls. He struggles to unseal his lips, which are dry and swollen.

"Is that my chart?" he croaks.

She turns, and looks at him over her shoulder. Her face is vivid with laughter. It's the roguish nurse again. He isn't sure if she is laughing at him, or at what she has written.

"What language is that?"

Instead of replying the nurse stretches up and writes a final line, above everything else she has written. As Giles watches, the language melts into English, and he sees his own name.

"What are you writing about me?" he pleads, but she won't tell him.

He falls asleep again, and while he's asleep she wipes off every single trace of the words from the wall.

186

And now he's getting better. One day passes, and another. He is drinking well, and his temperature is down. The penicillin is doing its work. He is getting better but he's almost too weak to stir. The nurses give him blanket baths. They expose one limb at a time, wash it in warm soapy water, towel it dry, cover it, move to the next. Afterwards they give him hot, sweet tea in a feeding-cup. Sister doesn't want him to have visitors. He needs to be kept quite quiet. At the end of next week, they hope, he will be moved to the King David Convalescent Home. His hands on the sheets look veiny and old. Old Giles. Is that who he is?

"Would you like to listen to the wireless?" Sister asks him.

"I don't think so."

He doesn't want anything. Not even a cigarette or a bottle of whisky. He just wants to lie here, perfectly still, unget-at-able, thinking of nothing and no one.

He lies there for a long time, listening to the tap of the nurses' sensible shoes outside his room, and the roar of London beyond the windows. They wear such ugly shoes. He cannot get back to that deep place where the nurse wrote on the wall. He must think. Inside him, in spite of him, the machine is turning. He cannot help it. The engine of survival has carried him so far, and he can't switch it off now. He must think, plan, act.

"Do you know what," he says to Sister the next morning, "I think I'll glance at *The Times*. And the *Daily Express*."

"You must be feeling better."

"I believe I am."

"Not too much reading at first."

He crunches toast and marmalade. His body is no longer the pure, empty thing that might have carried him away over the lip of the waterfall, wherever that goes. The papers come in, smelling sharply of newsprint.

Lily goes into the newsagent to pay their weekly paper bill. It is Saturday morning. Mrs Forfar flips the pages of her order book, finds their address and tears out the weekly tickets. Simon usually goes down with Bridget to pay the bill, while Bridget chooses her Saturday sweets.

"The rubbish they put in the papers," says Mrs Forfar as she turns to her cash-register and rings up the total. "It's a wonder to me sometimes, why people buy them." She laughs. "I don't know what I'm doing, saying that. I'll put myself out of business."

She likes Simon. She has a soft spot for him. Bridget comes home on Saturdays with extra sweeties in her bag, which certainly doesn't happen when she goes in with Paul and Sally. Lily says nothing. She is stiff, she knows. People think she's cold.

"Your change," says Mrs Forfar, stiff now in her turn.

Lily takes the coins, and the tickets, and leaves the shop. This woman pities her. At school, so far, they have said nothing. She walks along the Broadway with eyes burning into her. Don't be stupid, Lily, of course they are not looking at you. They have better things to do on a Saturday morning. That little boy is having a temper tantrum, so why should his mother care about Lily Callington? It is a beautiful, cold morning. The first of the real winter mornings. The air streams into Lily's lungs. The paper boy delivers *The Times*, but this week Lily has also bought the *Daily Express*, at a newsagent far from their house. She hid the newspaper in her shopping bag, and read it in the bathroom. There was a photograph of their house, with the hedge and their dolphin door-knocker. They had dug up a photograph of Simon, looking straight ahead as if he were staring into a police camera. But it's not a police photograph. It must have been taken a few years ago, because Simon parts his hair differently now. It's neither a good photograph nor a bad one. You wouldn't look at this man, and think: traitor. Spy. She reads the columns carefully. Neighbours in the quiet north London suburb were shocked by news of the arrest. Who was shocked? Who spoke to the newspapers?

Mrs Callington is believed to be a German refugee who came to this country before the war. "I thought she was English," said Mrs Doreen Oldfield, who lives a few doors away from the Callington family. "They seemed like a nice family." It is believed that the children attend a local school.

She doesn't think anything has been said to the children at school. Fortunately, children don't read newspapers.

Monday morning. Paul walks to school with Sally and Bridget. Normally, he hates walking with them, but now, with all the stuff about Dad . . . They walk close together, a phalanx of Callingtons.

Paul and Sally take Bridget round to the Infants' playground, and watch as she runs straight to Miss Goldberg and wraps her arms about Miss Goldberg's coat. Paul and Sally both remember the feel of that coat. It's brown tweed, warm and nubbly. Miss Goldberg is the nicest teacher in the whole school, and Bridget loves her.

Sally hurries indoors. She is Tidiness Monitor and has a lot to do before Assembly. Paul leans against the wall, in a patch of sunlight. He feels tired, although the day has only just started. Mum went to work early, so he and Sally washed up the breakfast things and laid the fires for tonight. Mum is going to get a full-time job.

Danny Coughlan comes and leans alongside him.

"Is it true what they're saying, your ma's a German?" Paul turns his head aside. The sun is so bright it makes his eyes water. That's because it's winter and the sun is low in the sky. "My uncle Joe was in prison for stealing scrap metal," offers Danny. "He got six months."

"My dad's not a thief!"

"Calm down, for feck's sake. I'm not saying anything."

"You'd better not."

"Or what? Are you the hard man now?" He jostles Paul in the ribs, friendly. "I told Ali Wigley to shut her cake-hole when she was going on your ma was a Nazi."

190

Ali with her long plaits and her crying. Paul has always been nice to her. He's never pulled her plaits, shouting, *Ding-dong!* and then run away.

"Who cares what Ali Wigley says. She's as thick as a plank."

"As thick as pigshit," says Danny.

Mrs Wilson has set Sally's class a composition. Usually there is a choice of three subjects, but today there is only one. Mrs Wilson writes it on the board, underneath the date. The subject is "Winston Churchill". Sally is relieved, because she knows quite a lot about Winston Churchill, but Penny Grant puts up her hand.

"Do we have to write about his childhood?"

"You may write about his childhood if you like, Penelope. But I want you all to think about how Winston Churchill served his country, and write about that. He was one of our greatest patriots. Now, who can tell me what 'patriot' means?"

Sally knows. She has her hand up before anyone else, but Mrs Wilson chooses Andrew Lammeter.

"Yes, Andrew?"

"A patriot is someone who tries to help his country."

"That's right. If you didn't know, write it down in your vocabulary book. So, Winston Churchill is a good example of a patriot. Can anyone think of another?"

"The Queen?"

"Good, Penny. Any other examples?"

"Princess Anne?"

Some people laugh, because Princess Anne is only ten, the same age as them.

"There's nothing to laugh about," says Mrs Wilson. "I'm sure Princess Anne is a patriot. Right. Pens ready? Off you go, and I want at least a full side from everyone before the bell rings."

Paul is waiting for Sally and Bridget after school. They walk home close together. Bridget skips and chatters about Miss Goldberg's brooch. Sally thinks about her composition, and the red line through her last paragraph, which said, "Winston Churchill was a great hero of war. I would like there not to be any wars, even though there wouldn't be any heroes like Winston Churchill." As well as the red line through it all, there was triple red underlining of the word "would", and in the margin Mrs Wilson had written, "Don't you know the difference between 'should' and 'would' yet?" She gave Sally five out of ten, and Andrew Lammeter got nine and a half. Mrs Wilson was the quickest marker out of all the teachers. She marked right through lunchtime. Sally always tingled when her exercise book came back after marking, because she was good at compositions.

It wasn't fair.

Bridget sings:

"Oh what a wonderful feeling
When the frost begins to bite . . ."

"It's all right for Bridget the Pidget," mutters Paul. "She doesn't understand anything. I bet she thinks

Dad's gone on holiday. She thought custody was custard."

Sally blurts with laughter.

"Is it going to snow, Sally?" asks Bridget.

"I don't know. I wish it would." Not a measly inch that quickly turned to slush under the wheels of the buses, but proper snow. Snow that falls all through the night and fills up the roads so nothing can move. They might close the school. She and Paul would make a snowman for Bridget in the back garden, and when they were so freezing they couldn't stay out any longer Mum would light a fire in the dining room and Bridget would play under the table. No one can see into their dining room, because it faces the garden.

Every time they go out, people are looking at them. That's why they walk to school together now. Mum thinks they don't know what was in the newspapers about Dad, but Paul bought the *Daily Express* with money out of Sally's Christmas tin. They lay on the floor in Paul's bedroom, and read the article. When they'd finished, they didn't say anything. Paul cut out the article with the photo of Dad and the photo of their house, and hid it under his mattress. Sally quickly read "The Gambols", then wrapped up the rest of the newspaper inside some sheets from *The Times* and stuffed it down to the bottom of the dustbin, with the ash from yesterday's fires on top of it.

People don't keep newspapers. They use them to light their fires, or they throw them away. Probably, by now, hardly anybody has still got a copy of that *Daily Express* with the story about Dad in it.

"Come up in my room when we get back," Paul murmurs to Sally.

Bridget is playing out in the cold, dusky garden. Her voice floats up to the bedroom window:

> "Forty years on an iceberg
> Out in the ocean wide,
> Nothing to wear but pyjamas
> Nothing to do but slide . . ."

Paul and Sally exchange glances. They feel infinitely older than Bridget, old and weary and heavy with knowledge. Dirty with it.

"I wish we hadn't bought the paper," says Sally.

"Don't be stupid. We had to. Listen, Sal. What're we going to do if they arrest Mum as well?"

"They can't! She hasn't done anything."

"Dad hasn't done anything either, you idiot."

"No, I know he hasn't, I didn't mean that, it was only . . ." It was only the difference between Mum and Dad. Dad has his own world. Dad disappears. No matter how tightly she holds him, gripping around his neck, breathing in his smell of soap and cologne, he's already on his way elsewhere.

"Alison Wigley said Mum was a Nazi. Danny told me."

Colour floods up into Sally's face. "Doesn't she know anything? Mum's Jewish, how could she be a Nazi?"

"Danny told her to shut her cake-hole. But he asked me: 'Is it true your ma's a German?'"

"Mum hasn't even been in Germany since she was younger than you. She only speaks English."

"And French and Italian."

"They don't count."

Mum is less German than anybody. They are more English than anybody. When they were younger — in Miss Goldberg's class — they would all surge across the playground in a chain, chanting:

"We won the war
In nineteen forty-four,
We won the war
In nineteen forty-four . . ."

They're both much too old for that now.

"You know the march Mum went on? I think she could get in trouble for that. Dad didn't want her to go."

"Thousands and thousands of people went on it. Erica took Clare. Do you think they're going to arrest a baby?" asks Sally with loud, theatrical scorn.

"Shut up. Mum'll hear you. You can't keep on saying it's not going to happen. If they can arrest Dad then they can arrest Mum. Who'd look after Bridgie?"

"Oma?"

They both think of the tiny, crowded flat in Brighton, and the smell of Oma's dog.

"Granny Callington's got loads of money."

"She never gives us any."

The Children Who Lived in a Barn is one of Sally's favourite books. Susan, who does all the washing and cooking, holds the purse with the money and takes care of the little ones, is not much older than her. And their parents do come back in the end.

"We could look after her."

"They wouldn't let us. They might put her in a children's home. They might put us all in children's homes."

"They couldn't if we ran away," says Sally, thinking of a field, a stream, a barn with a haybox and Bridget tucked up safely by capable, big-sister hands.

"Where would we run to, in the middle of winter? Bridgie would freeze to death."

Bridget sings in the garden:

> "You have to hug a polar bear
> To keep you warm at night . . ."

"She hasn't got a clue," says Paul. "I'm going to ask Mum if I can visit Dad."

"They won't let you." Why hadn't she thought of it first?

"I need to know what's happening. I don't think Mum realises she might be arrested. You remember how on Sunday she said Dad had only gone in to the police station to answer a few questions. She didn't know they were going to keep him in prison."

"We could warn her," says Sally.

"I thought of that. But I want to see Dad first."

196

"He's in prison," says Sally. It is the first time she has ever said those words aloud. Even in her mind, she has skirted around them. They sound as if they belong in a book, a quite different book from *The Children Who Lived in a Barn*. Prison means that even if something awful happened, if Paul didn't pass the Eleven-plus or Bridget got run over, Dad wouldn't be here. As the thoughts hit her, she understands that she no longer believes Dad will be back soon, next week or the week after or at the very worst the week after that. That's the way someone Bridget's age would think. "Dad can't do anything," she says.

They look at each other in the glare of the overhead light. It is quite dark outside now. Bridget must have come in, because she isn't singing any more. From where Sally is sitting on the rug, she can see the dust under Paul's bed, and his pyjamas. He always kicks his dirty clothes under the bed. If they lived in a barn, he would have to tidy up so as to be a good example to Bridget —

"I'm still going to go and see him."

Sally shrugs, a minute, expressive shrug that makes her look, for an instant, exactly like Mum. She thinks she's so grown-up, thinks Paul, but she's not even nine yet. More than a whole year younger than me. I bet she wishes she'd thought of going to see Dad first, and that's why she's making such a fuss.

"Do you think," asks Sally, colouring again, "it could be that Mum doesn't know things because of not being born here?"

That thought has come to Paul too, but he hasn't dared shape it into words. It makes him angry with Mum, and protective too, as if she's the child, not him. But he doesn't want Sal looking so scared.

"No," he says. "Mum's just the same as if she was English. Only a supersonic clodpoll like Alison Wigley would think anything else."

CHAPTER
FIFTEEN

Plan B

"That contraption looks rather medieval," says Julian Clowde.

"It feels it."

"I had a word with the sawbones. Anstruther. You'll be here for another week, I gather."

"Julian —"

"One moment." Like a big cat, Julian pads around the room, examining light fittings, bells, the telephone on its trolley, and then returns to his seat. He crosses his legs and waits. He hasn't lost any of his hair. Thick, white, wavy hair: you'd half want to stroke it, if you didn't know better. Cats, if they were any larger, would be unspeakable . . . What was that story of Archie's, about his cat? Bosie, he called it. Typical Archie; he was constitutionally incapable of calling a cat Fluff. Yes, that was it: Archie had influenza, quite badly. He felt like death. He couldn't even get out of bed to feed the wretched animal. On the second day, Bosie leaped up on to the bed and stood over Archie, paws on the pillow. Archie was drifting. He struggled to lift a hand to stroke the cat. Loyal little blighter, standing guard over his sick master . . . And then Bosie's claws scored him right across the face. Only just missed his right eye. It didn't care for the empty food bowl.

It must be years since he's thought of that. A good friend, Archie. If he were still alive, he'd have visited me like a shot.

"How was Venice?" he asks. Julian Clowde raises his eyebrows. Supercilious bastard.

"I suppose you must have some small idea of the difficulties you've caused me?"

Someone should kick him into the middle of next week — preferably on his way back from the opera house after a particularly delightful evening — and leave him in a gutter in his own piss and vomit, spitting teeth.

"Our friends are very, very fed up indeed, as you can imagine." Julian leans forward. "What the hell did you think you were doing, getting Callington involved? Special Branch has gone through that house with a toothcomb and there's no trace of it. The one thing we can be sure of is that he's got it. He's tucked it away somewhere. I don't need to remind you that it's got my initials on it. There's no conceivable reason for you to have had sight of it. There's no conceivable route by which Callington could have got hold of it on his own. Callington's going to plead not guilty, and why shouldn't he? He'll say the camera was planted. He'll bring out that file, and he'll tell the jury exactly where he found it. Why not? This is what Frith's been waiting for. He's going to get what he wants, through sheer criminal carelessness on your part. Why the hell didn't you ring me?"

"You were in Venice."

"I was in Venice," echoes Julian, coldly jeering, "not on the other side of the moon. How long do you think it takes to fly from Venice to London? Fortunately, others had a better grasp of the situation than you. I was back here the next day. But thanks to you, it was too late. I've done what I can to clear up the mess."

The contempt in him, like cold spit. The jeering schoolboy, bigger than you, older than you, knowing the ropes. Your own fault though, Giles. You forgot the rules.

No, I didn't ring you, Julian. You were in Venice, and besides — Christ! Do you think I don't know you? You've been looking for an excuse for months. You want me out of the way.

If Simon hadn't pissed about, the file would have been safely back with Brenda. The flat was clean. I made sure of that. You'd have had to accept that I'd handled the situation as well as possible.

But now . . .

You got rid of Petrenko. I was at your house when you took the call that told you he was safely out of the way. Or, in other words, the goods had been despatched. You'd been sweating blood about Petrenko, ever since the memo came through to you — to you! — that he was about to defect from the embassy in Vienna, and the dowry he'd be bringing across was information about Soviet penetration of British Naval Intelligence. You swung into action then. That telephone call told you that you'd been successful.

Petrenko had been despatched all right. You knew what that meant. Chloroformed, mouth taped, eyes taped, trussed up like a Christmas turkey and bundled into the boot of a car. On a plane back to a cell in Moscow and Christ knows what torments of the damned, before he died of "natural causes". You took that call, and after you put down the receiver you smiled at me and said, "Our friend Mr P. is going on holiday," and then you looked at your watch and realised you'd better get a move on, if you weren't to be late for Toby's private view. Petrenko could have blown us wide open, but you got wind of it, just as you always do. It's the advantage of your position. Why didn't I ring you and let you sort out the file? Because you'd have trussed me up like a turkey, too, to save your own neck. Metaphorically speaking of course, dear boy.

"For Christ's sake, Julian, I had concussion."

"You were drunk. I've put up with a lot for old times' sake, but you are not the asset to us that you once were. Time for a spot of leave, I think. But first, what are we going to do about Callington . . . He was one of your boys once, I believe?"

You know it. Every detail. You'll have photographs. Letters, too, no doubt. Everything that might be useful one of these days, thinks Giles. He is suddenly, extremely tired. He wishes a nurse would come in, take his pulse and say, "I'm afraid my patient must rest."

"Callington," muses Julian Clowde. "I can't say he's ever made much impression on me. You were very keen to bring him in, as I recall. He likes a quiet life, or so it says in the *Daily Express*. Apparently he goes train-spotting with his son." The suavity of his tone doesn't alter. "He's the chap next door, in fact. Could be you, could be me. The jury won't like that. They like their spies to look like spies. More comfortable for everyone that way. I can quite see their point. I wonder, does his wife — Does Lily know about her husband's little adventures? That could upset the apple-cart in Muswell Hill. Callington was being blackmailed, of course."

"What do you mean?"

"Use your wits, Giles. It's the key to the whole wretched business. The jury will see it straight away, if they're helped to do so. The Soviets had compromising photographs of Callington in bed with another man. They were threatening to expose him. You know where that would have led, and so did Callington: security clearance revoked, dismissal, end of marriage. No more train-spotting. Very likely a prosecution. If he were exceptionally lucky he might have traded a prison sentence for stilboestrol injections. Know what stilboestrol is, Giles?"

He doesn't.

"It makes your breasts grow, which is not so handy if you're a chap. Unfortunately it has the opposite effect on your balls: they shrink. All desires spent. It's frequently described as chemical castration. Not wanting any of that to happen to you is the kind of motive juries understand. So. The Soviets were threatening to expose Callington unless he did them a few favours. That all fits together nicely, doesn't it? The jury's unlikely to spot quite how hard it would be for

Callington to gain access to that file on his own. Once they know he's a little queer that the Soviets had the screws on, they'll believe anything of him. The only drawback is that it does rather drag you into the picture. Or photograph, to be exact." He pauses, hands steepled. "However, it needn't come to that."

"What do you mean?" Fool, Giles. That's the second time you've said that. Why can't you keep your mouth shut? He's playing you.

Julian raises an eyebrow. "It's not hard to follow, surely? Callington is presented with a choice. He can stick to a not-guilty plea — in which case, out come the letters, out come the photographs and it's perfectly obvious to any decent juror that he's guilty as hell. He goes down. Wife gone, children gone, friends gone, career gone, quite possibly *sans* balls in the near future. Not a very appealing prospect. That's Plan A. On the other hand, he can plead guilty. A first offence. He acted alone. The poor impressionable booby was taken along to a CND rally by his wife — cue more photographs, there's a nice one of them together on the steps of the National Gallery. He met this frightfully sympathetic chap. One thing led to another. Callington let slip where he worked and soon he was in deep, way over his head . . . No, that won't do. It's starting to sound like Plan A again. Scrub the sympathetic chap. Stick to Callington acting alone, led astray by CND drama-queenery. The end of the world is nigh and only Callington can save it by nipping into the office with a Minox and posting off the results to the Soviet

204

Embassy. A moment of madness leads to a lifetime of regret. That's Plan B."

Giles can't help himself. "I rather liked the look of the sympathetic chap."

It's as if he hadn't spoken. Possibly there's a twitch of Julian Clowde's lips. "Lifetime of regret," he repeats. "That might wash. Callington could carry it off. He's got one of those *Boy's Own Paper* faces. The jury doesn't hear a word about the briefcase. Your name isn't whispered. He'll get seven years, and Lily will be waiting for him outside the gates of Wormwood Scrubs. If I were him, I'd much prefer Plan B. What's your opinion, *old boy?*"

Giles has worked with Julian Clowde for donkey's years. With him and for him and under him. He thought he knew Julian backwards. But now he sees that after all those years of jokes and dinners and parties shared — let alone everything else — he, Giles Holloway, is no more to Julian than Petrenko once was. Whether he's stuffed in the boot of a car or shuffled off into a convalescent home makes almost no matter.

"I don't know," he says.

"Don't you?"

Julian leans back, his eyes half-closed. For a few moments he contemplates the ceiling, then suddenly, he stands up. For once in his life he's clumsy. His right foot catches the chair leg. He pitches forward, tries to save himself, knocks against the bed, puts out his hand and blunders into Giles's leg as it dangles from the pulley —

Even heavy Giles can't help arching up in the bed as if he's welded to a light-switch. Julian is on his feet now, looking down. "I'll have a chat with Callington. We need that file back. Don't make any more telephone calls. I'd have a good rest, if I were you. You shouldn't have any more visitors until you're quite recovered. Where are they sending you? The King David, isn't it?"

Giles cannot speak. He must keep perfectly still or he will throw up. The churn of pain rises to his lips and then slowly, slowly, recedes. He is cold.

"I've tired you out," says Julian Clowde as he leaves the room.

It's several days before Paul can put into action his plan of asking Mum to let him visit Dad. Night after night, Mum doesn't come home until after Bridget's bedtime. She has appointments in town until six or seven. They have to make the supper and look after Bridget. Soberly, side by side, he and Sally wash up and dry the dishes while Bridget plays in the dining room. One day, they all go to Erica's after school and have sausages and mash, and jelly with pineapple chunks for pudding. Bridget sits on Erica's knee for a story. She behaves like a baby. Mum comes to fetch them, wearing her best black suit. Her face is pale and her lipstick looks too red. She has a drink with Erica and then they all go home, with Bridget clinging and dragging on Mum's hand. Mum says she's tired and is going to go to bed at the same time as them. This has never happened before except once when she had flu.

The line of light under Mum's bedroom door disappears long before Paul goes to sleep. He hates the empty cave of downstairs. The radio should be on, with Mum and Dad's voices, the sound of the kettle boiling, the chink of glasses. Sal is awake too. She creeps into his room and says breathily in his ear: "You haven't asked her about you visiting Dad yet, have you?"

"I'm going to, tomorrow. She said she'll be home at five."

Sal creeps out, and Paul lies awake for a long time, thinking of what he will say.

The next evening, everything goes according to plan. As soon as Mum comes down from putting Bridget to bed, Sal — already in her dressing gown and slippers — announces that she's going to work on her Australia project in her bedroom.

"Why don't you spread out your project on the dining table? It's cold up in your bedroom."

"I don't want to have to tidy it away every night. It's our homework for all this week and it's got to be in on Friday."

"All right then. You can take the electric fire from our bedroom, as long as you're careful."

Sal skips away upstairs. She's a good liar, thinks Paul, better than he'd thought. But even now that the coast is clear, he finds he doesn't know how to start asking Mum about visiting Dad.

"Can I have a hot Ribena, Mum?"

"How much is left?"

Ribena is expensive, and it's bought mainly for Bridget. He and Sal both think this is unfair.

"I think there's quite a lot."

"Don't make it too strong, then. I'm going to do some marking."

Paul lights the gas and sets the kettle to boil. There's less than an inch of Ribena in the bottle. He pours carefully, but suddenly it rushes out into his tumbler. There's hardly any left. He tries pouring it back, but it oozes stickily down the outside of the bottle, and he gives up. Bridget gets Delrosa syrup as well as Ribena. On the other hand she also has to have a daily spoonful of that disgusting Virol. Sally and he used to pretend to swallow it but keep it in their mouths and spit it out under the bushes.

He puts a spoon into the tumbler, so the glass won't crack, and pours in the hot water. He'll wait until it cools down, then he'll drink it, then he'll go in and talk to Mum . . .

You've got to do it now, he thinks. Bridget might wake up, or the phone might ring.

Paul picks up the tumbler by its rim, where it isn't so hot, and goes into the sitting room. Mum isn't marking, although there's a pile of exercise books by her feet. She's lying back in the corner of the sofa, resting her head against the cushion. Her eyes are shut. In her right hand, the hand nearest to him, there's a cigarette with at least an inch of ash on its end. And the fire's not lit. He laid it all ready: that's one of his jobs. Mum's face is different when her eyes are shut. He doesn't like it as much.

"Mum? Are you asleep?"

She opens her eyes and smiles at him. "Of course not. I was resting my eyes for a moment, that's all. There's so much marking." She pats the seat beside her. "Come and sit down."

"Your ash is dropping all over the carpet."

"Ash is good for carpets," she says, standing up for a moment and rubbing the ash into the carpet with the toe of her shoe.

"I'll light the fire for you."

"I don't think we need it. It's quite cosy in here."

It isn't. The room is cold and Mum has only turned on the overhead light, not the standard lamp that always throws a soft, golden pool over the red leather furniture.

"It's freezing in here, Mum."

"Go and put on your Aran sweater. Coal is expensive."

"You know when Dad got all those logs from Highgate Woods, after they chopped up the fallen tree? I bet I could go up there and find wood."

"Why not," she says, but not as if she really means it or believes that it will happen.

"I could get wood from our copse as well."

She sits up sharply. "Leave the copse alone, Paul! It's nice to have all the trees and bushes."

"I only meant fallen branches —"

"It's all soaking wet. Leave it alone, please. I don't want you children tearing up the woodland. If you're really cold, go and sit by the kitchen stove. I've got to get on with this marking."

Coal has never been too expensive before. It's been a nuisance when the bills come in. That's what Mum always says as she bends to pick up the letters from the mat in the hall. "What a nuisance. The coal-man dropped in his bill yesterday, and now here are the gas and electricity as well." Mum frowns as she opens the envelopes, scans them silently, and then passes them to Dad. He looks at them and says, "That's not too bad, Lil," in a surprised and cheerful voice. She says, "I suppose not." Later on Mum gets out her chequebook and writes cheques at the dining-room table. There's always a fire in the dining room until Bridget goes to bed, and then a fire in the sitting room.

"Mum," he says, "do you think you'll be able to get a full-time job?"

She looks at him steadily. "The question is whether I will be able to keep the work that I have, I'm afraid, Paul."

"Why? You're a good teacher. They had to give you more hours."

"It's not whether I am a good teacher or a bad teacher." All at once, it's there, deep inside her voice. A tone that he never usually hears. Or maybe it's been there before, but he hasn't recognised it. Now he does. It's like the fingerprint of a different language, coming through from far away. There's the ghost of a "z" sound inside the "th" of "whether". He knows the sound, because Oma talks German sometimes with him and Sal and Bridget, when Mum isn't there. Nobody else would notice, he tells himself quickly. It's only because he knows Mum's voice so well.

"Well, what is it then?" he asks roughly, almost angrily. He wants so much to protect her. He doesn't want other people to notice those German sounds.

"I told you that there were stories about your father in the newspapers."

Why does she say that? Why does she say "your father"? She always just says "Dad".

"Yes." Lucky that he doesn't blush like Sal. Mum would guess something was up, and go on until she found out about them buying the *Daily Express*. He drops his eyes.

"A lot of people read those newspapers. The parents, for example. I'm not a permanent member of staff. Even if I were, the school might not keep me."

"Are they going to give you the sack, Mum?"

"I don't know. For the moment, I am carrying on, but it's not . . . There is an atmosphere. I don't want to worry you, Paul, but you're old enough to know how things are. We've got to be very careful with money."

"I could get a paper round, Mum. Forfars are always advertising for paper boys."

"We'll see."

"Will Dad get the sack too?"

Mum hesitates, then: "I don't know." At once, he's sure that she does, and isn't telling him. "So you see why we have to be careful."

"Granny and Grandad C. have got loads of money. They ought to give us some."

"I don't want to ask them for money. If I lose my job, I'll find another. Perhaps not a teaching job."

"But what else could you do, Mum?"

211

"Anything. There are all sorts of jobs. I could be a waitress, and get good tips." She smiles, and he's not sure if she's joking or not. "Don't worry. We're not going to starve. This isn't the nineteenth century. But we may have to leave this house for a while."

"We can't! It's our home!"

"I know. But there is a big mortgage — You know what that is? Money that we owe to the bank for buying this house. The bank lent us the money, and we have to pay so much back every month. It's quite a lot. Erica's friend Ruth knows some people in America. He is a surgeon and he's coming to Barts on an exchange. Erica thinks this house would be perfect for them, and they'd be able to pay a good rent. It would cover the mortgage. Don't look like that. I know it's difficult, but it's better than losing our home."

"Mum." The words in his head are a jumble. He has got to sound grown-up. "But after the trial, Mum, Dad'll be home. He hasn't done anything wrong."

"It isn't looking very good, Paul. Believe me, you can be innocent, and terrible things can happen to you."

He knows what she means: leaving Germany. Coming here with Oma. Mum never talks about it properly. Probably she doesn't remember. She doesn't even speak German, although Oma does, not just with them but with her friends, too. Oma is quite different in German and she teaches them the German words for everything. Not by telling them, like at school: just by saying things and then he and Sal say them back until they know them. It's easy-peasy. Oma doesn't speak German when Mum's there.

212

If Mum and Oma hadn't left Germany, they would be dead and he, Sally and Bridget would never have been born. But in England, things like that don't happen. That's why they have proper trials and the police can't lock you up just because they feel like it. Or take your home away.

"I have to make plans for the future," says Mum.

"But where would we go?"

"Somewhere cheap, as long as it's close to a good grammar school," says Mum promptly, and he can tell she's been thinking it all out for ages. "You and Sally have got to go on with your education. Somewhere in the country, probably, or by the sea."

He cannot believe any of this, but Mum is talking as if it's perfectly normal. If Mum is talking about grammar school, then she means years, not months. He's not even leaving primary school until next July, when he's eleven — and Sally not for nearly two years. Two whole years, with someone else living in their house.

"Has the surgeon — the American one — Have they got any children?"

"Yes. Three children, like us. All boys, apparently. They need to rent a family house, like ours."

Another boy will sleep in his bedroom. Other children will do their homework in the dining room. They'll go to school here: Paul's school.

"I think it's all rubbish," he says. "You're making it up. Dad's going to come home, and if you're stupid enough to let other people live in our house, he won't have anywhere to come home to."

Mum takes another cigarette out of her packet, lights it and draws in the smoke. "I hope you're right," she says. "Never mind. I ought not to have discussed it with you."

A wash of shame comes over him. "I'm sorry, Mum," he says. "I do want you to talk to me."

She crosses her legs, and continues to smoke, saying nothing, but it's not awkward because she smiles at him as if she knows why he was angry, and doesn't mind. Paul drinks his Ribena, which has gone cold without him noticing. It's freezing in here.

"It's hard for all of us to understand what's happening," she says.

He likes the way she says "all of us". It makes him feel safer, somehow, as if he's not alone in a confusion of darkness. He hates it when grown-ups pretend that awful things are straightforward and even somehow good for you. Mum sucks in a breath. Her voice is tight, the same way that his own stomach is tight. "You know Dad," she says.

"Of course I know Dad!" He's angry, indignant.

"Dad hasn't done anything wrong. You know that. But . . ."

The "but" sticks into him like the barbed wire at the back of the copse. "Mum —"

"I don't want you to talk to anyone about this."

"I won't. I promise."

Another of those sucking breaths. He is so close to Mum that he can see the swallow in her throat. Her arm comes around him, squeezing him. "The date for the trial hasn't been set. We don't know, Paul . . ." She's silent. He wants her to say it. He wants to put his hands over her mouth so she can never say it. "Paul, Dad might — It's possible that Dad will go to prison for a long time."

Neither of them hears the stifled noise that Sally makes from behind the door, which she has pushed open, just a little bit, so that she can hear better.

She'd gone up to her bedroom, as she and Paul had planned, but even though Mum had said she could, Sally didn't fetch the electric fire. She hated the sparks that came out of it. She got the scissors and glue, and her big sugar-paper project folder. The thing she wanted to do most was the cover. Her plan was to cut out a cardboard comb, mix powder paint and paste until it was stiff, spread it over the outside of the folder and make swirls with the comb, which she thought would look like the Aboriginal drawings in the *National Geographic* magazine. This cover plan had been warm inside her for days. When she thought about it, the frightened feeling in her stomach went away for a bit.

She lay on the lino, sorting out her pictures. But down here, close to the floor, she could hear voices, although she couldn't hear what they were saying. She rested her head so that her ear touched the cold lino, but she still couldn't make out any words. Her stomach hurt. Their voices went on and on. Paul was supposed to be finding out whether he could visit Dad or not — that shouldn't take all this time. It sounded as if he and Mum had secrets together.

She goes down the stairs so lightly that she can't even hear herself. Bridget is fast asleep. Bridget's only a baby and she doesn't understand anything. It was stupid, thinking that they could be like the children who lived in the barn, if Mum got arrested. There aren't any barns in Muswell Hill. Mum can't be arrested. But what is she telling Paul? The talk goes on and on. If it was good news, if Mum had said, "Yes, of course, Paul, you can go and see Dad, I should have thought of it myself," then Paul would have rushed back up to Sally's bedroom, to boast about it. It doesn't sound like good news.

She sees they haven't closed the sitting-room door, and slides herself noiselessly into position.

"I don't want you to talk to anyone about this."

"I won't. I promise," she hears Paul say.

How dare he promise? He's only down there talking to Mum because she, Sally, has agreed the plan with him. Half of it was her idea. Mum is murmuring again. Sally catches some of the words, but not all. She will have to risk it. She moves forward, and pushes the sitting-room door a little wider. Now she can see them. They're on the sofa, side by side. Paul is right up next to Mum. Sally sees Mum's arm come out along the sofa back, and then go around Paul's shoulders. They are so close that they are like one person. Mum's head comes up as if something has jerked inside her, and she says, not in a murmur now but clearly: "It's possible that Dad will go to prison for a long time."

Sally hears the sound that comes out of her own mouth. She freezes, waiting for them to turn, but they don't seem to have heard her. She shrinks back, as if them not seeing her is the most important thing in the

216

world. Here are the stairs, with Mum's stair carpet hiding the sound of Sally's feet. She holds tight to the banister rail. It's like going up the stairs in the ferry when they went to the Isle of Wight. The sea was very rough even though Dad said it was only a short crossing. The ferry stairs swung up and down at them and Bridget nearly fell, because she wouldn't hold on.

She has got to get back into her room. The doorknob spins round without opening, the way it sometimes does, and for a minute Sally can't remember how to push it in and then try again. But she gets it right and the door opens. Mum says don't shut your door completely, that doorknob's going to come off and you might get stuck. Dad was going to mend it.

Sally shuts her bedroom door. The overhead light glares on the lino and hurts her eyes. She switches it off, feels her way over to the bed and burrows down and down, under the counterpane, under the eiderdown, in between the cold sheets. She curls up into a tight ball with her eyes shut and her hands over her ears. When Paul comes in, she hopes he'll think she's asleep.

CHAPTER
SIXTEEN

Dr Maggot

Deep in its nest of soil and leaf debris, the briefcase begins to breed. Damp leaks into the pigskin. The lock is no longer true. This was Giles's school briefcase, kept for sentiment rather than security. Woodlice truffle along the stitching. Maggots cluster where the pigskin is rubbed away, as if this were a wound they might debride. Already, the file within the briefcase is swollen with the seepage of autumn rain.

Rain slides down the windows of Julian Clowde's office. His desk is clear. Brenda has just left. In her long, belted mac and headscarf she looks like a housewife going shopping. But her mind is not the mind of a housewife. She is absolutely loyal, resourceful, discreet, intelligent, tireless. She was married once, but thought better of it. Brenda is also one of the few people who never laughs at Giles Holloway's jokes.

He runs a hand over the leather top of his desk. The day's work has crossed it and left no trace. That is as it should be.

The smell in Giles's hospital room was really quite unpleasant. Giles is a liability, but he has been contained. In the longer term, he must be pensioned off. Simon Callington has been isolated effectively and his position will be made clear to him in no uncertain terms. He will co-operate.

The missing file niggles at Julian Clowde. It's messy. He likes his desk clear. The wretched thing may turn up at any time.

It's highly unlikely that Callington has destroyed it. Either he's hidden it, or he's given it to someone.

Julian Clowde passes his hand over the waves of his hair, slowly, as if he were stroking the pelt of a beloved cat. His eyes are half-closed. There is something missing: a last hole that must be stopped up. The wife. Of course, it makes perfect sense. If Callington has given that file to anyone, it will have been to her.

He can picture Lily Callington quite clearly. A slight, dark woman, with something about her that grated on him. Exactly the kind of woman to make trouble. Jewish, of course.

Julian Clowde sits for a long time, thinking, calculating, stroking.

The wound in Giles's leg is not healing as it should. His temperature is up again, his pulse rapid. He mutters restlessly. Mr Anstruther has been telephoned, and will be in to see the patient at nine o'clock.

Mr Anstruther was not always a pinstriped god, walking the corridors of the Latimer. Once he was a captain in the RAMC. He landed on Sword Beach, and while the troops hid and hunted in the terrible *bocage*, Captain Anstruther worked sixteen hours a day, up to his elbows in blood, gristle and bone splinters. When he could, he stripped naked to sluice himself with a pail of water. The healing of wounds was his obsession. Usually several hours elapsed before a wounded man could be got to the operating table. It might be longer. A soldier might have lain under a hedge for a day and a night, with soil blown into a compound fracture of the leg. There was the new "wonder-drug", penicillin, saving lives that would have been lost even two years earlier, but even penicillin could not do everything. Sometimes, necrotic tissue continued its advance, eating through flesh and bone. Maggot debridement might be deemed old-fashioned, but it could salvage a limb when everything else failed.

Captain Anstruther was precise about the timing of his maggot dressings. They must not be left on the wound an hour too long, because maggots that had devoured the necrotic tissue might move on to healthy flesh. He was always present when the cage dressing was removed. He could tell instantly, by the smell of the wound, whether or not he would see pink, clean tissue. The men called him Dr Maggot behind his back, and Anstruther could not have cared less. If it was their own stinking, necrotic wound that had been cleansed, they sang a different tune. While penicillin steamrollered over the field of infection control, Anstruther remained quietly passionate about maggots.

Giles Holloway has a strong family history of vascular disease. Claudication is present in his lower legs. His wound has abscessed and the infection is not responding to antibiotics. Pain and fever are present.

Anstruther's glance sweeps over the patient's chart. He talks, low-voiced, to Sister, with whom he works easily and well. For a successful consultant, Anstruther has very little side. He is so sure of himself that he does not need any. They both agree, in a few murmured half-phrases, that Mr Holloway isn't "doing" as they would wish. They both know that he stank of whisky when admitted, but they are too experienced to need to smell the alcohol on a man. They can perceive its effect throughout the organs of his body.

Draining the abscesses has not been successful. Acute osteomyelitis is now present, and this is failing to respond to methicillin.

"He seemed to be doing rather surprisingly well over the first four or five days. Disappointing," says Anstruther. Sister nods her agreement. "Has he had visitors?"

"One or two. No family."

"I see. Well, we must press on. We'll continue with the methicillin, and I intend to prescribe maggot debridement in addition."

Sister nods. She is used to Mr Anstruther's ways, and the almost boyish light that comes into his eyes at a chance to deploy his beloved maggots. Nurse Foster, who will have to affix the dressings, may be less enthusiastic. Mr Anstruther can't see any reason for disgust. Maggots are clean, beneficial little creatures. *Have you a cat at home, Nurse Foster? A dog, hmm?*

The creature will be swarming with parasites and bacteria, you may be sure of it.

Giles lies as still as still. His head is huge. It may float free of him if he's not careful, to bounce against the ceiling like a balloon. The nurse with the handwriting on the wall hasn't come back. That chap — the tall striped-column chap — is here again. Giles knows he knows him, but can't remember who he is.

"Could we light a fire?" asks Giles, as politely as he knows how. It doesn't do to get on the wrong side of these people.

"Don't you know that there's a war on?" counters the other. But Giles knows that isn't true. He's not so far gone. The war is over. Did they think they could trick him, dressing up as doctors? He knows what they are up to.

"I'm not going anywhere with you," he says clearly.

"No one's going anywhere," says the voice. It's Anstruther. Giles remembers him now. The sawbones, Julian Clowde said. He was going to send Giles to the King David Convalescent Home for Officers.

"I'm frightfully sorry," says Giles, "I don't think I can walk."

"No one wants you to walk. Nurse is going to put on a fresh dressing. You'll soon feel more comfortable."

It seems a long time since Julian Clowde was here, and since then Giles hasn't been very well. His hands, too, are huge. He wishes they would light that fire. It's so cold in here.

222

His leg is out of the pulley and lying on the bed. It is enormous. He squints at it. Like a barrage balloon.

"What's that smell?"

"It's nothing, Mr Holloway. I'm just changing your dressing."

Two days pass, as the maggots inside their cage dressing go to work. They liquefy and absorb Giles's dead and dying flesh, cleansing the wound with a precision far beyond the finest surgical instrument. At the right moment, the sated maggots are removed. Nurse Foster, pale and sweating, disposes of them and applies a fresh dressing under the direction of Mr Anstruther. It's all going well. Clean tissue has started to appear. The patient is quiet now. The temperature is down, the pulse steadier. It is all very satisfactory.

Giles wakes to a pale splash of light on the wall. He turns his eyes towards the window, where winter sunshine outlines a black mass of twigs. For the first time in days, he knows exactly where he is. His head is his head, resting on his pillow. His hands — he flexes them — are the right size. He is as weak as a baby but even weakness is a pleasure when his body has nothing to do but float here under the gaze of those twigs. They are perfectly motionless. Lozenges of sky appear within their cradle. Giles traces the pattern. Even though the twigs aren't moving, the pattern seems to change and shift, becoming more perfect until his eyes blur with looking at it. But perhaps he isn't even looking at the twigs. No, they are looking into him, printing themselves on him, through his skin and through his flesh, into the centre of him. Everything else has been washed away. Even the pain is still.

Not to have pain. To be still, not to thresh or cry out. He tests himself and finds that he wants nothing. He is neither hungry nor thirsty. There's nowhere he wants to go, and nothing and no one that he wants to see. The splash of light. The size of it about the same as the size of his hand. The light trembles, but the twigs don't move. He feels his body, lying, resting, pressing down on the white sheet. His wreck of a body that is cast up here and good for nothing. Nobody wants it any more, not even him. He doesn't want the old body back. This is enough: his eyes, watching; his ears, hearing the tap of feet.

The door opens and Sister steps quickly, lightly to his bedside. She takes up his right hand. She holds the little watch that is pinned to her breast, and times his pulse. With great effort, Giles opens his lips.

"Am I dying?" he asks.

She smiles, and shakes her head. "No," she says. "You're much better today."

He doesn't know how to name the pang inside him. Is he afraid, because he has to live? All this will go away. His life will start to push at him again, darkly.

"I'm sorry," he says, embarrassed, because Sister must have noticed the tears that have leaked out of him. She shakes her head again.

"There's nothing to be sorry about, as far as I can see," she says. "You're doing nicely now. Mr Anstruther will be pleased."

She goes away again. For as long as the splash of sunlight stays on the wall, he lies and watches it.

CHAPTER
SEVENTEEN

HM's Spy

"Mrs Callington, would you pop in for a word with the Headmistress at the end of the morning?"

Lily lifts her head slowly. Harrold looks as if she has eaten something choice, and is sucking at the remnants between her teeth.

"Of course," says Lily, and turns back to Barbara Watson. They are drinking their coffee together. Every day since the story in the newspapers about Simon, Barbara has kept a place beside her for Lily in the staff room at break-time. She hasn't mentioned Simon, but she fetches extra biscuits and presses them on Lily, saying, "You mustn't get any thinner." She's a kind woman. Lily is tired of the little looks that flicker over her, from other staff and from the older girls. Barbara is a shield.

"I'll get you another cup of coffee."

"I'll have to go," says Lily. "It's five to already."

"You can take a few minutes more. Don't look now: that wretched Harrold is still hovering by the door. She's got her eye on us."

"On me."

"What an irritating woman she is. I can't stand the way she comes in here at break-time, just when one wants to relax. Spying on us." Too late to catch back the word, Barbara realises what she's said. She rushes on. "The Harrold has no idea what it's like to spend the day in front of a class. There she sits in that damned office, like a spider in its lair."

Lily's weary face lightens, just a little. "Do spiders have lairs?"

"I am sure that Harrold has one. She casts off all semblance of humanity as soon as the outer door is closed. Lily, dear . . ." Barbara's eyes are bright. She looks almost as if she might cry. "I don't want to be a bother, but I really feel that I can't go on saying nothing. Is there anything I can do?"

"It's very kind of you," says Lily, more stiffly than she intends, "but there's nothing, really." To her surprise, Barbara doesn't give up.

"It isn't kind in the least. I'm worried about you. Have you any idea what HM is up to?"

"I can guess."

"She can't get rid of you. Look how many pupils you have, more this term than ever. The parents think you're marvellous."

"None of that will mean anything."

"Oh dear. Oh dear, I don't know what to say. Perhaps if I had a word? After all, I have been here for twenty-seven years. One of the oldest inhabitants. HM only came five years ago."

"No, Barbara! Don't. It won't do any good, and she'll hold it against you. Look how Harrold is watching you now."

Barbara turns her head. Yes, Harrold has her eyes on both of them. Harrold is HM's spy; she came with her from Ashburton's. She's always in and out of HM's office. You can never get a private word. Perhaps that's the idea.

She'll hold it against you. Barbara thinks of her room: her fire, the smell of coffee brewed from freshly ground beans, and the pile of marking. Home. Easing off her polished brogues and putting on those rather jolly Tyrolean slippers she bought on holiday with Freya, before Freya moved to the High School in Edinburgh. Outside the window darkness has fallen, but it doesn't matter. These winter nights are cosy. Rain beats against the glass, and you think: I'm glad to be indoors. You can feel sorry for those outside, roaming the streets. It's the long summer evenings that she finds difficult. Streets full of strolling couples; babies out in their prams for an airing before bed; cries from the Lido and laughter that gusts from windows and back gardens.

She's never sorry to go to work. Her classroom. Her girls. They all know her, and she knows each one of them. They scrutinise the young teachers, taking in every detail of their clothes, their hair, the rings on their fingers. Their eyes rake for clues. Adult life is a mystery which captivates them and repels them in equal measure. How are they going to become women? They don't look at her clothes, because they are always the same. Heathery in winter, navy with touches of cream in summer. They wouldn't like it if she changed. The younger ones lean against her desk, unselfconscious, while she goes through their work with them. As the holidays approach, the excitement mounts. One or two of the more thoughtful girls may ask politely, "What are you doing in the holidays, Miss Watson?" and she'll reply, "Oh, lots of plans. Friends, travel. Some wonderful books I've been meaning to read all year." They stare at her, blank as foals, then canter off together. Relieved, duty done. Inside Barbara Watson a little point of dread expands as the weeks of holiday gain upon her. What would it be like, what could life be like, without school?

"I won't sit with you tomorrow," says Lily.

"Oh, my dear girl, surely —"

"No." Lily clears her throat. "You mustn't be dragged into all this. You don't know —"

She breaks off, and Barbara doesn't dare to say any more. She sees, now, how much it costs Lily to put on that air of composure and come into the staff room.

"I must go," says Lily. She stands, drops her shoulders, straightens her back. Barbara's eyes sting. She looks down so that Lily won't see her face, and when she looks up again, Lily has gone.

There's a small fire bubbling in the grate of the Headmistress's room. Two tub chairs are placed one on either side, at inviting angles. Between the chairs is a low table, with brown chrysanthemums in a silver vase.

The Headmistress sits with her back to the window, in the farther of the chairs.

Lily had expected a formal interview with the desk between them. She walks to the chair, and sits, drawing her knees together.

"Let me ring for coffee." HM presses a small brass bell-push to her right. There's no sound, but Lily pictures Harrold scurrying with trays and cups. Behind HM's head, clouds move slowly. The sky is clogged with damp.

"Not a very pleasant day. Ah, here it comes."

A token tap on the door, and the tray enters, followed by Miss Harrold. Her face is pursed with self-importance. The tray is elaborate: a silver coffee pot, coloured rectangles of sugar, a pot of cream and a jug of hot milk. There are Bourbon biscuits: children's biscuits. Miss Harrold slides the tray carefully on to the table and backs out of the room.

"We weren't sure if you would prefer milk or cream."

"Neither, thank you."

The coffee tastes faintly of metal, but it's not bad. Suddenly, as she swallows the first mouthful, the thought comes to Lily that Harrold has put something into it. Not poison. Something dirty, disgusting. She wants to run from the room and spit the coffee out into a flower bed, but she cannot. Don't be so stupid, Lily. You are imagining things, making a witch out of a petty woman. Her heart thumps and she feels her colour mounting. With an effort, she swallows.

"A biscuit?"

"Oh no, thank you."

HM takes a biscuit and eats it slowly. If she were alone, Lily thinks she might split the chocolate Bourbon open to nibble at the filling. Those chrysanthemums are shop flowers and they have no smell. Lily thinks of the wet, bruised flowers in her own garden, and the smokiness as she lifts their heads. What systems these women have. What has she told Harrold? *Bring the coffee, give me ten minutes, and then come in with an urgent telephone message. These things can be awkward.*

I'll walk out, Lily thinks. I'll go before she can tell me to go.

But she knows she cannot. She must have a reference from the school, or she won't be able to get another teaching job. She places her coffee cup back in its saucer, and waits.

"You look tired," says HM as she dusts crumbs from her fingers. She gives Lily the maternal smile she gives the girls from the platform on the last day of term, when they are noisier than usual. If there is to be control there must also be a measure of licence.

"I'm not tired."

"Teaching is difficult work. One must have authority. One must be able to command the girls' respect."

"I have no trouble with discipline."

"More coffee? No? But sometimes, situations change. The girls are very sensitive to a change of atmosphere."

"My teaching methods haven't changed."

HM takes another biscuit. Her face is tranquil. "I have to think of the parents," she says.

"Parham High and St Elfride's are giving extra private French conversation lessons to their O-level candidates this year," says Lily. "The girls are each having half an hour a week." These two schools gobble up scholarship candidates at eleven, and excrete them to Oxford and Cambridge at eighteen. They are HM's chief rivals.

"*All* the candidates? Not just the top divisions?" snaps out HM before she can help herself.

Lily nods. "The exam board has increased the proportion of marks allocated to the oral."

"I see." Rumination, as the face sets into heaviness. Lily is quite sure that Miss Cartwright, Head of Languages, will have sent a memo to HM the instant she heard of the change to the board's marking system. It's second nature to do so, in this place. But HM, for some reason, hasn't chosen to take it in until this moment.

"We shall have to have another *assistante*," she says.

And now Lily knows for certain. This is her dismissal. If HM had any idea of keeping Lily, she would have asked her to cover some of the extra hours. It will come any minute now, as soon as the woman had stopped calculating how to get the better of St Elfride's and Parham. But Lily is not going to let it happen. She refuses to be humiliated.

"I'm afraid that I shan't be able to offer any extra hours," she says smoothly. "You see, we're moving to the country. I had hoped to be able to finish the academic year, but I wondered if we might be able to come to some arrangement? My children will be

232

changing school, so it's better if they begin at the start of next term. I am most awfully sorry."

HM reddens. She swallows, and gives a slight, hen-like peck of the head.

She didn't expect this. She knows — she'll know all the staff contracts off by heart — that I am employed by the term and on flexible hours. I am not paid for the holidays. I do not have to give a term's notice. And she cannot sack me now.

Lily knows she must get out before Harrold's discreet entrance and sly glance. None of that, not any more, not ever. She would rather clean floors, like her mother.

"I'll ask Miss Harrold to organise the paperwork," says HM. A heroic comeback. She is calm again. She may even take another biscuit in a moment. "I quite understand your decision."

Of course you do, thinks Lily. There will be no resistance, and no scandal. I'm going quietly, which is probably what you wanted in the first place. I've even saved you the trouble of sacking me. What a fool I am.

Lily stands up, and to her surprise, HM also gets up, holding out her hand. This close to her, Lily can feel the charisma, the sheer will by which she rises above more than a thousand formless girls and women, quells their mutinies and makes them want for themselves what she wants for them. Lily doesn't want to touch her, but she takes her hand. Its pressure is light and dry, instantly given and instantly released. Her eyes are implacable. For the first time and with shock, Lily realises the intensity with which HM has wanted her gone.

She believes what she's read in the newspapers. She believes that Simon has betrayed his country — her country — and that he has been exposed and will be found guilty. She believes he has brought shame on his family. Because I am his wife, I must be part of what he's done. I was wrong to think she was a hypocrite who only cared about the reputation of the school and the opinions of the parents. She does this from the bottom of her heart. She despises and condemns what she thinks I am.

Now it is real.

Lily has no job, and no income beyond the next couple of weeks. She stands by the netball court and watches the girls run, red-cheeked in the cold. It seems to her that hours have passed, but it's still lunchtime and the girls are still playing. They're children, after all, in spite of everything that is done to shape them. Wild shrieks rend the air where the juniors grab hands and play Chain-He. It's forbidden. They are not the sort of girls who need to play games like that. Board school games, old Miss Turville calls them when she is on duty. She doesn't seem to have noticed that there are no board schools these days. In a moment the game will be broken up. Yes, here comes Miss Turville with a heavy leather netball in either palm, for the children to practise shooting at goal.

Lily has two more pupils, one at three and one at three-thirty. If only she could go home. Tomorrow the

American is coming to look at the house. She must tidy, and make the children's rooms presentable. Soon Lily will have no job, and they will have no home. That will be her achievement. Paul hated it when she told him about the American boys. Sally's bedroom has a sign on it: "Private! No Entry Except by Request. Signed: Miss S. Callington". Simon made the sign. She'll have to tell Simon that the Americans have taken the house. If they take it. They must. Simon's face will close up, even against Lily. He can't bear what he has done to them. He is helpless. He can't do anything to help them.

"Lily." It's Barbara again, coming up behind her, too close, so that her breath smokes in the air beside Lily. Lily doesn't want to talk to her, or anyone. If Erica were here, maybe — but even then, Erica has her house, her husband. The baby and Thomas are safe. "Lily, are you all right?"

"Do you mean, have I still got my job? No. I've resigned, because we are moving away from London."

"You resigned? She didn't —"

"She didn't sack me, if that's what you mean. She would have done, but I got in first."

"Oh, Lily, dear."

Her voice is thick with emotion, but Lily feels nothing, nothing. Poor Barbara, her eyes are full of tears. "It's all right. I was expecting it," she says. She sees the effort Barbara is making, to control herself and not to upset her, and it seems like something that is happening a long way away and has nothing to do with her.

"But how will you manage?"

"I'll get a job. We are letting the house to some Americans."

Barbara's hand flies to her mouth, as if someone has died. "Your home, Lily!"

"It's only a house. There are plenty of other houses where we can live. I couldn't afford to stay in London, even if I'd kept my job. The tenants will pay the mortgage."

How hard she sounds, Barbara thinks. It's shock. It's how Lily is. If you didn't know her, you might think she was as hard as nails, sometimes. She won't let anyone near her.

She wants to touch Lily, to comfort her, but she daren't. She scolds herself. Really, Barbara, this is not about you and your silly old feelings. Be practical. Lily is losing her job, and heaven knows that husband of hers won't be able to give her any money. No wonder she looks worried half to death. "Lily, dear," she says cautiously, "you know what a dull creature I am. All I seem to spend money on is coffee and cigarettes. I put away half my salary: I simply don't need it." Oh dear, was that the right thing to say? Does it sound odiously smug? But Lily seems to be listening. Quickly, she goes on. "There it sits in the bank, mounting up like old newspapers. No good to anyone. If I could help at all, you've no idea how much it would please me."

Lily's face changes. "You're a good friend, Barbara," she says, and now Barbara hears it: the German accent of Lily's early years, the "d" of "good" shading very lightly into a "t". In spite of herself, there is a jar. "But it's all right, I don't need money," Lily continues. "We have savings."

She won't let me know how she really feels, thinks Barbara. She never will. Once she's left the school, I shan't see her. Perhaps it's better that way. Outside school, we'd find that we had nothing in common. She remembers herself stepping back into the shop doorway, so as not to meet Lily with her little girl. For a moment she imagines herself stealing to the front door of Lily's house, after dark, with a bundle of banknotes in an envelope, and pushing it through the letterbox.

She pictures Lily, stooping to pick up the envelope and knowing straight away that Barbara had posted it through the door. She wouldn't like it. She'd find a way to send the money back, and it would embarrass her. It would spoil her memory of me.

What self-indulgent idiocy. Barbara, my girl, you are going to have to give yourself a good talking-to. Spoil her memory of you, indeed. She won't be thinking of you. A Christmas card once a year if you're lucky. And why on earth do people say that, as if Christmas might come twice a year?

"That's better," says Lily. Quickly, fleetingly, she takes Barbara's hand, squeezes it, lets go.

"What?"

"You're smiling."

"Am I?"

The smile wavers, becomes uncertain and even pleading.

"It's freezing out here," says Lily. "I'd better go in. Two more lessons to go."

"See you later," says Barbara, and keeps smiling as Lily walks away.

CHAPTER
EIGHTEEN

How Prison Works

Simon doesn't know how prison works, but he watches and listens. He knows that he has the right to refuse any visitor. As a remand prisoner, he also has the right to wear his own clothes, receive more visits than convicted prisoners, write letters . . .

Quite soon he understands that for many of the others on remand, prison is like a station on the very end of a Tube line. Epping or Cockfosters, say. You always know that these are real places, even if you never travel that far. For these men, it's the same with the Scrubs, or Wandsworth, or Pentonville. They may not have been to that end of the line, but they know someone who has. There's a boy in here for the first time, that the other men call Gobbo. He looks like a boy of fifteen although he is four years older. He has a sharp, pretty face, which might get him into trouble but won't, because anyone that went near him, Gobbo's dad would get him. He'd be shivved in his peter.

Simon listens. Gobbo looks like a confirmation candidate. He's always talking about his brother or his cousin or his dad's mate, all of whom are or have been in prison. Soon, he'll be in communion with them.

He'll be doing his bird. Gobbo goes on about his case and his brief and his trial date, and the other men put up with it.

What Simon hadn't known was how quickly prison would change him into a prisoner. He can't read most of the prison map yet, but he isn't the same Simon Callington who walked along the Embankment, swung on and off the Tube and sat Bridget on his knee to hear her sing "Catch a Falling Star". That other man's daily hot bath and splash of cologne after shaving seem impossible luxuries, and yet there the fool was, carrying on as if all that was perfectly normal and would go on for ever. Simon, lying awake, knows enough now to be glad he's not in Pentonville. That's the end of the line all right; you don't want to end up there. He watches his former self mooch around his house, whistling, pouring himself a drink or asking Lily whether she fancies the concert that's on the Third, or the play. But it's not always like that. The other Simon Callington sometimes sits in his red leather armchair by the fire for hours without speaking. He stares into the fire but doesn't talk to Lily because he's feeling — Christ! What can he have been feeling to stop him saying a single word to her? When he was in his own house, free to do whatever he wanted, with Lily sitting opposite him? Lily glances across at him, notes the look on his face, says nothing and carries on with whatever she's doing. Marking, probably, or some of the children's mending. Simon would like to step back into the past, and beat himself up.

Instead, he does what the fool forgot to do. He returns, slowly and carefully, to the room where he sat so often without even thinking about it. There's the fire. In its heart is a slump of red ash, from the logs he brought home when they felled the trees in Highgate Wood. He and a couple of others filled the boots of their cars for five shillings. Now for the chair in which he sits. Comfortable; yielding. He thinks of Lily's face when the men delivered the new furniture, and took off its protective sacking. They heaved the old brown sofa out into the garden, for the children to jump on. Lily and the children sat in a row on the new red sofa, all of them smiling.

The leather armchair has its own smell, especially once the flames have warmed it. There might be a gin and tonic on the little table that the children call the pastry table, because of its fluted edges. Quinine and juniper. A saucer of the salted peanuts for which he and Lily are both greedy. Lily's skin and hair; her perfume. All taken for granted.

Now there's the smell of men together, like the smell of school but worse, because men smell worse than boys. Sweat and feet and breath. The smell of his own excrement, collecting overnight in a bucket in the corner of his cell. The smell of all of those buckets at slopping out. He hadn't known what that meant. By morning, he can't even smell the bucket, because he's deadened by a night in the stink of his own piss and shit. The warders' faces, when they came in fresh from the outside air for their morning shift, tell him how disgusting his cell is. After slopping out there is time to wash and shave, but never enough time. The soap doesn't lather properly. He knows better than to say anything. He learned that when he was eight years old. You didn't ask questions and you didn't cry if Mr Arkwright hooked his stick round the handle of the lav where you were sitting, and pulled the door wide open so everybody could see you with your shorts around your ankles. Older boys said the lavs didn't even use to have doors. They were going to take them all off again, said one, with his eye on the new bugs. You listened and didn't catch anyone's attention. You kept quiet.

Lily is allowed to bring in fresh clothes for him, because he's on remand and not yet a convicted prisoner. She takes away the dirty clothes to wash. He thinks of her gagging at the prison smell as she unfolds them and pushes them down into the twin-tub.

He's been put in a single cell, although most cells are shared. It may be because of the nature of the charge against him. It's hard to believe that two or even three prisoners can share a cell this size. He has paced it out, and it's seven feet by eleven. He tries some physical jerks he remembers from the RAF, but there's not enough space. He remembers Lily switching on the wireless for *Keep Fit with Eileen Fowler*. Bridget must have been about two then, and Simon was at home for a week when he had flu and then bronchitis. He was still as weak as a cat. Lily had rolled back the rug in the sitting room and Bridget was scarlet with excitement as she pranced on the bare floorboards. Both of them were laughing so much they couldn't speak.

242

An hour's daily exercise outdoors is another of his rights as a remand prisoner. The men walk in Indian file, silently, because talking is not permitted. However, Simon soon realises that other prisoners know how to speak without moving their lips, in a low murmur without sibilants so that they can't be heard by the warders. Simon doesn't yet call warders *screws*, even to himself. The word is part of a language that he'd have to become a different person in order to speak. Or perhaps he is already becoming that person, without knowing it. He eats prison food. He excretes prison excrement made out of that prison food. He washes in prison water and he drinks it too. His body moves, not because it wants to but because it's time for it to do so. Simon believes that even in this short time his muscles have started to atrophy, and that soon his legs will become an old man's legs, with thin, flabby thighs and spindle shanks.

In the exercise yard there is weather, and sky. The sky is grey and cold, or blue and cold, or sometimes there's yellowish fog that comes down on them like another wall. If it's raining, the exercise period is cancelled. He likes to watch the rain. It has come from far away: from Ireland, perhaps, or the Atlantic beyond. The best thing is if they've been outside for almost an hour, and then the rain comes. When exercise is cancelled, a feeling of suffocation flashes over him. So far it has been cancelled twice.

He'd like to walk faster. He can't get into a rhythm when they shamble round at the pace of the slowest, while the warders watch. Although the walls of the exercise yard are high, you can still hear the traffic. The cold air is good. He breathes it in and smells London. There are no weeds in the yard. They make sure that none poke through the asphalt. Round they go, with Kipper coughing and hawking phlegm in the back of his throat. He says that he has emphysema and that if he gets more than a year, he'll be dead before he's out. He is coming up for trial in two weeks' time. Think of dying here. Or do they let you out, to go into a hospital for your last days?

Through the traffic, Simon sometimes hears the shriek of a train. He listens for it as he walks, and just before the end of exercise, it comes. If there were a net that could catch such sounds, it would be slung over the yard so that prisoners could never hear them. Now there are three good things from today's exercise: cold air against the skin of his face; the way the man in front of him glanced at the sky, sizing it up like a farmer and not like a prisoner; and the whistle of that distant train.

There are many rules. There's a list of them on the back of the door in Simon's cell, which he is supposed to have read. The rules make prison sound organised, but while it is full of restrictions, it is also chaotic. It is full of contradictions. Frightening, yet dull. Enclosed and guarded, but not safe. The building clangs, day and night, as doors are unlocked and slammed shut again. It is like living inside an engine which is being built and demolished and rebuilt around you. You can never get away from the noise. On a good night, the prison vibrates around you, but on a bad one the screech of metal and voices penetrates every crevice of your brain.

244

There are locks on cells, locks on landings, locks between the wings.

At night the warders tramp from door to door, slide up the covers on spy-holes and peer in. Simon lies still with his eyes closed until the cover slides back and the boots tramp on to the next cell. Sometimes there are ferocious outbreaks of shouting, swearing and banging on cell doors. Prisoners bang with tin mugs, boots, plates, spoons, and the short metal pole that secures the bed and is meant to be fixed fast but can sometimes, with strength, time and ingenuity, be detached. Sometimes that metal stump is put inside a sock, where it forms a cosh. Simon has never seen this, but he's heard of it. Such things rarely happen on the remand wing, because the prisoners here have more to lose. The sound rises to a crescendo which makes him fear that the prison is about to burst inwards. If that tide swept from cell to cell, he doesn't know where he'd be taken.

Simon has already noticed that not only are the paving stones of the prison uneven, but they are also pushing up from their bed. The building is damp, as if one of London's hidden rivers runs beneath it. He pictures brown water, quick with rats. This is the time of night when he would throw on his overcoat and walk along the ridge of Muswell Hill and down and round, street after street, until the wind had blown such thoughts out of his head. He turns from his back to his side, and wraps his blanket closer. The walls of his cell are cold and greasy to the touch. He pulls his hand away and wipes it on the blanket. Better not to touch these walls. They are sweating out all the lives that have been lived in here: if you call it life.

He got himself in here.

He goes back in time again. It's evening. He's sitting with Lily. They've got a bottle of cider to drink while they listen to the play. The telephone rings, and Lily goes to answer it. She comes back and says, "It's Giles Holloway for you." Instead of getting up and going into the hall, he whispers to Lily, "Did you say I was in?" and she understands at once, enters into the conspiracy and says, "No, all I said was, 'Just a minute.'" "Go back and say you can't find me. Say you think I must have gone down to the pub for cigarettes." "All right," says Lily, and she smiles. She's pleased that their evening isn't going to be broken up. Off she goes to the hall, and he hears her apologising, "I'm sorry, Giles, he's gone out. I think he must have gone to the pub."

Over and over, he sees himself rise to take Giles's call.

CHAPTER
NINETEEN

A Bendix in the Scullery

Lily wakes suddenly to find herself sitting up in bed, her nightdress damp and clinging. She must have had a bad dream but she can remember nothing. Perhaps she heard Bridgie? She listens, but there is no sound from the children. The wind has got up and the window sash is rattling. The hands of the alarm clock glow green: half past three. She must go back to sleep, because she's got to be up at six to clean and tidy before Dr Wiseman comes to see the house. If Simon were here, he'd get up and wedge the window with an old handkerchief.

Lily throws back the blankets and gets out of bed. She doesn't need to put on the light: she reaches into the top left-hand drawer of their chest and takes out a soft, folded handkerchief. She ironed a pile of them yesterday, for Simon.

She crosses to the window and parts the curtains. The window is open a few inches at the top, for fresh air. She'll have to close it. As she stretches to push the sash window up, she catches movement under the branches of next-door's cherry tree. The shadow is still, and then it moves again. It's just outside the front gate.

There's someone there. Lily freezes. If she keeps perfectly still, they won't see her. A moment later a flame jumps in the darkness, and then disappears. She waits. A red point of light appears, and then dims. Lily lets out her breath. Of course. He's lit a cigarette, and now he's smoking it. The branches of the cherry tree thrash in the wind, confusing the shadows underneath them. Is he still there, or has he gone?

She's not imagining things. Inch by inch, she lets the curtains fall together. Thank God she didn't put on the light. If he was busy lighting his cigarette, he may not have seen her.

Lily retreats to her bed, and wraps herself in the blankets. She ought to check that the children are all right. In a minute, she tells herself. She must think. Perhaps they've put a policeman outside the house to watch the comings and goings of any night visitors. Perhaps they still think she is part of it all. They may still come to arrest her. What would the children do? Who would look after the children? Erica might take them for a week or so, but any longer would be impossible in a house that size, and Tony might not want it anyway. Whatever happens, they mustn't go to the Callingtons.

What if it isn't a policeman? Her skin prickles. The briefcase. The police came looking for it, but perhaps they aren't the only ones who want to know where it is. The police might arrest her, but those others wouldn't care what they did, as long as they got what they wanted. They might do anything.

Now the suburban street is dark and full of shadows. She has dropped her guard: she has taken too much for granted. *England is an island, Lili. That is why we will be safe.* But all at once it seems as if anything might happen here.

By morning, Lily's fear has hardened into resolution. She must get the children away as soon as she can. By half past five she is up, noiselessly putting away the toys and washing. She wipes the surfaces, and polishes the tables. The children have barely swallowed their breakfast before she whips the crockery into the washing-up bowl. As soon as they are off to school, she tidies their rooms ruthlessly.

Dr Wiseman is coming at ten-thirty to see the house. If he likes it, he will get a contract drawn up. His family's passages to England are booked, and they arrive on 17 January. On the telephone he was efficient but preoccupied, in the way of a man who is used to considering his own time more important than that of the other person. If he decides to take the house, he would like to move in at least a week before his family arrives.

Dr Wiseman is short, solid and dark, with a brush of hair, and he shakes Lily's hand with old-fashioned courtesy.

"Mrs Callington? A pleasure to meet you, ma'am."

It reminds her of the war. GIs always said "ma'am". She asks him in, and offers him a cup of coffee. He thanks her, but says he doesn't believe he will. His next clinic is at mid-day.

She shows him the kitchen first, and is not surprised when he looks around with bright, expressionless eyes and makes only the politest of murmurs. To an American, her kitchen must look shrunken and primitive, with a fridge fit only for a doll's house.

"There's a knack to the stove," she tells him, hearing herself sound more English than she ever feels. "If you bank it up well at night, and pull the damper right out again in the morning for at least twenty minutes, then you should have plenty of hot water. We never let the stove go out, unless we're going away or in the middle of summer, when you can use the immersion. I know things are different in America."

"That's OK," he says. "We'll work it out." He looks at the twin-tub. "I plan to order a Bendix for my wife. It's what she's used to back home." He steps forward and peers into the scullery. "I see you have plumbing in here."

They go upstairs. She wants him to like the house, to take it, but she doesn't want him here. In Bridget's bedroom he goes to the window where the view is, and says, "Scott will like this."

"Scott's your son?"

"That's right. We have three boys. They'll be attending the neighbourhood school."

His manner is so certain. He doesn't ask her about the school, because he isn't interested in her opinion. This will be his home, and his life. She's no part of that. He moves aside courteously so that she can lead the way into her own bedroom. In the heat of a man's preoccupation with his own family, she is cold. She'd always thought herself self-reliant, without realising how much she relied on the understatedly united front that she and Simon presented to the world. Simon would always put her and the children before all others. She didn't have to notice that, until it was gone. Now her marital status will be the subject of cold enquiry rather than the nod of recognition that says: *Yes, you are one of us.* This man probably thinks that she's separated from her husband, or, at best, a widow. She finds herself saying "we" with emphasis, as she would never have done before.

He'll be a good tenant. He will pay the rent that will enable her to keep this house. It's weakness and stupidity to think of anything else. Lily crosses her bedroom and says, "There is the same view from this bedroom, and then the two bedrooms at the back look over the garden."

He is no gardener. He'll get a man in to mow the grass and keep the hedges trimmed.

"Don't bother with the back, by the copse," she says quickly. "We leave that part wild. The children play games and make camps there."

That's fine by him. Will the house do? Yes, it will do. He will be able to send his wife an address now, and a description, so that she can look forward and think of it as her home. They're having linen and kitchen equipment shipped over, along with their personal possessions and the kids' stuff. He wants it all in place before they arrive, and some plumbing and electrical work, if Mrs Callington is happy with that? A colleague has recommended a contractor.

He is sure of himself. He's had his struggles, no doubt, but whatever these were they've left his confidence intact. His wife and children are coming over on the *Queen Mary*. By the time they get here, the Bendix will be in the scullery along with the closest approximation to an American fridge that London can provide. Their own drapes, as he calls them, and some pictures. His glance runs over the bookshelves. "You seem to have quite a library," he says, but not with appreciation.

"The books will be stored in the loft," says Lily.

"That's fine."

He asks no questions about why she's leaving the house, or where she's going, and Lily is grateful for it. He makes no observations about the children's clutter of toys, or their names on the bedroom doors. It's enough for him that they will soon be out of the way.

He looks at his watch as they go downstairs. They talk about dates, banks, agreements. If he's surprised that it is Lily and not her husband who is negotiating with him, he doesn't show it. Perhaps he puts it down to the customs of another country, worth noting, but, in the end, a matter of indifference to him.

The front door closes on him. Immediately, Lily goes into the sitting room and begins to lift books from the top shelf. There's more dust than she expects, so she goes back to the kitchen and fetches a damp cloth. Shelf by shelf, she clears the books into boxes, and then wipes the shelves clean. By the time the children come home from school, all the books from the sitting room are piled into boxes and waiting at the foot of the stairs. Paul and Sally will help her to carry them up to the loft-ladder.

Bridget goes into the sitting room. "Mum! All the books have gone," she shouts, and then she hears the echo of her own voice, sounding quite different now that the books are no longer there to absorb it. She starts to hoot out notes, testing the echo, while Lily and the other two children tramp up and down the stairs with boxes of books. Already, the house has changed. It has begun to have the daring of an empty house, in which anything might happen.

CHAPTER
TWENTY

Can You Hear the Sea?

It's almost dark. Lily and the children have changed from the London express on to the branch line. There's a stretch of single-track railway ahead. As each train goes through, the driver hands over the key he carries to the waiting train at the other end. There is only ever one key, and it must be taken before the train can go forward. In that way, there will never be a collision on the single-track line. Paul already knew about the key system and he explains it to Bridget, who drums her heels into the upholstery until dust flies. The making of this journey is the one thing that has lightened Paul's mood, but he knows that soon they won't be travelling any more: they'll be *there*. No London; no school; no Danny; nothing that he knows anything about. He won't think about Dad. Their bags and suitcases are up in the racks. Two trunks have been sent ahead. Nothing else is coming with them. Sally preached at him yesterday about how much worse it must have been for Mum when she came to England, but even Sal is silent now, with her cheek pressed against the cold glass of the window.

254

Lily is glad of the journey. It is a breathing space: for a few hours, at least, she can do nothing. The train is carrying them to their destination. It feels as if she hasn't sat down for days. Every evening, until late in the night, she has sorted, cleared, labelled, packed. The loft is full of their belongings. She has cleaned until her hands are raw. Mrs Wiseman has got to like the house. She must come in, look around and turn to her husband with relief and satisfaction: "Why, this is just what I thought it would be like, from what you said. I think we'll be happy here." If the tenants leave, there is no money to pay the mortgage. Finding the cottage was easier than she thought it would be. She decided on the Kent coast, because she would be able to visit Simon from there, and yet it was quiet, remote and cheap. The children would like the sea. She had picked out five villages from the Ordnance Survey map at the library. They were all on the railway: that was essential, because of visiting Simon. She telephoned the pub and the post office in each of them, to find out if there were any cottages to let. She'd struck lucky in the Smugglers' Rest at East Knigge, where the landlord put her on to Mrs Woolley. The rent is less than a third of what the Wisemans are paying her.

"It's nothing fancy, mind," Mrs Woolley had warned. God knows what that meant. Well, they'd find out.

Lily closes her eyes. She'll rest them, just for a moment. The children are quiet: they're tired too. The train canters on through the darkness. It knows where it's going, at least, she thinks. She has left everything that she knows, but she doesn't have to think about that, not yet, not until the journey is over. Her hair smells of train-smoke. The train from Berlin didn't smell like this. The smoke was different. It was a big train and it went fast, until it stopped at the border. They had to show their papers. She had forgotten all that but now it is as clear as clear.

"It's so dark, Mum," says Sally. "We won't be able to see anything when we get there. It's never as black as this when you look out of the windows in London."

She sounds scared. Lily rouses herself. Children are sensitive: they pick up your thoughts. "No, but just think how nice it will be to wake up in the morning and see it all for the first time," she says, as if Sally is as young as Bridget. "The beach is only half a mile down the lane. You'll be able to run to the sea whenever you like." She does not repeat what Mrs Woolley has told her: "It's not much of a beach. We don't get many visitors, even in the summer."

The cottage has two bedrooms upstairs and an attic where a bed will have been set up for Paul. Downstairs, a kitchen and a living room. There's an outside toilet. No bathroom. However, there are washbasins in both bedrooms, and "a bath can be taken in the kitchen if desired". Lily wonders why, since Mrs Woolley has already got running water, she hasn't installed a bathroom. But if she had, the rent would be higher.

There is a grammar school five miles away, and the school bus runs through the village. For now, the children will go to the village primary school. There's a station in East Knigge, although the railway is mostly used by freight trains from the quarry. Mrs Woolley told

256

her all this and would have said more, but already Lily had used up almost nine minutes on the call.

"We'll soon be there," she says to the children. The carriage jolts and sways. Every so often the train slows and stops at empty platforms. A guard shouts, a lamp flashes, and they are off again.

At last, the train loses speed, slides under a footbridge and comes to a halt with a hiss of steam. It's the end of the line: East Knigge. They are here. They clamber down from the carriage, cold and stiff. There's no one on the platform but the guard. The train isn't going any farther, and it waits, panting, for its journey back along the single line. No one else has got off the train, and no one seems to be waiting to board it. The air is damp, and smells of salt. The man in the ticket-office goes to look in left luggage, and sure enough, their trunks are waiting. But there's no porter. They can leave the trunks there until morning. They'll need a taxi, with those cases. It's a fair old walk out to Beach Road.

"Is there a taxi rank outside?"

He laughs. "You from London?"

"Yes."

"Turn right as you go out, and Joe's number's on a card in the phone box."

They come out of the station into darkness, and stand in a tight clump, with their bags and suitcases, until the taxi comes. Ten past six, and it feels like the middle of the night. Bridget is too tired even to complain. She leans against Lily and asks, "Is this Kent?"

257

"Yes, we're here now."

In one of Lily's bags there is bread, butter, cheese, tea, a tin of Nescafé, a tin of baked beans and a tin of peaches. She's packed the tin-opener too, just in case there isn't one. There's a shop in the village, but it will be shut now. Lily asked their landlady to arrange for three pints of milk a day. Today's bottles should be waiting on the doorstep.

At last, the taxi comes. It's a decrepit Jowett driven presumably by Joe, who must be at least sixty. In no time he has stowed bags and suitcases into the boot and the back of the car. If the little 'un sits on Lily's knee, they'll be off in two twos. Lily is almost suspicious of such cheeriness. Is he about to overcharge her? But he seems to know where he's going. The road gets bumpier. They are flying through the darkness, jouncing on the hard leather seats. Lily grips Bridget, who has woken up completely and is craning out of the window. But there's nothing to see.

Joe puts on the brakes and they all slide forward.

"Here you are."

The track is pale underfoot. On their left, set back, is a darker bulk. It must be the cottage.

"You'd think they'd have left a light on," says Joe, who has already unloaded everything, taken Lily's half-crown, ruffled Bridget's hair and given back the change. She offers a tip, but he refuses.

"I'm not a taxi-driver as such," he says, "I'm retired, but it keeps me on my toes."

Lily has an absurd, fleeting hope that he will carry their luggage into the cottage, find the lights and show them where everything is. But of course he climbs back into his car, and as they troop towards the gate he does an impressively rapid three-point turn, honks his horn and is on his way.

Darkness and emptiness flow towards them.

"I don't like it here," says Bridget.

"You're so stupid," says Paul. "We haven't seen anything yet."

The key will be left under a white stone to the left of the front door. There's no stone. Lily bends down, scrabbling, until a cry from Sally shows the stone and the key on the other side of the door. Of course: Mrs Woolley meant on the left from inside the house. Three bottles of milk glimmer through the dark. Lily feels over the wood of the door until she finds a keyhole. The key has to be jiggled in the lock but at last it turns, and they push in all around her, as if the creatures of the night are at their backs.

"Wait, wait. Let me find the light-switch."

Blindly, her hands sweep the wall. There it is, the blessed light-switch, and then a burst of light as they stand staring. They have stepped straight into a room, with furniture.

"There isn't any hall," says Sally.

Perhaps the room will look better by daylight. There is a brown, worn carpet and two floral armchairs with grease marks where heads have rested. But at least someone's laid a fire.

"That was kind of Mrs Woolley," says Lily, wanting to start the children off on the right foot.

"Who's Mrs Woolley?"

"She's a silly old sheep. Baaa!" shouts Bridget, who is beyond tiredness now.

"That's enough. Sally, get the matches out of my blue bag and light the fire. Paul, get the milk in from the doorstep, then you can help me carry these suitcases upstairs. Bridget, you can take the red bag into the kitchen."

The range in the kitchen was supposed to have been lit for them, but it's cold. It heats the water, too, so there won't be any hot for washing. Never mind, she'll look at it later. There are fireplaces in both bedrooms. The whole place smells of damp.

"It's cold here. I don't like it. Why can't we go home?"

"You know why we can't go home. Don't pretend to be an even stupider baby than you are," says Paul as he swings up another suitcase.

"That's enough, Paul. Bridgie, go and sit by the fire that Sally's making, and you'll soon be warm."

I make a baby of Bridget, Lily thinks. That will have to stop. She reaches up to the kitchen shelf for a blackened saucepan. She can heat the baked beans over the fire and then at least the children will have something hot. If there's a toasting fork, they can have toast too.

"Are there sheets on the beds, Paul?" she calls up.

A pause, then: "No. Just blankets and eiderdowns."

She should have asked the taxi-driver to go back to the station for their trunks. Never mind, they can sleep without sheets for one night. She runs up and down stairs, unpacking and putting in place what's needed for the night, telling the children to hang their night-clothes near the fire to warm them, to find their thickest jumpers and their hot-water bottles and bring these downstairs too. They do as Lily says with an alacrity that she finds almost painful. They want so much to believe that there is order in all this and that their mother knows what she is doing. When the fire is hot enough, she sets the kettle to boil and fills the children's hot-water bottles one by one. Now it's time for the baked beans. Paul kneels by the fire, toasting bread, while upstairs Bridget yelps at the cold as Sally washes her face and hands.

They sit in a half-circle around the fire, on a blanket from upstairs. The hot toast is deliciously sodden with tomato sauce and butter, and the children eat wolfishly, in silence. The coal scuttle is full. Thank God the woman did that, because Lily would never have found the coal bunker in this dark. The core of the fire glows red. There's one piece of toast left. If Bridget goes to bed as soon as she's finished eating, then the first day will be almost over, thinks Lily. She must get the range going, and then the house will warm up. Who knows how much better these rooms will look with sunlight coming into them? And she'll clean the whole place from top to bottom.

She sighs, and changes it to a cough when Sally glances quickly at her face. The children look so tired. She must put the chamber pots under their beds, for night-time. They can't go out to that toilet in the dark.

"I want to sleep in your bed, Mum," says Bridget.

"Listen," says Lily. "Can you hear the sea?"

They are all still, listening. A long shushing sound, close but not loud. It must be the sea. It can't be anything else.

CHAPTER
TWENTY-ONE

Don't Get Cold

Giles's leg is doing well, but they haven't moved him to the King David yet. His temperature stubbornly refuses to return to normal, and the slightest effort makes him breathless. The maggots have done their job. The wound is bright pink and clean, which Sister says is an excellent indicator of healing.

The little dark nurse, Nurse Davies, brings a kidney dish and his toothbrush, with the paste already spread on it. For Christ's sake, surely he ought to be able to squeeze out his own toothpaste? But his hands tremble as they hold the brush and after he has finished, rinsed and spat he falls back on the pillows sweating with weakness.

"Let's get you more comfortable," says Nurse Davies. "Upsidaisy." She's very strong. With one arm she levers him forward and up, and then she holds him there as she plumps up the pillows and puts them back in place, before gently lowering him into position again. "Better now?"

"Thank you." How long has he been in here? He must ask Anstruther. Ridiculous not to be able to remember, but one day melts into the next in an atmosphere of relentless good cheer. Anstruther says that the next stage will be a cloud of new growth around the broken bones. It won't look pretty but that's what they want to see on the X-rays. The metalwork will stay in for at least a year, possibly two. Some people never have it removed. Bodies are remarkably adaptable things, and there are plenty of chaps still walking around with shrapnel from the trenches inside them.

Giles clings to these remarks. Soon he will be out of here, out and about, one of thousands of old coves who have more metal inside them than the Bank of England. The wound — everyone calls it that, impersonally, as if it's only accidentally part of Giles — is a textbook example of maggot therapy. He's been lying in a hospital bed for days — weeks — doing bugger all except when he is released from all the contraptions and Sister bullies him on to his feet. So why doesn't he feel better? That's not a question he can ask Anstruther or any of the nurses. He hasn't had a drink since the night of the fall. Doesn't even feel like it. The thought of a glass of whisky makes him nauseous. Smoking's off the cards too: the one time he tried, he coughed until he choked. He is diabolically weak. It feels as if not only his leg but his entire body has been smashed up, beaten to a pulp deep inside where no surgeon will be able to get at it. The worst thing is the way he sweats at night. It must be the drugs they give him. He wakes up cold and drenched, with his pyjamas soaked through and the sheets clinging. They say his temperature is still wrong.

"Nurse Davies is going to take you along to the Orangery this morning," says Sister. "Mr Anstruther thinks it may be beneficial."

The Orangery is a big conservatory on the ground floor. It faces south, and even in winter it is warm when the sun shines. The nurses help him into a wheelchair, and he goes down in the lift, like a child in its pushchair. The Orangery is a surprise. It is so bright that it makes his eyes sting. There are rows of day-beds, tubs of dusty lemon trees and a smell of trapped, heated air and citrus leaves. It has already been explained to him that exposure to sunlight, even through glass, is good for bone healing. It is the Vitamin D in sunlight that does the trick. Giles would have thought this could have waited until he was in the convalescent hospital. If he's well enough to be wheeled down to the Orangery, then why the hell aren't they transferring him to the King David?

The day-beds, too, are wheeled. Nurse Davies and another nurse help him out of the wheelchair into the bed. He lies back, utterly exhausted, sweating and out of breath. He feels a hand take his wrist and fingers on his pulse.

"Just lie quite still. You might not think it, but it's quite an effort, the first time a patient comes down here."

Her voice is so kind that tears gather behind his eyelids. For Christ's sake, man, you're getting maudlin. With an effort, he unsticks his eyes. The nurse is gazing into the distance, her face perfectly calm. Everything must be all right. After another half-minute she releases her hold on his wrist, lays his hand down carefully at his side and nods as if thoroughly satisfied.

"I'll just take your temperature," she says, whipping a thermometer out of its holder and inserting it beneath his tongue. His mouth is so used to this routine by now that it opens meekly at a word. But he is still out of breath, even though he's lying down. She seems to know this, because she calls another nurse and they raise the back-rest on the day-bed so that they can prop him up into a sitting position.

"I'll have a word with Mr Anstruther," says the other nurse, who seems to be in charge of things here.

"Yes, Sister," says Nurse Davies.

The day-beds are set to face the light, and here the patients lie, waiting for the pale winter sun to creep from behind the clouds again. Giles drowses, and then wakes suddenly at the rasp of a snort from the back of his nose. Has he been making that noise all the time? No one turns. Each is in his own world, preoccupied with the advance and retreat of his own pain. And Giles lies there, one of them.

Enough snow has fallen in the night to coat the roofs of the prison, and the air is raw. There's slush in the exercise yard, and the screws stamp their feet to keep warm. Christmas, thank God, is over. Simon has taken to attending chapel. One must do something. His mother has put in a request for a visit, but he has refused. He cannot have her here, to see him stripped bare. She'd sit there, taking in everything, asking the same idiotic questions she used to ask when she came down to visit him at school. She might make observations about the other men and their visitors, in her voice that was always slightly too loud.

"What does it matter if they *do* hear, Simon? For heaven's sake, why are you always so touchy?"

After the visit, she'd take the train back to Stopstone, rearranging the day in her head as she planned what she would say to Pa and his brothers. Her day had been simply frightful, but it was over now. His brothers would telephone Stopstone that evening to hear how things had gone. They would be very manly and stern and careful of her.

He must get money for Lily, he thinks suddenly. Perhaps he ought to have allowed his mother to visit him. He could have tried to make her see that whatever she thought about him, it mustn't affect Lily and the children. They are her grandchildren, for Christ's sake. Lily's mother, who has nothing, puts ten-shilling notes into birthday cards and sends each child a five-shilling book token at the start of the summer holidays. His own mother talks endlessly about the terrible drain of running Stopstone. She will pretend to think that Lily can manage perfectly well, with her job and the little house in Muswell Hill. He hasn't told his parents that Lily has left London. He hasn't even told Pargeter. The less that they know, he thinks, the better for Lily and the children.

Pargeter is running out of steam. Every case, even the most hopeless, can be transformed by conviction. He smiles at his own double-entendre. The other side will pick up every sign of weakness and make sure that the jury does too. They won't even know why they don't believe a word that comes out of Callington's mouth; they simply won't believe him.

There's a smell to a case which has little to do with the facts. And this one not only smells bad, but the facts are against Callington as well. He's as stubborn as a mule, and refuses to accept that the jury will want to know a little more than that "someone" must have put the camera in his desk, although he has no idea who that someone might be, or why they might want to incriminate him. Pargeter taps his pen cap. The whole thing stinks to high heaven.

If he had any choice in the matter he wouldn't put Simon Callington on the stand. He might well come apart spectacularly. Pargeter has his reputation to consider. He can't afford to be made a B. F. by Simon Callington in Court No. 1. Clients who hold back material facts from their own defence and think that they won't be pulled apart by the other side are the worst, and thank God he hasn't had to deal with too many of those in his career. Soon, it's going to be time to have a very frank word indeed with Callington. And now there are the Portland arrests. God knows whether that will make matters better or worse for Simon. The evidence against the Portland trio looks as if it will be pretty damning. Anyone who reads the newspapers — any jury — will now know that spies can perfectly well live next door, in a bungalow in Ruislip, without a cloak or dagger in sight. Or in a terraced house in Muswell Hill. But on the other hand that bungalow seems to have been an Aladdin's Cave of evidence, whereas at the Callington home they found nothing at all. So it cuts both ways.

Even so, Pargeter is losing hope of getting home on this one.

After conviction, Simon knows that he might be sent to the other end of the country. How will Lily manage then? She'd have to find the fares to visit him, on top of all the other expenses. She said she was pleased about the rent that she'd negotiated with the Americans, but still worried about how their savings were dwindling. She's found a part-time job as housekeeper to a retired solicitor called Austin, who had lost his wife in April. It always amuses him when people use that expression, as if the wife might be somewhere in the attic or coal cellar, waiting to be found. The solicitor's house was already going to pot. A nice man, Lily said. When she went for her interview, she found him in the scullery with his sleeves rolled up, peeling potatoes with a scout knife. He had taken off so much peel that there was hardly any potato left to cook.

She was happy with the housekeeping job. Things were cheap in East Knigge, compared to London. The woodshed was almost full. The farm sold milk and eggs for two-thirds of what they cost in Muswell Hill. They wanted to charge her visitors' rates at first, because they knew she was from London, but they didn't try that any more.

"What do people there think you've done with your husband?" he asked Lily on her last visit.

"I don't know," she said.

"Perhaps they think you're a brave little widow."

Her mouth twitched, but she answered calmly, "Of course they don't think that. Why should they?"

"The children must say something at school."

"I don't think anyone's very curious. We're outside the village, and the lane doesn't go anywhere. Only to the beach. Nobody sees us. You might be coming home every weekend, for all they know."

She had put a card in the village shop window, advertising private French lessons.

"Do you think that's a good idea?" he asked.

"How else am I going to get pupils? I've written to the grammar school in St Mary Regis but I haven't heard anything."

"Simmery Regis? Is that where Paul will go?"

"It's Saint Mary really, but they say Simmery."

And so do you now, he thought. She was picking up local ways. God knows what people in a little village in Kent thought when they saw a postcard advertising French lessons. He kept getting pictures in his head and they wouldn't go away. There was Lily in front of him, sitting on one of the mean iron-framed chairs that were put out for visitors. She wore her navy suit and her hair was up in a chignon. She looked cool and remote but he knew that she had dressed like this on purpose, to give herself confidence as she walked in through the gates. She glanced from side to side, nervously. Her mouth was set.

He knew he should praise her courage and good sense. It was all he could have expected and more, but

270

his heart was so flooded with bitterness that he didn't dare open his mouth. He could do nothing for Lily or the children. The more he tried, the more he was a drag on them. He'd suggested to Lily, before they went to East Knigge, that it might be a good idea to change the children's surname. His name would be in all the papers when the trial came on. The children would be going to a new school, and it was a chance for a fresh start. She'd refused. The children were who they were. She could never explain to them why they couldn't be Callingtons any longer.

"But you changed your name when you came to England," he'd said. "You changed your language. That was a much bigger thing. You told me that you never spoke German, even at home. You changed your whole life."

"That was different. It was to fit in, not to hide anything." Even as she said it, she wasn't sure it was true. They had hidden themselves in Englishness. Her mother had known what they had to do.

But Simon knew what English villages were like. As soon as the trial opened, someone would see the name Callington in the papers. There would be details about his family. They might even say that his wife and children had left the family home in Muswell Hill for an unknown destination. Journalists used that kind of language, to make something perfectly innocent sound sinister. Anybody who lived in an English village miles from anywhere and had never been to London would be perfectly capable of putting two and two together in less time than it took to walk home from the village shop, newspaper under arm. Not very curious! They'd have been talking about her for weeks. A woman with three children, suddenly appearing in East Knigge, with no connection to the place, no sign of any husband, not much money from the look of it, taken a job with Mr Austin, shouldn't wonder if she was after his money. Nothing would be said to Lily. No questions would be asked, but the news would seep into every house in the village. Lily would be watched, weighed up, judged and condemned.

He must say something, he thinks now. There she sat on the chair. She had travelled for four hours to get here. She looked tired.

"The children like the cottage," she said. "They finish school at half past three and then they run down to the beach and don't come back until dark. They collect driftwood and last week they found some sea coal. There was a colliery near the beach once, apparently, and coal washes up. Paul seems to know all about it."

"I can imagine."

"Sally told me that the teacher asked all the children who had ever been to London to put up their hands. Only two hands went up."

"Sally's and Paul's?"

"No. There were two others, out of sixteen. People don't go anywhere."

She'd already told him that there were only thirty children in the whole school. Bridget was in the Infants' class, and the elder two were together in the Junior class.

"Thank God Paul took the Eleven-plus in London."

"He says they don't bother much about it. No one's gone to the grammar from East Knigge for three years."

Lily didn't add that the children's accents were already changing.

"I can't be Queenie, I gotter git 'ome," she'd heard Bridget yell across the playground. No, it wasn't quite "git". It was a new sound that she'd never heard from Bridget before. Lily had opened her mouth to correct Bridget, but caught the words back. She herself had done the same when she first came to England. Lili had become Lily.

"I brought you some soap," she said, "but they wouldn't allow it. I gave in a postal order too."

"You shouldn't have done that. You and the children need all you've got." His anger had risen again. How could she be so naïve as to think they'd let her bring in a cake of soap? "And I don't want money."

"It was stupid about the soap. I can see that now," she said, looking down at her lap. She was upset. Why hadn't he been nicer about the soap? he asked himself. They were terrible, these visits. You could say nothing. It was as if he wanted to hurt her, because they were so terrible. He could not stop thinking of her in another man's kitchen, peeling potatoes for him.

"You'd better go," he said. "It's going to take you hours to get back, and the children are on their own. What if it started to snow again and the trains were cancelled?"

"They'd be all right. There are three of them; they look after one another."

"They have to, I suppose."

She looked up and her eyes flashed. "I'm doing my best for them, Simon."

"For God's sake, I know you are." Was he supposed to keep on praising her, cheering her on? Visiting time was almost over. He half rose from his seat, then sat again. He felt utterly defeated, as if they had been apart for a thousand years. She knew it. Her mouth quivered. "I'm sorry, Lil," he said.

Eagerly, instantly, she answered, "It's all right," even though she must have known, they both knew, that nothing was right. "I'll come again next Thursday."

"It's too far for you to come every week. You look worn out."

"I want to come." And then, to his amazement, she leaned forward and said in a murmur that he could only just make out, like the murmur of the exercise yard, "Seeing you is the only thing that keeps me going."

She needed him. She didn't mind the hours on the train or the cold eyes of the female warders, brought to search female visitors. She was fumbling with her gloves now. Soon she would walk out into the grey January afternoon, but he wasn't angry with her now. All that had dissolved. He felt as if she were Bridget venturing to school for the very first time, her hand in his, and then saying, "You can go now, Daddy," when he could see that her whole being longed to hide itself in him. She had to go. He wanted to lift her to him, hold her, keep her.

"Put your scarf on," he said to Lily. "Don't get cold."

274

CHAPTER
TWENTY-TWO

The Full Picture

In Kent the snow lies thick and the light is yellow. After school, Sally, Paul and Bridget race to the end of the lane and on to the pebbled beach. They never go straight home unless it is pouring with rain. It doesn't rain as much here as it used to in London, and it's colder. The other children talk about being snowed-in, and the time that the school bus got stuck in a snowdrift.

Mum is never there after school. One day a week she goes to London, to see Dad. The other afternoons she is at Bourne House, looking after Mr Austin.

"Can't he cook his own dinner?" asked Bridget rudely.

"He is paying me, Bridget. It's a job. Besides, he's a nice man. His wife died nine months ago, and he's very lonely. Once I've got everything straight up there, I shan't be working every afternoon. I'll finish after I've washed up his lunch things."

The three children look at each other. How many months has Dad been gone now? Not as many as six. Not even three, but it seems as if years have passed since the time when six o'clock meant Mum running upstairs to comb her hair because Dad would soon be home. When they look back they almost feel sorry for those idiots, that other Paul, Sally and Bridget, who didn't know any better than to think their lives would go on like that for ever.

They go to the beach most days, and scour up and down the tideline for driftwood. Once they found a plank that must have been eight feet long, and they dragged it home. Paul has learned to use the axe to chop wood, but for the plank he needed the saw. They aren't the only ones who scavenge for wood. Sometimes the beach is dotted with dark, crouching figures who drag sacks behind them. They are not friendly. When the sea coal washed up after a weekend of rough weather, everybody pounced at once. Some had waders so they could go deeper and get the most coal. You have to dry it out or it won't burn properly. Mum doesn't understand any of this. She thinks they go to the beach for fun.

When it gets dark they have to go back to the cottage, and then it's Paul's job to light the fire and stoke up the stove. Sally makes the children's tea: bread and butter, jam sometimes, boiled eggs sometimes, cake if Mum made one at the weekend, cocoa. They all have second helpings of everything at school dinners.

"Does your dad work in London?" Susie Patch asked Sally.

"No, he works away. He's in the Navy," said Sally instantly. It was what she and Paul had decided to tell everyone. Even when they talk about Dad to Bridget, they say he's in the Navy. She's so little that otherwise she'll forget and say the wrong thing at school. Already, they think she believes it.

"Dad's on a ship, isn't he, Sally? That's why he can't come home."

"Yes, but don't talk about it to Mum. It makes her sad, because she misses him."

"I'm sad too," says Bridget, but she doesn't look it. She is rosy and noisy and she talks back to Paul and Sally in a way she'd never have dared in London.

The tide is high now, and water almost touches the rim of snow above the tideline. There's too much snow for them to go wooding. Paul has recently learned another thing, which is that when a load of seaweed washes up after a storm you can collect it and the market garden half a mile the other side of East Knigge will pay tuppence a sack. There are people in the village who will pay, too: Mr Austin and Mr Porter, and the two old ladies who live in the house by the church. But the Pearce twins sell to them and they would beat Paul up if he tried to muscle in. It doesn't matter. He and Sal can easily drag sacks as far as the market garden.

Bridget digs with her mittened hands and picks up stones to chuck into the water. Her throw is poor and they fall short. Paul takes the largest stone from her and shies it professionally so that it skips and skips and then sinks. He bends down and brushes snow aside until he finds one of just the right shape and flatness, and then he casts it out with the flick of the wrist that Dad taught him on the ponds of Hampstead Heath. If the stone skips seven times, then Dad will come home. Skip, skip, skip, skip. Skip. Paul clenches his stomach, willing it on, but the stone goes down.

He's going to plead guilty. He is guilty. He can barely remember picking up that briefcase or the way it felt in his hand as he brought it home. The briefcase is irrelevant. It's the cause but it's not the reason why shame hangs over him like fog. Lily knows nothing about Giles Holloway, because he, Simon, has never said one word about him. He remembers Giles telling him once that Tolstoy gave his diaries to his wife to read, the night before their wedding. There she read about the woman by whom her future husband already had a child. You have to imagine a girl of eighteen, Giles had said, a girl brought up in unimaginable ignorance, which was called purity, reading of her husband's lust for gypsy women and of the child he had fathered. It was the night before her wedding, when she was full of the hopes and dreams that had been stuffed into her since she was a child. Those diaries would change the marriage, no?

It was the kind of talk Giles loved. There seemed to be no end of long afternoons, with the light fading and a chill making its way through the glass of the window. They would unstick themselves from their sweat of sex and Giles would roll on to his back and talk about the stabbing of Christopher Marlowe or that photograph of Lord Alfred Douglas where you can see the vanity and venality of the man as clearly as if it were printed in words across his forehead. He talked about taking the train from Moscow to Mongolia, about Ankara in 1937

278

and Berlin in the autumn of 1945. He was in Kreuzberg one day — in the American sector, Simon. There was a column of *Trümmerfrauen* — rubble women — cleaning bricks. The wind blew back one woman's coat, and on the lining there was her Frauenschaft badge. The others closed around her, protecting her from Giles's gaze. *Was geht es Dich an? What's it got to do with you?*

Simon can't remember what he said when Giles was talking like that, about worlds Simon hadn't begun to encounter. Perhaps he said nothing. It wouldn't have mattered. They weren't the kind of conversations where you had to bat the ball back, or, worse still, bat the ball back in style. He ceased to be Giles's lover and became his child. He could lie there and browse on what Giles knew, taking from it whatever he wanted. There were rolls of fat under Giles's chin, and his hair was thinning. From this angle, he didn't look good. In his clothes, with his car and his style, he was invulnerable, but not now. Simon was the stronger here. He was young; he was immortal. Death and age would never happen to him. It made him feel tender towards Giles, at first.

He never talked to Lily about Giles, not one word. He put it all behind him and hid those months with Giles, even from himself. But now they won't be hidden. They pull his sleep apart. He remade himself with Lily. When the children came, he was in a world that he'd never dared imagine. He unlocked the door; he went in; that happiness was his. It was Lily whom he loved. He didn't want the past. There was no future with Giles, and there never would be, outside Simon's room. He didn't want Bobbie's or the Nightshade, or the constant, careful checking of public behaviour. He didn't want the secret society which was all he'd be allowed, as long as he was with Giles: signalling to others, and being signalled to himself. He rejected it, along with Stopstone and his parents, his brothers and his school, and he made himself believe that it was nothing to him any more. He'd been a boy with Giles, impressionable and over-eager. His real, adult life was what mattered. He'd chosen Lily, just as Giles once chose him. Lily and he, together. He put his faith in the present, and the future.

There's no present in prison, or none that anybody wants. By day you live in the near future. The next smoke, the next meal. It's not good to look too far ahead, but an hour's time is always likely to be better than now. At night, the present dissolves and there's nothing to hold on to but the past from which Simon has been trying to escape for as long as he can remember.

He could talk about Stopstone with Giles. There was his mother in the glare of the sunlight, with a bed of salvias behind her. Her cat stretched and stabbed the air to catch a butterfly. And there was Simon, six years old and cowering behind the bathroom door as his brothers ramped up and down the stairs. They were looking for him. That night they pulled him out of his bed and hung him out of the window, but when they swung him back and dropped him on to the floor he got away. He ran downstairs to where the light was, and burst in among the grown-ups. What a figure he cut, snotty and shivering in his wet pyjamas. They were about to go in to dinner. His mother dug her fingers into his shoulder, and marched him to the door.

"What a fuss about nothing. Off you go to bed." She softened her voice, because there were guests, but her fingers were hard. He wanted to kill his mother. If he could have done it, he would have done it. He was wicked, he knew that. No one must ever know.

The past rushes at him like an animal. Only one place — one bed, one endless series of afternoons full of hard white Cambridge light — has ever sent it growling away. Giles knew everything. Giles did not think him wicked. Giles roared with laughter, until the bed shook.

He is the sum of those long afternoons with Giles in his bedsit on the Madingley Road, as much as he's the sum of his years with Lily. He's the father of three children but that can't wipe away the fact that in his own way — the only real way Simon has ever known — Giles fathered him and made him what he was.

If thou, Lord, should'st mark iniquities,
O Lord, who shall stand?

He must get out of here. He can't stand it. The routine grinds on day after day, mimicking normality. Slopping out, scraping a blunt razor over his cheeks with soap that won't lather. He smells the stink of himself. Breakfast: the porridge that is no worse than school porridge. Jostling dirty bodies, teeth bared. The man whose name he doesn't know, who stands too close. Men who are dulled and yet at flashpoint. Bread with a smear of marge and bright pink jam that tastes of wood. Simon eats it with his left arm curved around his plate, as if someone might snatch it away. His right hand grips his mug of tea. There'd be a fucking revolution if there wasn't any fucking tea, even in here. So says Proctor, he with the nervous whinny in place of a laugh. He is charged with fraud, and has taken a shine to Simon.

"You're an educated man, I can tell," he says, and away he goes into a mass of rambling, confused detail about his case. He interrupts himself, brings himself back to the point, sheers off again into knowing what ought to be done better than any lawyer. He is stupid, cunning and arrogant. Simon can't make sense of any of it, but soon he understands that this doesn't matter. Proctor sucks his teeth, shakes his head and is satisfied that the complexity of his case has defeated Simon, the educated man. For what is education anyway but a nod and a wink above the heads of the world. Professors, doctors and lawyers: they're all conmen at heart, and Proctor's on to them. But he's servile, too. He carries his case about like a patient going from doctor to doctor with a rare illness that he has diagnosed himself.

"I'm sorry I can't help," says Simon. "It's not really up my street." That was a mistake. Proctor looks at him narrowly. Is Simon trying to come it over him? Quickly, Simon adds, "You need a legal brain. But you seem to have a pretty good grasp on it yourself." It's the kind of appeasement he's grown used to here. One thing he saw straight away was that anyone who thought he was any better than anyone else was in trouble, unless he could back it up with violence.

Simon expects to hear no more of Proctor's case, but the next day he's back, his head bobbing too close to Simon's, garbling the detail of his latest meeting with his brief.

"You want to watch that one," says Reg Miniver, passing close as Proctor slopes off at last. "He's got a nasty side to him."

They are taking Giles down to X-ray again. Mr Anstruther has popped in to see him about an hour ago. It's not an X-ray of his leg this time. Mr Anstruther would like to check that his chest is clear.

"Of course. Best to get the full picture," says Giles, as if he and Mr Anstruther are on a par in treating this recalcitrant thing which is Giles's body. He waits for Mr Anstruther to go away again, and when he does, Sister comes in quietly.

"We won't bother with the wheelchair today," she says.

"I don't know how far I can walk."

Sister smiles. "No, I meant that we'd wheel your bed down. The orderlies will be here in twenty minutes, and Nurse Davies will go down to X-ray with you."

They are looking after him. They understand what he can do and what he can't. A wash of relief almost comforts Giles, but not quite.

"A general anaesthetic can cause breathing difficulties for quite some time," says Sister, as if she has heard the questions he hasn't asked.

"I don't feel very well," says Giles, without meaning to, without even knowing that the words were about to come out of his mouth. This time Sister says nothing reassuring. She just nods, as if Giles not feeling well was to be expected, and sets about making him comfortable for the journey.

Giles faints during the X-rays. It's entirely his own fault. He told the radiographer that he was fine holding his arms up for the side-view, when he was already seeing blotches of darkness. They must have got him back on the bed, because when he became conscious Nurse Davies was holding a mask over his face and telling him to breathe deeply.

"Feeling better?"

"Yes." He feels bloody awful.

"Good. We'll get you back upstairs in a minute and then you can have a sleep."

He hears murmuring, conferring. Nurse Davies is on the telephone to someone. Not only can he not hear clearly, but he doesn't even want to.

"I'm frightfully sorry," he says with excessive politeness and his eyes shut. "Did you get all the pictures you wanted?"

"Yes," says the radiographer. "Perfectly satisfactory images."

Perfectly satisfactory. This time it is not a wave of relief, but a sea of it on which Giles drifts, content, all the way back up to the ward. Sister brings him, incredibly, a drink of hot Bovril. He hasn't had Bovril for years, not since he was a child. He drinks some of it and then falls asleep.

By the time he wakes, winter dusk is already thickening outside his windows. It makes him think of buses looming through fog, and taxis at walking-pace. It's good to be inside, in the white, clean bed. They have an amazingly clever way of changing the sheets so that he doesn't have to get up. They roll him on one side, draw the sheet from under him, roll him back and draw the other side out, and then they do the same to replace it with a clean one. They work together, as efficient as anything he's ever seen. They can give him a blanket bath without ever chilling his body. Wonderful girls.

Nurse Davies is going off duty soon, but she takes his blood pressure, temperature and pulse first, and notes down the results on his chart without comment, as usual.

"Good about the X-rays," he says.

She glances at him. "Mr Anstruther is going to pop in at six o'clock," she says, "and after that I go off duty. Sister Ransome is on tonight. Now don't go fainting on her, will you?"

"Keeps you on your toes," he says, but a fit of coughing interrupts him. By the time it finishes he's bathed in sweat.

He must have dropped off again because when he opens his eyes Anstruther is at the side of the bed. He draws up a chair and sits.

"How are you feeling?" he asks.

"Bit tired."

Anstruther nods. "I've had a look at those X-rays."

Something in his tone sharpens Giles. He raises his head to look Anstruther full in the face. "And?"

"I'm afraid there are some abnormalities."

Giles doesn't speak. His whole body tenses, surging with adrenalin. He searches Anstruther's face. Something's there, in the eyes or is it around the mouth? *He knows something that I don't know.* No one, *no one*, is going to know things about Giles that he doesn't know himself.

"I thought as much," he says.

"I was concerned about the possibility of a pulmonary embolism following surgery, given your state of health, but we seemed to be in the clear. However, with the increase in breathlessness and the pain in your side that you reported to Sister, I thought we should take a chest X-ray."

"How does one treat a pulmonary embolism?"

They are on the same side again. The situation is under control. But no. Anstruther still knows something. He is embarrassed.

"I'm afraid . . ." Anstruther clears his throat and looks at the floor and then up again. Suddenly Giles sees that behind him the door is open and Sister is hovering. Now, at once, clearly and forever, Giles knows that he has been barking up the wrong tree. They are not in this together. Something awful, irreversible, is about to be said. He must stop

286

Anstruther. He must stop this humiliation of them knowing and him not knowing.

"It's bad news, I gather," he says.

"Yes. I'm most awfully sorry. I'm afraid the X-rays showed a mass in your right lung. A growth."

"A cancer, you mean."

"I'm sorry to say that it looks like that. Of course we shall do further tests —"

"But you don't need to. You can tell."

Slowly, Anstruther bows his head. "I'm afraid it does look pretty clear on the X-rays. There is a small mass in the left lung, but the right lung is more severely affected."

"I see."

"If you wish, I can show you the X-rays."

"I'll take your word for it." Cold, staccato, withdrawn. That's the style. That's the only way to get through this. If only Sister doesn't come in with pity in her eyes.

"I've sent copies of the X-rays across to a colleague of mine in thoracic surgery," says Anstruther. "He'll come in to see you tomorrow morning, to discuss treatment options."

Treatment options? Lung cancer was a death sentence; everybody knew that. Even so, a small, weak part of him leaped with hope.

"What do you mean?"

"Barnes-Wilson will assess you. It looks as if there may be significant pleural effusion. That can be drained, which will improve the breathlessness. Surgery on the lung itself doesn't immediately look like an option, but it's not my area." How much more comfortable he is, now that they are back on professional ground. "Barnes-Wilson is absolutely the top man in the field. He's doing interesting things with radiotherapy, too."

I bet he is, thinks Giles. He does interesting things and then he goes home afterwards, in the pink. Anstruther seems not only far away but also too bright, too distinct, as if someone's shining a light all around him from behind. Giles is not going to faint again. He will not do that in front of Anstruther.

"Thank you," he says. The words make hardly any sound but they clang in his head as if mad bell-ringers are at work there. "Going to sleep now," and he shuts his eyes, shuts himself off until he is sure that Anstruther has gone. The tumult inside him slowly calms itself. He, Giles, the pulse of him, is still here. When he opens his eyes, he will see his hands outside the hospital sheets. His leg is healing itself. What the hell is it doing that for? Doesn't it know that there's no point? Now he realises that he forgot to ask Anstruther the question that everybody is supposed to ask: *How long have I got?*

"I've brought you a cup of tea." It's Sister's voice. She knows he's not asleep.

"Thank you," he says, opening his eyes.

"Let's raise you up a bit . . ." She is at it again, with her small, strong hands. Another pillow slides behind him, and he is half-sitting. She has brought the tea in a china cup with blue flowers on it. It is steaming and fragrant. "And ginger biscuits. I know you like them."

288

Imagine Sister bringing tea with her own fair hands. What a revolution in etiquette. He half smiles.

"I forgot to ask him how long it'll be before I conk out," he says.

"You mustn't talk like that. Drink your tea. Mr Barnes-Wilson is very good, you know."

"But not a miracle-worker."

Sister looks him full in the face. "No."

"Thought not. Will they be moving me?"

"I shouldn't think so. We can look after you here as well as anywhere."

She knows that Barnes-Wilson won't decide to operate. He might as well die here as anywhere, that's what she means.

"That's good," he says. "I don't want to move."

She holds the cup steady so that he can drink. He can't manage the biscuits, but it was a nice thought.

"Leave the light on," he says, as she's going out. They try to start the night so early in hospitals. "I don't want to be lying here in the dark."

CHAPTER
TWENTY-THREE

The Owl

A slant of winter light touches the motes drifting silkily from the pile of flour Lily has just sifted into the mixing bowl. She takes a knife and cuts shavings of butter into it, then rubs in the fat. Cold water to bind it, and on to the marble slab where it will rest until the apples are ready.

Mr Austin keeps his Bramleys through the winter in the shed he calls the apple shed. The shelves are slatted so that air can circulate, and each apple is wrapped in newspaper. Their skins are wrinkled now, and the flesh no longer crisp and fizzing with juice, but the flavour, he says, is better than ever. They keep until April sometimes.

All those apples, in their wrapped rows, each set a little apart from the next so that if there is rot, it won't spread. She has peeled and cored, chopped and sweetened, added a clove and a grating of nutmeg, and the fruit is beginning to melt into a mush. Lily takes the pan from the stove and sets it on the back doorstep to cool, with the lid off. Steam rises in plumes. There is just time to make the custard before she rolls out the pastry. Mr Austin likes Bird's custard, not the real thing, and he prefers it cold.

"Leave it in the pantry with a plate over it."

"There will be skin on top."

"That's all right, I like the skin."

All that trouble over growing the fruit, and he eats it with a concoction of cold factory cornflour. He also claims a strong partiality for baked beans. "Butter and Marmite on the toast first, then the baked beans, piping hot. Beats caviar any day."

The pie is finished, the edges crimped and the pastry lid glazed with beaten egg. She'll put it into the oven now, and he will take it out. He seems to like a little system of notes with instructions. The pie will last him two or three days.

"You can't beat a wedge of cold apple pie, with Cheshire cheese. Or Lancashire."

Lily smiles. She knows by now that for all his words, really he is indifferent to food. He goes through the motions for her sake, out of his superlative politeness, because he knows how much trouble it all is for her. The whole kerfuffle, the business of keeping alive. He pretends to an appetite that he can't feel, because eating alone kills the taste of everything. He's very thin, but probably he always was. It's that type of build: lean, almost boyish, stooping.

"I'll see you tomorrow, Mr Austin. The Irish stew for dinner is on the larder shelf, and I've left a note on the kitchen table about heating it up. You can warm up the apple pie, or have it cold. I've cut ham sandwiches for your lunch, and for pudding there's the treacle sponge from yesterday, with the rest of the cream. Don't forget the gingerbread at teatime: the tin's on the top shelf. It's all in the note."

"It all sounds absolutely delicious."

His wife was everything to him, and did everything for him. They had no children. He doesn't play golf, or bridge, which is how she'd thought a retired country solicitor would pass his days. He reads a great deal, listens to music and takes long, solitary walks. The garden? Oh, that was all Louise. She made it out of nothing. She planned the beds, the walks, the orchard: all of it. Drew it all out on sheets of paper when most of the garden was a wilderness. It had been let go for years before the two of them came to Bourne House, thirty years ago. The place had belonged to an aunt of Louise's, who lived to be over ninety.

Lily has thought of suggesting that perhaps he might get a dog, but decided against it. She didn't want to seem presumptuous. Besides, it was hard to imagine a dog bounding through this quiet house.

"I'll see you tomorrow, Mrs Callington."

"Yes, I'll be here at nine."

"Good."

He is very lonely. A reserved man, and dignified, with his sudden sweet smile. He keeps his routines going but hasn't a clue about how to run the house. Louise must have done all that, too. As for cooking, he hasn't the foggiest, he admits. That's why Lily's notes are so marvellously handy. If it's not a frightful bore, he'd like her to write down a few recipes. Easy ones, of course. He can boil an egg and heat up a tin of beans, but

292

that's about it. Still, never say die. He'll get the hang of this cooking business in the end, if he sticks at it. If Mr Austin had had a daughter, he would never have abandoned her. Lily thinks of her own father, in a city called Fez where she has never been.

"Goodbye, then. See you in the morning."

"I look forward to it," he says, with the old-fashioned courtesy that is part of his being. The same courtesy makes him appear to take for granted Lily's sudden arrival in East Knigge, and the absence of her husband. But *The Times* is delivered every day. He will read the reports of the trial, when it begins. She wonders if she ought to say something now, before she has to. It might be better. But no, she decides for the third or fourth time as she walks away down the drive, she can't afford to say anything about Simon. If she keeps quiet, Mr Austin may never make the connection. Callington is not such an uncommon name. He assumes that Lily is in East Knigge to stay, and has already said that next year the children must come and pick as many plums and apples as they want. "There's only so much fruit that one can send to the Harvest Festival, and most of the apples aren't keepers. Louise used to bottle the plums."

"I could make jam," Lily said, but Mr Austin shook his head.

"Can't have that," he said. "I ate enough plum-and-apple pozzy in France to last me a lifetime."

Lily smiled, to hide the fact that she had no idea what he was talking about.

Now she walks briskly. Last night's frost hasn't yet melted from the hollows under the trees, where leaves lie thick and crisp. Birds scuffle in the undergrowth. This afternoon she has laundry to do, and mending, and then a letter to Simon. Her mind is so much set on all this that she isn't pleased to see a figure standing on her doorstep. A woman, with a silly little yapping dog. Cold, alien moment of unrecognition, and then Lily realises that it's Erica, with Coco on a lead. What is she doing here?

"Erica!" she calls, waving and hurrying forward to hide her own reaction. Erica waves too, and Coco lunges to the end of the lead in recognition. There is Erica's thick, soft tweed coat, the scent of her skin as they embrace.

"I thought you were never coming! I was going to give up and get the train back to London."

"I didn't know — Why didn't you tell me?"

"How could I? You're not on the telephone."

"You could have written."

"I could have, I suppose. But what does it matter? I'm here now."

Erica didn't want me to know she was coming, in case I told her not to, Lily thinks. And she was right: I would have told her not to come.

"Come in and have some coffee. I've just finished work."

"You've found a job? Trust you, Lily!"

"It's not a teaching job. I'm keeping house for an old gentleman — a widower."

294

"You really are extraordinary. Here you are in the back of beyond and you've already found a job and no doubt the widower's fallen in love with you. And what about the children? Have they got jobs too? I've always thought a spot of child labour would do Thomas good."

In spite of herself, Lily is warmed by Erica's flattery. "They're at school. Damn, the key always sticks. Push the door, could you?"

"What a ducky little cottage."

"It's not bad, is it?"

"It's lovely. You've made it lovely."

To Lily the cottage looks cold and unprepossessing. She stoops to light the fire.

"You are so organised. I always have to clear out the grate."

"Paul does that, and he lays the fire every morning before school."

"Oh God, you really do put me to shame. Thomas could no more lay a fire than he could fly to the moon."

"But where's Clare, Erica?"

"Tony's looking after her. He's to look after her, and fetch Thomas from school, and make the supper. You know what Tony's like, he wasn't keen —"

"He didn't want you to come here."

"Don't be like that, Lily. He didn't want to be landed with the children, that's all it was. I had to say I'd bring Coco, or he'd have rebelled."

"I'm glad you did," says Lily, stooping to caress Coco. At the touch of the silky coat, Lily's eyes, in spite of her, sting with tears. Why did Erica come? I can manage, I can keep going, as long as nobody comes.

She daren't look up. With her face averted, she says, "Have you had lunch?"

"I had sandwiches on the train. Coffee would be wonderful. Lily —"

"I shan't be a minute."

But Erica catches sight of her face, and follows her into the kitchen. "Don't bother with that now. Let's sit down. You don't want me to see that you're upset but how could you not be? It's awful. The whole thing. Let's not pretend —"

"I'm not pretending. I'm trying to make some kind of a life for the children."

"I know that. Don't be cross with me, Lily. I'm your friend. That's why I came."

Lily leans against the sink and rubs her eyes hard. They are sore. She must look awful. "I'm sorry," she says. "I'm tired, that's all."

"Every time I see the people who are living in your house, I want to spit at them."

"What are they like?"

"I don't know really. She hasn't been here that long. They've got three boys."

"Yes, I know."

"None of them is in Thomas's class. I hope they're paying the rent on time."

"Yes, they are. It was good that you heard about them, Erica."

"So what's going to happen?"

"What do you mean?"

"Come on, darling. *What's going to happen.* Are you coming back to London? Are Simon's parents going to cough up some cash so that you can go back to the house, or don't they care? What's going to happen at the trial? I'm assuming he's got a good solicitor. Do you think he'll get off?"

"Erica, please . . ."

"No, Lily. There's been enough of this. You not saying things and me not daring to ask. Your vanishing act. That bloody Mrs Wilson had the nerve to say to me in the playground: 'Such a pity about the Callington children,' as if the children had some contagious disease that couldn't be discussed."

"What did you say?"

"I said: 'Why is it a pity?' The silly cow shouldn't teach children if she can't face reality. She said, 'Oh, well, you know, everything that has happened.' I wasn't going to let her get away with that. I said, 'No, I don't know. What, exactly, has happened? What have those children done?' And so she had to say that of course the children had done nothing."

"But what difference does it make, in the end, what Mrs Wilson thinks?"

"You're doing what they want, Lily. Letting people brush you under the carpet — as if you're a bad smell —"

"A bad smell under the carpet?"

"You have every right to come back to your house and the children have every right to come back to the school. The Mrs Wilsons may not like it but they'll get used to it."

"I haven't got the money to pay the mortgage unless I let the house."

"But you could get it. You could frighten those Callingtons — they need it. Make them say out loud: *We refuse to keep a roof over our own grandchildren's heads.* Make them afraid that everybody in their neighbourhood is going to know just how vile they've been. Those kinds of people care about what the neighbours think."

"Everyone does."

"Not everyone, Lily."

"I didn't mean you."

"I should hope not."

"I don't want to ask anything of Simon's family."

"Don't you see, that's exactly what they want? You hiding yourself down here, slaving away cleaning houses? No embarrassment for the Callingtons. No need for them to think about how it is for you and the children, because you're conveniently out of sight. Look at your hands, Lily! What future is there for the children here?"

"Don't, Erica."

"I'm sorry. Look, I brought you some flowers, darling."

Erica delves into her bag and gives Lily a beautifully wrapped tricorn, with "Broadway Florist" scrolled across it.

How many times has Lily been in that shop? Zinc buckets crammed with narcissi or roses or chrysanthemums . . . The chill, and the green smell of pollen, leaves and crushed stems. Flowers for Erica when she had Clare; flowers for her own mother before those punishing trips to Brighton; flowers for the house at Christmas. She sees herself, Sally on one side, Paul on the other, Bridget in the pram outside. The assistant gives her the bunch of hyacinths and white narcissi that Lily has chosen. They are wrapped in green and white paper with the name of the shop on it. Outside, red buses push their way through the grey afternoon. Their headlights are on, although it's only half past three. The shop-bell rings as Lily opens the door to leave. There's Bridget, bouncing against her pram harness, glad to see them. Lily pushes up the brake with her foot and off they go. They pass the greengrocer's and the children want to touch the leaves poking out of the boxes of tangerines. People hurry past, other mothers, also holding the hands of children. Lily knows most of them.

Lily opens the flowers Erica has brought her. They are anemones, still in bud, and limp with cold. She must put them in warm water to revive them.

"Thank you, Erica."

"I brought a box of Maltesers for the children as well."

"They'll love that." Lily pauses. She touches the crumpled petals of a dark crimson anemone. It looks almost dead, but she knows it isn't. "I do want to come back."

"I know you do."

"Everyone thinks Simon will go to prison."

"How long for?"

"I don't know. Years."

"You can't stay here for years!"

"Simon has done nothing wrong, and they're going to lock him up for years. Being down here is nothing compared to that."

Lily thinks, suddenly, of the file. Her stomach clenches. She can't stop seeing that page with the initials on it. Not Giles's initials, and certainly not Simon's. Julian Clowde saw those documents and signed the page to say he'd done so. His was the last set of initials.

She remembers the party where she first met Julian Clowde. It was full of theatre people; Giles took them along, not long after Simon began working at the Admiralty. Noise surged around them, and when she was introduced to Clowde he heard her name wrong. He bent over her, charmed, charming, as if there were no one else in the room. He told her how delighted he was to meet her. Smiling boyishly at his own enthusiasm, he told her that he was the most tremendous fan. She began to have her doubts then, to protest, and when he swept on into a discussion of *Lucia di Lammermoor* and what a voice such as hers, a lyric coloratura, might bring to the role, she put her hand on his arm to interrupt him.

"I'm not a singer," she said. His face was extraordinary. Its surface shivered, and he was a different man. Sharp with suspicion, almost angry. He drew his arm away as she added, "I think you're confusing me with someone else."

"You're not Lily Stanton?"

She shook her head. At the time she had no idea who Lily Stanton was, but afterwards she found a photograph of the singer and saw that there was a resemblance. Julian Clowde raised his eyebrows at her, as if she'd tried to trick him, and then turned away.

Erica takes Lily's wrist and shakes it gently, as if waking her up. "Don't, darling. I hate it when you look like that. There hasn't even been a trial yet. We don't know what's going to happen. They might find him not guilty."

"He isn't guilty. You believe that, don't you, Erica?"

Erica holds her gaze. "Yes, of course I do. You would know."

"But that means you believe he's innocent because I do, not because you do."

Erica's eyes have filled with tears. "It's so horrible, Lily, that all this is happening. I still can't believe it's real."

"No."

"Did Simon say that you should leave London?"

"We had to leave. We couldn't pay the mortgage unless we let the house. You know that."

"But it was all so quick, Lily."

"It had to be."

"I'm worried about you, all on your own down here."

"We've got somewhere to live, and I've got a job. Here it's easier than London, for now anyway."

Erica thinks that she has never heard Lily sound less English. Without meaning to, she lowers her voice. There's been so much in the papers about the Portland spy arrests. "No one said you'd better take the children out of London?"

Lily glances at the window. "No, of course not."

"You just went."

"You knew I was going."

"Yes, I knew . . . I can't believe how quiet it is here."

"That's why I like it." Lily knows what Erica thinks: How can you stand it, alone here with the children? There's not another house in sight. The thought curls into her own mind. The cottage is so remote. If anything happened, no one would hear. *No*, she tells herself, *you are not going to think like that*. "It's peaceful," she says. "No one bothers us. I'm all right here, Erica, really."

Could she say to Erica: *I'm in a dark room. I'm feeling my way around the walls. Every time I find a door and open it, there's only more darkness*. No, she couldn't say that.

"I wish you'd come back, Lily. I miss you."

Imagine having the confidence to say such a thing, thinks Lily. Has she ever told anyone that she misses them? No, not even Simon. But then they are never apart — never have been apart — only now . . .

Barbara Watson wanted to be a friend, a real friend, and I didn't let her. It was for her own good. She must have known that. What if she'd lost her job too? But Erica is a true friend. Why can't I say: *I miss you too?*

Wir sind ja in England, Lili. Hier darf man nicht Deutsch sprechen.

All through the war her mother was afraid. She hoarded pills from the doctor, bottles of them in a drawer. It was in case of a German invasion. They came close; they came very close. The whole country was on

302

tiptoe, holding its breath in spite of the clanking of troop trains, the rumble of heavy lorries, the wheeze of machinery and then the throb of engines overhead. Lily would slide the drawer open, look at the pills, and slide it shut again.

"You should get a dog," says Erica, and Lily smiles.

"That's what I wanted to say to my employer, but then I thought I'd better not. He's very lonely, since his wife died."

"A big dog, Lily, not a crybaby like Coco. One that'll bark like hell if it hears anything."

"I like Coco," says Lily, stroking the slender, silky back again. "The children will be so excited to see her."

Erica looks at her watch. "The four-oh-five is the last train I can get."

"They come out at half past three. If we walk to the station, we'll pass them on their way to the beach. They usually go down there after school."

"I'll write to those Callingtons, if you won't," says Erica.

"No, Erica."

"Oh well, darling —" Erica breaks off, and blows her nose fiercely into one of Tony's handkerchiefs. She shakes back her hair and smiles. "Come here." She puts her arms around Lily and squeezes her tight. She smells of bluebells and her hair tickles. If I'd had a sister, Lily thinks, it would have been like this.

For a moment, when Erica sees the three Callington children come down the lane shoulder to shoulder, a gang, red-cheeked, hardy and bigger than she remembers, she doubts herself. They look as if they belong here. Paul is carrying an empty sack.

"Coco!" screams Bridget, peeling away from her brother and sister to pounce on the dog. "It's Coco!"

They are familiar again: three children she has known all their lives, almost. Bridget jumps around her, imploring to be allowed to hold Coco's leash. Paul and Sally smile but hang back. They are not just bigger, they are older too, in that way of children who can leap a year in a couple of months.

"How's Thomas?" asks Sally at last, shyly.

"He's fine. He'll be so jeal when I tell him I've seen you."

Sally smiles. She'd forgotten how Erica said "jeal", and made it sound a normal thing to be, instead of shameful.

The children want to be away, Erica can tell. They flash glances, signally.

"I'm awfully sorry, Erica," says Paul, sounding like his father, "I'm afraid we've got to go. You see, there's been another wash-up —"

"And we've only got an hour before it's dark. Everyone's down there already," says Sally.

"Off you go, then," says Lily, as if this business of the tide and the dark is perfectly usual. The children say goodbye to Erica, dip to stroke Coco one last time and gallop away down the lane.

"What are they going to do?"

"Pick sea coal. A wash-up means that a lot of it has come up on to the beach."

"Oh, so that's what the sack was for."

304

"They collect quite a bit, when there's a wash-up. Coal is so expensive. And they get driftwood all the time."

They have a new life already, Erica sees. Even new words. No wonder the children looked different.

"Thomas would love it here," she says, as if Lily has brought her children on an especially marvellous seaside holiday. And Lily, in spite of everything, is pleased.

"They do look well, don't they? They're so much more independent down here. All the children are."

"We baby them in London, I suppose."

"Yes, when you think that Paul is going on for eleven . . ."

But Lily knows that she had wanted to baby them. They were to have an uninterrupted childhood, but now, of their own accord, they are sloughing it off. Paul is already older than Lili was when she came to England. He is stern with Bridget about the sea coal. She has to collect her share, not muck about looking for shells. "It burns better than ordinary coal, doesn't it, Mum?" Paul says with pride as he tips their haul into the coal scuttle.

And now here is Erica, actually walking at her side. Lily has always envied that coat with its belt and long, swinging skirts. Erica had it made years and years ago, out of a bolt of cloth she bought at a mill up in Scotland. The New Look was in. Erica could carry off the style. She has the height and the long, elastic walk; the elegance, thinks Lily, who knows that she herself is not elegant.

At the station the two women embrace. There is no one like Erica. Once a friend, always a friend, Erica said to her once. Erica took the children when Lily went into labour with Bridget. Lily walked three-week-old Clare up and down, up and down so that Erica could snatch some sleep before Thomas came home from school. Erica lent Lily her black velvet cloak and babysat so that Lily and Simon could hear Joan Sutherland sing Desdemona in *Otello*. Erica paced up and down the autumn garden, alight, blazing, as she told Lily about Bertrand Russell's speech in Trafalgar Square.

The platform is deserted.

"It'll come out of the siding," says Lily.

They watch the clock's minute hand shiver into place. There's no station buffet, not even a chocolate machine.

"Here it comes."

Clanking and hissing, the little branch-line train crosses the points, reaches the platform and lets off a gout of sooty steam.

"Do you want to go in the Ladies' compartment?"

"No need. The whole train's empty," says Erica.

The compartment smells of train dirt. Erica puts down her bag on the seat carefully, so as not to disturb the dust. Under the luggage rack there are glass-covered posters for Margate, Broadstairs and Folkestone. The thought of visiting those places makes her shudder. She pulls down the strap to lower the window and leans out. The guard is walking up the train with his flag and lantern, and Lily is the only other person on the platform. As the train jerks and starts to move Lily keeps pace with it, then falls back. Erica waves for the last time, the train rounds a bend and Lily disappears.

Erica sits back while flat landscape slides past the windows. Darkness is settling on it already. What a place. How can Lily stand it? The train judders and slows, as if it can't make up its mind whether to go on or to stay here. More than anything, Erica wants to be back in London.

In the middle of the night, Lily wakes. Her eiderdown has fallen off and she's cold, but that's not what woke her. It was the owl that did it. It comes most nights, drifting past the window. She thinks of it tilting in the darkness, balancing its wings as it scours the ground below for a flicker of movement.

Suddenly, she is sure beyond doubt that there is someone outside the cottage, watching it, just as there was in London. The walls seem to dissolve and leave her naked. If she looked out she would see them, standing on the lane, turned towards her window. They know she's here.

There aren't any neighbours. If anything happened, no one would know until morning. Maybe not even then. It's too dark for her to look at her watch, and she daren't switch on the light.

The children are all asleep. Her blood rushes in her ears, almost blotting out the sounds outside. The owl calls again. Or is it the owl this time? The children know how to make the sound of an owl between their cupped palms, for a signal. It won't be children out there at this time of night. No car. She'd have heard a car.

Soundlessly, Lily gets out of bed and feels her way across the lino to the window. The heavy rep curtain is drawn tight. Whoever is watching will notice even the slightest twitch of movement. Lily presses herself as close as she can to the window and listens, but although she waits until she's cold all through, she hears nothing.

CHAPTER
TWENTY-FOUR

A Useful Idiot

It's night. In his cell, Simon turns over, dragging the blanket with him. It itches, and the bed is too narrow. Each time he comes to the edge of sleep, he jolts back to awareness like a man about to fall over a cliff. Julian Clowde has been to see him. He should have refused the visit. Why didn't he? It was the same weakness that had made him agree to go to Giles's flat and find the file.

"You'll plead guilty, of course."

Clowde's groomed, implacable face, incongruous in the prison interview room. He made no enquiries. He expressed no concern for Simon's predicament.

You'll plead guilty, of course. How the hell had he got permission to see Simon in here, alone, as if he were a solicitor? Simon stared at him, shocked. That was the moment when everything began to fall into place. Those three sets of initials on the file, JRC the last. Julian Clowde was the last man to have sight of the file. It should have been returned immediately, but it had ended up in Giles's flat, for Giles to photograph.

Long ago, back in Cambridge, Giles had said to him, "There's a chap I'd like you to meet." Julian Clowde had been very friendly at first. There were overtures, withdrawn so quickly when Simon didn't respond that he ended up thinking that perhaps he'd imagined them. But he'd known, really. He'd felt the truth, even if he'd blocked it from his conscious mind. He was a fool. He didn't act on what he sensed. He told himself Julian was a cold fish, and let it go at that.

"You'll plead guilty, of course."

"Why?"

Julian Clowde's eyes were like lizard's. "A guilty plea will work in your favour, as I'm sure you must realise. You'll be able to enter a plea in mitigation. You were naïf. You came into contact with CND activists and they made use of you. Have you any idea how many Soviet agents are active in London at this moment, or how deeply CND is penetrated?"

So that was the game. "No," said Simon. "I wasn't aware of that."

"Precisely. You had no proper idea of the consequences of your actions. You took those people at face value. A useful idiot — I believe that's the correct expression. You were a useful idiot and so you were used. It will prevent a lot of unpleasantness, for you and for your family. Your wife has no idea that you and Giles Holloway were quite such great friends. I can't imagine that thought has ever been far from your mind. And let me assure you" — he had leaned forward, and there was no feeling anywhere in his features — "let me assure you that the jury will be provided with some very interesting letters, should you be foolish enough to think you might cut a fine figure in the witness box.

That room of yours on the Madingley Road — now what's the correct expression?" He picks out the words with tweezers of contempt. "Ah yes. A *love nest*. Lucky old Giles." Julian Clowde gives Simon a look he'd had from him just once before, when he first came to the Admiralty.

"You're a great friend of Giles Holloway, I gather? He speaks very highly of you."

The signal had been given. Simon had muttered something or other in response. A week or so later, when the invitation came to dine with Julian Clowde at his club, he had declined clumsily. And that, he'd thought, was that. Clowde had raised his eyebrows and walked away. Idiot that he was, Simon had thought that there were no hard feelings, not after all these years. Now here was Clowde visiting him in prison, in his perfect suit. In his position, everything became easy.

He was what he'd always been, but for the first time, Simon saw it. It was like that damned kaleidoscope he'd got for Bridgie from Hamleys. You shook it one way and you saw one thing. Julian Clowde, a man on top of his job and his entire department. Cold but decent. He even put up with Giles's antics, for old times' sake. You shook the kaleidoscope another way and you saw a grin of contempt. He was letting the mask drop, because it didn't matter any more whether or not Simon saw what was beneath it. No one would believe Simon now. Simon was disposable. His word against Clowde's? What a joke. Simon was discredited, and Julian Clowde was a man who never forgot a slight.

Clowde had a lifetime of distinguished public service behind him. Soon he would retire, and get his K. He would spend his time visiting friends in the capitals of Europe, writing his memoirs — Giles said he was a marvellous calligrapher, in his spare time —

"Lucky old Giles," said Julian Clowde, and he shook his head. "The jury won't like it, you know. They're very down on that sort of thing. They'll understand exactly what was going on, and they know that our Soviet friends are extremely keen on a spot of blackmail. Why try to teach an old dog a new trick, when the old ones work so well? So there you were, and there was your old friend Giles. You were in and out of his office. Giles goes out every lunchtime, everyone knows that. He's reliably absent for an hour or more. You knew that. It won't look good for Giles, it has to be said, but there's plenty of evidence about his drinking, and that makes a man sloppy. There will be witnesses to the state of his desk. You took advantage of his weakness. It may not look good for Giles, but it will look a great deal worse for you. Giles had an extraordinarily good war, as he may or may not have told you."

Julian Clowde's face was set. For an instant Simon wondered: Is it possible that he's sincere? Does he care what happens to Giles?

"Giles wouldn't have had access to that file," said Simon. "It can't have been on his desk."

There was a pause. Julian Clowde raised a hand and passed it over his silver hair. "I'm not talking about a

312

file," he said, and his eyes gave their peculiar flicker. "I'm talking about the other evidence against you."

Christ. He had let Clowde get away with all that. It was like being operated on while paralysed, but without anaesthetic. He'd let it happen, because in one respect Clowde wasn't lying. Simon had done what Clowde said he'd done. He'd lain on that narrow bed in the room on the Madingley Road, and he'd been king of the world. He'd thrown his mother's cheese ration out of the window. He'd made Giles wait while he finished his essay and then he'd let him do whatever he wanted. They had both done whatever they wanted.

They'd got his letters to Giles.

He saw himself with sheets of paper spread on the desk, writing and writing. The hard, white light of Cambridge winter days, and the excitement that went up in him like a rocket at the desire in Giles's face.

Call it what it was. He had written himself down on that sheet of paper, folded it, and put it into Giles's overcoat pocket. He had been beside himself, outside himself.

He had been himself. He had loved Giles.

For God's sake, what was he saying? What was he thinking? He'd betrayed Lily before he even knew her. He'd given away to Giles what could never be given twice. What Lily never knew would half kill her if it came out. She came new to him. She'd never loved anyone before. She told him that. Never trusted anyone enough. She found it hard to trust.

He sat there in the interview room with Julian Clowde, paralysed. What the hell did Clowde put on his hair, to make it gleam like that under the light? This is just how he'll look when he goes to the Palace to collect his K.

"I'll leave you to think about it," said Clowde, and he stood up. He was perfectly confident. He knew that Simon would do what was wanted, because he had no alternative. "I hope your wife is enjoying her new life down in Kent, by the way. East Knigge, isn't it? She could hardly have chosen a more out-of-the-way spot. Sensible of her. But on the other hand, it's very isolated, isn't it? Oh, I was forgetting, of course you've never seen it. I hope she's careful to keep her doors locked at night."

Someone's been down there, he thought, his heart pounding. They know where Lily and the children are.

"You bastard, Clowde," he said, and felt a weight fly off him, as the weight of the cheese once flew as he hurled it from the window. He could have killed Clowde with his bare hands. He could have broken his neck. "I know what you are."

But as he said it, at the moment when his anger surged, he knew something else. Clowde has threatened Lily — why? Why even think of doing that, when he'd got Simon completely trussed up? Clowde knew that Simon was trapped. He knew he would never risk Lily seeing those letters. So there must be something else —

Lily.

The file.

Clowde wanted it back, of course he wanted it back. For Clowde, that file was dangerous, because Simon could never have had access to it, no matter how many times he'd dropped in and rifled through the documents on Giles's desk. That file was proof. Clowde suspected that it was Lily who knew where the file was. That's why he threatened her.

"I doubt if your knowing or not knowing anything is going to make the slightest difference, in this case," said Clowde.

"You touch her and I won't care what I do."

"I think you will."

But he was suddenly less sure. His eyes flickered, as a lizard's eyes flicker before it darts into a hole in the wall. He stood up, went to the door, rapped on it.

Simon sweats, pacing his cell. That's what you do, it turns out, when what was safely tucked away in books becomes real life. You're in a cell and sure enough you pace it. There's nothing else you can do. Nothing left. He will warn Lily: he'll find a way. No, they won't touch her. It would be too great a risk. It would be in all the papers. They want everything to die down as soon as possible. Simon must get his seven years, or whatever it turns out to be. Giles will be eased out of the way. Pensioned off, probably. He's too big a risk now.

So Giles kept his letters. Simon remembers the swarm of words that came to him, and how he shaped them. Giles in his mind, Giles's hands opening the envelope, Giles's gaze on the paper. He has never written such letters to Lily. He never thought of writing to her, even when they were first together. He didn't know whether she minded or not. Besides, she knew he wasn't keen on writing letters. Never had been. At his prep school they had to write a weekly letter to their parents, before supper on Sunday evenings. Simon would dash something off in fifteen minutes. As long as you said you'd had roast beef and Yorkshire pudding for lunch, and included the scores for the last set of house matches, your letter would always be passed.

"You mean they read your letters home?" Lily asked him.

"Yes, you had to give the envelope to your housemaster unsealed. If you licked it by accident they made you do the whole thing over again."

"My God. No wonder you don't like writing letters."

He feels a rash of shame now, all over his body. If Lily ever read those letters he'd written to Giles — if Lily even knew of their existence —

It would be the end. She trusts Simon as she trusts no one else. If he'd told her straight away, it might have been all right. *There was this chap I knew when I was at Cambridge.* He could have come out with it then, right at the start. It would have been difficult but she would have seen he was trying to be honest with her.

Tolstoy gave his wife his diary to read, just before their wedding. Giles told him that, and then he said something more about it later: he said that what Sonya read in the diary must have become a running sore in the marriage. It was self-indulgent, he said, to tell all;

316

you were trying to clear your own conscience at the expense of the other person.

But the truth was that he hadn't avoided talking to Lily about Giles out of consideration for her. It was because he was afraid. She might have been disgusted, even frightened. She might have said that after all she couldn't marry him, because it was too much of a risk. She might have thought that he was only pretending to desire her, or that he was marrying her in order to appear normal. He'd had no idea how she might react and after weeks and months it became impossible to say to her: *You know, Lily, I ought to tell you that before I met you I was in love with another man.*

He said nothing, and it began to seem right to say nothing. What happened with Giles was quite separate, and anyway the whole thing was over before he even met Lily. It didn't even seem like concealment any more: it felt natural to be silent. He loved Lily. She was his life now. Everything else was irrelevant.

She'll go now, though. All she'll be able to see is a shabby deception, a betrayal as long as their marriage. She'll leave him. He sees her putting on her coat in the hall, and tying the belt tight. She calls for the children, and obediently they come down and get ready, without looking at their father. No scuffle for shoes, no argument about a scarf. Bridget takes Lily's hand and they all troop out of the front door. Paul is at his mother's side. They don't look back and no one says a word. Down the front path they go, and up the street, the children a phalanx around their mother. Gone.

CHAPTER
TWENTY-FIVE

Cold Obstruction

They've put an oxygen cylinder by his bed. Giles doesn't need it all the time, but he feels safer with it there.

The pleural effusion was drained yesterday, and his breathing is easier. Or, as Sister puts it, he is "more comfortable".

She asked him if there was anyone he would like the hospital to contact. He went through them all: his colleagues, the old friends from a thousand parties, the boys, but the thought of it made him tired. He didn't want any of them.

Only Simon. He'd like to see him, but he's in prison. So much for that. What would be the point of it, anyway? Simon wouldn't want to see him, not now. Even if none of it had ever happened and Simon were able to come, it would be no good. He'd perch on that chair by the bed, feeling sorry for Giles but bored and uneasy, wanting to get away.

Ma Clitterold has been in several times. She brings grapes, and newspapers, and his letters, which he never bothers to open. She sits stolidly, without making conversation. Her bulk is as disapproving as ever, but she won't abandon him. He is her gentleman. She'll be there at his funeral, dressed decently in black, her feet overflowing her shoes. He might give her the Kandinsky, but she won't care for it or know what it's worth. She wouldn't give it to a jumble sale, out of respect. Julian would like the Kandinsky, but he's not getting it.

The Kandinsky will still be there, and Giles will not. Here it comes: a wave of terror, topping the sea wall, turning his insides to water. And there it goes again.

There are no leaves on the branches outside his window. Very likely there never will be again, as far as Giles is concerned. The moment for asking Anstruther how long he has got seems to have passed. Nobody talks about death. He can quite see why not, from their point of view, and most of the time he goes along with it. They are busy people and have to get on with their work. They don't need weeping and wailing and gnashing of teeth. But sometimes the breath of health and the cold outdoors on their skin gets to him.

Ay, but to die, and go we know not where;
To lie in cold obstruction and to rot . . .

Yesterday he'd muttered the lines while Nurse Davies was changing his drawsheet. She must have caught some of it, because she immediately began to chatter about the bunch of huge, hideous daffodils brought in by Ma C.

"Lovely flowers you've got. Aren't you the lucky one? I'll just top up that water for you when I've finished making you comfortable."

Giles felt ashamed. What the hell did he think he was doing, quoting about the most dismal speech from *Measure for Measure* at a girl who was doing her damnedest to make sure his arse wasn't covered in bedsores?

He has been examined by Barnes-Wilson, as a matter of form. Beneath the professional manner, boredom and even irritation showed. A patient for whom one could do nothing was clearly not of interest to Barnes-Wilson. The nurses, afterwards, seemed more consoling than before. Or perhaps it was that he noticed the difference. The nurses were not irritated with him, even though day by day they looked after him and he only grew weaker and more ill. They did not blame him for it, and remained interested in the small things that might make him, as they were always saying, "more comfortable". Trivialities, these would have seemed to him once, when he was well. Hardly worth the bother, especially when a chap's going to die anyway. He knows better now. The nurses won't let him lie for long in one position. They help him to turn, and rub his buttocks with methylated spirits. Ten times a day, they expertly rebuild his pillow-mountain, and ease him back into position when he slips down. He's so damned weak.

When Anstruther told him about the cancer, what had he thought of first? Pain, probably. Oh, and extinction, of course. Good old extinction, always worth sparing a thought for that. What he didn't think about and didn't know about was this weakness that changes everything. Weakness swallows him deeper into itself each day.

He dreams of falling from shocking heights, and wakes with a jolt, sweating, struggling for air. Nurse Davies has left the bell within reach. He puts his finger on it, but he doesn't push the button. He knows that he's breathless from panic, not want of oxygen. If he keeps very still, his breathing will steady. He hears footsteps, and the nurses' night-time voices. They're only just outside. No need to call them. He turns his head to see the luminous hands of his travelling clock. Only ten to two. Ma C. brought in his little folding clock in its brown leather case that has been all over the world with him. Who'd have thought it would end up here? There it is, ticking away, just as it ticked in Vienna and Istanbul. My God, what sights that clock has seen.

You have to end up somewhere. No good being surprised. That's weakness. Giles has seen surprise on the faces of the newly dead. They were torn out of their lives. They didn't expect it, those young men dying in ditches, behind orchard walls, on little roads that were white with dust. It's only looking back that he really sees how young they were. How young we all were. It didn't strike him at the time. No wonder they looked surprised and even offended. This was the full stop, with their lives snatched away from them. You only had to make one mistake, because death never made any.

He understands it now. It's taken a long time but now everything is falling into place. You have your time and then it's over. So easy to say and so meaningless, until you understand, really understand, feel with every weak inch of you that it applies to you, not only to all those others. Soon he, Giles Holloway, will lie on this same bed, perhaps with that look of surprise on his face. The nurses will kindly plug all the holes in his body so that he won't leak over the sheets, and lastly they'll cover his face. Someone will close his eyes, holding down the lids for just long enough while gazing rather abstractedly into the middle distance, just as they gaze at their watches while taking his pulse.

The skin is pouched under his eyes. The flesh is being raked off him. Not a pretty sight, Giles old boy. No one would want to touch you now. The nurses have to, because it's their job. There doesn't seem to be anybody much left, otherwise.

It's like being at a party, in a crowded room, holding forth, everybody round you, laughing, the faces shiny and the mouths open. Every time your glass empties someone fills it. You breathe in smoke and hot perfume and you come to a climax: roars of laughter, waves of it, billows of it over the heads of the guests and out through the open windows. You are raised up. You are invincible, your words like a thousand swords flashing in the air over your head. *Old Giles is on terrific form tonight*. And then, between one drink and the next, they are gone. The room is half-empty. More than half-empty. The wreaths of cigarette smoke are cold. Your hostess stands by the door with a fixed, weary smile, looking straight ahead of her. You stumble, and can't remember where you put your coat.

"Goodnight," you say. As you lean in to kiss her cheek she turns away so that you brush on nothing.

"Goodnight, Giles," she answers, and her voice is cold, admonitory.

You go down the steps, grasping the railing, and don't know what it is that you've done. The square is full of massed, inky shadow. You'll walk home to sober up. Damn her anyway, silly bitch, a wet blanket if ever there was one. Shouldn't give a party if she doesn't like parties. They were laughing. They loved every moment of it.

No one much has come to see him. The best of them are dead anyway. His real friends. Mulching the ditches of Normandy. That line out of *The Waste Land* about the ships at Mylae and some character called Stetson. The ships at Mylae. Quinqueremes and triremes. You'd have been in a damned sight of trouble at school if you didn't remember about Mylae, and Giles still does. The defeat of Hannibal Gisco at sea, in 260 BC. Pretty bloody unlikely to have a chap called Stetson at Mylae, but there you are.

That bloody T. S. Eliot. What the hell did he know anyway? Where was he in the war he wrote about so well? The First World War. He was at Oxford. All that stuff about corpses sprouting. Corpses don't sprout, Tom old boy, not in any war. They swell up until the features disappear. They fall apart. They rot in ditches instead of leaping over them.

Some of us survive and end up in Berlin and there are women still wearing their damned Nazi badges on the inside of their coats as they dig their country out of the rubble.

Wirtschaftswunder, that was the word for it. Economic miracle. Led by pretty much the same bunch of old Nazis that had run everything through the thirties and forties, as far as Giles could see. And the same bloody fools let them do it, and talked about building a fortress against Communism in the heart of Europe. *Giles, old boy, your Russian's rather good, isn't it? We need chaps like you to keep an eye on what the Soviets are up to.* Men who had about as much conscience as my hairbrush, prating about freedom.

Sister has asked him about his next of kin. When he was first admitted, he gave them Ma Clitterold's name, making a joke of it. But Sister was serious: she wanted more. A brother or sister, perhaps? Perhaps not, thought Giles. Lucy was two years younger than him, and what she didn't know about breeding English springer spaniels wasn't worth knowing. The last time they met, Lucy had held forth about the dogs' ear infections while posting potted-meat sandwiches into her mouth. She didn't ask Giles about his own life: never had done. Probably well aware that she wouldn't like the answers. She couldn't imagine why anyone would want to pig it in a London flat, when they might live in the country.

Lucy is a parody of what she has set out to be. He remembers her at six, dipping her finger into warm puddles of gin and tonic after one of their parents' parties. She was always afraid when the noise rose, voices blurred, and doors flew open with a crash. Well, she got away as fast as she could, down to deepest Dorset, where she married a man without curiosity, had no children, bred her dogs.

Lucy would bury him. He could rely on her for that. She probably *would* send the Kandinsky to a jumble sale. He ought to do something about that bloody Kandinsky, but he's too tired. He can't be bothered. There's no one much he wants to see.

The nurses are very good. Sometimes, when they hold a beaker to his lips, he sees those same hands making him comfortable for the last time. He's stopped being afraid of drowning in the fluid that gathers in his lungs. He couldn't ask Anstruther about it, but one night he asked Sister. She said there was no need for him to worry about that. They would continue to drain off the fluid, and when the time was right, they would increase the morphine to make him more comfortable. She explained what morphine did when it was administered in the right doses.

"Mr Anstruther is very good on morphine," she said, and wiped his face.

Good on morphine, Giles gathers, means giving a patient lots of it. Well, he's all for that. When the time comes that's what he'll want: the warmth of it trickling through him and the distance it brings.

In the morning, Sister stands by his bed, holding his wrist. "Have you thought any more about your next of kin?" she asks mildly, keeping her eyes on the watch that is pinned to her uniform.

He grunts. Lucy won't do. He doesn't want Lucy here, getting in the way when he's dying. Or worse still, that husband of hers. He supposes that if one had a child, things would be quite different. A son, for instance.

It's this weakness that makes him think of Simon Callington. Simon in prison. It's done, it's over, what the hell is the point? If Giles were himself, he would put Simon out of mind, quick-sharp. But he's not himself.

Those digs Simon had on the Madingley Road. A wretched narrow little bed. Simon wasn't like all the others. He was there with Giles because he wanted to be, and as soon as he stopped wanting, he'd be gone. It made things easy but at the same time it made them more difficult than Giles had ever known. You couldn't press Simon. He would write his essay, and finish it too. He would heat up his baked beans as if it were the best meal in the world. He didn't seem to have any family that he cared about, and he threw his mother's cheese out of the window. Nothing had ever made Giles forget that glancing smile Simon gave him as he turned away. And those letters. There'd never been anything like those letters. He'd kept them all.

He'd been drinking whisky that afternoon in Cambridge, while Simon wrote at his rickety desk. Nothing in that room was made properly, or worked properly. Simon didn't care. The whisky bottle was by the bed, and Giles drank steadily, but not too much. The gas fire popped, because one of its elements was broken. Simon drank his own glass of milk, and then the glass he had poured for Giles. He was talking about his forthcoming National Service, and Giles was thinking about nothing much, when suddenly it hit him that if there was another war, Simon would go to it.

It must be how people felt when they had children. Giles had flinched. His flesh had crawled at the thought of Simon's flesh, battered, broken open, rotting. At his eyes, full of shock and offence at his own dying. He'd wanted to gather Simon into him and hold him there so that no war would ever be able to tear him away. But that was all nonsense, of course.

There was never an afternoon like that one again. Never in his life.

Simon can't come to see him, because he is in prison. There's nothing to be done about that. He won't want to see Giles, even if he could. He must hate me now, thinks Giles.

You can't make an omelette without breaking eggs. Was Simon an egg? Ridiculous, when you looked at it like that. But someone has to suffer. *Today the struggle*, and all that. History was stronger than either of them. Inevitable, that was the word. Better not look too closely at what you believe, Giles old son, or you may find that there's nothing there. He's followed that rule for a good many years now. Trotting home with his files.

Clowde has what it takes. Very soon he'll be Sir Julian. I'm not like him. That poor bastard Petrenko thought he was getting a passport and a new life in exchange for the bank vault of information he was going to open. But Julian wasn't having that. He knew which numbers to call: he always did. Petrenko must have been careless, they said later. The Soviets must have got suspicious, guessed that Petrenko was about to fly the coop. Petrenko was trussed up in the back of a car, mouth taped, ears taped, eyes taped. And then a flight back to Moscow. He'd have been begging them to kill him long before they obliged. They had him taped all right. He'd been going to spill the beans. The Julian bean and the Giles bean and God knows what other beans beside. You can't make an omelette out of beans.

Compared to Clowde, Giles was a bit of a joke, with his excellent Russian and his loudmouthing at parties. He got out his Minox and his measuring chain and photographed trivia for other trivial men to look at in offices God knew where. And so one thing leads to another, and that is your life.

Simon is in prison.

Simon with him in that room in Cambridge.

Not Simon with his three children and his pure-as-a-lily-in-the-dell. Not that Simon. The boy: his boy. The only one out of all those boys.

Who are you trying to fool? Simon wasn't a boy then, and he certainly wasn't yours. He was there in that room with you on that afternoon you're making so much of, but only because he wanted to be. As soon as he stopped wanting it, he was gone. Simon took a good look at you guzzling your dinner at the club and decided that he could do better. He thumbed a lift back to Cambridge, wrote more essays, no doubt threw more cheese out of the window. What he wanted wasn't you.

328

He's in prison. They don't pick oakum in prisons any more, or make them work treadmills. It's a soft life, compared to Oscar's. "Everything about my tragedy has been hideous, mean, repellent, lacking in style . . ." They don't make them wear uniforms with big arrows on them any more, either, so that people can spit on them on station platforms when they are transferred from prison to prison.

Giles turns his head on the hospital pillow. I am mean, repellent and lacking in style. I look in the mirror and see that I am hideous. But I am not the one in prison. I have nurses, and a soft bed. They will look after me as I sink down into death, and help me not to suffer any more than I have to.

No, I'm not like Julian Clowde. I'm worse.

"I should like to make my will," says Giles to Sister, the next morning. "I want to see a solicitor."

"Is there a family solicitor I could telephone?"

"Ross and Witherside. Holborn. They're in the book. Ask for Ross."

"I'll give them a ring now."

"I'll need my pen, and writing paper. I must make some notes before he comes. And something to lean on. An envelope. I must have an envelope."

He starts to cough. His chest heaves, thick with disease. He can't get his breath.

"Gently, Mr Holloway. Let me prop you up a little more."

"Can't —"

"It's all right. Breathe in slowly, through the mask."

Better now. A lifeline. He won't drown this time. Cast up on the bed, soaked in sweat. Sister holds the mask to his face. Hiss of oxygen and the cylinder squatting there, making him safe. He keeps going.

"I'm just going to give you an injection," says another voice, a male voice this time. A doctor. Not Anstruther.

The windows are mauve, because another day is going. The day went so fast. One minute it was morning and now it's almost dark. He must have been asleep for a long time. He feels better. The mask has been tidied away, but the oxygen cylinder is by his bed, waiting for him to need it. He panicked, that's all it was. There was never any question of drowning.

Sister stands in the doorway, dressed in her cape. "You've had a good sleep," she says. "I'm going off duty now. Sister Donnelly's on tonight."

He likes Sister Donnelly. Euphoric, he loves them all. What the hell was in that injection?

"Oh, and you've got a visitor. Do you feel up to it?"

"Who is it?"

Simon, he thinks crazily. Simon, out of prison and twenty again. My Simon. My boy.

"He said his name was Clowde. Julian Clowde. A silver-haired gentleman."

She's impressed. People always are. She'll go off duty and leave me with that devil.

"I don't want to see him."

"Are you sure?" Her voice humours him. "It might do you good to have some company."

He holds her eyes. "No. Don't let him in."

Her face changes. She nods, a quick, professional nod, and turns, to find Julian Clowde standing behind her, gleaming under the light. Her cape seems to spread, to widen, blocking the doorway.

"My patient is tired," she says. "He isn't well enough for visitors today."

"I'll only stay a few minutes."

"I'm afraid I can't allow it."

"My dear lady . . ." he protests smoothly, and makes as if to push past her, but years of lifting and carrying have made Sister strong. Giles sees her put out a hand, flat against Clowde's chest, stalling him.

"I won't have my patient disturbed," she says, and then, raising her voice, "Nurse Davies! I want you here a moment."

But Clowde has already stepped back. He's a head taller than Sister, but he won't want a row. He never does. That's the genius of the man. When things might go against him, suddenly Julian Clowde isn't there. He melts away, never implicated. Not once seen to be baffled or confounded, in all the long years that Giles has known him. He has already stepped back, as if nothing was ever further from his mind than bullying his way to Giles's bedside. He sweeps a hand over his hair.

"Another time, then," he says, his voice light, as if it was all nothing. A mere bagatelle. That's one of Julian's favourite phrases. Sister will doubt herself, watching that elegant, silver-haired figure walk off down the corridor.

She watches him out of sight, then comes into Giles's room, shutting the door behind her. "I'm going to leave instructions that no visitors are to be admitted. They must send up their names and you can decide if you want to see them."

She understands. She hasn't been fooled, unlike all those others whom Julian Clowde has fooled over the years. The silver hair cut no ice with Sister. She saw that Giles was afraid. She'd know about fear; yes, she would recognise it.

Giles nods. He wants to thank her but doesn't trust his voice. He is so damned weak. But he must tell her that he's got to see a solicitor now. Ross or anyone else, it doesn't matter, as long as they can come straight away. Before they do, he must write a letter. Get Sister Donnelly to give him more oxygen, and anything else she's got that will keep a pen moving in his hand for long enough to finish his letter.

CHAPTER
TWENTY-SIX

Points of Desperation

Lily in the evening, by the sea-coal fire, with the children asleep upstairs. Or so she thinks. They can be silent when they want. Paul and Sally sit on Paul's bed up in the attic, wrapped in blankets like Indian braves, talking in voices which don't reach beyond each other's ears. They sit like this most nights. Bridget's asleep, Mum's downstairs, and they are free. They talk about Dad, and what's going to happen to him. They talk about Mum, and what she'll do without Dad. They never reach an answer.

"I hate those books where there's a mystery but the children solve it and they all go home for tea."

"They're rubbish."

"Do you think the people who write them know they're rubbish?"

"Why should they care? They just want to finish their books off."

"If Dad did get out of prison — just suppose, I know it's not going to happen — do you think he'd get his job back?"

"They're not going to let someone who's been in prison work for the government."

"That's what I thought," agrees Sally quickly.

It has been a long day. Lily's day off. She walked to the station, took the branch line and then changed to the London train. She's used to the journey now. She didn't bring a book, or buy a newspaper. She sat with her hands in her lap and looked out of the window. She might have been going up to town for a day's shopping.

When she got home again, the children were waiting. Bridget jumped round her, over-excited. She'd told Bridget that she was going up to see the people who were renting their house. There were some things that needed sorting out. The elder two knew she'd been to the prison. They were wary and knew better than to ask questions in front of their little sister.

"Dad was well," she said to them later, when Bridget had gone to bed. "He sent you all his love."

Sally's eyes darkened. She doesn't believe a word I say, thought Lily. She ought not to look like that, at her age.

At last she's alone. Every moment of the visit is tightly rolled up inside her. Now she can spread it out, and pore over it.

Simon was pale. "It's the indoor life," he said when she asked him if he was well. "How are the children?"

She told him about Paul's visit to the grammar school where he'd be going in September. He'd liked the science labs.

"Good," said Simon. "Do you think it's a decent place, Lily?"

"It has a very good reputation."

"He's a clever boy, he'll do well," said Simon, as if he were talking about someone else's son.

"Yes," said Lily.

"Is there a proper lock on the front door?"

"What?"

"The door of the cottage. Could someone get in round the back? Have the doors got good locks?"

"I don't know. They look all right. I haven't really noticed, it's so quiet down there —"

"Get a locksmith."

She held his gaze. "I will."

He mustn't be worrying about things like that. His fingers were beating on the table in nervous rhythm. She wondered what song he was marking out. He loved those old music-hall songs, but when he sang them to her they meant nothing. She thought the words silly, though she never said so. He whistled while he worked on Paul's train set. Something was always going wrong. A buckled rail or a tender that wouldn't couple. Paul was almost as good as his father now, when it came to working out where the problem lay. Now the train set was put away in the loft of their old house, and Paul might be too old for it before they went back.

Simon made her feel safe. They were safe together. When they met each other's gaze over the heads of their children, what they felt was for them alone. No one else could touch it. Now she was cut loose, and the children too. Dr Wiseman had looked round their house in Muswell Hill and thought only of what would suit his own family. He hadn't cared tuppence about the Callingtons. Why should he?

All over Berlin, thousands of deserted apartments were taken over by new inhabitants. Soon it was as if the new people had lived there for ever. Those who'd gone weren't missed. Good riddance to them: let them go to the East or wherever it was that they'd gone. That was for the government to deal with.

Dr Wiseman comes from America. Of course he puts his own family first, it's only natural, and if you didn't have his rent you wouldn't be able to pay the mortgage. You'd have to sell the house.

The lock on the back door in Muswell Hill was so weak that a child could push it open. It had never bothered them, until the day the police came.

"There are bolts on the cottage doors, front and back, as well as the locks," she said. "They're rusty but if I oiled them they'd work."

Simon glanced quickly at the warder on his left, then back to her. She understood that there was something he had to tell her, but they were listening. She tensed, and gave him an almost imperceptible nod, to let him know that she was listening too.

"I wish I'd worked harder in French lessons at school," he said, out of nowhere. She frowned, to show she hadn't got it. "Must be wonderful", he went on, looking at her, "to be able to say whatever you like in another language. I end up talking absolute rubbish."

She had it now. He was telling her that he would try to say something to her in French. His French wasn't good, and besides the warders wouldn't allow them to talk in a foreign language. But if he were quick, something could be said.

"I'm used to it," she said. "You should have heard what the children used to come out with, at school."

He nodded. He knew she'd understood. "I like that scarf you're wearing," he said conversationally. "It's new, isn't it? It looks like a French design. A Monsieur Nuage . . ."

The warder glanced at him, looked away again. He was a decent man and didn't like sitting staring at man and wife.

She sat silent, willing herself. Her brain whirred and caught. The words had meaning because they were not words, but a name.

Mr Cloud . . .

She'd got it. Julian Clowde. It was something about him.

"Yes, it's pretty, isn't it?"

"Very. He's such a good designer. A master designer."

Now she had it. She could touch the words.

"But they're temperamental, those types," went on Simon. "You have to be careful not to upset them. It's the artistic temperament. I used to know another designer like him — not as senior, but still pretty good. The pressure got to him, though. He started drinking and then he lost his touch."

"I think I know the one you mean."

"Yes. The problem is that these chaps have regular customers, and customers like that want new stuff all the time. They get impatient."

"I suppose the designs become well known."

"Sometimes, although the designers don't want the limelight. They're happy to do the work and let others take the credit."

"Oh, I see," said Lily. The warder on Simon's left wasn't happy. He was wondering what the hell they were going on about. They hadn't much time now.

"Tricky lot, these artistic types," said Simon. His eyes were points of desperation. Did she follow him?

"I count myself lucky that you haven't got an artistic bone in your body," she said, and although he didn't smile, for the first time his face warmed and lightened. He had understood her. He knew that she had understood him.

"Where did you buy your scarf?"

"Oh, Liberty's. They're pricey, but you can be sure you're getting the real thing."

"You'd never buy anything from a door-to-door salesman, would you?"

"I'd shut the door in his face."

"You shouldn't open the door, Lil. Not even if they're selling high-quality stuff like Monsieur Nuage."

"I shan't."

He wanted to give her a shotgun, a tank, a machine gun. He wanted to weep because she'd understood him. How had that happened? But he knew, really. He'd always known what it was that set Lily apart, even when she wanted so much not to be. Lily had lived in fear before she knew why she was afraid. She'd grown up knowing that people hated her. Perfectly ordinary people, the kind of adults who ought to be helping her to cross the road, hated Lily and wanted her gone. That was the climate of her childhood. It was the rain that fell on her every time she went out of that apartment she rarely talked about, into the streets of Berlin.

"I almost forgot," he went on. "You know those leather gloves I lost? I think they must have fallen behind the children's wellingtons. Could you have a look?"

He'd been right. He knew it now for certain. Lily had taken the file. He was sure of it when she gave him again that tiny, almost imperceptible nod.

"Oh," she said, "I should have told you. I found them and put them away."

That's my girl, he thought. You found them and put them away. He has never known Lily do any job other than thoroughly. Monsieur Nuage can whistle for it now. But he knows, too. That bastard knows.

"Remember," he said. "Keep the doors locked."

The fire is slumping into red ash. Lily will let it die down now. She'll put on the kettle for her hot-water bottle, then go out to the privy. It's a windy night. Giles Holloway, Julian Clowde. There are others, no doubt. They will be holding their breath, waiting for Simon to go down and so release them all. It will all be pinned on Simon. That's what they want.

She is the only one who knows where the briefcase is. She wonders how long it will take for it to dissolve into the earth. Probably the brass fittings will remain and be identifiable. Even if the Wiseman children were to play in the copse, it's very unlikely that they would ever find it.

Suddenly it comes to her that she won't go out to the privy tonight. All that darkness seems to be bulging against the back door. She'll use the chamber pot.

Lily gets up. In a box on the top kitchen shelf there are some odds and ends from Simon's toolbox. It was Paul who'd thought of bringing them: "We're bound to need these, Mum."

How sensible he was. A hammer, a couple of screwdrivers, sandpaper, a can of oil, a paper bag of hooks and nails. Lily gets the sandpaper, the oil and the rag. She'd tried to put the bolts across earlier, and given up because they were too stiff. Rusted in. She could have asked Paul to oil them. He'd have been glad to do it, but she didn't want to alarm the children.

Now, Lily fetches a kitchen chair and props it by the back door. As the wind gusts it brings the noise of the sea. She wouldn't hear anything if someone were moving about in the garden tonight. Panic prickles at her neck. She climbs up, and directs the nozzle of the oilcan into the top bolt. There's another at the bottom. Mrs Woolley has told her that years ago this was a coastguard's cottage, and smugglers round this way had guns: "So did the coastguard, mind, in these out-of-the-way places."

There's a lot of rust. Lily works away at it with the oily rag. It would be easier to do this by daylight, with the door standing open, but she can't leave it now. She twists the sandpaper, and flakes of rust loosen. After a while, the bolt eases.

Lily treats all the bolts, top and bottom on both doors, then slides them home. In the hearth there are two pokers: the stout everyday one, blackened with soot, and a slim, whippety brass poker that looks as if it belongs to a fire-set. Lily pauses, then picks up the brass poker and puts it behind the front door. She does this quickly, ashamed of herself.

The children will notice the bolts, unless she's up before them. She'll explain that out in quiet country places, people do bolt their doors. She isn't sure that Paul will be fooled. She has seen his eyes on her. He knows that she visited Dad in prison today. Neither he nor Sally asked questions beyond — once Bridget was safely out of the room — "Did you give Dad our love?"

"Of course," she said. "Of course I did. And Dad sent his love back."

Later, she said to Bridget, "Dad loved the drawing you did for him. I sent it with my letter."

"Did he put it up in his cabin in his ship?"

"Yes, straight away, he said."

She saw Paul and Sally exchange glances. Just before Lily left Simon had said, "Tell the children —" But nothing more. She couldn't bring herself to make up any further message for them. It was all right to say that he sent his love. That wasn't a lie, even if Simon hadn't spoken.

The doors are safe now. I shan't go to bed tonight, I'll stay down here by the fire. And then, if anything happens . . .

Lily brings down her pillow and a blanket and curls herself into the armchair. Now that the light is off, there's a faint glow of red in the hearth. The cottage grows cold quickly. You can't keep warmth in it. Lily drowses, starts awake, drowses again. The wind is dying down. Good, that means she'll be able to hear footsteps if anyone comes. But would she hear anything? The earth is so soft — deep and soft — good for burying things . . .

She sleeps. It's the night before Paul's birth. Lily walks and walks around the hospital's central corridor. She has discovered that she can do a circuit. The ugly linoleum gleams under the lights. Sometimes a nurse goes by, but no one stops Lily. Her bed in the antenatal ward will be growing cold.

A muscle surge comes from deep inside her, lifting her stomach up. It tightens and then it lets go. This has been happening for hours now. Lily looks at her wristwatch and finds it is ten to three. She has been walking like this since just after midnight. At first she lay in bed, shifting position, trying to make herself comfortable. It was impossible. Her back hurt too much. She clambered out of bed, stuck her feet into her slippers and put on her dressing gown although she was too hot. The nurse at her desk looked up. Lily smiled and pointed.

"I can't sleep," she whispered. "I'm going to sit in the dayroom."

"Are you all right?"

"I'm fine. I'll read for a while."

She didn't want to tell the nurse anything. She'd had a show that afternoon, and some contractions. They'd told her to come in, and then nothing more had happened. It was as if everything inside her froze as soon as she got to the hospital. The nurses were brisk. Doctor would examine her, but it didn't look as if anything was happening. Simon had visited her at half past six, and sat by her bed for an awkward hour before the bell rang and he had to go home. They would send Lily home too, in the morning. She wasn't going to make a fool of herself again, imagining she was in labour when the nurses knew it was a false alarm.

It was all right as long as she kept moving. The surges were now so strong that she had to stop and lean against the wall until they passed. But it can't be labour, she thought. In labour, women writhed on beds and screamed. She would keep quiet. She would keep on walking.

Outside the windows, it was still dark. Simon would be at home, asleep. Her side of the bed would be cold. She gasped, and held on to the wall, and then she moved on again. She must walk. No one must know. It was better to be alone.

Later, a midwife saw her holding on to a window-ledge. Lily couldn't speak when the woman questioned her.

"My goodness, dear," said the midwife when she had got Lily back into bed and was examining her, "you're halfway there. Whatever were you thinking of, wandering about like that?"

Lily wakes. It's still dark but she thinks it's close to morning. She's stiff all over from sleeping in the chair. She stumbles to the light-switch, turns it on and looks at her watch. It's quarter to six. The night is over.

CHAPTER
TWENTY-SEVEN

Monsieur Nuage

The crust on Mr Austin's rabbit pie glistens gold. Rabbit pie, potatoes, cabbage, the gravy boat. Lily carries everything into the dining room, where Mr Austin is already unrolling his napkin.

"My word, that looks good!"

"I hope so. Be careful, the plate is hot."

She cuts into the pastry. Savoury steam gushes out. He will take five potatoes, or even six, and yet he is so thin. But he won't enjoy them. So much politeness: he is so grateful, always. She puts the gravy boat at his right hand.

"Smells delicious," he says, and then, "You know, Mrs Callington, I'd very much like you to stay and have lunch with me. You'd be doing me a favour. This rabbit pie could feed a regiment."

"I thought you might have it cold, for supper tomorrow," she says. "I'd like to stay for lunch, but I've got the cleaning to do this afternoon, before the children come home from school. They go down to the beach, you know, but they need something to eat first. It's very kind of you."

"I know how busy you are. Keeping those Young Turks fed and watered is pretty much a full-time job in itself. And this barn of a place on top of it. Not kind of me at all, you know, about lunch. Selfish, in fact. Well, one of these days." He pauses, and then adds more briskly, "Might be worth telling them to be careful with Bridget on the jetty. There are underwater obstructions farther out, from the war. You can get a tidal race."

"I've told them not to go out on it. Paul and Sally are very sensible."

"Of course they are."

"I enjoy coming here," she says, because it's true and also because of his thin face and the shyness in it when he said *one of these days.*

"That's awfully nice of you," he says.

"I'll see you tomorrow."

"I look forward to it."

He is lonely. Very likely he thinks she is lonely too. He's an educated man. He reads his *Times* every day. Will he have recognised her name? Callington is not such an unusual name, but there were photographs in the papers, and an article underneath about "the suburban house where Simon Callington lived with his wife and three children. A quiet house in a quiet street, like thousands of others all over England . . ." But not like them, the papers insinuated. Without ever quite saying it, they told their readers that this particular quiet house was different, because it contained a traitor who had hidden himself in plain view, in these calm, orderly streets where a cat stretched itself in the sun and children made their way home from school with

346

satchels on their backs. These were Englishmen's streets.

In the photograph their house looked so bland that it was almost sinister. The newsprint smeared on her fingers as she bundled the paper out of the way. Mr Austin wouldn't read those rags. There was no photograph in *The Times*.

Lily hurries through the village, and out on to the coast road. Mrs Woolley has said she can paint the bedrooms, if she likes. Lily has ordered white emulsion from the village hardware store, and it is to be delivered at two o'clock. She hopes to start work later in the afternoon, when she's finished cleaning. Paul and Sally will help when they come home. They are both careful.

She wraps herself in a print overall. Sunlight pours in and bounces off the walls as she dusts, sweeps, mops and polishes. There is no vacuum cleaner here. Never mind. The place is small and easily cleaned now she has put most of Mrs Woolley's clutter into the cupboard under the stairs. Lily's spirits rise. There's a clump of early daffodils in bud on the south-facing bank behind the cottage. She'll bring a few indoors and they'll flower on the windowsill. The paint should be here soon — Mr Harding said that he'd drop it round —

There, that's the door. Lily runs downstairs, wiping her hands on her wrapper. She's excited at the thought of laying clean white paint over the shabby walls. It was an extravagance, but worth it —

She pulls the door open wide.

And there he is. She knows him at once, as if some part of her has always known he'll come. Monsieur

Nuage. He cuts a smart figure on the cracked path. His hair is like corrugated iron, but white. He has taken off his hat and holds it in front of him, as if he's attending a funeral. A dark overcoat and a dandyish yellow scarf at his neck. She sizes him up rapidly. He's five feet ten perhaps. She remembers the cut of him from the parties she attended with Simon. That coat flatters him. He's not so well made. How strong is he?

Her hair is tied up in a scarf. With that and the wrapper, she must look like Mrs Mopp.

"I'm afraid I've caught you at a bad moment," he says.

"Not at all."

"May I come in?"

There's the sound of a car engine. Something coming along the lane from the village. It'll be Harding's van, and she doesn't want anyone to see Julian Clowde on her doorstep.

"Come in," she says. "This will be a delivery for me." He steps inside so swiftly that she realises he doesn't want to be seen either. "Do sit down," she says, pointing at a chair by the cold fireplace. A grey van rattles to the gate and stops. A lad jumps out.

"Paint delivery for you, Mrs Callington," he sings out, and opens the double doors at the back of the van with a flourish. He swings two large tins of paint to the ground. "Shall I bring these in for you? Heavy, they are."

"No, it's all right, leave them here on the doorstep. I'm cleaning and the floor's wet. Have you got the brushes?"

He whistles. "Lucky you said. They're in the back." He dives down, and brings up a brown-paper parcel. "Here you are. You got a big job on then, cleaning up this place."

"Yes." She smiles at him. How nice he is, with the low sun gilding his quick face. A decent boy. She'd like to give him a cup of tea, but — "I'd better get on," she says. "Everything's upside down."

"No rest for the workers, eh?"

He executes a dashing three-point turn, and rattles off again. Lily steps back into the dark cottage, carrying the brushes. There is no one in the room.

"Mr Clowde," she calls sharply, thinking of him upstairs, prying in her bedroom, but he emerges from the kitchen at once. "It was only the delivery boy from Harding's," she says. "No need to hide."

"My dear Mrs Callington, I was thinking of your reputation. This is a small place."

She lifts her shoulders. "I'm afraid I can't offer you anything. I'm in the middle of decorating."

"I shouldn't dream of giving you any trouble."

Then why are you here? thinks Lily. You could have sent someone, but you've come yourself, all the way to East Knigge . . .

"Did you get a taxi from the station?"

"Do you know, I walked. It was such a beautiful day," he says, as if the day is over, or has stopped being beautiful.

You didn't want anyone to know you were coming here, thinks Lily. But just imagine how conspicuous you must have been, walking through the village in your yellow scarf. Food for hours of gossip.

"It's a pretty village, isn't it?" she asks satirically.

"I've no idea. I took a footpath from the station, over the fields."

She looks at his feet, disbelievingly, but sure enough he is wearing thick brogues, and there is mud on them. Damn him. Mud on her clean floors. He hasn't even bothered to wipe them. That's how much he thinks of her. Well, better to know that. Her heart is beating quickly. She feels alive twice over, and her mind shuttles from thought to thought so quickly that she has woven them into cloth almost before she's conscious of them.

Simon warned her about Julian Clowde. Now he's here. Did Simon know or suspect that he would come, or was it someone else whom Simon feared, someone Julian Clowde might send? And for what purpose? To warn her, to silence her, to make her talk about the briefcase?

They don't know where it is. She's sure of that.

"I wasn't expecting you," she says calmly, off-handedly she hopes. "No one from the department has even been to see me."

"Very remiss of us. But you can understand why, I hope, with so much going on. It has been rather a time." He looks at her, his eyebrows raised. "Do you fancy a spot of fresh air?"

She tenses. Is someone else out there, waiting? He's uneasy. He doesn't like being in here — why not? He

350

flicks a glance around the room. He doesn't want to talk here.

Oh, for heaven's sake, she almost says aloud. You can't think there is a hidden microphone. Where would I get such a thing? What world do you think I live in?

But there's the briefcase. That other world has already touched her. Perhaps he thinks she went to talk to someone about the briefcase. But how could she do that, without him hearing of it? Julian Clowde's desk is where everything stops. So who else could he be worried about?

"Of course, we can go out if you like," she says. "The track only goes down to the beach. It'll be quiet there now. People come at low tide to pick sea coal but it's high tide now."

"It sounds positively Dickensian."

"Coal is expensive." They are outside the front door when suddenly she looks down at herself. She is still wearing her print overall. "Excuse me a moment, I must just fetch my coat."

They walk side by side down the rutted track. She has the strange sense that the longer she keeps Julian Clowde here, the better for Simon. The sun is low now, and behind them, throwing down shadow. The children will be coming out of school soon. Ahead is the white intensity of sky over water. High tide. The beach will be deserted.

"Yes," muses Julian Clowde, "it's been a tricky time for everyone. Confusing. Or perhaps less so, from your point of view. Women usually know what their husbands are up to, even though it's sometimes expedient to pretend ignorance."

How contemptuously he said that.

"Let's not beat about the bush," said Lily, and even after all these years she can't rid herself of pleasure at finding occasion to use such a typically English idiom. "You're saying that Simon has been photographing confidential documents and passing them on — to *Russians*, is that it? — quite regularly. Like those Portland people. You are insinuating that I knew about it. Is that the case?"

"You mean, is it the case that I think that?"

"Let's not split hairs. That's what you're saying. That's what you're all saying. That's why Simon was arrested, and it's what the trial will be about."

"Because of what we said, do you mean, rather than because of what he did?" A faint, insulting emphasis on the pronouns. "Oh come on, Mrs Callington, I'm not having that. Injured innocence won't wash at this stage of the game."

"None of it is a game, as far as I'm concerned."

He leans forward as they crest the small slope which runs down in a shingle bank to the water. "Desolate place, isn't it? I suppose that jetty must have been in use once. Your husband has had every chance. He's a small fish — any jury will see that, if they get the right direction. He was made use of. The Soviets are frightfully clever at spotting the weakest link. I doubt if he'll get more than seven years. Your job, my dear Mrs Callington, will be to keep the home fires burning. We shan't abandon you. You shouldn't have taken it

352

personally. No one from the department came to see you — well, of course not. Not immediately. What did you expect? If you'd only been a little more patient . . . Whatever possessed you to drop everything and come rushing down here? We'll make sure that you and the children are taken care of."

"Who will?"

"I beg your pardon?"

"Who is this 'we' you keep talking about? I'm not sure I understand."

"Mrs Callington, I don't think you are listening. I've come here to tell you that you have nothing to worry about. You must reassure your husband. He has nothing to fear."

"Apart from seven years in prison, you mean?"

For a moment she sees something move in his eyes, like the click of a camera shutter. "There are worse things than that," he says lightly, evenly. Their feet crunch over the pebbles. It's just as Lily knew: the beach is deserted at this time. She drops her shoulders and breathes out slowly.

"Perhaps you'd like to tell me what those worse things might be," she says. Again that flick. Surprise, or calculation. She isn't quite what he expected? Or is she flattering herself? He has the air of a man who holds himself ready to expect everything, and can adapt himself so quickly you won't even see the change.

"Utter disgrace," he says.

"Utter disgrace? You keep saying things that haven't got any meaning."

"Not for you, perhaps. Let me put it another way: *Eine wahre Schande*. Is that clearer?"

"I don't speak German."

"But you are aware that physical relationships between men are illegal in this country. Sexual relationships, to be more precise."

"I don't know what you mean." She has stopped, and is facing him. Behind her is the sea, and his face is exposed by its light. He's implacable, like a machine that will keep on coming at her. How could she ever have dismissed him as a typically buttoned-up English public-school gentleman? That was what she'd called him, to Simon. Stupid, ignorant complacency. Now she's frightened of him. He mustn't see that she's frightened.

"Let me show you something," he says. He unbuttons the top button of his coat, and takes an envelope from his inside pocket. He turns it so that the address faces her. "Look at the postmark," he says, but she's looking at the handwriting. Simon's handwriting. The letter is addressed to Giles Holloway. "Take it. Open it."

"I don't want to. It's not addressed to me."

"I can read it to you, if you prefer."

She takes the letter. The hatred in him makes her quail. It's not so much that he hates her personally. She's not significant enough for that, but she's in his way and has to be got out of it.

She opens the envelope, torn open carelessly years ago. She takes out the folded letter. There are several sheets. She lowers her head, and turns slightly away from Julian Clowde as she reads.

You think I'm writing my essay, but I'm not. I'm writing to you. "Bloody freezing out there," you said when you took off your coat. "And not much better in here." You shook out your handkerchief and blew your nose like a trumpet. Your shoes creaked as you walked across the room to my bed, and then you sat down heavily, your knees apart, and said, "Well? Aren't you going to give me a drink?" I love the shoes you wear. You told me where you'd had them made. I could pick your shoes out from a thousand pairs. You think I don't know much about you, but I do. I know how heavy you are and how your breath stinks when you've been sleeping after too much whisky. Whatever too much whisky is. That's one of your sayings. You lie on your back and snore with your mouth open. It doesn't make any difference to me. It should do, shouldn't it? You don't like the way you look. I shouldn't think anyone else guesses that.

"Don't grow old, Simon," you say, and I say, "For Christ's sake, Giles, you're still in your thirties."

In a little while I'll get up and yawn and say, "I've finished my essay," and you'll be pleased because it means I've stopped pissing about and we can go to bed, or have dinner, or whatever it is you want. Probably bed, even though we've been in bed for hours. It's what I want too. I smell of you, Giles. I can smell myself. You were so quiet afterwards that I thought you'd fallen asleep, but then you started telling me about returning those gold cufflinks to the shop. I know you were browned off that I wouldn't accept them. God knows what they cost. I also know why you told me what the woman in the shop said, when you explained that your nephew hadn't liked the cufflinks. "The ingrate!" I can just see her, puffing herself up, utterly on your side. You laughed about that. Really laughed, from your belly. But you liked it, didn't you? You like getting people on your side. You'd rolled off me by then but there's never any room in my bed. You were crushed against me still. I don't want any bloody cufflinks, Giles. I'm not one of your boys.

I'll put this letter into the pocket of your coat, for you to find later. You'll probably chuck it on the fire without realising that it's a letter. Never mind. Even thinking about you doing that makes me want to laugh, but I won't, in case you get suspicious. There isn't much to laugh about in the social and economic consequences of currency debasement in the sixteenth century. You're whistling to yourself now, and doing those conductor movements with your index fingers. You'll say: *For Christ's sake, Simon, stop writing that bloody essay and come to bed.*

I don't want to stop writing my essay. I don't want time to move on. I want you to keep on sitting there, looking a bit fed-up, reading your book while you wait for me to finish. I want to hold back, because this is the best part, isn't it, when everything's still to come. I don't want to stop writing to you.

How cold it is. The beach and the raw sound of the sea. That man watching her. The lines burn.

Lily remains bent over the letter. There is blackness inside her, like the time she bled so heavily after Bridget was born. They had to raise the end of the bed.

This is the best part. Everything's still to come. He wrote that. Simon wrote that. He wrote it to Giles Holloway.

I smell of you. What you say after you make love. She has said that. She's licked his skin and tasted it.

She can't look up and meet Julian Clowde's eyes. He's read the letter. God knows who else has read it.

All this, and Simon's never said a word.

There's too much spit in her mouth. She will have to swallow it or she'll be sick. Simon loved Giles Holloway's shoes.

I want to hold back, because this is the best part.

Of course she knows that there are men who want men. They go to Clapham Common, or public lavatories. They are had up in court. But this letter, Simon's letter . . . What a fool she has been. Naïve. Stupid. Did he expect her to guess? Was he waiting for her to come out with it one day: "Oh, Simon, by the way, about Giles Holloway, I've been wondering . . ."

No, he has hidden it from her. He has wanted to hide it. She was never meant to know.

I don't want to stop writing to you.

She and Simon have never written love-letters. Perhaps they were never apart for long enough. But some couples would still write; they would seize a piece of paper and write, even when they were close enough to speak to each other. When they were in the same room. Lily's mother said: "Simon is a typical Englishman. He is shy of his own emotions, and he doesn't want to display them." It was true that Simon never kissed Lily when her mother was there.

We've always been together. There was never any reason for us to write love-letters. If she ever said that aloud — if Simon ever said that — did they look at each other quickly, to see if the other one was convinced, and then as quickly away?

He knew how to write a love-letter, but it was not to me.

Lily presses her lips together, and carefully folds the sheets of paper that she wants to rip into shreds. Her fingers shake, but she controls them. She puts the letter back into the envelope, and pushes its torn edges into place.

"There you are," she says, holding it out to Julian Clowde. She sees his face but she won't look into it.

"Don't you want to keep it?"

"Why should I want to keep it?"

It hurts to speak, because her throat is tight. She must control herself. This man is dangerous, Simon has warned her. Her thoughts veer away from Simon like frightened horses, and then slowly back to him. She must show nothing to Julian Clowde.

When Lili burst through the door of their Berlin apartment, crying, her mother said: "If Frau Müller says anything like that to you again, Lili, don't respond. Come straight up in the lift. Ignore her. Don't show her that you're upset."

I won't think of anything except the children. The children must be safe. The tide is very high. There's hardly any beach. No one will be coming to pick coal until low tide. It shelves so steeply here. If the water wasn't so cold and dirty you could dive straight in from the shingle-bank.

No, Lili, we can't go to the swimming-bath. You know perfectly well why not, so don't keep asking.

"Your husband must plead guilty, and then no one will ever see the letters."

Of course, you have more than one letter, thinks Lily. Even if I'd ripped up that one, you've got more, somewhere safe. And you'll have made copies, too.

"I don't know why you're saying this to me," she says. She needs time. Why has he come here? Something's happened.

"It will all come out otherwise, I'm afraid," sighs Julian Clowde. "It explains everything, you see. Poor Simon was being blackmailed. He lost his head. He took files home and photographed them."

"There are no files," says Lily.

"What do you mean?"

"No one has produced them, have they? You haven't got evidence against Simon. The men who came to our house found nothing."

"My dear girl, you know about the camera that was found in Simon's desk."

"Yes, I know about that."

His voice sharpens. "What do you mean?"

Lily doesn't reply. She shouldn't have said that. He mustn't guess that she's been warned against him. Somehow he has moved her without touching her, so that now she has her back to the sea and he is above her. She glances behind her. The grey tide almost fills the bay now. It's as if coal-dust has got into the water. You can't see through it. Her heart is beating thickly now. She mustn't think about Simon now. She must think only of Julian Clowde.

The sea is behind her and he is blocking her way to the land. She must not panic. The children will be coming out of school, but they know the tides better than she does. They won't come down here. No one will come.

CHAPTER
TWENTY-EIGHT

There's No Ship

Bridget is crying when Sally goes round to the Infants' entrance to fetch her. It's not the usual Bridget hullabaloo. Her face is blotched and her body shudders. She looks as if she's been crying for a long time. The teacher comes out behind her.

"I'm afraid Bridget has been a bit upset," she says, as if Sally is grown up.

"I'll take her home."

"*Mum, Mum,*" weeps Bridget.

Paul catches up as they are going through the village.

"What's up with Bridgie?"

"She wants Mum."

"Come on, Bridget the Pidget, cheer up. Don't you remember? Mum's going to be at home today."

But when they reach the cottage it is empty. Everything is upside-down: Mum's been cleaning. The fire isn't lit. Bridget is now hiccuping with sobs: "I want Mum. I — want — Mu-um."

"She'll be sick if she goes on like this," says Paul.

Sally kneels in front of Bridget and puts her arms around her. "She'll be back soon."

"She won't. She won't," weeps Bridget. "She's gone."

"She thinks Mum's gone away like Dad," says Paul.

"She hasn't, Bridgie, she hasn't, I promise you."

"Yes, she — has."

"Bridgie, we can't hear you if you keep bellowing like that. Listen. I've got half my Mars Bar left. Do you want it?" says Paul.

Bridget's eyes are slits in her swollen face, but she nods her head.

"I thought you would. Now. Stop crying, tell us why you think Mum's gone away, and you can have the Mars Bar."

Sally wipes the snot off Bridget's face. "Come on now. Tell us. Look, Paul's brought the Mars Bar. No. Stop crying first and tell us and you can have it."

"Dad's ship's at the beach. Mum's going away on Dad's ship. I saw them."

"Bridget," says Paul loftily, "that is ridiculous. You didn't see them."

"Don't, Paul." For Bridget is off again. She drops the Mars Bar on the floor and her face shudders as more tears spurt.

"I did see them — I — *did* — see — them — I — *did* . . ."

"Christ," says Paul, sotto voce, "he's not even on a bloody ship."

"Paul!"

"All right then." He bends down to Bridget. "Listen. If you're a good girl and stop that racket I'll take you to the beach. You can have a piggyback."

"Can — you — Can — you — go quickly?"

"Like the wind."

Her arms are wrapped around his neck. Her hot, wet face is pressed to him. It's a bit disgusting, but for once Paul doesn't mind. Something of her fear has got into him too. And into Sal. Where *is* Mum? Why isn't she back?

"What a hole," says Julian Clowde, and he looks around him with contempt. His hands go up and straighten the scarf around his neck. Suddenly, overwhelmingly, Lily's afraid of him. She sees what hides behind that face of an English gentleman. Cold contempt for all the fools who don't know what he really is. Simon used to say how clever he was. *A tremendous charmer when he wants to be, you've no idea, Lil.*

"You should think about your children," he says.

The children. She watches him. Now he has crossed the line into darkness.

"We must think about Lili. This might be our only chance."

"You're being hysterical, Elsa. They're not interested in children; they're interested in Jewish money and Jewish businesses. Besides, even those lunatics can't make out I'm Jewish, just because of Oma. My father was awarded the Iron Cross, for God's sake. You're my wife and Lili is my daughter. We are perfectly safe."

"If you won't think about your own child, I will."

Lily's fear dissolves. Simon and the letter vanish from her mind. Everything in her peels away from the core that was always there and never shows itself. This man speaks to her about her children. This man is threatening them.

She backs away from him, along the shingle, and he follows. Not too fast, not openly threatening. A man like Julian Clowde will make sure he can back off until the last moment.

The jetty. She's forgotten about that. The shingle piles up here at the top of the beach so it's almost flat with the wood. The jetty is a rotten old thing from the days when coal-boats worked this coast. Crabs crawl round the metal stanchions at low tide, and weed drips off the underside of the planking. It's dangerous. She has told the children not to go out on it. It's slippery and the currents around it are strong. She means to cross the jetty and get back on to the shingle on the other side but he's done it again. He is above her, blocking her. She's giving ground. He fingers his yellow scarf again. She doesn't think she's moving but the beach is shrinking away from her. She's going backwards down the jetty.

Simon's brothers are here too. They caught her off guard. They got hold of her because she was half-asleep in the hot sun. That won't happen again. She's on guard now. She puts a hand to the large single button that closes her coat, as if she's clutching at her heart in terror. Now the button's undone. Her left hand slides inside the coat and touches the thin, whippy length of the poker which is jammed into the belt of her overall. Her hand slides out again, free and empty. He is watching every move but he has to glance behind him, quickly, to be sure that no one is coming. She has the advantage of him there.

Her animal self knows now that he means to kill her. That's why he's looking round. That's why he walked from the station over the fields. No one must know he's been here. She sees a flash of him walking the footpath over the muddy fields, back to the station, having taken care of everything. She is a thing he's got to get out of his way. *The briefcase. They know I had it. They know I saw that file. I am in the way.* She steps backwards again. Already the water is deep on either side. Thirty feet of rotting wood and then it stops.

She is up on the balls of her feet. Hair rises on her neck and on her arms as she edges backward, drawing him on. She knows, her feet know, that the planks are coming to an end. He is still moving closer, and Lily Callington vanishes as if she has never been. She is Lili Brand in the hall of their apartment block, jabbing at the lift button as Frau Müller's poison drips into her.

Bald wird der ganze Wohnblock judenfrei sein. Judenfrei — verstehst Du das?

Lili faces the brass railings and presses the lift button. Her mother has told her not to say a word. She wants to pee. If the lift doesn't come she will wet herself and Frau Müller will see the puddle on the floor. The lift clanks but does not come.

Ja, judenfrei! Verstehst Du, was das bedeutet?

And now the sea clucks under the boards and the rage of all those years thickens Lily's voice: "*Ich werde Dich töten, Du schreckliche alte Hexe, Ich werde Dich töten* —"

Her hand is on the hilt of the poker. He is standing between her and her children. He will kill her and they will be alone. He has his scarf undone now, ready. He will strangle her and he will tip her in. She is swaying, light on her feet, watching for his move. Draw him on, draw him almost to the water — He thinks he's got her —

He lunges for her. Light and quick, she slips sideways. He almost has her but his muddy boots skid on the slimy wood. He is right on the edge now, all his weight too far over. His legs scissor like a clown's. Even now he lunges to bring her down with him but with all her strength she shoves him away. He falls backward, grabbing at air, twisting as he goes down. His head strikes against the iron stanchion. He is in the water.

She falls to her knees, shivering. He is on his back, and the water sucks at his black coat. The heavy cloth takes in water, bearing him down. Those brogues too. Now the sea begins to pull him. She is on her knees on the dank wood, watching as he is carried away. He doesn't thrash, or shout for help. He is still facing upwards but she thinks he is hanging in the water. He can't be standing. His face is barely above the surface. She watches as water washes over it and his features wobble like jelly. His mouth and nose break the surface again. His head is tipped right back now and his eyes are white. His arms flap at the sea but he makes no sound. The water covers his face again, but up he comes, eyes wide, glazed, staring. He sucks for air like a fish before a wave fills his mouth.

She cannot reach him. He comes up again, further out, and she thinks he breaks the surface, but perhaps it is only her imagination. No, he is there. The sea is carrying him. She sees his face, his eyes looking at her but not seeing her. Another wave comes, and then she can't see him any more.

Lily looks around, but the yellow scarf has gone. Perhaps he was still holding it as he fell. She cannot remember. Slowly, she gets to her feet. There is blood on her knee, and her stocking is laddered. There must have been a nail in the wood. She turns and shades her eyes. The sea shines to the horizon, flat and silvery. Nothing breaks its surface. Mr Austin said they must be careful of the tide race. She cannot get her breath.

There was no one in sight. He made sure of that.

Her legs are shaking. Very carefully, she puts one foot in front of another. The surface of the jetty is so slippery and the shingle looks far away.

"Mum!" a voice cries, and then another: "MU-UM!" Paul and Sally fly over the lip of the shingle-bank, on to the beach. Bridgie is on Paul's back.

"MUM!"

"Are you all right?"

"It's Bridgie —"

"What's wrong?"

"She's been crying and crying —"

Julian Clowde has gone. He has melted away as if he'd never been. There are her children, calling for her. In a few more steps, she will be with them.

Lily lifts Bridget off Paul's back. Bridget clings with her arms and legs like a monkey, wrapping herself around her mother. She's still heaving with sobs.

"Oh my poor little duck, what's the matter?"

"She thought you'd gone off on Dad's ship."

Bridget is soaked with tears and, sure enough, she has wet herself too. Better not tell Paul that.

"What does she mean, Dad's ship?"

"You know, Mum. That's why Dad's away, because he's on his ship in the Navy," says Sally. Her lips are folded together and her face is pale.

"There's no ship," says Lily. "Look, Bridget. Look at the sea. Can you see a ship?"

Slowly, Bridget shakes her head.

"There's no ship, Bridget," says Sally.

"There's no ship, Bridget," says Paul.

"Why were you right out on the jetty?" asks Sally as Lily kneels to undo Bridget's buttons and set her coat right. "You always say it's dangerous."

"I wanted to see where the coal-boats used to tie up."

"What were you doing down here anyway, Mum?" asks Paul. "You never come to the beach."

"I thought I'd look for coal, but it was high tide."

"I knew you were here, Mum," says Bridget, leaning against her mother. "I told Paul and Sally, didn't I, Sally? I said you were at the beach."

"Don't start that up again," says Paul, but not unkindly.

368

Lily looks into Bridget's face, and the eyes where thoughts swim like fish. Are they hazel today or are they brown? So open, so transparent. Her little girl.

"How did you know that, sweetheart?"

Bridget shrugs. Her eyes become opaque. Whatever she knows, or has known, it's slipping away now and soon even Bridget won't be able to recapture it. The moment passes.

"Why have you got the poker stuck into your belt, Mum?" asks Bridget in a quite different voice — for Lily's coat has swung open.

"I thought I might use the poker to dig bits of coal out of the shingle," she answers slowly.

"That's not how you do it, Mum," explains Bridget. "You just use your hands."

"It was silly of me, wasn't it?" Are Paul and Sally buying this? She can't tell. Sally's face is still, attentive.

"I don't think you ought to let anyone see you carrying a poker like that, Mum," says Paul.

Lily crouches down so that her face is level with Bridget's. "It *is* dangerous on the jetty," she says. "Look where I fell." Bridget stares at the blood on her mother's knee. "I could have gone sideways. I could have hit my head and fallen right into the water, and nobody would have been able to save me."

"What if you'd swum to a ship?"

"There's no ship, Bridget. Even if there were, I would never go on it. I would never leave you."

CHAPTER
TWENTY-NINE

Perfect Aim

Was it so hard, Achilles,
So very hard to die?
Thou knewest, and I know not —
So much the happier I . . .

The lines drum in Giles's head. He's not dead yet. Hasn't floated off in a cloud of morphine. It's not going to be as easy as that.

It won't be long now, he tells himself as the dark goes on and on and refuses to give way to morning. Oxygen most of the time now. He's written the letter, given it to old Ross. Ross came. Good of him. The will was simple. All to his sister, for dog-breeding no doubt. The Kandinsky to the Tate. Lucy would only put it in the bin. That would be no good. Wanted to give the Kandinsky to Simon. Make it up to him. But it doesn't work like that. Might cause more trouble for Simon.

He sweats. It's hard to sleep sitting up but he can't lie down. Sister left a lamp on by his bed. She knows he doesn't like the dark.

"You're looking better this morning, Mr Holloway," says a young voice.

Silly fool of a girl, what did she know. His mouth tastes like hell. Nurse Davies isn't in today. But the awful thing is that he does feel better. Perhaps this is how it's going to be, dragging on like this, better and not better, dark and not so dark.

If thou, Lord, should'st mark iniquities,
O Lord, who shall stand?

Simon sang that.

The letter. Ross has taken the letter. He promised he would lock it in his safe and post it when I'm dead.

Clowde. That devil. What if Clowde gets hold of it somehow? A letter is only a piece of paper. It can be intercepted. Burned. A letter isn't enough.

Sister adjusts the knob on the oxygen cylinder. The gas hisses and Giles breathes in; then he signs for her to take the mask away. They will put him in a tent if he needs it. He raises his hand to attract Sister's attention. She bends close to his mouth.

"Do you believe in hell?" he whispers.

"Hell?" she repeats, to make sure.

"Yes, hell."

"You won't be going anywhere like that," she says, half-smilingly, all her lovely, plain consoling face bent on him.

He shakes his head. "Sorry," he says, "my breath stinks," and then he's too tired to talk for a while.

Evening comes. There's a bright liveliness about the place. Voices and footsteps. They are changing shifts.

He feels so much better. It's almost incredible. He could get up now and walk. He rings his bell. Sister hasn't gone off duty yet, and in she comes.

"I feel so well," he says, fixing her with his astonishment. She comes over to the bed and rests her fingers on his pulse. She counts silently and as usual she gives a small, satisfied nod.

"Good," she says.

"Perhaps I'm getting better."

He sees her face then. It's not pity, no. He feels for a word that he doesn't think he's ever used. *Compassion.* He's not getting better, of course he isn't, they all know that. He knows that. So why does he feel all at once as if anything is possible?

"I want you to telephone someone for me," he says rapidly. "His name is Frith."

Sister is off duty now, but she has left instructions with the new night sister. It only took an hour for Frith to arrive. There's a woman police officer with him. She has a shorthand notebook and she sits on one side of Giles's bed while Frith sits on the other, beside the pillows.

Giles's private room is dark outside the pool of lamplight that falls on him and on the woman police officer as she writes. Frith sits more shadowily. Every few words, Giles has to stop. Sometimes Frith gives him the oxygen mask: the night sister has shown him how to do this. Sometimes he moistens Giles's lips with the little sponge that lies on the bedside locker, in a kidney dish of clean water. The door is open and every so often the night sister leaves her station to survey the scene. Sometimes she steps to the bed and checks Giles's pulse and once she checks his blood pressure. He is becoming uncomfortable. He is heaving himself up on the pillows with each breath. If it weren't for Frith and the policewoman, the night sister would call Mr Anstruther. It's time for the morphine dose to be increased.

Giles closes his eyes. They are sunken but his nose is prominent, almost beaky. His colour is dusky. It's hard. He wants them all to go and leave him alone, but they can't go yet. There's more to say.

The lamp burns on. Frith sits forward, still, attentive. This is his moment. He has earned this. The girl's bent head shines as she takes down Giles's words in shorthand, every one of them. Frith will have his avalanche of evidence and it will sweep away Julian Clowde.

Giles is going down. The words come out struggling. It's very hard now. The night sister has called Mr Anstruther and he is here, a dark column by the white bed, waiting. As Frith stands up, he steps forward, and in goes the needle, into the crook of Giles's arm.

The room rushes away.

O my boy, his arm drawn back, his perfect aim.

CHAPTER
THIRTY

Arrival

The little train chugs along the branch line. It stops endlessly, but Simon doesn't mind that. He's in no hurry. In fact, he's afraid of arriving.

The compartment is empty now. He stands up and walks from one window to the other, pulling down both straps as far as they will go so that cold air floods in. He leans out and the wind fills his mouth and drags at his hair. He would like to smell of the air, not of prison. He has slung his bag up on the luggage rack. At the station he thought of buying something for the children, some chocolate, perhaps, or comics, but he had hardly any money. They gave him a travel warrant but he didn't want to use it, and the train ticket took most of the cash they'd handed back to him. He could have gone to the bank, he supposes, but he wasn't sure they would give him any of his money. Everything will need to be started up again.

The case against him has been dropped. It was Frith who told him that, not Pargeter. Simon hasn't even seen Pargeter, which is peculiar when you come to think of it. Frith looked the same as ever, although presumably he must have had some luck with his investigations or he wouldn't be here, saying those extraordinary words: *You're free to go.*

"What do you mean?"

"There are a few formalities to be completed, but the case against you has been dropped, and consequently you are free to go."

There was no hint of an apology.

"What the hell do you mean by that? Is that all you have to say? You arrested me, you've kept me here for months, and now that's it, let's all go home?"

"Not all," said Frith. "Not Mr Clowde, for example."

"What do you mean?"

"He appears to have gone to visit friends."

"He has friends all over Europe." Did they know?

"And beyond," said Frith, in his strong, flat voice. "We think that's where he is. However, he hasn't surfaced yet."

Clowde had gone. They knew. Christ. They must have been on to him, but he got out in time. Someone must have tipped him off.

"I gather he's very fond of ballet," said Frith. "He'll get plenty of that, where we think he's gone," and for the first time, a smile of satisfaction edged his lips.

"You wanted him to go," said Simon, astonished.

"He wasn't going to do us much good here."

"Has it been in the papers?"

"Not yet. There's some tidying up to do. But you needn't worry. It'll be made clear that charges against you have been dropped and that there was no case to answer."

Christ, perhaps Giles has gone too. How he used to joke about Moscow. What was it he said? *Like Birmingham, but without the bright lights.*

"What about Giles Holloway?"

Frith leaned towards Simon. "He's dead," he said, while his eyes watched sharply. Simon sucked in a breath.

"Who killed him?"

"Why do you say that? He died of natural causes."

Giles dead. Just like that.

"When did he die?"

"Two weeks ago."

"Why did no one tell me?"

"Would you expect them to?"

Simon looked at him. This game was going to come to an end. He wasn't going to have it. Question in return for question, nothing ever clear. He'd had enough.

"Yes, I would expect to be told," he said. "Giles Holloway was one of my oldest friends."

"Was he such a good friend to you?"

> If thou, Lord, should'st judge iniquities
> O Lord, who shall stand?

"I'll decide that," said Simon. "Have they held his funeral already?"

"Yes. It was very quiet."

All those friends. All Giles's boys. They'd tiptoed away at the end.

"I want you to go now," he said to Frith.

He sat for a while after Frith had left, not wanting to move. He'd have sat longer, but they came to get him. A screw, one of the more decent ones, who was pleased for Simon. All the time they went through the

376

procedures, getting him to sign things and sign for things, he thought of Giles going down into the earth, a handful of soil, a few indifferent mourners. That sister of his. Lily would say that Giles had got what he deserved. She'd be angry with Simon for sparing a thought for Giles, after what he'd done to him.

You're only going to get a bloody Third, you know. Why don't you stop that and come here?

Two stops left. He'll walk from the station to the cottage. Lily says it's about a mile and a half. She doesn't know he's coming. She doesn't know that he's out of prison. They offered to send a telegram but he made excuses: she wasn't on the telephone; he didn't want her to hear the news from anyone else. Giles is dead, Clowde has disappeared, and he, Simon, has been released.

Lily is putting on her coat to leave when Mr Austin comes in from the garden. He is carrying a basket of apples. His Bramleys, stored all winter, wrinkled but still good.

"I've picked out the best," he says. "Here you are. They won't keep for much longer. Apples for the Young Turks."

"Please don't give me all these. You won't have any left for yourself."

"My dear, I insist."

He has never called her "my dear" before. Lily takes the handle of the basket.

"Are you all right?" he asks.

"Yes, of course."

"You don't look well."

"I'm fine, really."

"You don't look well," he repeats gently. "I know that things are difficult for you at the moment, Mrs Callington." He lifts his eyes and, for once, this shy man looks her full in the face. His eyes are grey. They are lucid. He knows, she thinks. Probably he has known all the time. "But they will get better, I can promise you that. There was a time in my life when things seemed pretty pointless, for one reason and another. That was after I came out of the convalescent home. They sent me there, you know. Get the old leg working again: that was the idea. It's still got shrapnel in it now. They were very good there, but ... sometimes I felt like chucking it all in. I felt I was no use for anything. A few months later, I met Louise. Ah well, there we are."

He's embarrassed now, to have said so much. He's not sure how I'll respond.

"He didn't do it, you know," she says.

"I know that."

"How?"

"He wouldn't be married to you, if he were that sort of chap."

She smiles. His innocence moves her almost to tears. If only you knew what I'm really like, she thinks, you would take away these apples and never let me into your house again. I pushed that man as hard as I could. I watched him drown.

"It's not so much what you see," he says abruptly. "It's what you see in yourself. But you can't keep on looking at it."

He's telling her that he, too, has done things that frighten him.

"I know," she says.

They are silent for a while.

"I must go. I'll make the children an apple crumble for supper. They'll love it."

"That's the ticket. See you tomorrow."

"Yes, see you tomorrow."

Lily makes the crumble extravagantly, with butter, and prepares the apples with cinnamon and brown sugar. Her hands are still shaking, but not so much. She should drink less coffee. She'll make Bird's custard, because the children, like Mr Austin, prefer it. Usually Lily would be soothed by cooking, but it doesn't work today. Her whole body is restless. She feels as if there's something she ought to do, something important that is clawing at the sides of her mind but she can't remember it. She looks at her watch. Half past two. Not long before the children come out of school, although as the evenings grow lighter they come home later. She's tempted to walk up to the school to make sure they are all right, but Paul and Sally wouldn't like that. What is this feeling? Restlessness, yes, but something else too. She thinks of the children coming down to the beach. If they'd got there ten minutes earlier —

She mustn't think of that. She must remember what Mr Austin said.

She pushed Julian Clowde as hard as she could. He was off balance and she shoved him and he fell. Again she sees his legs, scissoring. Those white eyes, turned up. He hit his head so hard. Perhaps he was unconscious even before he went into the water. But his arms flapped. Only his nose and mouth were above the water, and his arms flapped, and then the sea carried him away.

I did nothing, she thinks. He would have killed me and so I let him die and I didn't even try to save him.

That letter is in the sea with him. It was written in ink: she can see the words now. They'll have dissolved into a wad of pulp. She can forget them. It will be like a letter written in German.

But I do speak German, she thinks. I understand it. I must remember what Simon wrote.

She remembers herself on the jetty, with Julian Clowde watching her. She was consumed with anger, shaking with it. Why was she so angry? Simon had betrayed her, he had shamed her, he had loved another man. Because it was love, not something to do with public lavatories and police fines. He was twenty years old. He had never seen Lily then. He'd never dreamed of hurting her. It was only that he loved Giles Holloway. There, she has said those words to herself.

She thinks of Simon's eyes, when he talked to her about Monsieur Nuage. They were points of desperation, begging her to understand him. When she said that he hadn't an artistic bone in his body, his face had warmed and lightened. He understood that she meant:

I trust you. I know that you are not like Julian Clowde. You are not a traitor to anyone.

"You're very hard sometimes, Lily." Her mother had said that, and Lily had immediately suppressed it, because it was her mother being unreasonable. Am I hard? thinks Lily, leaning on her hands, which are flat on the kitchen table. She remembers Simon's face, and the plea for understanding. And on my face too, she thinks. I wanted him to understand me.

The clock ticks on. Ten to three. She can't stay in here. The crumble is ready to go into the oven. She'll walk — not down to the beach — the other way.

She sees him coming, far off. He is a small, indistinct blot on the rutted track, but she would know him anywhere. The shape of him. The way he moves. She stands utterly still. He is walking slowly, laggingly, like Bridget when she's had a bad day at school. He looks as if he doesn't quite want to arrive.

She sets off running. She stumbles in the ruts and comes on, running faster. As she runs she opens her arms and begins to cry out incoherently, his name, her name, other words all mixed up, English words, German words, all the stream and fountain of language that is within her when the dam breaks and the words cry out for themselves. She runs, runs, runs, her legs flying and her arms open and she sees that slowly, tentatively, his arms too are opening like wings, wider and wider, to receive her.

Acknowledgements

The epigraph to Chapter 29 is taken from the poem "I Saw A Man This Morning" by Patrick Shaw Stewart, written in 1915. I am grateful to Lawrence Sail for his help with translations into German.

Other titles published by Ulverscroft:

THE LIE

Helen Dunmore

Cornwall, 1920, early spring. A young man stands on a headland, looking out to sea. He is back from the war, homeless and without family. Behind him lie the mud, barbed-wire entanglements and terror of the trenches. Behind him is also the most intense relationship of his life. Daniel has survived, but the horror and passion of the past seem more real than the quiet fields around him. He is about to step into the unknown. But will he ever be able to escape the terrible, unforeseen consequences of a lie?

THE GREATCOAT

Helen Dunmore

In 1945, newlywed Isabel Carey arrives in a Yorkshire town with her husband Philip. One cold winter night, Isabel finds an old RAF greatcoat in the back of a cupboard. Once wrapped in the coat she is beset by dreams. And not long afterwards, while her husband is out, she is startled to hear a knock at her window, and to meet the intense gaze of a young Air Force pilot, staring in at her from outside. His name is Alec. As Isabel's initial alarm fades, they begin a delicious affair. But nothing could have prepared her for the truth about Alec's life . . .

THE BETRAYAL

Helen Dunmore

Leningrad in 1952: a city recovering from war, where Andrei, a young doctor and Anna, a school teacher, are forging a life together. Summers at the dacha, preparations for the hospital ball, work and the care of 16-year-old Kolya fill their minds. They try hard to avoid coming to the attention of the authorities, but even so their happiness is precarious. Stalin is still in power, and the Ministry for State Security has new targets in its sights. When Andrei has to treat the seriously ill child of a senior secret police officer he finds himself and his family caught in an impossible game — for in a land ruled by whispers and watchfulness, betrayal can come from those closest to you.

COUNTING THE STARS

Helen Dunmore

Living at the heart of sophisticated, brittle and brutal Roman society at the time of Pompey, Catullus is obsessed with Clodia, the Lesbia of his most precious poems. He is jealous of her husband, of her maid, even of her pet sparrow. And Clodia? Catullus is "her dear poet", but possibly not her only interest . . . Their Rome is a city of extremes — civilisation and violence are equals, murder is the easy option and poison is the weapon of choice. Catullus' relationship with Clodia is one of the most intense, passionate, tormented and candid in history. In love and in hate, their story exposes the beauty and terrors of Roman life in the late Republic.